# Broken Oaths

*Patricia Marques*

# Broken Oaths

HODDER &
STOUGHTON

First published in Great Britain in 2024 by Hodder & Stoughton Limited
An Hachette UK company

1

Copyright © Patricia Marques 2024

The right of Patricia Marques to be identified as the Author of the Work has been
asserted by her in accordance with the Copyright, Designs and Patents Act 1988.

A CIP catalogue record for this title is available from the British Library

Hardback ISBN 978 1 399 70726 8
ebook ISBN 978 1 399 70728 2

Typeset in Sabon MT by Hewer Text UK Ltd, Edinburgh
Printed and bound in Great Britain by Clays Ltd, Elcograf S.p.A.

Hodder & Stoughton policy is to use papers that are natural, renewable
and recyclable products and made from wood grown in sustainable
forests. The logging and manufacturing processes are expected to
conform to the environmental regulations of the country of origin.

Hodder & Stoughton Limited
Carmelite House
50 Victoria Embankment
London EC4Y 0DZ

www.hodder.co.uk

*To Kiba, who still goes on park walks with
me in my dreams.*

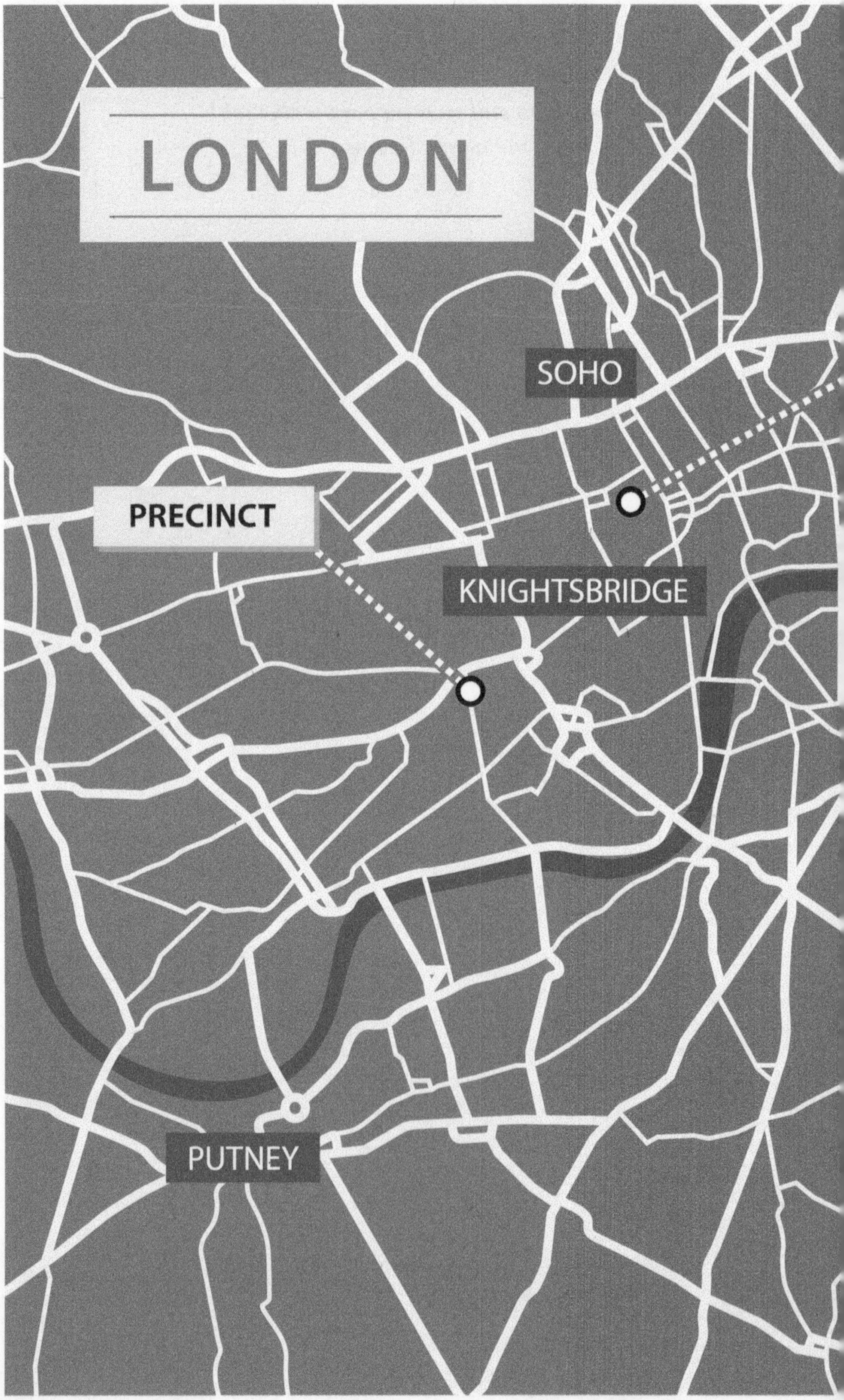

LONDON
SOHO
PRECINCT
KNIGHTSBRIDGE
PUTNEY

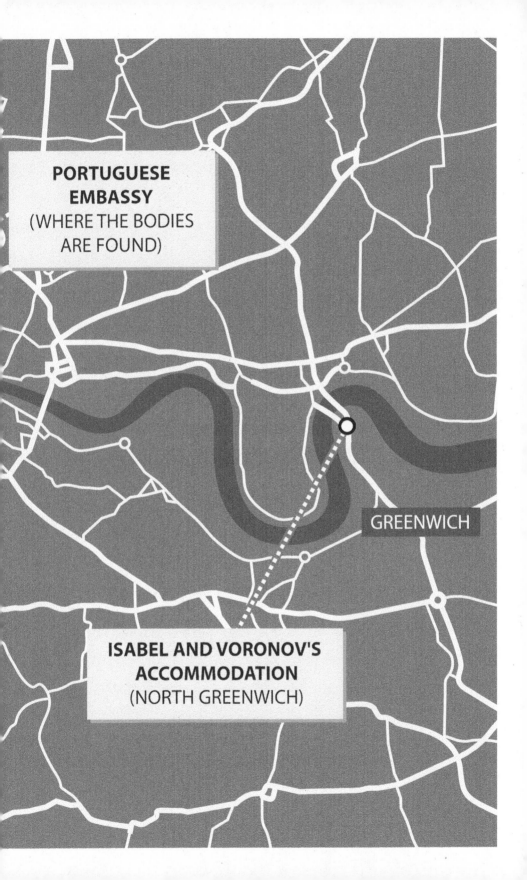

PORTUGUESE
EMBASSY
(WHERE THE BODIES
ARE FOUND)

GREENWICH

ISABEL AND VORONOV'S
ACCOMMODATION
(NORTH GREENWICH)

# I

'Merda,' Inspector Isabel Reis mutters, hand cupped protectively over her mouth as she strides up the stairs ahead of her partner, Inspector Alexander Voronov.

The perp they'd arrested and brought back to the Anjos precinct is still yelling the place down as uniformed officers drag him away to get booked. He's calling her every name under the sun, spittle collecting in the corners of his mouth, veins popping in his neck. His anger is a gnarled thing, rusted red and filling the room. There's no coherency to it, no thoughts clinging to it.

She'd known in the moment they'd answered the call – pulling into a gated community, the neighbours gathered outside trying to intervene – the rage spilling from him had an amplified sharpness to it that had left Isabel dazed for a moment. It had made sense when they'd managed to get their hands on his ID. The man was a level-five Gifted.

It had thrown Isabel for a second. Just a second. That had been enough for him to clock her in the face with his elbow.

Isabel pokes gingerly at the inside of her lip and winces. At least she can't taste blood anymore. The cut is there though, a split that feels a little wide to the tip of her tongue and the swell of her lip is still growing. Her cheekbone is a bright spark of pain. She's going to have a black eye tomorrow.

This one had been an accidental blow. Nothing compared to his girlfriend who had tentatively opened the bathroom door to them, neck a rainbow of colours and eyes nearly swollen shut. Isabel makes a mental note to check in on her later.

She hopes the girlfriend presses charges. But she's not hoping too hard. She knows how these things go.

The late summer heat is still going strong with forecasts predicting that it may last long enough to tip over into October. Isabel's hair is up in a haphazard ponytail, but tiny curls have already escaped from its hold. She can hear the velvety whirrs of multiple fans doing nothing but circulating warm air around the open space of their floor. Despite that, if it weren't for the building lights, the inside of the building would be in shadows. Clouds had settled early in the morning, blanketing the whole sky.

It feels oppressive.

Isabel stops at the top of the stairs. She hears Voronov calling her name from behind her.

She takes a deep breath and with that sinks inward.

A couple of months ago, she would have had to start from the beginning, finding the quiet in the space of her mind and slowly, painstakingly, build a wall to protect it from other people's unwanted thoughts. Now the wall is there, tall, heavy, a circle of protection around her mind. Not perfect. She sees where the cracks are, little lines that glow white in her mind's eye.

It feels like minutes, rather than seconds, as she seals each and every one of those cracks until there's nothing but a seamless barrier.

Getting knocked by another Gifted person's power had unbalanced her for a moment, just enough to leave a few chinks in her armour. Nothing she can't overcome with more time and practice.

There's a presence at her back.

Isabel stiffens. Eyes straight ahead and still unseeing.

The presence stretches, unfurling and yawning open behind her.

'– bel—'

Isabel yanks away from the soft touch to her arm and whirls, jaw set.

Voronov stills, hand still outstretched.

The presence she'd felt lingers for a moment longer then dissipates.

'Sorry,' she says, 'I was just in my head.' Her heart is still racing, like the quick pitter-patter of a frightened rabbit's.

'It's fine,' he says.

'I'll be there in a sec,' she says, jerking her chin in the direction of their section. 'I need to take care of this.' She gestures at her mouth and cheek.

Before Isabel can follow through, she hears the sound of fast-clipped steps and spots Carla Muniz coming straight towards them.

'I thought I saw you both arrive,' Carla says, as she stops next to them.

Carla is a petite woman with short, straight, dark hair and a strong nose. She's always dressed professionally, even in weather like this. Case in point, her buttoned navy shirt and grey trousers topped off with a classy thin gold watch on her wrist. Not a hair out of place.

'Are you okay?' She frowns, eyes widening as she takes in the sight of Isabel's face properly. A junior inspector at the precinct, Carla's partnered with Inspector Daniel Verde, a long-time colleague and friend. Recently, along with Senior Crime Scene Specialist Jacinta Cacho, they'd all grown closer as a team, having worked two significant cases that caught the attention of the media and, unfortunately for their chief and Isabel in particular, politicians.

'Fine,' Isabel replies, straightening.

Voronov steps back from Isabel.

'How are you not sweating in that?' Isabel asks.

Carla waves hello to Voronov. 'I'm used to it,' she says, 'I wasn't just stalking you guys by the way; Chief Bautista is looking for you.'

'Did she say what it's about?' Voronov asks.

'No,' Carla says, 'but she has someone with her. Not police.' She gives them both a look. 'I think she's government.'

When they reach their section, Carla hangs back. Isabel catches sight of Daniel's close-shaved head peering over the divider at them, lifting a hand in greeting as he watches them head down the hallway towards Chief Bautista's office.

3

'Someone from government?' Voronov says, voice low.

Isabel pulls an ice pack away from her face. There's a bloom of rusted red spotting the paper. She prods at the inside her lip. The metallic taste lingers. 'I hope not,' she mutters.

When they reach the chief's office, Voronov knocks quickly before opening the door.

Chief Bautista looks up at them, doing a double take when she catches a glimpse of Isabel's face. The woman sitting across from her is dressed in a sharp, pale-blue suit, black hair pulled into a neat bun at the nape and a visitor's lanyard hanging from her neck.

'Inspector Reis, does that need to be seen to?' As always, the chief's voice sounds as if she's knocked back a drink of something that could strip paint and followed it up with twenty-four hours of straight chain-smoking.

'No, Chief, I'm fine. You called for us?' she asks as Voronov closes the door behind them.

'Good. Reis, Voronov, this is Milena Amorim,' she says, 'she's a representative from the government's Consular Affairs Department.'

Isabel nods a quick greeting at the woman. Next to her, Voronov greets her more politely with a handshake.

Milena Amorim is sitting very upright, but her fingers are locked tight around the strap of the bag resting on her lap.

'Senhora Amorim has come to us with an unusual situation and their department has requested our assistance.'

'Our assistance with what, exactly?' Isabel asks.

Chief Bautista gives a heavy sigh, and then right there, in front of the representative, she pulls out a packet of cigarettes from her pocket. She slides one out and lights it up. Amorim wrinkles her mouth in distaste.

The chief strokes a thumb over the arch of her eyebrow and blows out a curling stream. The smell of smoke taints the room. She rests her hands on the desk.

'I'm sending you both to London.'

4

# 2

'How long will you be there for?' Sebastião asks.

Her brother's eyes are a little bloodshot and the skin beneath them is darker than usual. He stands next to his car, watching her saying bye to her dogs. She rubs her hands over Tigre and Branca's heads, leaning down to give them kisses and ignoring the tight feeling in her throat.

'I'm not sure,' she says.

He looks over her shoulder at Voronov waiting a little further away, giving them space to have a private conversation. His travel bag is down by his feet.

Sebastião sighs, running a hand over his head. He's recently shaved it, leaving nothing but a short stubble in its place. He's in casual clothes, jeans, and a T-shirt. She's lucky he hadn't been delivering a service at his church this morning. He holds the hat he'd been wearing in his hand. Once upon a time it had been black but had been rendered a very dark shade of grey by multiple wash cycles.

'I wish you weren't going right now,' he says, quiet enough that it almost gets lost in the sound of traffic. He gives her a wry smile, sadness rounding out its edges. 'You haven't talked to me in a while.'

Isabel drops her gaze to the floor. Her mouth and eye are still throbbing, and every small move of her head makes her wince. 'We talk all the time.'

Sebastião watches her quietly for a moment. 'I didn't know you were on sleeping pills.' At her sharp look, he shrugs. 'They were on your bedside table. I packed them too.'

Isabel rubs at the bridge of her nose. 'It's nothing for you to be worried about.'

'I'm not used to you lying to me. Or avoiding me.' It's not said with censure, but the quiet disappointment in the words cuts her quicker than anything else could have. Embarrassment and guilt are quick to tangle together and send a hot flush up her throat.

How do you explain to your big brother that someone you were responsible for putting in jail almost a year ago has found a way to literally get inside your mind? And that every night you're too scared to close your eyes to sleep because you don't know if you'll hear their voice in your head again? Speaking to you. Trying to draw you out.

The feel of plastic sliding over the bridge of her nose has her jerking her head up in surprise and flinching at the quick flash of pain at her mouth. She instinctively puts a hand up only to realise that Sebastião is sliding his own shades into place over her eyes. He follows it up by tucking his cap over her head too.

'There,' he says, 'now you don't have to worry about people staring as much.'

Right. Although the pain is very much present, Isabel forgot that her face looks as if it's been used as someone's punchbag.

Sebastião tugs her into a hug.

*Ah, maninha, you worry me. Be safe. Lord, please keep her safe.*

His thoughts slip in, carrying the same warmth as his hug. Isabel closes her eyes and allows herself this. A moment of accepting comfort and reassurance from someone she loves. She hugs him tight and ignores the stinging in her eyes. She feels a desperation and a craving for reassurance that has nothing to do with her leaving right now and everything to do with what's in her head.

She hears Branca and Tigre whining and shuts her eyes tighter because it's making her feel like hands are squeezing around her heart.

'Isabel?' Sebastião asks, easing back from her a little. 'Belinha?'

In that small space, tucked away in her mind, shrouded in shadows, a presence shivers and unfurls.

It's as if someone spills a line of ice water down the centre of her back.

Isabel jerks back, breaking the hug.

She can hear Sebastião saying her name. She's still holding on to him, hands squeezing his arms tightly. Even through the panic she registers the skin-crawling sensation. Sebastião cups her shoulders, concern slanting his eyebrows.

Tigre and Branca's whines rise in pitch and passers-by shoot glances over at them, their attention going from the dogs to her face, to the two men standing near her.

Isabel pulls in a calming breath and lets go, steps around him to kiss the dogs' heads, giving their wriggling bodies a few last scratches.

'Thank you,' she says. She forces herself to meet Sebastião's gaze. 'I'll let you know when we arrive.'

'Call tia, too,' he says, 'she's already upset that you haven't been by to see her lately. And stop stalling and speak to Rita. I know things are difficult between you right now but she's our little sister. It's about time you both resolve this, don't you think?'

There's a lot Isabel can say to that, but now isn't the right time. She wonders how much Sebastião knows about what took place. So, for now, it's easier to say nothing. 'All right.'

Knowing that he won't get much else out of her, Sebastião gives a strained smile and then waves at Voronov. 'Safe flight.'

'Thanks,' Voronov says.

With one last wave and with the dogs in the back still whining, Sebastião gets in his car.

Isabel watches him drive off, joining the queue of cars ready to leave the drop-off area before grabbing hold of her luggage and turning to head inside.

Voronov falls into step with her, as silent as her.

The airport has enough activity going on to set Isabel's teeth on edge.

People are walking around, dipping in and out of the shops surrounding the seating areas, others charging their electronics and the majority clustered around the food places further back, queuing to grab something to eat before settling in and spending the rest of the time checking the monitors for their flight gate.

It's easy for Isabel to spot Voronov's head towering above other people's, even from her seat on the floor a little further away from all the bustle, her back to the wall, bags set next to her. It's not like she can avoid the crowds entirely. The airport is one of those spaces where there is no escaping the people, the loudness, the crowding of emotions all overlapping each other in a cluster of colours. Even with a decent wall up, it's hard for Isabel, as a telepathic Gifted, to manage. So, she's put as much distance between her and them as she's able to.

Besides, the chief had told them there was something they needed to look at so she'd wanted a space where she could ensure there would be no one peering over her shoulder.

Isabel is itching to see the file now, but neither she nor Voronov have seen it, so she forces herself to wait till he returns.

She hadn't been lying to her brother when she'd said she didn't know how long they would be away for. The chief hadn't been able to tell them. In fact, the chief had told them very little. Amorim had been practically silent in that room. Considering Isabel and Voronov were being sent to London at her department's request she could have done them the courtesy of giving them actual solid information.

The feeling of heading to a different country with barely any basics doesn't sit well with her. She'd attempted a quick internet search to see if anything relevant popped up but there was nothing. It doesn't help that Isabel, or her team haven't had the best of experiences with government officials in the last few years.

'There's been an incident at the Portuguese Embassy,' the chief had said, and gestured to Amorim who had shifted in her seat to face both Isabel and Voronov where they stood by the door.

'Inspectors,' Amorim addressed them, 'at around 7.30 this morning, Emanuel Francisco, our London ambassador, was in a call with our Secretary of State for Foreign Affairs and Cooperation, Rogério Pessoa. And something . . . unusual took place. We tried to get hold of the London embassy for a solid twenty minutes, but they were unresponsive. Eventually we called the authorities in London.'

'What did they find?' Voronov asked.

'There was no response.'

Isabel had stared at her, confused. 'What about when they gained entry?'

Amorim brought her hands together and sat straighter, the motion almost prim. Isabel got the sense that she was about to hear something irritating. 'They can't enter the premises without the permission of the ambassador.'

Isabel looked at the chief. There was a scowl on her face and she was taking a drag from her cigarette.

'Okay,' Isabel said, 'but the ambassador was inside. He's part of the reason why they need to enter the premises. You can't grant them permission?'

'This is a potentially sensitive situation,' Amorim said, 'we want our own people there to supervise the entry of the British police into the premises and keep us apprised of any updates.'

What?

Before they could ask anything else though, Chief Bautista cut in. She stood up, throwing an A4 envelope, unsealed, on top of the desk. 'Those are your tickets. Grab what you can, you'll need to head straight to the airport to make your flight. We need you there as soon as possible. I'll send you what we have so you can view it en route, call me when you get there.'

That had been that.

'Here.'

Isabel glances up.

Voronov eases himself down beside her, holding out a lidded paper cup and a bagged baguette.

'Thank you,' she says, taking them both from him.

He settles down beside her, arm pressing alongside hers. She expects him to shift away but all he does is set his own coffee on his other side before peeling the paper back from his sandwich and settling down to eat.

'Do we have it?' he asks.

'Yeah,' Isabel says. She settles the baguette on her lap and logs back in. 'It's a video.'

She plugs in her earphones and holds an earpiece out to Voronov. She brings up the video on the screen and clicks play.

The image that fills the screen is a typical video of a conference call.

Two windows: on the left-hand window you can see one man in the frame, with bookshelves at his back. He's wearing a jacket and tie, his grey hair neatly combed back from his face. The folds of his neck spill over the tight white collar of his shirt. In the frame on the right is another man, long and thin of face, with thinning hair, set against a white wall. Their names are displayed at the bottom of their own frame. Rogério Pessoa and Emanuel Francisco, respectively.

The two men are discussing something. Francisco seems tense and keeps wiping at his hairline, dotting at the shining drops clearly visible there.

They can't hear the words, but it's easy to see from their body language that whatever they're discussing has them both heated. There's a lot of gesticulating, slashing of the hands and huffing, but there's absolutely no sound coming through the video.

'Why no sound?' Isabel murmurs. Voronov hums in agreement.

Emanuel Francisco, the thin man, is mid-word when he stops moving.

Is the laptop or the app glitching?

Francisco's mouth is open, and his gaze has dropped to the surface of the desk. His shoulders are hitching in an odd pattern, almost like he's hiccupping, but no sound carries other than Pessoa's increasingly urgent voice, asking if Francisco is okay.

That's when Isabel realises that where there had been silence, now they can hear Pessoa's voice and Francisco's desperate inhalations. Isabel narrows her eyes. Someone deliberately removed the sound from the earlier part of their conversation.

Then Francisco's body jerks, his breathing becoming shallower and shallower. Isabel stares, waiting for someone to come in and intervene.

Pessoa curses and stands before disappearing from the screen.

What follows is an eerily still scene broken only by the sound of Francisco's desperate attempts to draw in air, his upper body collapsed against the desk, lifting jerkily with each attempt. Echoes of Pessoa's voice filter in through the connection, yelling in the background.

Francisco gulps for air again and slumps. He is still. His eyes are open and fixed on a point they can't see.

The numbers along the top of the call continue to tick away, only Pessoa's window frame flashing every time the off-screen yelling reaches the computer, muted by distance. The video stops at 7.47 a.m.

Isabel stops the video. She pulls out the earbud.

'That's it?' he asks.

She nods. 'That's it.'

His gaze flicks up from the screen to meet hers. 'Why are they sending us?'

Isabel sighs and glances back down at the screen. 'I'd like to know that too.'

# 3

They arrive at London Heathrow airport a few minutes shy of 5.00 p.m.

There's a young man in arrivals in police uniform holding a white placard with the names Reis and Voronov written in thick black marker. It helps considering he's tightly packed in by dozens of people on either side. There are balloons and even an overexcited chihuahua on a leash waiting there to welcome their person. The policeman is standing sharp and to attention. His gaze slides over them once or twice, clearly trying to guess who he's been sent to pick up.

Isabel walks a few steps behind Voronov, pulling her cabin luggage behind her, one of the wheels sticking every few seconds. She doesn't use it often and is always putting off getting a replacement, so she has to put up with it. She dreads to think what's inside it. Poor Sebastião had had to pack for her in a rush before grabbing the dogs and meeting her at the airport in Lisbon.

Isabel and Voronov had sat on opposite ends of the plane on the flight to London.

She wants food and painkillers. The whole flight had been a constant stream of thoughts and conversations, all circulating within the tight confines of the plane with nowhere to run off to. She'd been tense throughout the two-and-a-half-hour flight, unable to let her concentration slide because she'd known the onslaught of voices would have overtaken her if she had.

The man spots the two of them heading his way and eyes them with interest. Isabel adjusts the cap over her face. The pain of her lip and face has died down enough that she hasn't been wincing every time she so much as twitches. She's grateful for the sunglasses and hat that Sebastião had given her though.

'Inspector Reis and Inspector Voronov?' the officer asks when they reach him. He's got big brown eyes and a short ginger afro. He has light-brown skin and a smattering of freckles along his cheeks and neck. His voice is surprisingly deep.

Both Isabel and Voronov take out their IDs and the officer gives them a quick once over, lingering only for an extra second where Isabel's Gifted designation and telepathic affinity are listed. His smile has a nervous edge to it. 'I'm Detective Constable Duncan.'

Voronov smiles. 'Inspector Voronov,' Voronov says, reaching out a hand for him to shake.

Isabel stays where she is, one hand tucked into her pocket. She's too on edge for skin-to-skin contact right now. Still, she manages to put a smile on her face – then immediately regrets it when it reopens the split on her lip, making her hiss in pain and reach for it automatically.

DC Duncan steps forward, hand lifting as if to help. 'Are you all right?'

'Sorry,' Isabel says, her English coming easier than expected considering how long it's been since she's spoken it properly. Like Voronov's, it's marked by a heavy accent. 'I'm Inspector Reis. Unfortunately, I had a struggle during an arrest this morning.' She gestures at the glasses and hat. 'It's still very fresh.'

'Oh, right.' He blinks at her, not seeming to know what to do with that information. 'Well, um. We need to get going. I'll be driving you both to the embassy.' He lowers his voice and comes closer to avoid being overheard. 'The boss wants to get in there quick. They've been waiting for hours.'

It's not hard to read between the lines. Isabel would be pissed off too if instead of being able to access the premises right away, she was made to wait for some outsiders to come and let her in.

'Lead the way.'

The sooner they get inside that embassy, the sooner Isabel can be on a plane back to Lisbon and trying to figure out the mess her life is currently in.

# 4

Isabel had been to London before, years ago, with her brother, for a week. It had been close to Christmas, and she remembers the lights that had lit up the cold nights, people bundled into their coats as they poured on to the high streets. There's none of that now, only umbrellas floating up and down the streets as people hurry to where they need to be. It's supposed to be summer.

The Portuguese embassy is tucked away in a garden square in the City of Westminster, London.

There are officers in high-vis jackets guarding the entrance to the road, blockades up, and two of them walk to the car window to ask for identification. Their eyes flick to Isabel and Voronov from beneath hats dripping with rain.

The sky has started to darken with the oncoming evening. What had started out as a pitter-patter during their drive here has turned into something more persistent. In front of a tall red-brick building is a marked police van, officers gathering by the doors.

A small, well-cared-for garden sits at the centre of the square. Neat little benches and hedges, a small fountain at its centre. Isabel takes it all in as she opens the door and steps out of the car. Voronov gets out too.

'It's right over there,' DC Duncan says, popping up on the opposite side and resting an arm on the roof of the car before pointing to the correct place. 'DI Rampaul is waiting for you both.'

'Are you not coming?' Isabel asks.

'Uh.' He gives a firm nod that reveals a cleft in his chin, before slamming the door closed. 'Yes. Yes, of course.'

Isabel watches him walk around the car, and looks at Voronov, bemused. 'Okay.'

Except Voronov is already watching her, a contemplative touch to his expression. It's because recently these shared moments of amusement between them have become few and far between. Her fault. Just like the distance she'd insinuated between her and her brother. And everyone else that mattered. All the people she wants to keep safe.

Isabel clears her throat and shoves her hands into the pockets of her jacket.

'We'd be grateful if you could do introductions for us, DC Duncan,' Isabel says.

Easier to focus on the task at hand than all the other problems in her life right now.

They head over to the cluster of police staff.

'Boss,' DC Duncan calls out, 'sorry, we hit traffic on the way over.'

Someone peels away from the side of a building and a woman Isabel hadn't even realised was there walks towards them. It's a purposeful walk, like she knows right away who they are.

The way she's dressed reminds Isabel a little bit of Carla. Sharp but with a definite and unapologetic feminine edge. She's in a dove-grey suit that fits her form to perfection. The white shirt beneath it has a high collar that reaches halfway up her elegant neck and contrasts with her dark-brown skin. Her black hair falls in thick waves to cut off against her sharp jawline. She's a strikingly gorgeous woman.

'Inspectors Reis and Voronov, correct?' she asks. Her English has a hint of a lilt to it, and her voice is smooth. 'How nice of you to finally join us.' Her tone is dry, and she makes no attempt to greet them properly in any other way. Isabel hears a snicker from one of the officers standing behind her.

Isabel doesn't need her Gift to know what they're thinking. 'I would've asked the pilot to fly faster but unfortunately they don't take requests,' Isabel says. She feels a swell of satisfaction as the woman's eyes frost over and annoyance flares, orange-red around her.

Voronov steps up, the look he gives Isabel only mildly censoring. 'I understand we need to get inside. It seems like you and your team have been waiting for some time. I'm Inspector Voronov. This is Inspector Reis.'

Isabel doesn't miss the slow once-over DC Duncan's boss rakes over Voronov's frame. 'DI Rampaul. I'm with the Met's Major Crime Investigative Unit,' she says, short. Then she cuts her gaze away and gestures to the man standing at her side. 'This is Mr Andrzej Grosz, he's the head of security here at the embassy. Mr Grosz,' she says to the man, 'your inspectors are finally here. How about you get us inside that building, now.'

Mr Grosz is a very tall, very thin man. He's as pale up close as he had been from a distance. There's day-old stubble along his jawline and the skin beneath his eyes is sunken and dark. His thick dark hair is brushed into a neat side parting and the blue polo neck he's wearing is tucked into belted black trousers. His shoes are so sharp and shiny that Isabel could probably use them as a mirror. In his hand he's clutching a thick bunch of keys.

'Good afternoon, Inspectors,' he greets them.

Isabel greets him politely. 'Mr Grosz,' she says, 'we appreciate your help with accessing the building.'

Surprising her, he switches to Portuguese for a bit. 'They told me I had to wait for you both and not let anyone in until you were here to escort them inside.'

Next to them, Rampaul's jaw tightens, her eyes narrowing on them.

Since they've already got off to a touchy start, Isabel responds in English. Stoking the fires won't help anyone here. 'Of course. Thank you for your patience.'

He nods, movements jerky. The keys jingle in his grip as he motions to the front of the building.

'You must be concerned,' Isabel murmurs as they go. She can feel it, the way it's gripping him, the need to get inside and check on the people he works with day in, day out. 'If you could open the door for us that would be helpful. And then I have to ask you to please wait outside unless we specify otherwise,' she says, as gently as she can.

'Yes, yes, of course, Inspector.'

Isabel looks back where DC Duncan hovers uncertainly. Rampaul doesn't pay him any attention.

'Isn't he coming?' Isabel asks Voronov. 'I thought he was part of her team.'

Voronov glances over at DC Duncan as well, who slides over to where Rampaul is walking behind them. 'Something's off there.'

'I thought the same thing.'

Voronov sighs. 'It's not our business.'

'I guess not.' They stop in front of the door and Mr Grosz steps up to the security pad on the wall. She can feel the stares of the English officers behind them, boring into their skulls. 'Is it me,' Isabel turns her head to the side to speak to Voronov and keeps her voice low, 'or are we in for a hard time here?' she asks.

Voronov glances down at her but he doesn't answer. Finally, as the silence threatens to become uncomfortable, he speaks. 'Yes. We are.'

Except she doesn't think he's talking about the same thing she is.

In front of them, the door opens with an echo that indicates a wide space inside. Mr Grosz steps back. 'It's open, Inspectors.' He hasn't opened the door all the way though, and from where they stand, Isabel can only see a sliver of the interior.

It's bright inside. Through the small gap Isabel sees a slice of shiny black-and-white chequered flooring and a strip of cream wall. A phone is ringing. All else is still.

Isabel wonders if they should be armed for this.

Behind them the wind picks up and the rain becomes more vicious.

She nudges the door open wider; the sound of the ringing phone spills outside.

17

They're faced with a very elegant foyer. The floor is so clean the light inside bounces off it. It's a tall entryway, with a set of stairs directly in front of the door. The steps are covered in thick, pristine, beige carpeting and a chandelier hangs from the ceiling. The hallway runs deeper into the property on the left side. There are two doors along the wall and one right at the end. The second door and the one bringing up the end of the corridor are both closed, but the first one is wide open. The ringing phone sounds as if it's coming from that room. The light is on in there too.

'Hello?' Isabel calls out, eyes directed at the top of the stairs. 'Anyone here?'

The phone keeps ringing. No steps, no voices. Nothing.

'Other than that phone, I don't hear anything,' Voronov says.

'I don't either.'

The Met Police team behind them are talking under their breaths.

Isabel pushes the noise to the back of her head. She steadies herself then reaches out. She feels her Gift stretch, probing gently, parting the silence to try to capture even the slightest tint of emotions in the air or a stray whisper of a thought. It's difficult. The team behind her are loud and she's having to hold up a wall to block out their noisy thoughts while simultaneously opening herself up to whatever could be in this building.

She registers Voronov speaking to them, voice hushed, asking for them to be calm, be quiet.

Withdrawing her Gift, she sighs. A touch of pressure settles over the back of her left eye, almost imperceptible. 'I'm not getting anything.'

Voronov nods.

Just in case, Isabel calls out again. 'We're inspectors with the Portuguese Judiciary Police, the Major Crime Investigative Unit is also present. Is anyone h—'

Isabel reaches for Voronov, catching his arm.

He stays still at her side. 'What is it?'

She points.

18

There, through the open doorway of that first room, right in the corner. It looks like the curled tip of a finger.

'DI Rampaul,' Voronov says, 'is it possible for us to have shoe covers? Do your team have any with you?'

Isabel keeps her eyes zeroed in on that small glimpse.

'Ma'am, here!'

DC Duncan is cutting through the group clustered around the front of the building. He's got one arm up, warding off the rain that the wind has turned into pellets. He's holding out a see-through bag containing bright-blue plastic boot coverings within.

Isabel thanks him. As she and Voronov put on the coverings, she doesn't miss the stare Rampaul aims DC Duncan's way.

'DC Duncan, would you mind keeping Mr Grosz company? I think it may be best if only a few of us go in and do a sweep of the building,' Isabel says, 'just to be sure.'

'Inspector.' Rampaul's tone is sharp.

Isabel stops on the first step.

Rampaul is glaring up at her. 'I think you're misunderstanding something. You are not in charge here.'

Isabel stares right back. 'I'm not misunderstanding anything. Until we've checked the building, however, there is nothing for you to be in charge of. Rest assured we'll follow your lead in any ensuing investigation, Detective. Your team might be dealing with a crime scene, so it also gives you time to make sure everyone is outfitted appropriately, no?' She doesn't wait for her to respond. 'Let's go, Aleks.'

The plastic of the shoe covers crackles. The noise feels disrespectful in the silence of the building. Isabel looks back. The sense that someone will be there an eerie, nebulous feeling that hovers.

They walk to the first door. They're careful, although Isabel is pretty sure that there is no one else in the building.

They reach the open first room.

Isabel stops.

They almost appear as if they're sleeping.

The hand she'd spied belongs to a woman who is lying on the floor, head close to the corner of a coffee table. A slim gold watch glints around her white wrist. Beneath the swirl of her brown hair is a red stain. A white mug is on its side close to her stomach; a dark-brown splash of liquid has soaked into the plush carpet.

There are two desks framing a seating area. Magazines decorate the top of the coffee table and the two-seater sofa opposite it is a rich dark-blue velvet. The other two people, also women, are each at their desks, one face-down on her keyboard, the other sunk into her chair, eyes fixed on the ceiling, unseeing. The red light on the switchboard phone atop her desk blinks in time with the ringing.

Isabel gathers herself and crouches down as Voronov carefully goes around her. She checks for a pulse on the woman on the ground. There's no warmth to the wrist and it feels stiff to the touch.

The ringing stops. The silence that pours in feels unnatural in its suddenness.

'Nothing,' Isabel says.

'These two are also gone,' Voronov says, coming back from the desks.

Isabel rests her hands on her knees as she balances there, taking in the room anew. 'We need to check on the ambassador,' she says.

But given what they'd seen in that recording and what they've walked into here, the sheer vacuum of life she feels within the building . . .

She's pretty certain of what they're going to find.

Isabel stands and with one last glance at the bodies in the room, she heads out.

The next door down is a bathroom, and the door at the end of the hallway opens into a compact kitchen and beyond it, a long stretch of very neatly maintained garden. In the kitchen, slumped over a round table and still in their chairs are four people dressed in the same uniform. Unwrapped sandwiches and cold teas and coffees litter the table. The crisp white collars of their shirts under black jumpers suggest they were security.

They head back to the front of the house. DI Rampaul and an uncomfortable, but stubborn-looking, DC Duncan stand just outside the door. At least they now have the appropriate attire on.

'Three dead in the main Reception area, four in the kitchen,' Isabel says as she heads for the stairs. 'I think you and your team can get to work, Detective Inspector, we'll continue our sweep of the place.'

Rampaul cuts her a glare before she addresses her team, and soon they start pouring into the entryway.

The whole building is lit up. Isabel thinks they have maybe a first and a second floor to check.

There are three doors on the first floor; the layout roughly follows that of the ground floor below. A small room directly above what would be the entryway has its door locked but it seems like the light inside is on. As Voronov knocks on the door and calls out, Isabel continues to the next one. It opens a few inches before hitting up against something.

She holds it open against the weight.

Isabel has to crane her neck to see. A man in a pale-grey suit is collapsed on his side, facing away from the door, and the door is butting up against his feet. There's a mobile phone on the carpeted floor close to him. She's pretty sure that like the three women downstairs, he's also gone. She has to check regardless. She forces her way in, careful as she creates enough space to wiggle inside and check for signs of life. There are none.

'What is this . . .' She shakes her head.

Voronov is waiting at the foot of the stairs leading up to the next floor. He's staring up, grim resignation on his face.

'There's another in that office,' Isabel says as she draws close. 'And the locked door with the light on doesn't bode well. There aren't any signs I can pick up on. What did you find?'

'There is one more in the corner office on this floor,' he says, attention still on the stairs.

She stops next to him and follows his gaze.

Right there, sprawled on the landing upside down and torso taking up the first chunk of the staircase up to the second floor, is a woman. A notebook and a pen lie on the floor and there are dozens of A4 papers scattered across the steps. Her straight black hair is spilled on the stairs, leaving her face completely uncovered.

Her eyes are open, and rolled back in her head. From this angle it's as if she's staring at them. Her mouth is open wide, stretched long, her cheeks are hollowed out and her tongue pokes out against her lower lip. The fixed expression is oddly grotesque and despite having seen so many people in so many different states of death, Isabel feels a chill at the sight.

They can hear DI Rampaul downstairs, directing her team. Isabel calls down to say there are at least three more bodies on the first floor and one room that needs to be forced open.

'Let's go,' Isabel says, and they continue on their way up to the next floor, careful to ease around the body.

They reach the second floor and there is an empty bathroom, which is the first door they come across. There's another beside that that they try but when they open it, they find only a small empty office with a window facing directly into the building behind this one across what's probably a really narrow alley.

'I guess it's this one,' Isabel says, stopping outside the last door. She opens it.

Right there, slumped over the table, in an exact replica of what they had seen in the video, is the ambassador.

His dead gaze is fixed right on them.

# 5

'Isabel. I've found something.'

Isabel turns from where the ambassador, Francisco, is being wheeled out of the embassy building and to the waiting vehicles. Sitting on the back of one of the ambulances with a thermal blanket over his shoulders and a cup of something hot in his hands is Grosz. DC Duncan is with him, head bent over as he listens to something the man is telling him. The light from the ambulance has bleached his complexion into a sickly colour.

Voronov is standing at the top of the stairs, waiting for her.

The building has now become a hub of quiet activity, the crime-scene officers setting about their tasks with minimal communication. They had found twelve dead in total.

'Coming,' Isabel says. She starts back upstairs and glimpses Rampaul and the senior officer from the crime-scene unit standing at the end of the corridor. As she goes, Rampaul's gaze flicks up and catches hers. The skin between her eyebrows wrinkles briefly, as if she's caught sight of something unpleasant, before her expression wipes clean once more and she turns her attention back to the CSO.

'There's one more room,' Voronov says, voice low. He tilts his head to indicate the top of the building and Isabel can see where the stubble is starting to come through on the underside of his chin.

Isabel frowns. 'There's another room up there?'

She follows Voronov as he leads the way.

'There's a corridor leading to one last room,' he says. 'It seems to wrap around to the back of the building. It's through the small supplies room on the top floor.'

Same floor as the ambassador's office.

There are two CSOs inside when Voronov walks her past it.

The supply room that Voronov leads her to is at the end of the hallway, its door the length and width of the bookend wall.

Voronov pulls the door open. It opens outwards. Directly opposite the door is a unit of shelves mounted on to the wall. It's holding sealed bags of toilet rolls along the lower shelves and the higher ones have rows of handwash bottles, boxes of paper towels and tissues.

The height of the shelves extends above the doorway, beyond their line of sight.

Voronov flips on the light switch and gestures her in front of him.

She murmurs a thanks and pokes her head inside, eyes sweeping the small space. There's about room for one person to fit inside it. Two at a push or for the very motivated. But on the left is a narrow door. There's a lock below the doorknob but the door itself is ajar.

'It wasn't locked when I tried it, and it opens up into another hallway.'

Isabel taps it lightly and it swings open with a squeak of its hinges.

The corridor it exposes is long and windowless. It has the same plush carpet as the rest of the building and right at the end of it is another door.

The lights here are different, just one hanging from the centre, and it has a distinct yellow tone. Instead of adding warmth to the space, it leaves the corners of the corridor in shadow and pools at the centre like an ominous spotlight.

'Are you getting anything?' he asks.

Isabel shakes her head.

Every stray thought she can sense is coming from the police working throughout the building.

'No,' she says, 'there isn't anyone here.'

What they find beyond that secondary door is a compact and simple, self-contained annexe room. The light inside is on. The furnishings are sparse. An opened sofa bed in a corner, a TV mounted on the wall and a coffee table. There's a partition and behind it, they find a small shower, toilet and sink concealed from the rest of the room. The sink is packed tight with body-wash, face cream, toothpaste and a box of period pads. There are no windows here either, only a small square skylight above the workstation-cum-kitchenette along one wall. It holds a kettle and a few mugs. There's an opened box of tea there and an unfin-ished sandwich on a small plate. Cluttered together at the edge of the counter are more toiletries. A tub of body cream, a single and near-empty bottle of perfume and a couple of boxes of painkillers.

The sheets on the sofa bed are tangled and there are items of clothing strewn over the back of it. An open book lies pages down on the pillow. A small suitcase is open in a corner, revealing more clothes and shoes inside.

Isabel kneels beside it, peering inside but not touching anything.

'Someone has clearly been here a long time,' Isabel says.

Voronov comes to stand by her. 'No sign of any ID. No wallet or purse. No personal electronics.'

Throw in the unfinished food, the chaotic state of the room. The lights that have been left on.

Isabel glances up at the skylight that shows them only the night sky.

'Whoever they are or were, I think they were in a hurry to leave.'

It's nearing 8.30 p.m. when they get back to the MCIU headquarters in Knightsbridge.

Despite the hour, there is a quiet buzz of activity. The building is unexpectedly cool inside, edging on cold, and Isabel struggles not to shiver as they follow Rampaul's lead through pale mint-green corridors that make Isabel feel as though they've entered a hospital instead of a police station.

Ahead of her, DC Duncan and Voronov flank the head of secu-rity, Grosz. Isabel and Voronov, more than anyone else, got a lot of looks upon arrival, the officers on duty not bothering to hide their hostile stares as DC Duncan signed them in. Most of the doors they pass are open, revealing small, empty, numbered rooms that are crammed with two to three desks when really there should be only one. Quiet conversations spill out from only a few of them. People are hunkered down with the terrible posture of the overworked on display as they hunch over their computers and squint at screens.

They're met at the end of the long corridor by a tall brute of a man with a wide stubbled face and shoulders Isabel has only seen on TV broadcasts of rugby games. Rampaul pauses briefly in her power walk.

'Tom,' Rampaul greets, and before continuing, she instructs DC Duncan to escort Grosz to room ten.

DC Duncan quickly nods and asks Grosz to follow him. Grosz, who has been subdued since identifying the bodies of his colleagues before they'd been taken away on gurneys, falls into step behind him.

'Inspectors, this is DI Tom Keeley, we often partner together on assignments. Depending on how it goes he may end up assisting on this case. Tom, this is Inspector Reis and Inspector Voronov from the Portuguese Judiciary Police.'

He seems about as impressed with Isabel and Voronov's presence as Rampaul had but manages to give them a nod in greeting and turns to Rampaul. 'Had the prints back on the Madden case. Come see me when you can.' He doesn't wait for Rampaul to respond before he leaves, and Isabel can't help but wonder about the levels of hostility that seem to exist within this team.

Rampaul motions with a jerk of her head for Isabel and Voronov to follow her.

She stops outside a room with the number 10 painted in white on the wall beside the door. There are scratches cutting across the digits, like someone has keyed the wall over and over again.

Inside Grosz stands beside the chair, staring at it like he doesn't remember what it's for. Isabel thinks, it's been a long day for him too. DC Duncan stands at the back of the room. He glances over when Rampaul fills the doorway.

'I'll be a moment, Mr Grosz,' Rampaul says. 'Can we get you anything? A tea, coffee? Water?'

Grosz doesn't seem to hear her.

'Mr Grosz?' Rampaul asks again.

The lurid brightness of the lights emphasises the dips and grooves of his face, making him look gaunt. 'Sorry. Just water. Please.'

'Of course,' Rampaul says. She beckons DC Duncan over and steps out of the room, pulling the door closed behind them. 'Adam, go and fetch a water for Mr Grosz, please.' She says this without once glancing at DC Duncan's face.

To his credit, DC Duncan doesn't show much of a reaction. 'Yes, boss,' he says and hurries to do as he's been told.

Rampaul waits until he's disappeared from view. She crosses her arms and faces Isabel and Voronov.

'Firstly, thank you. I appreciate that you've made quite a journey to get here and help us out. But I want to make clear that this investigation is under the jurisdiction of the Met's MCIU. My preference is for you to stay as out of it as possible, unless otherwise required. During your time here, DC Duncan will look after you. The Portuguese government want you here and given the circumstances, we're happy to accommodate that request but that's as far as it goes.'

Isabel isn't surprised that she's taken this stance. Her whole demeanour since they'd arrived on the scene had made her thoughts clear on the subject.

'Unfortunately, Mr Grosz has been given specific orders by one of your representatives and has made it clear that he refuses to speak without you both present. For that reason alone, I'm letting you stay throughout his interview but once that's done DC Duncan will escort you both to your accommodation. From that point on, I will keep you apprised of the investigation and its progression.' She stops there, clearly waiting for their response.

27

Isabel doesn't say a word. If she opens her mouth, she's got a strong suspicion that whatever words come out will lead to a reprimand by Chief Bautista.

'No questions?' Rampaul asks.

Yes, Isabel has questions. She wants to know who has spoken to Grosz. Who are these 'representatives'? Amorim? When would they even have had the opportunity to speak to him? At what point had Grosz been contacted to get him to the embassy for access to the building and who had done that? They're probably not questions for Rampaul though.

Isabel isn't surprised when Voronov answers her with complete calm. 'I think you've explained everything well enough, Detective Inspector.'

Rampaul's gaze settles on Voronov at his response. There's a subtle change there. Very subtle. The minuscule tilting back of Rampaul's chin, the way the curve of her lower back seems to deepen a touch and her shoulders open. The corner of her mouth twists upwards.

'Glad to hear it, Inspector Voronov,' she says. There's a change in her tone too.

Wow. A few choice words flit through Isabel's mind but in the end, she only huffs out a disbelieving laugh and shakes her head.

She senses DC Duncan returning long before she hears his steps. He's a little out of breath and clutching more than one bottle of water. 'I wasn't sure how long we'd be and thought it would be better to bring some for everyone.' He holds one out towards Isabel, eyes big and warm.

If he always exudes this type of energy, like a puppy wanting to please, then either he won't get very far, or people here will trample that out of him.

'Thank you,' Isabel says, taking the proffered bottle.

Rampaul turns away before DC Duncan can hand her a bottle and opens the door back into the room. 'You can wait out here, Adam.'

'Yes, boss.'

Satisfied that Isabel and Voronov understand what their role will be inside the room, Rampaul doesn't waste any more time.

Isabel cracks open the lid of the bottle, steps into the room and takes up a spot in the far corner where Voronov joins her.

Grosz looks at Isabel, eyes red-rimmed, back bent under the weight of what he's just discovered.

It's enough to sober Isabel up and have her set aside her irritation.

As long as they're here, then she'll do her best to help in whatever capacity they're allowed to.

Rampaul takes a seat opposite Grosz. She asks if Grosz would like anything else. When Grosz refuses, she gets to the point.

'Mr Grosz, I want you to take me through a typical day at the embassy,' Rampaul says.

Grosz's water bottle is down to half already. He slides it across the surface of the desk from one hand to the other, again and again. Swish, swish, swish, swish, swish.

Much to Rampaul's irritation Grosz is obviously relieved at having both Portuguese representatives present in the room. Some of the tension had visibly left him when he'd realised Isabel and Voronov would remain.

'I understand you must be shocked at what has taken place, but your input here could help us to understand what took place inside the embassy. Please try to answer my questions to the best of your ability.' Rampaul says, removing her jacket and hanging it over her chair. She crosses her legs and balances a refill pad on her thigh. She holds a pencil in her right hand, poised over the paper. She waits.

'Of course,' Grosz replies, but he lifts his eyes to Isabel and Voronov, including them in his address, 'I'll do my best to help.' He clears his throat before continuing. 'I coordinate the staff shifts, oversee our electronic security systems and report on any issues we may have. I also manage any new recruitments for our security team. At times we may require more capacity than when we operate in a normal period.'

'What constitutes a normal period?'

He spreads his hands, a shrug in his shoulders. 'Everyday business where it's our regular staff in the building. We have guests often, some are more high profile than others, so we have to take individual security teams into consideration or provide additional support.'

'Hmm.' Rampaul is recording his answers in her notebook, the *sk-sk* of the pencil moving over paper audible in the room. 'How many people work out of the embassy building?'

'On average we have around fourteen people who operate from there on a daily basis. Sometimes not all at once. But the receptionists and admin assistants, they're mostly in every day. Our cleaning staff also operate from the building daily. We have two. And then of course our security team. We work in shift patterns and in addition to me, there are four others. I'd say in total, working at the embassy we're a team of about twenty.'

'Who are the others?'

'The others?'

'You mentioned the admins, the cleaning staff, and your security team. Who are the others?'

Mr Grosz unscrews the lid from his water and takes a gulp. He screws the top back on with meticulous care and then sets it in front of him again. 'The ambassador, of course, the minister-counsellor, deputy head of mission, the first secretary, the defence, social and press attachés and the ambassador's PA.' He reels off the list easily.

Rampaul nods; she rips off a page from her notebook and places it in front of him along with her pencil. 'Please write all of their names down for me.'

Isabel glances at Voronov, frowning. She stretches up on tiptoe and he lowers his head to catch her low-spoken words. 'Why hasn't the Portuguese Foreign Affairs Department shared the list of staff with the English police already?'

Voronov shrugs and gives a slight shake of his head.

'Who was meant to be on duty today from your security team? Was today a "normal" day as you put it? Who from that list was meant to be there today?'

At that, Grosz stops writing. He looks from Rampaul to Isabel and Voronov and back again.

Rampaul tilts her head. 'You keep looking at the inspectors here. Why? Do you need their permission to say something?' She twists around in her chair and arches a brow at them, tucking her hair behind her ear as she does so.

Isabel tries her best not to show her irritation. She doesn't like Rampaul's tone. Particularly in front of someone they are conducting an interview with. Is this how they treat their colleagues here? No respect? 'No,' Isabel says. And then thinks, to hell with Rampaul not wanting them to interfere in 'her' investigation.

Isabel addresses Grosz. 'Mr Grosz, have you spoken to anyone else in relation to the incident today? Other than us and DI Rampaul's team here?'

Grosz pushes the completed list and the pencil back over to Rampaul, then wraps his hands around his bottle. He twirls it in place on the table, using his thumbs to rotate it. 'Yes, Inspector.'

'Could you specify who it is that spoke with you?'

'It was Mrs Amorim, the head of Consular Affairs in Portugal, and Mr Francisco's secretary, Miss Ramos.'

Milena Amorim. She didn't say a word of this to them this morning.

'Okay,' Isabel says, 'when did you speak with them and what did they say to you?'

'I think it may have been sometime around eleven? It was concerning the extra security we had in place over this past month.'

Rampaul lifts her head sharply and pins him with a stare. 'I thought you said today was a normal day.'

Grosz shakes his head. 'No Detective, you asked me to recount a normal day, which I explained.'

'Right.' Rampaul folds her arms. 'As clearly this wasn't a normal month for you, tell me what was different. Why the extra security? A big-name guest from somewhere else or some kind of special meeting? How much extra security?'

'We used an agency we partner with whenever we require additional security support. It's a Portuguese-owned agency, Moreno Security.'

'Where are they based?'

'Their office is in Chingford.'

'How many extras did you need?'

'We hired a team of ten.'

That seems excessive. 'Why?' Isabel asks and gets a veiled look from Rampaul for her trouble. Too bad.

Grosz swallows and grips the edge of the table in both hands.

Voronov pushes away from the wall. He pulls out a chair next to Rampaul and sits down.

'Mr Grosz,' Voronov says, 'why did you need an additional security team?'

'We needed them to monitor anyone going in and out of the annexe. We got so many because we rotated them in teams of four. We had to implement restricted access to the annexe as well. The only staff with clearance were the ambassador, his secretary, Miss Ramos, and me. Oh, uh, and the deputy head of mission also had clearance.'

Rampaul scans the list he gave her quickly. 'The secretary, Miss Ramos, wasn't one of the staff members found today. Is it normal for her not to be in the building when the ambassador is present and taking meetings?'

'She is there for the most part, but sometimes out on errands. I'm not told about staff whereabouts outside of the embassy. Cíntia, the office and facilities manager might know.'

'Mr Grosz, who was staying in the annexe?' Voronov asks, polite, but firm.

There's a pause and then he says, 'Dr Anabel Pereira.'

Rampaul frowns. 'And who is that?'

He takes a deep breath; he shifts in his seat. He picks up his water and drains the rest of it in one go. 'Dr Pereira is . . . an American fugitive.'

# 6

'The embassy has been harbouring a fugitive?' Rampaul says.

Isabel can still feel the echo of surprise in Rampaul and Voronov. She's right there with them.

'I thought you would know . . . the police were aware of her presence here. There were two officers stationed outside the embassy grounds every night,' he says to Rampaul, then to Voronov and Isabel, 'and the orders for additional security came from the Portuguese Foreign Affairs Department.'

He's right. They should have known.

Amorim had neglected to give them this key fact in the morning briefing and if the chief had known, she would have told them.

Voronov shifts forward. 'Dr Pereira. What is her full name?'

'Anabel Pereira.'

Isabel tugs her notebook from where it's crammed in her back pocket and scrawls the name down. She's not familiar with it.

'When did Dr Pereira arrive at the embassy?' Voronov asks.

'She arrived at the embassy end of July.'

They're in September now. This means she's been here for over a month.

What's an American fugitive doing seeking refuge in a Portuguese embassy? Her surname is a common Portuguese one, so there's most likely a connection there somewhere.

'When we were searching the premises earlier this evening you didn't mention Dr Pereira. Was she among the deceased you identified?'

Grosz shakes his head, his brow furrowing. His Adam's apple bobs. 'No, she wasn't there.' Then before they can ask any other any questions, Grosz drops his head into his hands. 'Sorry,

34

I – I . . . can we stop for now? I need to – I need to go home. Please.'

Isabel glances at Rampaul.

Rampaul is watching Grosz quietly.

'Please,' Grosz says again.

DC Duncan is the one who escorts Grosz to the entrance and ensures he's okay enough to get home on his own.

'Well. I think this is enough to work on for now,' Rampaul says.

Isabel looks at her, incredulous.

They had followed Rampaul after she finished with interviewing Grosz and leading him out.

They're in a brightly lit open office, with high ceilings and carpeted floor. It's certainly warmer in here than it had been outside. The squat windows look down on to a narrow street with lit-up window displays of boutique shops that have long since closed for the evening. A few modest restaurants too. Eight desks fit into the room and there's a small corner at the back which is only partially sectioned off with a compact kitchenette built in. Tins of tea and coffee, a kettle, toaster, and microwave are visible. There's a small fridge tucked beneath the counter and a tap and sink on the opposite side.

The people sitting at their desks, typing away or on the phone had all watched their progress through the office to the very back, where Rampaul's desk is.

Rampaul doesn't bother glancing at them as she boots up her computer. 'We'll be in touch if we need any more help. DC Duncan here will help you out with anything you need.'

When neither Isabel nor Voronov respond, DC Duncan hovers at the side of the desk, uncomfortable Rampaul stops messing about with her computer. She leans forward on the desk, folding her arms. 'I told you before the interview. We appreciate your help, but this is as far as your involvement goes. If we need anything else, we'll get in touch with you. We've done what was asked of us and waited for your arrival, we didn't overstep on your government grounds but that's it now.' She straightens up and turns back to her computer. 'DC Duncan, give them a ride to their place, please. Thank you.'

Voronov steps closer to Isabel, his chest brushing against her shoulder, and places a hand on her arm. 'Let's go. We need to speak to the chief anyway.'

It's the soft, cooling calm oozing into Isabel from his touch that draws her from that ragged edge, scathing words balanced on the tip of her tongue and ready to spill out.

She draws in a deep breath and nods. 'Fine.'

DC Duncan, head down and with cheeks darkened by a flush again, jogs lightly to catch up to them and take the lead. 'I'll lead the way to the car,' he says quietly.

It's not his fault, so Isabel forces herself to grind out a thank-you.

Voronov stays close to her, face impassive and head held high as they make their way out of the building. If Isabel didn't know any better, she'd think that Rampaul's rudeness hadn't bothered him one bit. But she does know better. All she needs is to stretch her senses just a little – the last thing she needs is her walls collapsing under the onslaught of the other voices and moods around them – and it's there. Displeasure, grey-tinged, rising from his chest and tainting the air around them.

DC Duncan leads them to the same black Ford Focus he'd driven to collect them at the airport.

'I'll sit in the back,' she says, 'might need to close my eyes for a bit.' There's a noticeable difference immediately after they leave the building. The entire time they'd been inside, it had felt like her head was trapped in a vacuum. The sheer amount of unregulated thoughts and emotions piling on to her barriers had left a lingering ache in her temples.

She gets in the back, and if it weren't for Rampaul being so condescending and disrespectful of them, Isabel would have stretched out over the back seats and tried to nap until they reached their destination. As it is, she doesn't want DC Duncan reporting back anything remotely negative.

As DC Duncan and Voronov get in the front seats, she ponders the differences in environment. In Portugal there's an elevated awareness that Gifted are part of the general population. Isabel hears things as she walks the street all the time but they're quieter. People have an instinctive caution because they know that at any time a Gifted person could listen in.

That doesn't seem to be the case here. People here seem to have their thoughts on blast and it's a powerful blow if you're a Gifted telepath who is not accustomed to this.

'Adam. That's what DI Rampaul called you?' Isabel asks.

Starting the car, DC Duncan looks at the rear-view mirror to respond. 'Yes, ma'am, that's right.'

'Do you mind if I call you Adam, too? And please, Isabel is fine.'

She catches a small smile and a nod from him before he turns his attention back to the road. 'Of course, yes, Adam works!'

Isabel smiles back. 'I'm curious about something.' The rain has let up as DC Duncan eases the car out of the car park and into the road. 'What is the situation here with Gifted?'

'Oh,' his eyes flick to her quickly before resettling on the road, 'that's – well. It's not a very pretty uh . . . explanation.'

'It never is,' she says.

Voronov glances back at her and their eyes meet for a moment.

'Well . . . it's not like we've ever had a huge Gifted population, we're pretty much like other countries in that regard. Gifted are a minority here, I think they number in the lower hundreds. During World War Two things changed for them. Not so much for the telekinetic Gifted. But they, uh, because of spying, you know? The telepathic Gifted were seen as too much of a risk here. Anyway . . . things were made difficult for some of them, in the UK I mean. Many left the country, emigrated elsewhere, mostly mainland Europe or the States. Others,' he shrugs but his tone becomes subdued, 'well. There are stories and theories and even some evidence to back those up.'

Isabel swallows, feeling queasy; her mind all too easily fills the gap.

'Their numbers shrank drastically. It has started to change again though, since the two thousands, a few telepathic Gifted popping up here and there, particularly with immigration, but nowhere near the numbers we had in the past.'

'I see.'

'If you're interested, there's a museum in King's Cross,' he says. 'It's a part of one of the universities around that area.'

Silence falls in the car, uneasy in light of what he'd just said.

Isabel thinks back to Portugal's own history and the tight grip the NTI had developed over time on the lives of Gifted. They dealt with their own persecution there. *We still do*, Isabel thinks.

'How far from here are we staying?' Isabel asks.

Chief Bautista had told them that the Consular Affairs Department arranged the place where they will be staying while here. They'd received the address as they'd been about to board, but Isabel has no idea where it is in relation to the embassy and the police station where Rampaul's unit is based.

'Oh. Well, there isn't much traffic right now, so it won't take too long. About thirty-five minutes to North Greenwich.'

'Thank you,' Isabel says.

Her phone vibrates in her jacket pocket. She realises she hasn't checked it or even messaged anyone to tell them they arrived safely and it's almost nine in the evening. She'd briefly looked at it as they'd left the airport to see if she had a connection and then put it away after that.

Her phone screen lights up the back of the car. She unlocks it and scrolls through the notifications. A message from Sebastião asking her if she'd landed safely from hours ago, a missed call from Chief Bautista and multiple messages from their team on their group chat. There was a missed call from her aunt too. The other name she sees on there gives her pause. A message from Michael, her sister's fiancé. Also, Isabel's ex.

The last time they'd spoken had been after an argument with her paranoid sister. Rita had become convinced that retaining a doctor-patient relationship with her ex meant Isabel was trying to get him back.

It had led to an ugly parting between the two of them with Michael showing up at Isabel's place nearing midnight. Isabel had ignored the ring of the bell and all the calls and texts that followed. She has enough on her plate without being pulled into manufactured drama.

Isabel locks the phone again and stuffs it back in her coat pocket. She'll deal with them all when they arrive at their place.

They fall into silence and Adam switches on the radio, a news station. A crisp, deep male voice reports on the weather.

Isabel lets the steady reporting soothe her overstimulated mind, the newsreader reminding listeners of the oncoming heatwave. She watches the passing scenery with detached interest. There are some things that catch her attention but she's too exhausted for them to hold her curiosity for more than a second. Besides, if they're going to be made to stay out of the investigation, God knows she'll be bored out of her mind. Maybe she'll wander around for a bit.

She thinks about Grosz's revelation that the embassy had been harbouring a fugitive. Something else Milena Amorim had withheld at the briefing that morning. Then again it might not matter, they might be on a plane back tomorrow morning. Maybe she didn't tell them because, like Rampaul, she didn't expect them to do more than scope out the situation and hand it over to the English police.

The thought doesn't sit well with Isabel.

At some point they turn off the main road and into a smaller one that runs alongside a group of tall buildings. It's clearly a residential area. They are located right next to the gleaming black river.

The whole area looks newly built. There are small sections between the buildings with trees and benches. A couple of shops sit right at the end and are still open. It reminds Isabel a little of the blocks in Portugal, except these are high-end, all the glass giving them a sleek finish. In Portugal they'd have cafés at the bottom instead, all of which would have been open at this hour and packed with regular customers. Here, everything is dark and aside from those two shops she's glimpsed, she can't make out what the other businesses are.

To her surprise, the car slows down and Adam pulls up by the pavement of one of the buildings.

'This is it. Maps says it's this one here.' Adam ducks his head to peer through the windscreen and up; he sounds disbelieving and a little impressed. 'It's nice.'

Voronov glances back at her as if expecting her to confirm whether this is the right place or not.

Isabel shakes her head. 'Don't look at me, all I have is the address. But I don't think our detective constable here would get it wrong.'

'Yes,' Adam says, glancing down at the app open on his phone, 'it says this is the place.'

Well. If that's what it's saying, then she guesses this is it. Isabel opens the door and gets out.

It's quiet. That's the first thing she notices.

The second thing she notices is that she can hear the river.

She hears the other door open, and Voronov gets out too.

The surrounding apartment blocks are even taller than they'd seemed from inside the car, and every single one of them has a sizeable balcony and a view across the city.

It was some view. Even from where she stands, Isabel can see the brightly lit buildings of the city across the river.

'All right. Let's go find our place, then,' she says and rounds the car to get their stuff out from the boot.

Adam hurries over to help her.

'No, no,' she says. 'Thanks, but I've got it. I'm sure you probably want to head back. We've got it from here.'

Adam smiles and nods. 'Okay. Here, take my number in case you need anything,' he says, fishing his phone out of his pocket, 'I'll be back in the morning after reporting in.'

They take his number and bid him goodnight before making for the entrance.

There are gardens in between the buildings and benches, leading down to the riverwalk. There are actually some people out, strolling down to the river.

They get into the building with a code. The Reception area isn't what Isabel expects. The lights are still on, and she sees sofas arranged in front of a help desk counter, unmanned. It stretches deeper into the building, but the view is blocked by the lifts.

A couple of people – Isabel assumes they must be residents – occupying the space look their way as they head straight for the lifts. Some are cradling cups in their hands, coffee or tea, Isabel isn't sure.

'If the government have the money to send us to a place this nice then you'd think they could fix the heaters in our building,' Isabel says and jabs at the call button for the lift.

'Are you complaining?'

Isabel snorts. 'Oh, I plan on milking this for what it's worth, don't worry.' She hears the tell-tale squeak and groan of the lift reaching them and a few seconds later the doors ding open, revealing a small space big enough for about five people.

'Ninth?' Voronov asks when they're in.

'Yeah, that's what it said.'

He presses the button, and the doors slide shut.

'According to the head of security, her name is Anabel Pereira, and she was a part of the American military, a research division,' Voronov says.

Isabel leans on the breakfast counter, her phone in hand and on loudspeaker; they're both still wearing their jackets, having connected to the Wi-Fi and called the chief right away.

'She wasn't among the twelve deceased identified by Grosz at the scene, and we didn't find anyone else in the building,' Isabel adds.

Even over the phone, Isabel can make out the distinctive sound of Chief Bautista flicking a lighter.

Isabel and Voronov share a look.

'What do you want us to do, Chief?' Isabel asks.

A deep sigh carries over the line. 'Stay put. I need to speak with Amorim and her people. There's always something with this lot. I'll update you both in the morning.'

'Yes, Chief.'

They say goodnight and hang up.

'I guess that's that.' Isabel eases herself up on to the stool. It feels like now that they've done all they need to today, the day is catching up with her. She stretches her arms over the breakfast bar and lays her head down. 'I don't think we have any food.'

'I saw some vending machines downstairs. I'll go and see what they have.'

Isabel lifts her head up. 'I can go.'

He waves her away. 'It's fine. I'll be right back.'

Isabel stays where she is for a bit after he goes. Eventually she slides off the stool to explore the apartment.

The interior matches the expectations set by the outside.

The bathroom is located immediately after the entrance with a small closet directly opposite that is meant to serve as a cloak-room, with built-in shoe racks at the bottom. Glancing at it, Isabel thinks that no person with a decent shoe collection would be able to fit anything of significance there.

Beyond the short corridor in front of the front door is the open space of the sitting room. It's a sitting room and dining room in one, with the kitchen, also open plan, to the left. The balcony, an impressive size and with a view of the river and the other surrounding buildings, is directly ahead. Then there are two bedroom doors to the right.

One of them, the one closest to the front door, has a low light on and when she draws closer to it she spots Voronov's bag by the neatly made double bed. Her bag is by the closed door next to it. He must've moved it there without her noticing.

Sliding doors separate the living-room space from the balcony. The city lights glitter, reflected in the ever-shifting surface of the river. She unlocks the balcony doors and steps outside. The wind whips her hair up and is cutting against her skin, leaving her chilled. Isabel wraps her arms around herself.

It's different from Lisbon. The darkness of the night sky here feels deeper, bottomless.

Looking out across the river it feels like they're on a little island, cut off from the main part of the city. Windows all around her are lit up, tiny rectangles of yellow making it seem like a festival of lights is happening all around her. The air is different too, even if the wet earth smell of rain remains the same. It lingers in the air. The clouds that pad the sky are menacing, crowding above the cityscape, and rolling too fast with the push of the wind.

The wind chafes at the sensitive skin of her mouth and cheek. Gently, she feels the area with a finger, wincing when the ache radiates out to encompass her entire face.

She's still out there when she hears the door to the apartment open and close. She listens to Voronov's steps as he walks over to the balcony. 'There wasn't much but I brought a few packets of crisps up, and water.'

Isabel tucks her hair behind her ears and turns to him. 'Thanks.'

'We should eat and then get some rest.'

She can't hide the relief that fills her at those words.

*Graças a deus.*

She'd thought he might take this opportunity to push. To ask what's been going on with her the past couple of months now they are finally alone and without fear of interruption. She knows he wants to.

She does owe him an explanation. But not right now. She isn't ready yet.

Isabel rubs at the bridge of her nose, running her thumb up and down, digging a little in between her eyes, to alleviate the pressure she feels mounted there. She nods. 'Yeah.'

A sudden gust of window almost rocks her. She takes that as a sign to get back inside and pulls the sliding door shut. When she turns, Voronov has left the doorway and is sitting on the edge of the sofa, fingers linked together.

'How's your face?'

'Still there,' she says and when that gets a reluctant smile out of him, she can't help her own answering one. She knows he's still worried. 'It hurts when I speak, but it's not too bad. It'll be fine.'

But then silence falls again. It draws out and neither of them move.

'I'm gonna take a shower first,' she says, 'and then try to get some sleep.'

'All right.'

She picks up her bag and heads over to the bathroom.

'Isabel.'

She stops and looks over her shoulder at him.

'We need to talk.'

Isabel pushes her hair back from her face. 'I know.' She meets his eyes and gives him a tired smile. 'We will.'

After a moment, Voronov nods. He doesn't say anything else.

Isabel goes into the bathroom and shuts the door quietly behind her.

# 7

Isabel slows down to a walk, continuing along the riverside until she comes to a stop, chest rising and falling sharply with each breath. She leans her hands on the railing and lets her head hang as her body slowly catches up with stillness.

Her hair is wet, curls sticking to her forehead, rainwater dripping from her chin, and her hamstrings and calves feel tight as stone. She licks her lips and tastes rain and the tangy saltiness of sweat. The rain had begun ten minutes into her run but there's an uncomfortable heat rising in the air.

Isabel makes quick work of stretching out her legs before she's speed-walking back to the tall building they'd arrived at late last night.

It's just as shiny-new in the daytime. The only difference being that where the view at night was of a glittering city, now it's of a river that reflects the murkiness of the sky with little boats dotted here and there.

It must be school time. There are parents hustling their children in their raincoats into cars or hissing at them to hurry. One little boy seems to be in his own world, riding his scooter at a leisurely pace, unmoved by his mother's words that are being forced out through gritted teeth and tight lips. Isabel shakes her head, struggling to keep a smile from her face.

On the ground floor of the building, what Isabel had thought were shopfronts the night before turns out to be a large super-market, with a bright orange logo and well-lit inside. Even at this time of the morning, Isabel can see how busy it already is, people roaming its aisles and some queueing at the manned tills. They'll need to make a trip to it later. She'd had a peek inside the cupboards in the apartment and all she found was cutlery.

Well. She should be grateful that there's anything at all.

Next to it is a gym and next to that, and of much more interest to Isabel, a coffee shop.

She goes in and she's surrounded by the warm familiar scent of coffee. There are people spread out throughout the shop: mothers with pushchairs having a morning coffee and chatting before they go on with their day, a businessman tucked into the corner digging for something in his bag, irritation stamping the air around him, a young woman clutching a tall takeaway cup swiping at the screen of her tablet, an electronic pencil between her fingers, chewing on her lip.

Isabel queues up, the state of her face drawing sneaky glances from staff and customers alike. Her bruises are much more colourful today. She'd winced when she'd seen herself in the mirror this morning. The apartment had been quiet as she'd got silently ready before slipping out for her run. Her body had been heavy from another night of sleep. She doesn't want to over-rely on the sleeping pills but without them, every time she closes her eyes—

The barista calls for the next person. Isabel shuffles forward with everyone else.

She walks out with two coffees, ham and cheese toasties and some muffins.

'How are they charging this much for coffee and a bit of food?' Isabel mutters. She feels conned.

Voronov is sitting at the kitchen counter when she walks in, laptop open. His hair is wet, and he's already dressed.

'Bom dia,' Isabel says, lifting the paper bag in her hand as she enters.

Voronov glances at the window then back at her. 'You went running in that?'

Isabel shrugs. 'It's not cold, but it wasn't the most pleasant run.' Now that she's out of the rain though, she feels her body growing uncomfortably cold in the wet clothes. 'Got us food,' she says, setting it down in front of him. She takes off her cap and drops it on the counter. Her hair is plastered to her head and clinging to the sides of her face and neck, and rainwater is gathered all along her hairline. She wipes at it, but it doesn't do much good.

Voronov rolls up his sleeves. 'Thank you.'

'Don't look so shocked.'

The smell of cheese and hot bread hits her nose as Voronov unwraps his toastie, making Isabel's mouth water. 'It's usually the other way around.'

Isabel huffs and drags one of the coffees over to her.

'I found some things,' Voronov says.

Isabel moves to his side to peer at his laptop.

He's got enough tabs open on his browser to make her eyes cross, but there are a few separate windows popped out.

'On the case we've been told to keep our noses out of, hmm?' She arcs an eyebrow at him, a smirk playing around the corner of her lips before leaning closer, using the mouse pad to click through. 'What's this?'

'I was curious. This is what came up when I searched for a Dr Anabel Pereira online.'

It's three articles; two of them are relatively short and the third one runs a little longer.

'Did the chief call yet?' she asks.

'She messaged telling us to call her. I was waiting for you to get back.'

Two of the articles relate to a prize won by a high-school student in New Bedford, Massachusetts. The student in question is Anabel Pereira, who according to the article is a Gifted student with an outstanding talent for science.

A picture is included at the end of one of the articles. A young woman standing with someone who is presumably her teacher, a large podium behind her that reminds Isabel of her old school and the way the gym had doubled as a place for performances and other school-wide presentations. The girl is awkward-looking.

Very tall, like someone whose body shot up too quickly and she hasn't grown into it yet. She has a strong jaw and full cheeks and she's wearing jeans and a blue button-down, with a cardigan over it. Her dark hair is drawn away from her face and pinned to the back of her head. It's started to go lopsided. She's holding a certificate in her hand and the smile she's aiming at the camera is uncomfortable.

She doesn't appear to be enjoying the attention.

The final and longer article talks about a project expected to have break-through results in optimisation of Gifts to allow for a more inclusive military force.

'Doesn't sound ominous at all,' Isabel mutters.

The research project was being led by a Dr Eliana Cross and a little further along, as part of Cross's quote, it mentions Anabel Pereira. The article says she was a part of the research team.

Isabel checks the date of the article. It had been published three years ago.

'Hmm.' Isabel looks at Voronov. 'So how does a promising, young American research scientist end up as a fugitive at a foreign embassy in England?'

'For now, you're both staying put.'

Isabel can see the brightness filling the chief's office in Lisbon on the screen. It might not be a blaze of sunlight but it's still a contrast to what's outside their window. That brightness doesn't extend to the chief's expression.

She's normally not the happiest-looking person as it is, but the lines carved into her forehead and downturn of her mouth as she speaks say that today would be a good day for people to keep to themselves.

'Okay,' Isabel says, drawing the word out, 'we stay. What are we doing exactly?'

'Milena Amorim is insisting on your presence there and she wants you assisting in the inquiry. I've spoken to Superintendent McKinley. He is the head of the Major Crime Investigative

Unit, and he's agreed to you both supporting DI Rampaul in the investigation but watch your step. They're not happy about it.'

Yeah, neither are we, Isabel thinks, huffing. 'Chief—'

'Reis, don't give me grief. I'm already pissed off about this situation. Assist them for now. I've agreed that you stay for the first week. After that, I'm going over Milena Amorim's head. If she wants you both there longer then I'm going to need their department to give me some actual answers.'

'What about the fugitive?' Voronov asks. 'Did they give us anything on her?'

Isabel didn't think it was possible for Chief Bautista's expression to sour any further. She's wrong.

'No. She claims she doesn't know anything. I've got Daniel and Carla in the station chasing the information down with Rogério Pessoa as we speak.' Pessoa is the Foreign Affairs official who had been on the call with Francisco at the time of his death. 'So far they haven't made it past his secretary. If we don't have anything by the end of the day, I'll be making calls myself and they won't like it.'

'Okay. Anything else, Chief?' Isabel asks.

'Just behave yourselves.'

Isabel frowns. 'We always do.'

Bautista doesn't immediately respond but when she does, she says, 'In a situation like this, you've got eyes on you.'

Voronov, who has been leaning on the back of the sofa, pushes off and nears the tablet. 'Do you mean the police here?' he asks.

The chief's eyes shift over to Isabel. 'We'll talk when you get back.'

A flash of hot cold washes over Isabel from head to foot as her mind instantly reaches for the most likely reasons for the chief's words.

Bautista doesn't elaborate further. 'The superintendent will send someone from the MCIU for you both so I'll leave you to get on with your day. Keep me posted.'

She hangs up before either of them can say anything else. Her face disappears from the screen to be filled by three emojis, asking them to rate the quality of the call.

Isabel flips the tablet closed and sets it down.

Isabel looks at Voronov. 'Great. Think they'll throw us a welcome party?'

# 8

Eyes track Isabel and Voronov's progress through the room as they follow Adam.

This time there's hostility. It compresses the air, frost-white and razor-thin. Hostility is nothing new to either of them.

At the far end of the office, Isabel notices Rampaul rising from her seat and watching them make their way over. Her eyes drift over the room, taking in all the heads turning in their direction, and the smallest frown lines her forehead. She types something short and quick and steps out from behind her desk.

DI Keeley, Rampaul's partner who they had been introduced to briefly last night, remains seated.

Yeah, Isabel thinks as she catches his sour expression, he's certainly not hiding how he feels about this situation.

Rampaul is holding a slim folder to her chest and tapping a pen against the partition. 'Inspectors,' she says, 'good morning. Follow me. You too, Adam.'

Adam pauses in his step before nodding quickly and speeding up.

Isabel glances at Voronov. 'Partner isn't coming?' she murmurs.

Voronov looks over his shoulder. 'Doesn't look like it.'

'Looks like some interesting conversations have taken place this morning,' Isabel says.

Rampaul leads them all into a room similar to the one they interviewed Grosz in yesterday. She holds the door, ushering them in. The room has one desk in the centre, no windows and three chairs that look about as comfortable as the floor itself.

The walls are painted grey, and the lights are powerful, brutally lighting up everyone's faces. Isabel is sure it's doing wonders for her bruised eye and mouth. Right now, she'd probably fit right in at a zombie movie set.

'Take a seat if you would like,' Rampaul says. She throws her folder on the table and drags a chair out, sinking into it with a heavy sigh.

Isabel and Voronov remain standing.

Adam takes in the look Rampaul gives him and with an apologetic dip of his head goes to one of the chairs and sits. He scoots closer to the desk, attention on Rampaul.

He seems nervous and like he too isn't entirely sure about what is going on.

Rampaul crosses one leg over the other, settling in, and steeples her fingers together, resting them on her stomach.

She's in jeans and a soft, thin powder-blue cashmere V-neck, her sleeves rolled up past her elbows. It's a more relaxed version of her than they'd seen the day before. Though Isabel is sure that her tongue won't have lost any of its cutting intelligence.

'I'll bring you up to speed on a few changes that have taken place since we last spoke yesterday,' Rampaul says. 'As I'm sure you know by now, you've both been asked to remain and assist with this investigation for the time being.' She pauses there. The corners of her mouth pinch before she rolls her lips inward as if mulling over how to continue. 'I'll be frank. My superintendent isn't happy.'

Adam flicks a look at Rampaul, eyes narrowing.

There's something else going on here, Isabel thinks, which is unrelated to her and Voronov's presence. Given what she's seen of this place so far, she can make a couple of educated guesses.

'He doesn't want others calling the shots on his turf. Since this involves both a foreign embassy and an American fugitive, it has the potential to become a diplomatic issue and we want to avoid that. I've been tasked SIO for this case. DC Duncan, you'll be working alongside myself and the inspectors here.'

Adam is startled. 'Boss?' Clearly, he hadn't been expecting that piece of information.

Rampaul sits up and rests a hand on the table. 'The presence of a fugitive on the premises makes this more challenging. Superintendent McKinley wants her found fast. He wants updates by the end of today. We've been told to keep this quiet.' Her jaw clenches before she smooths over her expression and continues. 'The number of investigators working this case is limited to the people in this room. For now.'

Isabel's eyebrows keep climbing up her forehead as Rampaul speaks and she doesn't bother to hide the incredulity she knows is stamped on her face.

Voronov stares at Rampaul. 'Surely if Superintendent McKinley wants fast results, it would be in this investigation's best interests to increase the workforce here.'

'Will your partner be assisting us at least?' Isabel asks quietly. She can feel Rampaul's agitation. It's frothing at her throat, barely kept in check by sheer force of will. Not a touch of it shows on her face. Isabel isn't sure if it's her question or the answer to it that she's frustrated by.

Rampaul takes a breath before she responds.

'Superintendent McKinley is of the opinion that with DC Duncan assisting on the case, as well as two very capable and experienced inspectors, we'll be able to do what we need to. Of course, the forensic unit will continue to support as needed. We can revisit the question of additional support, if needed, after we present our initial findings.'

Isabel's not going to correct her. She knows someone talking themselves down when she sees it. In any other case, what she's saying would be reasonable. Not this one.

But in this instance, they're dealing with an incident involving diplomatic individuals. The decision not to go above and beyond is either petty or short-sighted. Neither of those bode well for the future of the investigation. If this goes downhill it won't look good, and not just for the British police. Isabel and Voronov are involved in this now. Anything that goes wrong *will* reflect on them.

'Then I guess we don't have time to waste,' Isabel says.

Rampaul meets Isabel's eyes dead on and for the first time since their introduction yesterday, Isabel doesn't feel like the other woman wants to throw her out of a window.

Rampaul turns to her folder and flips it open. There are a couple of sheets in it but that's about it. 'At the moment we only have the report of what we found when we entered the premises yesterday at 7.12 p.m. and the few details Mr Grosz shared with us.'

Isabel and Voronov draw closer to the table.

Rampaul pulls a yellow legal pad from beneath the folder and produces a pen. 'As our starting point we have twelve dead bodies. Cause of death is as yet unknown. And we have a missing fugitive who is potentially the only one who knows what happened yesterday morning. Thanks to Mr Grosz, we are certain of the identity of all twelve deceased.' Seven had been staff members, four were outsourced security and one had been a guest.

Twelve dead and no cause of death . . . Isabel feels a ripple of unease. She glances at Voronov.

Voronov sets his backpack down on the floor by the table. 'We need to find Dr Anabel Pereira,' Voronov says, 'she's key to this case.'

Isabel folds her arms across her chest and sighs. 'Yes. And we need to understand the dynamics of the embassy. Mr Grosz mentioned the office and facilities manager. I think she's someone we should speak to as soon as possible.'

Rampaul nods. 'And the secretary, Ramos. We haven't heard a peep from her yet, which is odd considering the ambassador is dead.' What goes unsaid is how all these things would have already been followed up if the MCIU hadn't been made to wait for Isabel and Voronov to enter the embassy. It's a delay that Isabel has yet to see any solid justification for.

'We spoke to our chief this morning,' Voronov says. 'We have colleagues on that side trying to get us more information on Dr Pereira and the circumstances of how she came to be there, but as a fugitive, a Red Notice would have been issued.' In the case of a wanted international fugitive, INTERPOL will usually issue a Red Notice to inform police enforcement worldwide that someone is wanted. It provides identifying information and information related to the crime they have committed. Considering how unforthcoming the Portuguese government are proving to be in relation to Dr Pereira, maybe they'll have better luck there.

'We should also check to see if there was ever a report filed,' Isabel says, 'any record of police being aware of her presence here.' After a thoughtful pause, she adds: 'Depending on the nature of her offence, maybe even domestic counterintelligence and security?'

'All right.' Rampaul stands. 'We can start there. Adam, find me the officers who were assigned to keep an eye on Dr Pereira.' She looks at Adam. 'We want to talk to them before the day is out.'

Adam nods.

She turns to Isabel. 'I've been told you're a telepathic Gifted. How much of your ability are you able to use?'

Isabel and Voronov stare at her, both taken aback by her bluntness.

'What do you mean?' Isabel asks.

'I think if you know how to use that power of yours properly then I want you with me speaking to the members of staff. It means you can read their minds, right?'

Isabel frowns. 'Not exactly. There are rules in place.'

'What rules?' Rampaul scoffs. 'Inspector Voronov, I'm stealing your partner. Can I trust you and DC Duncan to check for live alerts, and any available records, on Dr Pereira?'

Voronov inclines his head. 'Of course.'

Adam stands so fast he almost knocks his chair back. 'Yes, boss. And I'll pull up a map of the area too. We can use it as a guide for identifying nearby businesses and residents and check for any surveillance points that might be of use.'

'Good. Let us know what you find.'

Voronov shrugs out of his jacket. He looks at Isabel. 'Call me if you need me,' he says.

Isabel swallows and nods. 'I will. Same with you.'

# 9

Andrzej Grosz lives in a semi-detached house at the end of a cul-de-sac. The road itself stands out from the ones they've passed by on their way. The ones Isabel has seen so far make her think of the English historical dramas oozing with old-world elegance they air back home, although less grand of course.

Grosz's street is different; the houses on either side are set a level lower than the pavement, with grass sweeping down to them like mini hills. These houses are large and flat roofed with white windows, and they have a distinct retro vibe. Most of the cars are parked on the road.

The road sign sticks up from the ground in the street and reads Acacia Avenue. A black cat twines around the legs of the sign before crossing the road at a leisurely pace to join another cat curled beneath a parked car. A lone older lady makes slow progress down the pavement on the other side of the road, pulling her check-print trolley behind her. Other than that, the street is calm as Isabel exits the car and slams the door shut behind her.

The ground glitters with the aftermath of rain, and rainwater is gathered in the potholes marring the road surface.

Rampaul slams her door shut as she gets out, a beep sounding as she locks the car.

'It's that one over there,' Rampaul says and points with her car keys at the last house on the right side of the road. A small pale-blue vehicle is parked out front. Not the kind of car Isabel would have associated with Grosz. She isn't sure if a man of his height can fit inside it.

Steam pours out from a central heating flue on the wall of the house. Hopefully that means he's home. 'You said there are rules,' Rampaul says, peering up at Grosz's house as they go.

It's not that bright out, yesterday's rain clouds lingering. But there's a glow to them that heats the air at ground level. The scent of rain lingers.

Isabel looks at her askance.

Rampaul points at her head. 'Your Gift. You said there are rules.'

'You don't have rules here?' Isabel asks.

'We don't have many Gifted in the force,' Rampaul says. 'And of the ones we do, none are telepathic Gifted.'

That you know of, Isabel thinks. Given what Adam told them last night and what she's hearing now, Isabel wonders what their system is for testing here, if their monitoring runs differently. If there even is a monitoring.

'Keeping my affinity to myself, unless consent is specifically granted by someone for me to do otherwise,' she says.

Rampaul glances at her. 'How will anyone know if you've broken the rules?'

'For case purposes, any information obtained through the use of my Gift, if consent was not explicitly given beforehand and recorded, becomes inadmissible.'

'That doesn't really answer my question,' Rampaul says. 'How can they tell?'

'They can't.'

Rampaul's lips curve into a smirk. 'Well, that's interesting, isn't it?'

There's a twitch of a curtain at the kitchen window of the house across from Grosz's. Isabel catches sight of an older lady staring at them quite blatantly from her house while sipping from a mug.

Maybe the gossiping culture and watching what the neighbours are doing is as much a thing here as it is in Portugal.

Isabel sighs and gives a slight shake of her head as predictably she picks up said neighbour's thoughts.

*Police? May be getting a show this morning.*

Isabel deliberately turns her back on the snoop. Rampaul is

already taking the steps leading down the miniature grass hill to the stone path that runs along by the houses.

A neat little number 31 is painted on to the front door.

Rampaul raps her knuckles on the door.

Isabel can hear the faint sounds of a TV from inside and what sounds like the whistle of a kettle. It's not long before she hears footsteps too. They get louder the closer they get to the door.

The door opens. Grosz's head almost brushes the top of the doorframe. His hair sticks right up, as if he's run his hands through it many times. His worn grey robe has a bleach stain on the shoulder and his black slippers have seen better days. His hairy ankles are exposed, and the lower half of his face is covered in greying stubble.

'Good morning, Mr Grosz,' Rampaul says.

He squints at them and shrinks away from the bright outside light. The skin beneath his eyes is a swollen purplish pink. 'Detective . . .' he says and then his gaze slides to Isabel.

Rampaul gives him a polite smile and flicks a glance behind him. 'We're sorry for coming unannounced. Can we come in?'

He looks weary but steps back into the house. 'Yes. Of course. Please.'

'Thank you,' Rampaul says, making sure to wipe her feet before stepping inside. 'We won't take up too much of your time.'

Isabel murmurs a thanks as she follows.

'Then . . . ?' he prompts, shutting the door behind him.

'If we could sit down and talk,' Rampaul says, 'we can explain the situation a bit better.'

'Okay,' he says, 'if you come this way.' He doesn't take them far into the house.

Isabel catches a glimpse of a living room with sliding doors that face an overgrown back garden. There's a plastic chair and a small table with an ashtray close to the doors. A small lamp by a saggy brown sofa is lit, casting a weak glow over one corner of the sofa where a paperback lies, split open, on the cushion. The sound of a TV is coming from inside the room but it's not within view.

Grosz takes them in through a door on their left which takes them into a tiny kitchen that is at odds with Grosz's size. The table is up against the far wall with three chairs tucked around it, and a window that overlooks the front of the house is directly above the sink. Pale yellow tiles with some kind of white flower pattern line the wall between the cupboards and the counter. There is a cluster of empty beer cans where the counter butts up against the fridge.

The whistling sound they'd heard when they knocked on the door is coming from the kettle on the stove. Grosz walks over to it, the soles of his slippers slapping on the floor as he goes, and switches off the flames.

'Sorry,' he says, and there's a rumble to his voice, 'I slept late.' He makes a gesture in front of his face. 'It's hard to . . . keep the things I saw inside that place out of my head, you know?'

'I understand,' Rampaul says.

Grosz gets a mug from a cupboard and opens a tin, plucks a tea bag out of it and drops it into the mug, before pouring over the steaming water from the kettle. He's quiet and lost in his own head, as if between one moment and the next he's forgotten their presence.

He turns and startles, like he's seeing them again for the first time.

This is not the man who sat across from them in the interview room yesterday.

Isabel tentatively reaches out. She wants to get a sense of his state.

What they saw yesterday was horrific. Is it the worst thing Isabel has ever seen? No. But even she found it hard to push back the images of all those people lying dead, as if someone had just cut their strings as they'd gone about their day.

If it can affect Isabel and others in her profession, then the impact on someone who doesn't deal with death as frequently will be tenfold.

She doesn't need to touch him, hasn't needed physical contact for something like this in a very long time. She sees it in her mind's eye as clear as if she were examining a photo album. Snapshots of the dead, flicking into the centre of Grosz's thoughts one after the other, again and again. There's a crystal quality to certain details – the too-wide eyes, fingers curled rictus-tight around the handle of a mug, mouths frozen in half-uttered sounds on gurneys before being covered in white sheets – that reeks of shock. Just behind that is the mind-numbing horror and denial the colour of a bruise.

'Sorry . . .' he says again. His eyes are fixed on the drink he's poured, tea bag staining the water brown. 'I'm . . .' He sets the mug down on the counter, the movement abrupt. Tea sloshes over the side. He covers his face with both hands and takes a deep breath, back expanding with it. He rubs his eyes and when he drops his hands, they have turned red. 'You want something to drink? Tea or coffee, or water? I think I have juice too if you like. Or . . .' His eyes drift over the empty beer cans and he seals his mouth shut.

Isabel can feel the agitation in him. The need to do something. Stillness is what probably led to the cans of beer that finally knocked him into sleep last night. It's easy to peer a little further into his head. The wounds are fresh in his mind, bubbling at the surface without her needing to go where she shouldn't.

Rampaul visibly gentles. 'A tea, if it's not too much trouble.'

'I'll have the same, thank you,' Isabel says.

As Grosz busies himself with the drinks, Rampaul wanders over to the window and glances out to the road. 'It's a very quiet road,' she says. 'I find it odd; I'm so used to noise.'

'I've been here a few years. Three now, I think,' he says. Steam rises from the mugs as he pours the water in. He dips into the fridge for milk. He releases the door and it slams closed hard enough to shake the fridge. 'It's nice. It is quiet, but that's because the residents here are older, not as many young families on this side.'

'Hmm.'

Isabel takes in the room. Nothing on the fridge, no pictures, no notes. Not even a fridge magnet. The mugs he's finishing up with are random, different logos from businesses Isabel doesn't recognise.

'Sugar?' he asks.

Isabel asks for two. Rampaul declines.

When he turns and holds out a mug for Isabel, the colour of the tea gives her pause. Milk. Right. She forgot they do that here.

She takes it with a murmured thanks, not as keen on it now but determined to be polite. Rampaul seems a bit more enthusiastic about her cup of tea.

The legs of Grosz's chair scrape loudly over the floor as he drags it back and it creaks alarmingly when he sits.

He gestures to the other two seats Isabel and Rampaul each take a seat.

Rampaul takes a sip of her tea, making a pleased hum before setting it down and addressing him. 'Mr Grosz, I know you spoke to us yesterday, but I wanted to speak with you again. We need a better understanding of the situation at the embassy prior to yesterday morning's incident. As you yourself told us, Dr Anabel Pereira was not in the building yesterday.'

Grosz nods and takes a sip from the mug. There's a faint silvery scar above his left eyebrow that Isabel hadn't noticed yesterday. 'You think she has something to do with what happened.'

Interesting that it's not a question but a statement.

'We don't know enough at this stage. But what makes you say that?' Rampaul asks.

Grosz scratches at his cheek, the scrape of his blunt nails over stubble audible. 'You mentioned her.' He doesn't elaborate beyond that.

'*Only* mentioned her, Mr Grosz.' Rampaul adjusts herself in her seat, locks her fingers together around the mug. 'Did you have a lot of interactions with her?'

Grosz shifts in his chair, his eyes slide away from them. He grinds his teeth together, making the muscles visibly shift under the skin of his jaw. 'My team didn't have that much interaction with her other than supervising her during her times out.'

Isabel frowns. 'Times out?' If she really was a harboured fugitive, leaving the premises would have been a risk. The British police would have been obligated to snatch her up and extradite her to America.

'She was allowed time in the embassy garden. It's big. It was a way that she could still step outside and get some air. But there always had to be two members of our team with her when she was out there.'

He paints an oddly lonely image. Despite herself Isabel feels a twinge of sympathy for the unknown woman. Cooped up for over a month and the only thing she can do is step outside into a garden and, by the sounds of it, never alone.

Isabel thinks about being stuck in her apartment for that long. Even if it is her home . . . she would have gone mad. Though in her case, things would have been more intense. Her neighbours' thoughts almost never shut off. Being trapped inside her home with no way to check out from that—

Well.

'What else?' Isabel asks. 'Was she allowed to roam free inside the embassy? How did this work exactly? It just sounds as if – and I'm assuming here – Dr Pereira entered the embassy of her own volition. This sounds like self-imprisonment.'

Grosz starts bouncing his leg. 'She was allowed to roam within reason. It's a working place. But she had access to the kitchen and the gardens, as I've said.'

'The offices? The Reception area?'

'Not the offices, that would compromise confidentiality. All offices are locked unless occupied by the relevant staff member so she wouldn't have had access to them unless there were people there. But I don't think she interacted with them.'

'How was she when you did see her?' Isabel asks.

His leg stops bouncing. 'I don't know.'

When he doesn't elaborate further Isabel looks across at Rampaul.

Rampaul leans forward. 'You must have interacted with her at some point.'

Grosz stiffens but doesn't respond.

'Didn't you?'

Reluctantly, Grosz nods.

'So, in that time you should have been able to form an opinion about her.'

His gaze flicks up. 'She wasn't normal,' he finally says.

Isabel stiffens.

Normal. She's starting to hate that word.

'In what sense?' Rampaul asks.

'In the beginning, when she first arrived, she would talk to people. But it was all fake, plastic smiles. And the way she looks at you . . . it made a lot of people uncomfortable. But then—' he cut himself off. The hand he has resting on the table curls into a fist.

'Then?' Isabel prompts.

'She started coming out of the annexe less. Not unless it was to speak to Mr Francisco or to go and sit in the garden. Caught her out there one day, sitting in the rain. Went into her room drenched after and didn't say a word to anyone. Left water all over the hallway. The girls in Reception didn't like the mess and they were upset.'

'How did the rest of the staff feel about her?'

'They gossiped, whispered about her, but that was normal. She kept to herself, was polite when she interacted with members of staff. That's all.'

Isabel was hoping for more.

'Mr Grosz, yesterday you told us you're in charge of the security team as well as the security systems,' She says.

He nods. 'That's right.'

'Is there a reason that you know of why Dr Pereira wouldn't have been in the premises at the time of the incident?'

'No. She can't leave. She'd be arrested the second she steps out of the building.' There's an unspoken question there; he wonders why they don't know this already. 'She was there the evening before and if she had left then whoever was on duty would have needed to report to me directly and to Cíntia. I would have been informed immediately and I didn't get any report of that nature.'

'Cíntia is on the list of staff names you gave us yesterday,' Rampaul says, 'what is her position?'

'She's our offices and facilities manager.'

'And was that usual? This kind of monitoring of Dr Pereira?' Isabel asks. 'She knows she's not allowed to exit the building. If she did, she'd risk being apprehended and sent back. Was the overnight security necessary?'

'It's what I was ordered to do.'

'By whom?'

'Cíntia.'

In her head, Isabel moves Cíntia to the top of the list of who they should speak to next.

'Are there cameras installed at the embassy?' Rampaul asks.

'We don't have a robust camera system. The budget doesn't stretch that far. We have cameras at the main entrance, one at the door to the garden and then one at each floor landing. We don't have anything inside the offices or common areas like the kitchen or Reception. We decided that it would be better to target main access points into the building due to our limited budget and because of the confidential nature of work carried out inside the embassy.'

That's something at least. 'We'll need the footage for yesterday released to our team,' Rampaul says.

'Uh,' Grosz shifts, 'we were told we couldn't return to the embassy today and I don't have remote access, but Cíntia can grant remote access.' He looks at Isabel. 'I thought you and your partner weren't going to be a part of this investigation?'

'We have no jurisdiction here,' she says, 'but we're assisting the Major Investigative Crime Unit for now. As you know, this incident was first reported directly to the Portuguese government and may have diplomatic implications, so they would like us to keep an eye on things just for now.'

For a moment, he's quiet, but eventually nods.

'Is there any staff member at all that you think may have had a significant relationship with Anabel?' Isabel asks.

He starts to shake his head but then seems to think better of it. 'Cíntia spoke to her the most. She would go up to Dr Pereira's room often since she was in charge of her meals. Aside from me, she was the only one allowed up on the annexe floor. I was only went up there once, which was the night Anabel Pereira was first installed at the embassy, and my team did one check a day of the floor itself but none of us went into her room. Cíntia is the only one who did.'

'Did Cíntia ever mention anything?' Rampaul asks.

'I think it would be best if you spoke to her yourself.' He gets up and exits the kitchen.

Startled, Isabel stands and glances over at Rampaul but before she can do more than push her chair back, Grosz returns with something in his hand. It's a torn-out page corner with a name and number scrawled on it in pencil.

'You can contact her yourself. I need to rest. I will follow up with the CCTV and make sure you both have access to it. But . . . for now, I'd appreciate it if you could leave.'

'Of course,' Rampaul says, 'just one more question. Has the ambassador's secretary, Miss Ramos, been in touch with you since yesterday?'

Grosz shakes his head and holds out the paper to her.

They take the number, thank him for his time and the tea and see themselves to the door.

Isabel pockets the piece of paper. Grosz disappears from view when he closes the door behind them.

Not normal.

That's what Grosz had said. He said Dr Pereira wasn't normal but also said she got along with the staff. No mention of her stepping out of bounds. Keeping to herself. So, what had prompted him to air that observation?

Isabel sighs and tucks her hands into her pockets as they walk back over to the car.

66

'Given how long Dr Pereira was there, I thought he'd be able to give us more than that,' Rampaul says.

'There are still the other members of staff, and there's this office and facilities manager, Cíntia,' Isabel says. 'From the sound of it she'll be able to get us more concrete information.' I hope, she thinks.

They stop and Isabel leans against the side of the car. The slight hint of sun that had been there when they arrived is gone and the threat of rain lingers in the air again.

Rampaul stops next to the driver's side. 'Did you get anything from him?'

From her tone, Isabel knows she's asking her for more than just her own take on Grosz.

At the window where Isabel had noticed the twitching curtains when they'd arrived, she sees a small woman unashamedly in front of the window now, mug still in hand and watching them.

'Like?' Isabel rests her hand on the car roof. 'I explained. I can't just prise open someone's head.'

Rampaul tilts her head to the side, mouth twisting as if in thought. 'I brought you instead of Adam for a reason.'

'I'm aware. You made that clear when you asked me to come with you. Listen,' she turns, 'what I can tell you from being in there with him is that, emotionally, he's at his limit. It was like a mix between being numb and being lost.' And beneath that, an undercurrent of horror that spiked up raggedly through the blanket of shock-stunned calm. 'Better to let him rest now.' She looks back at the house. 'You can always come back and speak with him again if you need to, no?'

Rampaul shakes her head and unlocks the car. 'You're not in Portugal anymore, Inspector. Aren't you supposed to do as the Romans do, when in Rome?'

Isabel gets in. 'If only.'

# 10

The radio show warns commuters of heavy traffic due to a police incident earlier on in the day followed by a summary of the public transport status. Listening to it makes Isabel wonder if everyone in London should just be walking from A to B right now.

'We got off on the wrong foot.'

That catches Isabel off guard.

The words aren't said with any inflection, more like an observation. Rampaul has her attention on the road. She slows to a stop at a red light and turns Isabel's way.

'You didn't exactly help your case,' Rampaul points out. 'Giving me attitude right off the bat.'

Isabel snorts, incredulous. 'You get what you give, no? Isn't that the rule?'

Rampaul shrugs and goes back to focusing on the road. 'Sometimes. With certain people, I suppose.'

'It's fine. If I were in your shoes, I wouldn't be very happy either. But as you said, it is what it is. We can make the best of the situation.'

Rampaul nods in agreement. The light switches to green and they're on the move again. 'This isn't my usual type of case.'

'No?' Isabel looks out the window. 'I really hope I'll be able to say the same.'

Rampaul checks the navigation map on her phone. 'Yeah. I read about you two.'

'Oh, you had time for that with all of this work on your hands?' Isabel asks. If she's being blatantly sarcastic, well, Voronov isn't here to tell her off for it.

'I made time. If I'm being forced to work with people I don't know, I should know who I'm dealing with, don't you think?'

She turns deftly into a narrow street, short squat buildings with shabby shops on one side and open blocks of flats on the other, their stairwells exposed and the spaces beneath them shadowed. The area has a brutal feel to it, the architecture blunt, the colours bleak.

A few youths linger on the far end corner of the street, hoodies up, heads turning as one when Rampaul leans out of the window to peer at the parking sign on the side of the road, before cruising further down to slide her car into a spot that's tight enough that Isabel is side-eyeing her the entire time.

Rampaul rolls her eyes and cuts the engine. 'No faith.'

They get out and walk to the closest set of stairs.

'Those two cases of yours are all over the internet,' Rampaul starts up the stairs and Isabel follows. She seems to know where she's going.

'We've had the bad luck of a couple of our cases catching more attention than we'd like, it's probably what contributed to them harassing my chief to have us sent over here to be a pain in your side,' Isabel says, tone dry.

'And your thoughts about what happened in the ambassador's office?'

'You've seen the video?' Isabel asks.

'Yes. Is there a version of it with sound?'

'I don't know,' Isabel says. 'We received the same version as you it seems.'

'Reis.' Rampaul stops and looks at her. 'Did they send you here because they think there's some kind of Gifted angle to all of this? Though how that would work . . . I'm not sure.'

'I don't think so,' Isabel says. 'I'd be more concerned about bureaucracy getting in the way of figuring this out. If that's something that you're considering we'd need more evidence to pursue a Gifted angle.'

Rampaul nods. 'I'm not ruling anything out, however unlikely.'

Isabel is a step behind her as they make their way up. 'There was an incident back in Portugal. A young woman caused a major incident in the city, affected a whole building with her telekinesis. And I've personally seen some things.' She thinks of the precision of Gifted just using their ability for fun in safe spaces. That kind of control isn't something to underestimate.

'That's . . . something.'

'That's one way to put it. But I think right now all we have for sure is a missing person.'

The building is mostly quiet as they walk out into the corridor for the third floor.

Despite the heat, most of the windows are open, curtains open too, people inviting this crippling heat in. The doors are all closed though and there's not much by way of people going about their lives behind closed doors.

The corridor faces a neat community garden. She can see the tidily grouped tools and crops which have been planted and are being cared for. How carefully everything has been set out to protect it from the elements. It makes her think briefly of the one at home that her dad used to tend.

Isabel can remember his days off being spent there as far as she can remember. Before he passed that was. The tree he'd planted when she was small is still there. The allotment itself belongs to someone else now. Her mother hadn't ever set foot there after he'd died and at the time, her brother hadn't been able to afford it. They'd had no choice but to let it go.

Clothes hang off the washing line, blowing gently in the breeze. The air has become increasingly humid as the day has gone on and some pieces have been out too long. The sky remains overcast.

The flat they're going to is the last one on this floor: Flat 33. There are iron bars on the window and the front door is painted a mustard yellow. When Isabel glances down at the doormat, she quirks the corner of her mouth at the words 'feline inside' and a picture of a black cat curled around the words.

Rampaul raps her knuckles on the door. 'Mrs Cheever? Are you in?' She raps again before standing back.

At first there's no sound, but then after a moment Isabel hears steps and the sound of a metal chain sliding free before the door cracks open.

A dishevelled woman around their age peers blearily at them from the slim gap.

'Yes?' She squints at them, one hand firmly gripping the side of the door. She's in a loose khaki tracksuit, the lower side of the top creased all down one side, like she's fallen asleep in it. Her hair is barely contained by the clip pinning it to the top of her head, chunks of it falling haphazardly around her face. She slides a pair of glasses she's holding in her hand on to her nose and the wrinkles in her forehead smooth out. There's a noticeable accent in her speech.

'Mrs Cheever?'

Rampaul tugs her police ID from inside her jacket and shows it to her. 'I'm Detective Inspector Rampaul with the Major Crime Investigative Unit and this is Inspector Reis of the Judiciary Police in Lisbon. We'd like to come in and speak to you about the incident that took place at the embassy.'

Isabel stares, bemused, at the cat making itself comfortable in her lap.

Mrs Cíntia Cheever walks over to the sitting area and sets a tray down on the large wide coffee table. The table makes the small living-room space feel even smaller. Three mismatched mugs filled to the brim sit next to a plastic tub of sugar and a clean spoon.

The milk, Isabel notices with a sense of resignation, has already been poured into all three mugs of tea.

On the mounted TV, four women sit along a table in a well-lit studio which has erupted into applause. Mrs Cheever quickly grabs the remote and turns the sound down.

Isabel strokes her fingers into the cat's lush black fur, and it stretches appreciatively on her thighs. The little bells on its collar jingle. 'Thank you,' Isabel says, as Mrs Cheever sets a mug on a coaster in front of her and hands the other to Rampaul.

71

'No problem, no problem.' Mrs Cheever settles down on the carpeted floor on her knees as she adds sugar to her own tea. 'I didn't realise they'd sent someone Portuguese over to deal with this.'

'My colleague and I are only here to assist with the incident,' Isabel says and gestures at Rampaul. 'DI Rampaul is leading the inquiry.'

'I see.' She adjusts the hem of her top, tugging it down in a way that stretches the collar. She takes her mug in hand. 'How can I help? I wasn't there yesterday. I don't usually work Tuesdays, it's the day I visit my mother at her care home.' Her eyes take on the faraway look of someone going deep into thought. She rubs her thumbs back and forth around the rim of her mug.

The cat on Isabel's lap twists and jumps down, slinking its way to Mrs Cheever. It climbs delicately on to her knees and butts its head against her stomach.

Mrs Cheever blinks down at the small animal. She sets her mug down and scoops the cat up, gathering it to her chest. She strokes her hand over its head and back. 'I wasn't there,' she says again.

'We're aware,' Rampaul says. She pulls out a pocket-sized notebook and a blue ballpoint and rests them on her lap. 'But there are still some blanks you can help fill for us. You know we've spoken to Mr Grosz?'

'Andrzej?' The cat wriggles out of her hands and climbs up on to her shoulder. She continues to stroke it absently. 'Yes. I know he spoke to you and helped identify the – the people found in the building.'

'Mr Grosz has been very helpful regarding the security arrangements of the embassy. We'll be speaking to remaining members of staff who are employed by the embassy,' Rampaul says. 'We'll need your assistance with gathering their contact information, phone numbers, addresses, etc. I'm assuming you have access to the records of all those on the staff?'

Mrs Cheever flinches at the word 'remaining'. She twists her face down to rub her cheek against the cat. 'Yes. We moved to a cloud system last year. We're not supposed to access work information and files from devices outside the embassy, but yes, I have access.'

'As the office manager and the one in charge of overseeing the facilities, you worked closely with Mr Grosz regarding security arrangements. Did anyone at the embassy also contribute to decisions on the security arrangements?'

'Judite. Judite Ramos. She's Mr Francisco's—I mean, the ambassador's, secretary,' she says.

Isabel remembers Grosz briefly mentioned Ramos during their first interview with him at the station yesterday.

'Has Miss Ramos been with the embassy for a long time?' Rampaul asks.

Mrs Cheever frowns, cups her mug in both her hands and brings it to her mouth for a careful sip. 'She's been there longer than I have,' she says, 'I started at the embassy about five years ago. But I think she's been there ever since Mr Francisco was appointed as ambassador.'

'How long ago was that?'

'I'm not sure.'

'Is that something that you can check?'

'Yes. We have records for all of our current staff members.'

'What about those who have left the embassy?'

'It depends how far back.'

'That's fine.'

'And do you know why Miss Ramos wasn't at the embassy yesterday morning? Did she have a meeting elsewhere, perhaps?'

Mrs Cheever shakes her head. 'I don't know, maybe. There are last minute changes to hers and Mr Francisco's calendars all the time.'

Rampaul asks a few more questions about the timetables for supply deliveries and other companies or suppliers with access to the building. Mrs Cheever's responses are in line with what they have been told by Grosz.

'What about in-house staff schedules and rotas?'

The cat has started trying to climb up on to Mrs Cheever's head and she jerks when one of its paws catches on her hair. That startles it and it jumps down and crawls under the table.

'Yes, I have those too. For senior officials, like Mr Francisco, I won't as much due to confidentiality, but I can see where things have been marked as busy or out of office, on his calendar. When you speak to Judite she can give you a more accurate schedule for Mr Francisco.'

'Right.' Rampaul makes a note of that. 'Is there anything else you think we should be aware of?'

Mrs Cheever tucks back a whisp of hair. 'Like what?'

There's a sudden pulse of emotion there, and Isabel tips her head, chasing after it like a spoken word she hadn't heard quite well enough.

Rampaul catches the shift in Isabel's body language. She glances at her, askance.

Isabel scoots to the edge of the sofa cushion and leans forward. She rests her elbows on her knees and meets Mrs Cheever's gaze.

Mrs Cheevers eyes widen and her face pales. She's been caught in something. She doesn't know in what, but she realises that much.

'Anything at all. Is it okay if I call you Cíntia?' Isabel asks, giving her a reassuring smile.

'Of course.'

'Cíntia, as DI Rampaul here explained I'm an inspector with the Judiciary Police in Lisbon. I'm also Gifted, I have a telepathic affinity.' She keeps her voice as soothing as she can. This is uncertain ground for her. She has no experience of how the general public here react when faced with someone who can potentially listen in on their thoughts, given what DC Duncan had told them.

If Isabel thought Mrs Cheever had gone pale before, the way the skin around her lips whitens is alarming. 'You—' She leans away from them. 'I thought – here, we don't—'

'There's nothing for you to be concerned about. I promise. I don't do anything without someone's consent. In fact,' Isabel allows herself a wry smile, hoping it'll help put the other woman at ease, 'if I *did* do anything without your explicit consent, not only would it be inadmissible at court, but I'd lose my job.'

'Sorry . . .' She looks at Isabel, or more accurately, in Isabel's direction. She can't quite bring herself to make actual eye contact.

'It's fine,' Isabel says. 'I understand it can be disconcerting.' She wonders how much worse her reaction would have been if she knew that nowadays it takes Isabel more effort to keep other people's thoughts out of her head than it does for her to slide into someone's mind and leaf through it like she just walked into a library and picked up a book.

'Sorry,' Mrs Cheever says again and this time her gaze falls to her hands where she's now gripping them tightly together on her lap.

'Like I said, I'm not allowed to do anything without your permission. However, one thing that Gifted people like me are able to do is pick up on emotional cues. You see, people feel quite loudly,' Isabel says, touching a hand to her own chest, 'and when DI Rampaul asked you if there was anything else you might want to tell us, I felt a change. Something a little like panic.' Isabel pauses there and lets that sink in. 'I want you to tell us about that.'

At Isabel's side, Rampaul waits patiently, her expression neutral.

Isabel hopes Mrs Cheever correctly interprets what she's trying to say.

Don't lie to us because I'll know.

Mrs Cheever runs both her hands over her hair, shifting to sit on her knees again. Clearly agitated. 'I don't like to gossip,' she mutters.

On TV, the chat hosts are continuing to talk in the background as Isabel and Rampaul wait her out.

When she speaks the words come out rushed. 'I saw Mr Francisco leave the doctor's room.'

75

'You mean Dr Pereira's room?' Isabel asks.

Mrs Cheever nods.

'Is that normal?'

She shakes her head no.

'Then I'm assuming it wasn't appropriate for him to be there?'

'Yes.' Mrs Cheever turns her hands palm up on her lap, examining them, then runs her thumb along the lifeline of the opposite hand. 'That was the place she was allocated when they agreed to house her at the embassy until the ambassador could resolve her situation.'

Isabel narrows her eyes. 'Were you there the day she arrived?'

'Yes. I hadn't been notified and neither had Andrzej. That was unusual. For a situation of this severity, Andrzej and I are always informed.'

'Did she show up by herself? Was she escorted there?'

'She arrived with Judite.'

Ramos, the ambassador's secretary. That means there must have been communication beforehand with Ambassador Francisco. Why else would his secretary have known to meet Dr Pereira and bring her there?

'When were you and Mr Grosz informed that she would be staying at the embassy?' Isabel asks.

'When Judite arrived with her. That was the first time we were told.'

So, they'd already granted Dr Pereira refuge.

Isabel can hear the scritch of Rampaul's pen on paper.

'Okay. So, she's given the room at the very top, correct?'

'Yes. It was the only room that could be used for housing someone.'

'Did you ever see anyone else coming out of her room?'

'No. Her meals would be ready downstairs in the staff kitchen. She liked the garden. She went out there a lot too.'

That matched with what Grosz had told them.

'Go on,' Isabel says.

'Well – usually meetings between the ambassador and the

76

doctor took place in his office. I know because I'd have to order refreshments, so I had to be informed and Judite was always present for them. I don't know the particulars of what they were all discussing, but I know that Mr Francisco was speaking to our government – that is, the Portuguese government – on the doctors behalf. They met often.'

'The times you saw Mr Francisco coming out of her room, was it daytime? Nighttime?'

'Daytime. The admin team and I work from nine to five. Sometimes the secretaries will do a bit of overtime because of meetings running over or meetings with people in different time zones.'

'How many times did you witness this?'

'Two – no – three times.'

'Can you give us a more specific time frame?'

Mrs Cheever does. Twice in the morning. One time after lunch. 'He followed her after lunch. They were walking up the stairs together. I had a worker in that day trying to fix the sink in the upstairs bathroom; we were both inside when I saw them walking towards her room.'

'Aside from them heading to her room, did anything else seem odd to you? Did either of them seem different or agitated or anything of the sort?'

'I couldn't really see their faces,' she says.

'I see.'

'Was there anything else?'

The cat edges out from under the table towards Mrs Cheever, its nose sniffing delicately at the air.

She reaches out to pet its head, hand cupping over the cat's ears, and as if from deep inside a dream, she asks: 'What happened in there? The embassy?'

They can't answer her.

'It's suspicious,' Voronov says, 'but it's not incriminating.'

Isabel switches the phone from one ear to the other as she

brings Voronov up to speed on the new information they'd learned from Cíntia Cheever, namely Ambassador Francisco's unusual visits to Dr Pereira's room. She glances behind her to see if Rampaul is done.

She's waiting outside what Rampaul had called a chicken and chips shop, leaning on a small slice of wall next to a Turkish food market. The smell of fried potatoes and grease spills out from the open door. Inside, a few students in their school uniform and bulky backpacks are squeezed around one of the small dark-blue plastic tables, boxes of chicken and cans of Coke crammed on to the surface.

Rampaul is at the counter, also on her phone, waiting for their order.

'If it's unusual enough for her to report it, it's possible something else was going on. We can't reach Francisco's secretary though,' Isabel says. 'She would have tried to get in touch with Francisco or the embassy by now, don't you think? So, we should have heard from her.'

A burst of loud laughter and shouts draws her attention to the pub on the corner of the street. Baskets overflowing with petunias in blues, whites and pinks hang above the pub windows, adding a touch of old-world charm to the building. People are crowded on to the benches outside, others standing but tightly grouped around. Isabel can see through the windows into the well-lit, packed interior.

The pub is one big ball of voices, physical and internal, swelling outward and coloured in many different emotions. They batter at the barriers shielding her mind.

'Judite Ramos?' Voronov says.

Isabel drops her head into her hand and digs her thumb into the space between her eyebrows. 'Yes, that's her,' Isabel says, 'Cíntia sent the staff records through?'

'She's sent over the information you requested, and we have remote access to the CCTV files for the embassy. We're logging everything right now. One more thing, I got through to the manager at Moreno Security. They confirmed Grosz's account of the rota. They have the other six who were on rotation at the embassy. They've said they'll hold them for you until three; their boss wants them spoken to as soon as possible so he can let them off on leave.'

'Okay, I'll tell Rampaul. Food should be almost ready; we can go straight there.'

'We'll check at the staff records and get Ramos's address. We can pause things here for now and go see if she's home.'

'All right. Keep us posted.' Isabel hangs up.

A plastic bag being shaken right next to her face and the strong smell of fried chicken has her turning around to find Rampaul standing beside her.

'Let's go, Reis. I want my food before it gets cold.'

## 11

Moreno Security is situated in a large commercial building in an industrial park in Chingford. The plaque on the wall next to the heavy blue double doors leading into the building tells them they're based on the third floor and when Rampaul rings the buzzer for that floor, a soft accented female voice tells them they'll be right down.

Behind them, the sun is struggling to penetrate through the clouds. The humidity in the air has worsened and Isabel wonders if a storm is coming.

She presses a hand to her stomach, feeling uncomfortably full since they'd eaten earlier.

'You all right?' Rampaul asks, noticing the motion.

Isabel drops her hand and nods. 'Yeah. I'm fine, food just didn't settle great.'

One of the doors swings inward with a loud echoing sound that makes it seem as if a large mechanism has been unlocked and from behind the door a small woman who is possibly in her sixties steps out. She peers up at them.

'Good afternoon,' she says. It's the same woman who had spoken to them via the intercom. She's dressed in an old-fashioned grey pencil skirt that stops above the ankles, a white shirt with pearl buttons and neatly done-up collar. Her grey-brown hair is combed back into a bun at the nape of her neck and her glasses, secured by a silvery chain, are perched on the end of her nose. 'I'm sorry, we're having a problem with our doors, we're trying to get them fixed but it's taking the company some time.' She sighs and shakes her head. 'We have to come down every time to let people in, so frustrating.'

'That's no problem,' Rampaul says.

'I'm Sofia, the receptionist here at the company. It's been a bit stressful here since yesterday. Mr Moreno is waiting for you. If you follow me,' she adds as she beckons them inside.

Her dainty steps echo in the large hallway. Ironically there's an empty security desk to the right of the hallway and a bathroom directly behind that. Aside from that there are two sets of lifts and a set of stairs leading up into the building.

They take the lift.

'Here we are,' she says as the doors open right on to the floor. Sofia springs into action, all non-stop motion as she strides past the Reception desk with its huge computer, a mug, a small plate with biscuits and a pale-blue cardigan on the back of the chair there.

Beyond it, the floor is divided into two parts. There's a recreational area with a sofa and TV, a kitchenette too. There's a big whiteboard on the wall and Isabel can see names and dates scrawled on it in red board pen. On the other side of a makeshift blue-partition wall is a meeting area, with a long table and several chairs tucked into it.

There are two people occupying the sofa, both of them on their phones, though they peer up at Rampaul and Isabel as they follow behind Sofia.

'Just through here,' Sofia says, her kitten heels clicking on the floor as she walks. 'You're both very pretty for police officers,' she adds, 'very pretty. It must not be easy for lovely young ladies like you both. Seeing horrible things, such horrible things. We're all still in shock here. Mr Moreno wants to send everyone home early today; he says we need time to process. Mr Moreno is a very kind man, very kind. He has a good eye for people, I've worked for him for twenty years. Never had a reason to complain.'

Isabel glances at Rampaul, who gives Isabel a pained look.

Despite the friendly chatter, the woman is a bag of nerves, her anxiety bubbling up around her, and that film of shock that had coated Grosz's interactions with them is present in Sofia too.

A place like this, Isabel gets the sense that they're a tight-knit team.

Sofia leads them into a turn on the right. There's not much else here either. The corridor is short and there are two doors, one on the right marked WC and the other only a few feet further on at the end of the hall.

Sofia leads them straight to it and raps quickly on the door.

'Can I get either of you anything to drink?'

'We're fine, thank you,' Rampaul says.

From inside, someone calls out for them to come in.

Sofia opens the door. 'The police are here,' she says and then ushers Isabel and Rampaul in like they're children, all encouraging and patting them on the arms.

A man strides over to them, walk strong and assured, hand out in front to shake their hands.

'I'm Antonio Moreno, head of Moreno Securities,' he says. Moreno is a stocky man, dressed in grey slacks and a smart, V-neck navy jumper with a gold watch on his thick wrist. His handshake is short and firm.

The office is decently sized but sparse with a lot of light coming in through the large windows. There's a neat desk with a laptop open on it. A paper tray and a small plant in a white pot sit in the right-hand corner of it. A couple of padded chairs are placed opposite it, both occupied. A woman stands behind them, hands braced on the backs as she curls over them to speak in hushed tones to the two seated people.

Rampaul nods in greeting. 'Mr Moreno, I'm Detective Inspector Rampaul. I'm with the Major Crime Investigative Unit here in London. This is Inspector Reis of the Judiciary Police in Lisbon. Thank you for making the time to see us today. I understand this must be a distressing situation for you and your team. We'd like to get to the bottom of it as quickly as possible so we can give you some answers.'

'Of course, whatever I and my team can do to help. Unfortunately, I've since sent three of them home . . . they were not in the best state. I couldn't keep them here in good conscience. I have explained that you will want to follow up with them, and Sofia will give you their addresses so you can speak with them privately. However, Luca, Elvira and Sônia have stayed behind to talk with you. I hope this is okay?'

'That's fine. We'll follow up with the others as you've said.'

Isabel eyes the people behind him, letting his exchange with Rampaul fade into the background.

The three wear yellow T-shirts which have what Isabel assumes is the Moreno logo in miniature on the chest.

None of them are making eye contact with her, their eyes on the floor, their collective grief contained within this space.

'My men and women always form strong bonds. Most of the time they are paired on assignments or in teams, they get to know each other very well. So, this is . . . this is a shock to us all,' he says.

'We understand,' Rampaul says. 'Come on, Reis.'

When they approach, Isabel sees that the man – who must be Luca – sitting on the chair is holding the hand of the woman seated next to him.

As they get closer, the woman who had been bent close to talk to them straightens. Her eyes are red-rimmed and dry, her skin pale and too tight. Her closely cropped head is a dyed-white blond that clashes with her dark brows. Her eyes skip from Isabel to Rampaul before she steps back and folds her arms over her chest, settling into a wide stance and giving them a hard stare, clearly on the defensive.

The guy is giving off the same kind of defensiveness as the standing woman. He pins them with a glare from beneath heavy brows. He has a shaved head and a thick beard and goatee. He doesn't let go of his colleague's hand.

The woman on the chair wipes roughly at her face, never letting go of the man's hand. She's a petite woman. Her face carries the marks of someone who has had to deal with severe acne in the past. Black curly hair is secured with a clip at her neck. Her head stays down. Moreno sticks to their side, clearly having no intention of leaving his staff alone with them.

'Detectives, this is Luca and Sônia,' he indicates the two sitting on the chairs, 'and Elvira,' he says with a nod to the woman standing. 'This is DI Rampaul and Inspector Reis. They are investigating what happened at the embassy.'

'My condolences,' Rampaul says. 'We know this is a distressing time for you. Andrzej Grosz told us you and your colleagues have been working at the embassy this past month on a rotational basis. When was the last time you were on duty?'

Luca sits up, blows out a breath and rakes his nails over his head. He blinks fast. 'I was on shift on Monday with Johnson. The daytime shift.'

'Johnson?' Rampaul asks.

Moreno clears his throat and when he responds his voice is raspy with supressed emotion. 'One of our team who was found at the embassy yesterday morning.'

Rampaul nods. 'I see.'

Luca's mouth trembles. He holds himself rigid and the heaviness of the room increases.

'We were on night duty Saturday and Sunday,' Sônia says. She still hasn't lifted her head.

'Elvira and I were assigned the indoor detail,' Luca says. 'There were two others manning the perimeter. We were due back on rotation tomorrow for the Thursday daytime shift.'

'Did you notice anything unusual during your shifts in the last few days? Any members of staff acting strangely, or contractors or deliveries, for example?' Rampaul asks.

'Nothing,' Luca says, 'we signed in, debriefed with the on-shift team on arrival, de-briefed with the next-shift team on leaving. Everything was fine. Guests signed in at the office. No one accessed the annexe floor. Everyone who was not a staff member was always escorted to and from meetings.'

There's conviction and truth in his words, no wavering and Isabel, listening in and waiting to catch any stray thought that may hint otherwise, finds nothing but gnarled confusion and disbelief.

'Any changes to routine?' Isabel asks. 'With regular suppliers or any other individuals who don't work directly within the embassy?'

Sônia shakes her head, as does Luca.

Isabel glances at Elvira. She shakes her head as well.

Rampaul is silent for a moment. 'Dr Pereira is missing. She wasn't among the deceased found at the premises yesterday. Mr Grosz has said that your presence there was primarily to keep tabs on her and it's urgent that we locate her as soon as possible.'

Sônia's head snaps up, bloodshot eyes wide with surprise. 'Dr Pereira is alive? B-but we were told everyone in the building died?'

'She wasn't in the building. We need to locate her urgently.'

Elvira frowns; she straightens away from the chairs. 'What? That's not possible. If she had left the building, those on duty would have alerted Andrzej. There were officers watching the place,' she says. 'If she's not in there then she should be in *your* custody.' Her voice has grown steadily more aggressive as she speaks, and her last word rings out in a shout which must be audible beyond the room.

Rampaul's gaze remains steady and under her silence, Elvira seems to recognise who she's talking to. She shrinks back, rubbing a hand over her face.

'None of this makes sense,' Sônia says, 'none of this makes any sense.'

Rampaul stares at Isabel and says nothing.

Waiting.

Waiting for me to use my Gift, Isabel realises.

She almost laughs, incredulous.

Clearly their conversation earlier hadn't put her off the idea of having Isabel put it to use.

Except Isabel is using her Gift as much as she's willing to. There are a lot of emotions and thoughts swirling in this room. She feels their weight. Has felt their weight since the lift opened its doors to the third floor.

Isabel looks at them all. Their reaction to learning that Dr Pereira wasn't found with the others is different from what she'd expected. Not the reaction of people who had just done their jobs and gone home, not like Grosz who clearly saw her only as an additional duty, a complication. There had been no attachment to her in the way he'd spoken.

The three in this room seem more emotional about her. Their concern is genuine, even when buried beneath the horror of the colleagues they've lost.

'Did you grow close to Dr Pereira during her time at the embassy?' Isabel asks.

Discomfort, the first time since their arrival; Isabel catches a hint of it, faint, but there. She traces the emotion to Luca. His earlier fierceness has since fizzled out, and he seems undecided about what to say next.

Then he sets his shoulders, chin jutting, and answers her.

'We were told to keep our distance and not to engage with her. Just keep an eye on her. The people who worked there did as they were told. So did we at the start. But you can't keep someone in there like that and not treat them like a human being. I don't know what she did to land herself in that situation – but that woman has been through some things.'

'Did she tell you that?' Isabel asks.

'No. She never opened her mouth about any of that. Never complained once. Not once. She did as she was told, took her meetings with Ambassador Francisco and sat in that garden when she could. That was it. But when you spend enough time with someone you can tell.'

Isabel walks closer and leans a hand on the desk. 'And how did she seem to you?' she asks.

'Tired,' Sônia says softly, 'and hurt.' She swallows. 'Not physically. But like she was hurting inside. I felt like she was scared but putting on a brave face. You wouldn't know the difference though, if you weren't with her that often. And the others don't spend time with her like that. But with us, we were there to watch

86

her and watch anyone near her. We saw. We all saw. Elvira sneaked in books for her.'

Unlike the other two, Elvira's defensiveness is still there, projected loud and clear, but there's a softening behind that, when she meets Isabel's eyes.

'She saw me reading once on my break,' Elvira says. Her hands clench on the back of the chair and her teeth are gritted. 'Said she liked romance too.'

Isabel nods.

'I know you're all hurting right now from what has happened to your colleagues. As DI Rampaul has said, it's important that we find Dr Pereira as soon as possible. At this moment in time, we have to consider all possibilities, including that she may be hurt somewhere as a result of what took place. It seems you all felt a sense of responsibility towards her that went beyond what you were paid to do. If there's anything you can tell us, even if you think it might have nothing to do with this, then now is the time to do so.'

They fall silent.

And then:

Sônia turns to Isabel.

'People in that place like to turn a blind eye to a lot of things happening. Everyone in there, including us, has had to sign non-disclosure agreements. But I think you need to talk to Miss Ramos.'

Rampaul tilts her head, eyes narrowing, hands in her pockets. 'And why is that?'

'Because if you want to know more about Dr Pereira, maybe she can tell you why the ambassador regularly visited the annexe after hours.'

Isabel looks at Rampaul.

A theme is beginning to take shape.

# 12

'Detective Inspector Rampaul!'

Isabel and Rampaul have just walked into the station when a harried officer on the front desk cuts around the other people in the Reception area to get to them.

Outwardly, Rampaul doesn't react, but Isabel hears her thoughts ring loud over all the din: *What now?*

'We have a DC Chloe Bridges and an investigator with the NCA, Rupert Mackey, waiting to speak with you. They're here about your current case. I've asked them to wait in room 12.'

'Right. DC Duncan and Inspector Voronov?'

'They haven't returned yet.'

'Thanks.'

'NCA?' Isabel asks as they take the stairs up.

'National Crime Agency,' Rampaul sighs and pinches the bridge of her nose, 'I sincerely hope they're not here to get into a pissing match with us.'

Isabel catches her side-eye.

'You and Inspector Voronov are more than enough.'

Investigator Mackey and DC Bridges make an interesting pair.

DC Bridges is a tiny blond woman with a dimpled chin and big baby-blue eyes. She's dressed in a white T-shirt, denim jacket, jeans, and white trainers. She could pass for sixteen. Mackey is a small man, shorter than Isabel, dressed as if he's about to play a game of golf, his hair neatly combed into a side parting. He's maybe late forties, early fifties.

Mackey sits on the edge of the desk, composed and at home with Bridges standing at his side like a sentinel.

'We came straight here when we realised the MCIU was overseeing the embassy case,' Mackey says. He's got an accent Isabel isn't familiar with, definitely English, but not one she would associate with London. 'Bridges and I were tasked with keeping tabs on Dr Pereira. Resources are thin on the ground but as an international fugitive who took off with US military property, a little bit of collaboration was in order.'

'You weren't there yesterday,' Rampaul says.

Mackey shakes his head. 'No. Last week we were told changes were going to be made to her surveillance. They told us to take yesterday off, said someone would cover and that from next week we would be reassigned.' He scoffs. 'It was the first and only day we've been off this in months. Got back today to yellow tape and a closed building. The Met kept passing us around until we got a call telling us a DC Duncan was asking around about the surveillance detail for the Portuguese Embassy.'

'Right,' Rampaul says, 'well. Shouldn't they have sent someone to replace you?'

Mackey gives her a pointed look. 'That's what we're trying to figure out. NCA told us cover would be in place, so we left it in their hands. Now they're saying there was an administrative error and no one was ever assigned.'

'An administrative error?' Rampaul repeats, deadpan.

Mackey drags in a deep breath, like someone praying for patience. 'Trust me, you're not the only one unimpressed with that little piss-poor excuse. We're following it up. We're out a fugitive. Our arses are on the line here.'

He's not lying. He's seething and Isabel can see the molten orange of it suffusing his person. He seems to keep it from manifesting physically with ease, however.

Rampaul lets it go. 'What did the NCA tell you about her? How much information did they give you?'

Bridges clears her throat. 'Dr Pereira is a level-eight Gifted. Worked for the US military right after high school. She stayed there as part of the Gifted in Combat Military Research Division

89

and became a prominent figure in Gifted research. She's mentored by Dr Eliana Cross, a world-renowned figure in the field. Dr Pereira travelled extensively as a result of her position and status, attended a lot of conferences; she was a major contributor to research papers, that sort of thing. A little over a month ago, she stole an undisclosed piece of US military property and has been a fugitive since then. She took refuge at the Portuguese Embassy in London.'

Mackey grunts. 'That's all we were given. Questions weren't encouraged. They assigned us to her about a month ago. You could say the assignment was a simple one. Keep an eye on the embassy and arrest Dr Pereira on sight if she sets foot outside of it.'

'That's it?' Rampaul asks.

'That's it,' Mackey confirms, 'tedious at best. No indication that she may be violent or a danger to anyone around her, so they saw fit to only allocate two people to surveillance. Normally they would have kept it to just the one, but apparently our American friends put pressure on the authorities to do a little more than that, so to placate them, they threw me in to sweeten them up. So, imagine my surprise when I turn up ready for duty after one day off and find out the embassy has been levelled and there's no sign of the person we've been keeping tabs on.'

Bridges doesn't comment. She remains as she has been, maintaining her ramrod-straight stance. But like her senior, she's not happy about the situation.

'Right,' Rampaul says, 'then how do you feel about helping us out?'

Before Mackey can respond, Rampaul's phone goes off.

'Sorry,' Rampaul says, 'one moment.' She pulls her phone out and frowns as she sees the name on the screen. She takes the call. 'What is it?'

Isabel folds her arms across her chest and waits.

Rampaul's mouth parts but she doesn't speak.

Then she rolls her lips together and nods. 'All right. Hold the fort. Call the forensic unit. Reis and I are on our way.' She glances at Mackey and Bridges. 'Sorry about this but we have to go. I'll have DC Duncan call you both later. There are a couple of things we could use your help with but right now I'm afraid Inspector Reis and I are urgently needed elsewhere. We'll leave you to sign yourselves out.'

Mackey sits forward in his chair as if he's about to ask her to wait, but Rampaul's locked a hand around Isabel's arm and pulled her out of the room.

Her emotions bleed through as if melting through her skin and infiltrate Isabel's body.

Isabel pulls her arm out of her grasp as the door to room 12 swings shut behind them.

'What is it?'

Rampaul raises her hands in apology and then puts her phone away.

'Adam and Voronov have found Judite Ramos dead in her home.'

# 13

It takes them half an hour to get from the MCIU headquarters to Judite Ramos's house. Rampaul is silent behind the wheel. Her eyes don't stray from the road ahead, but the corners of her mouth are pinched, and her fingers tap impatiently at the steering wheel whenever they're forced to a stop at traffic lights. Her thoughts are threatening to spill over, and Isabel has to block hard to keep them from piling on her in the small interior of the car.

One of Ramos's neighbours had seen Adam and Voronov investigating the outside of the house when they hadn't got a response at the door. According to the neighbour Ramos's car was right there parked out front and hadn't budged.

The street they arrive in, even to someone unfamiliar with London, is an upscale one. Isabel thinks the place where she and Voronov are staying is impressive as it is. It has nothing on this place though. This street oozes money.

Tall, white, pretty, terraced houses fill both sides of the road. They are the kind that often make appearances in movies or shows Isabel has seen set in England.

A police van has already arrived, parked in front of one property in particular that has its door open.

There are police officers stationed at either end of the road; pedestrians are being closely monitored as they head to their properties in the street, while some are pointed in a different direction. The whole street is cordoned off.

Isabel spots Voronov's tall frame as he comes out of the house, eyes searching the road, and when he spots them getting out of Rampaul's car he heads over.

He nods at Rampaul. 'DC Duncan is inside speaking with the forensics team.'

'Thanks.' She nods at them both and heads inside.

Isabel stays back, tucking her hands into her pockets as she surveys the bubble of activity.

'What happened?' she asks him.

Voronov shifts so that he's standing next to her facing the same direction. 'When we arrived, we tried the door but got no response. We were searching for a way to see inside the house. The neighbour,' he glances to the house directly next to it, 'works from home so she sees Ramos around most times.'

Isabel sees a woman in her thirties standing at the door, her arms crossed, staring wide-eyed. She's in pyjama bottoms, slippers and a baggy jumper. The glasses perched on her nose are thick-rimmed.

'Her workstation is on the first floor next to the window. She's a translator. She works odd hours because her work is mostly Japan-based. She said she saw Ramos go into the house on Monday evening but hasn't seen her since then.' He turns around and Isabel follows his line of sight to a silver Vauxhall Corsa. 'Her car hasn't left either. Neighbour says she's also noticed the light in the kitchen has been on. We went into her garden, and we could see it too.'

So, she comes home the evening before the deaths at the embassy and doesn't come out at all.

'We managed to get over the garden fence and look through the kitchen windows and saw her.'

Isabel rubs at the bridge of her nose. 'Did the neighbour see anyone else come in or out of the house?'

'No. Adam managed to get in through the bathroom window. It was open, he was able to squeeze through. He was on the phone to Rampaul when the boyfriend arrived.'

'Boyfriend?' Isabel asks.

Voronov points to one of the police vans stationed on the road. Its back doors are open and there's a blond white man sitting in

93

the back. There's a blanket over his shoulders and a paper cup in his hands. He's staring fixedly at the house Rampaul and Adam have now disappeared into.

As if sensing he's being watched, the man's attention shifts from what's happening inside the house and locks unerringly on them. His gaze is dulled.

'Voronov, Reis.' Rampaul has come back out and is gesturing impatiently at them. 'Get your arses in here.'

Isabel sighs and heads her way.

The grave expression Voronov has been wearing lifts for a moment, wry amusement adding a small curl to his mouth.

'What?' she asks. It comes out more defensive than she would like.

He hangs back to let her in through the small gate leading up into the house first. 'It's interesting seeing how you are when the shoe is on the other foot.'

Isabel rolls her eyes. 'Please. You hate having to take orders from someone else just as much as me.'

His amused huff in response is all she needs as confirmation.

Any humour disappears completely after they've put on the protective footwear and stepped inside the home.

The interior matches the outside.

The hallway floor is made up of a pretty mosaic tile and the stairs are carpeted; it's thick and lush and immaculately maintained. The kind that makes you want to kick your shoes off and luxuriate. High, white ceiling and an open sitting room that captures all the sunlight. Its décor is all white and warm creams. Everything is in its place with only a set of pink orchids adding a splash of colour. Some letters have been haphazardly thrown on the surface next to them and there's a blazer draped over the back of the corner sofa and a woman's black bag nestled into the corner of it, patent beige heels discarded on the fluffy white rug.

The classy and yet domestic scene is at odds with the smell permeating through the house. It's not too bad yet, still tolerable.

Not what it would be like if they were to walk in here a day or two later.

Isabel covers her nose and mouth, the attempt at protecting her senses instinctive more than anything else. She knows from experience that there's no way to keep from inhaling that smell.

'It's been a few days,' Voronov says.

Isabel nods as she makes her way past the sitting room and into the dining area. Rampaul has disappeared somewhere into the back and Isabel can hear the movement of people, the click of camera shutters, from that end.

It's the kitchen. A huge space, just as neat as the entrance and the open-plan sitting room and dining area they walked past. And just like everything else it's high-end too. There's a breakfast bar and a door that leads out into a long garden. Isabel can see a shed through the glass of the garden door and a deck area with a table and chairs.

Rampaul and Adam are standing by the breakfast bar.

Voronov's expression is grim.

Looking past the officers working in the room, Isabel sees it. It's hard to miss.

The body of a woman is still atop one of the bar stools. She's wearing a black pencil skirt which exposes her bare ankles. They're tied together and to the stool; her hands are tied behind her back. She's slumped forward on to the breakfast bar; her head is resting cheek down on it.

A dainty watch gleams on her wrist. Her fingers are curled up, the nails perfect ovals in a French manicure. From where Isabel is standing, she can't see her face. But she can see the straight dark hair in a soft ponytail spilling over the counter.

She can see the congealed blood that's dripped on to the floor from the other side.

Around her, the team are busy cataloguing the scene, circling the body and taking photos. Rampaul stands off to one side, her arms crossed, and her features wiped clean of any expression. In the other corner, Adam is nodding along to something one of the crime-scene officers is saying and jotting it down. His eyes keep straying to the body and his face is a little on the pale side.

Voronov walks around to the other side, eyes taking in the scene before them. 'She was shot,' he says.

Isabel glances at him, eyes sharpening. She walks closer to the body too, careful to not get in anyone's way.

She can see the face now.

'This is definitely Judite Ramos?' Isabel asks.

'Adam says the boyfriend, Timothy Allen, confirmed it,' Rampaul says.

Her brown eyes are open. Her lipstick is a deep red, accentuating her thin mouth which hangs slack. She's wearing pearl stud earrings. The mascara on her eyelashes is thick and some of her lashes stick together. There are tear tracks down her cheek.

At her temple is one perfect black circle and a rivulet of red which has curved its way down her jaw to her neck. It's stained the collar of her white silk shirt.

'Mr Allen said he last spoke with her the day before the embassy incident took place,' Voronov says. 'The forensics team told us that their first impressions show no forced entry anywhere in the house, but it will take them longer to confirm and prepare the preliminary reports.'

'Any sign of the weapon?' Isabel asks.

'Not yet.'

Adam joins them again. 'They haven't found any personal electronic items so far. No sign of her phone and no sign of any laptops or tablets. She has an office upstairs but there's no desktop.'

'We tried calling her when we arrived,' Voronov says. 'The house phone rang. We could hear it from outside but when we tried her mobile phone the service was saying it was switched off.'

Isabel frowns. 'This morning it was still ringing, wasn't it?'

Voronov nods.

'Do they think she was alive this morning?'

Voronov shakes his head.

Isabel's gaze drifts back over to Ramos and her open eyes. She sees the distorted reflection of her silhouette in them.

# 14

Evening is settling over London, bringing with it a reprieve from the freak unrelenting heat the city has been experiencing.

Timothy Allen sits, unmoving, in one of the chairs at the station. His face is turned away from them, eyes focused out of the window and on the building opposite. His gaze still has that vacant quality to it.

Isabel and Voronov are outside the interrogation room, watching as Rampaul and Adam try to coax the man out of his shocked state.

Timothy Allen is twenty-eight years old, works for an architecture practice based in South London. He is twelve years younger than his deceased girlfriend.

Standing on the other side of the one-way-mirror, all Isabel is getting from him is confused shock.

His mind is trapped in a fog of disbelief, looping in on itself every time he comes close to understanding that his partner is dead.

'Mr Allen,' Rampaul says. Her voice is steady, tempered with patience. 'Are you sure we can't get you something to drink?'

'No, thank you,' he says very softly. His voice is much deeper than Isabel expected, and it takes her by surprise.

'We'll try our best not to keep you any longer than we have to.'

He nods, the movement tight.

'You told DC Duncan that you and Miss Ramos were boyfriend and girlfriend,' Rampaul says. 'How long had you been together?'

Voronov shifts in place beside Isabel. Arms crossed over his chest, eyes forward, watching through the interview room's one-way mirror.

'A few years.' His voice is slow and he's mumbling his words, making Isabel strain to hear what he's saying even through the clear audio coming into the observation room.

'And when was the last time you spoke to Miss Ramos?'

'Last week.' He lifts his head but it's as if it weighs too much and he drops his gaze back down before he even makes eye contact with Rampaul and Adam on the other side. 'Wednesday.'

Rampaul links her fingers together. 'You didn't speak to her after that? No phone calls or texts? Didn't stop by to see her or vice versa?'

He shakes his head. 'We argued. I . . . wasn't ready to speak to her.' As if moving through treacle, he reaches into his pocket and fumbles his phone on to the table. His fingers are shaking as he slowly unlocks his phone and slides it across the table to them.

Rampaul gestures for Adam to take it.

'What did you argue about?' Rampaul asks.

That seems penetrate the stupor he had sunk into since they'd seen him sitting outside Ramos's house. His shoulders stiffen and awareness comes back into him. Isabel sees it clearing right before her eyes, the fog fading and clarity returning, shaky but there.

Rampaul narrows her eyes when he doesn't respond. 'Mr Allen. What did you argue with Miss Ramos about last Wednesday?'

He takes a deep breath, chest expanding with it, and lets it out in one long audible rush of air. He lifts his head and grips his hands together on his lap. 'Her job,' he says. 'We argued about her job.'

'It must have been serious if it led to you not speaking for that amount of time. Can you elaborate?'

He stares at Rampaul, eyes like stones. But the question has triggered him enough that his mind is working now, thinking beyond the shock of today, and Isabel catches the vestiges of past arguments. Not just one. Sees them like one-time Polaroids, snapshots of faces distorted in anger and frustration. She recognises the kitchen they had found Ramos in, recognises too the outside of Ramos's house, but there are more.

Whatever they argued about, it hadn't been their first time. The quick succession of memories are all edged with anger, disgust and shame, but even as Isabel sees him shifting through those emotions, the memories dull, becoming blunted by denial and the settling in of loss.

'As secretary to the ambassador Miss Ramos must have had a heavy workload. Maybe lacked time for a relationship?'

No. Isabel narrows her eyes. That's not what these arguments were about. Isabel folds her arms and steps closer to the window.

'What do you think?' Voronov asks.

'He didn't do it,' Isabel says.

Voronov turns, his gaze boring into the side of her head. She knows what he's thinking without having to hear it.

'He's projecting very loudly,' she says, and then, dropping to a mutter, 'like everyone else in this city. It's exhausting.'

'You haven't mentioned it,' Voronov says.

Isabel sighs. 'Complaining won't change it.'

'Does it have to?'

'Why? What are you going to do?' she says, giving him a side glance, humour curling the corner of her mouth. 'Protect me from it?'

Before he can respond, Timothy Allen answers Rampaul.

'It wasn't anything like that,' he finally says, 'it had nothing to do with time commitments, nothing to do with the job itself.' His gaze falls to his hands, where his fingers are locked tightly together. 'It was the ambassador. The things he would have her do.' A muscle jumps in his jaw as he grinds his teeth. 'He'd call at all hours. No respect. She cleaned up his messes. All the time. It took me a while to realise the kind of messes.' He falls silent again.

'Can I confirm that the person you're referring to is Ambassador Emanuel Francisco?'

After a tense silence: 'Yes.'

'Go on.'

He shakes his head. 'Does it matter?' He rubs his hand over his face. 'What could this possibly have to do with what happened to Jude? Why are you here questioning me like this?' Then he frowns, that fog clearing a bit more. 'Hold on. You were already there when I arrived. You guys were inside. What were you doing there? Did someone report it? I'm the only one with keys. No one else could have . . . did someone at her job report her?'

Rampaul tilts her head, like a curious cat that has caught sight of something interesting. 'Why would they report her, Mr Allen?'

Adam gently sets Mr Allen's phone, which he'd been examining, back down on the table. He doesn't hand it back. When he speaks to him his tone is gentle. 'Is it related to what you mentioned before? The kind of messes, you said, that Miss Ramos was assisting the ambassador with?'

Timothy Allen makes a sound like a laugh but there's no mirth to it and his hollowed stare remains the same. 'Mess. It wasn't a mess,' he mutters.

He drops his head into his hands. They can all hear his breath whooshing in and out.

'He was molesting people. And she was helping him cover it up.'

# 15

According to Timothy Allen, Judite Ramos had been deteriorating.

They'd been dating for three years, and as far as he knew everything was okay. She liked her job and the people in it, and was good at what she did.

There were moments though when she would get tense and take time away from him. During these times she consumed alcohol excessively and barely slept at home. It always coincided with an unprecedented number of errands for the ambassador.

He'd called her out on it a few times because he hadn't been happy with her inebriation. They had argued about it.

Last month it had started again, and it had been particularly bad.

This time when he confronted her about it, she'd been in a drunken fit and broken down.

What she had called errands had actually been confiscating of incriminating evidence, liaising with private investigators hired by the ambassador to dig up dirt on women coming forward to make allegations of sexual assault against him. There had been hush money. A lot of hush money, and she'd been the middleman for every single instance that had reared its ugly head.

Judite Ramos was paid handsomely for her discretion and her assistance in hushing it all up.

'We argued on Wednesday because I could tell it was happening again,' he says, 'and I couldn't take it anymore. I wanted her to report it to the police. She refused to.' He shakes his head, still stunned by her point-blank refusal. 'I don't understand it. She just refused to. And now . . .'

He swallows.

And now Judite Ramos is dead.

'Her death is significantly different from those that took place at the embassy,' Rampaul says, 'I mean, she's been shot in her kitchen. The others all keeled over at their desks.'

The four of them have spread out in the case room after letting Timothy Allen go.

Isabel sips from the mug of coffee Adam had handed her, keen to get a hit of caffeine in her system. It helps when she has to reset her walls and sometimes eases the headaches she gets as a result of the constant stream of thoughts attempting to seep into her head.

'Doesn't change the facts though,' Isabel says, 'twelve people dead, several of those who knew them hinting at a history of assault by the ambassador, and now another member of staff is dead, and she was well aware of, and had a hand in, hushing up said alleged assault history. It would all be one impressive coincidence if that's what it is.'

Adam clears his throat. He's sitting on the edge of his chair, a little stiff, but there's a determined set to his jaw. 'Well,' he says, hands clasped together, 'we have the CCTV footage to finish looking at and the rotas and shifts sent in by the office manager to go through, but maybe, I was thinking with Agent Mackey and DC Bridges willing to assist, we could have them help canvass the area around the embassy and fan out from there.'

Voronov, who is standing next to Isabel, his own coffee long finished, makes a noise in agreement. 'It would make sense to use them. Especially as Superintendent McKinley is expecting a swift turnaround in locating Dr Pereira. Miss Ramos's death complicates things though.' He looks at Rampaul. 'If we're going to treat Miss Ramos's death as related—'

'Which we should,' Isabel interjects.

'It might be more efficient to investigate it simultaneously,' he finishes.

Rampaul lets out a deep sigh. 'Right.' She's quiet for a moment. 'Yeah, let's put Mackey and Bridges to work. Whatever time they can spare. And since you were both first on the scene and you're already the point of contact for forensics on this one, Adam, why don't you and Voronov lead on the inquiry into Miss Ramos's death. Talk to that neighbour again, see if she has anything to add and see if anyone else in that road saw anything. Keep me posted on the forensics team. The autopsy may take a while after we sent twelve bodies down just a couple of days ago.' Under her breath but still audibly, she adds, 'Marlow's going to bitch about that.'

Isabel has no idea who Marlow is but thinks he's probably someone who is a part of the autopsy process.

'Oh, and Adam, Timothy Allen said Ramos was being paid off by the ambassador. Check into her finances and the finances of the ambassador as well.'

'Yes, boss.'

'Reis and I will finish off with the remaining members of staff, see if they share anything else of note. Then we'll go from there.'

While they'd been dealing with Timothy Allen, Isabel and Voronov had received a text from their colleagues in Portugal, Daniel and Carla, updating them on their attempt to reach Amorim.

'Our colleagues back home have been attempting to speak with Milena Amorim from the Consular Affairs Department. She was the one who spoke to us and our chief to send us here,' Isabel says, 'and Rogério Pessoa, who was on the call with Emanuel Francisco when he died. So far, no luck, but they'll be heading over to speak to them in person first thing tomorrow morning.'

Rampaul nods. 'All right. Let's hope they get something useful.' She looks around at the room and at the empty cups of coffee. 'Top up your coffee and let's make some headway on what Cheever sent over.'

Isabel and Voronov straighten up to do just that.

It's going to be a long night.

# 16

They get the opportunity to meet the person Rampaul had referred to as Marlow the very next day.

They leave the apartment that morning after getting a call from Rampaul. Adam is already downstairs; he's rubbing his eyes roughly as they get down there.

There's a mist hanging over the river. It's 7.45 a.m.

'Morning,' Adam says, 'you guys had a good night?'

Isabel makes a so-so motion, mouth cracking open on a yawn. The bruised side of her face twinges but it's much better than it had been two days ago. The bruising makes it more dramatic.

She'd copped a few hours of sleep at a time on the sofa last night, the TV on in the background and her laptop wedged between her and the back of the sofa. She doesn't even remember closing it, so must have nodded off mid-reading.

That she was able to fall asleep so deeply is a minor miracle.

She can't shake the anxiety that takes over whenever it's time for her to get some rest.

Sleep means vulnerability.

It's hard to allow yourself that vulnerability when there is someone else with open-door access to your mind whenever they want. Particularly when that person is a high-level Gifted murderer.

Isabel hasn't got a good night's sleep since the day she'd heard Gabriel Bernardo in her head, speaking to her as if he was in her body with her.

Voronov had woken her in the morning with a gentle shake, telling her that he was starting coffee and that Rampaul had called for them to join her as preliminary autopsy results were in. He hadn't asked why she'd chosen to sleep on the sofa instead of the perfectly nice double bed in their temporary lush accommodation. Isabel can feel the time where she'll have to sit down and be open with him about what's happening closing in.

Adam arrives to pick them up and it takes them roughly thirty-five minutes to reach the wide residential street that is their destination.

They've left the mist behind, and the sun is out, bright, and unapologetic. The street, long and sloping dramatically down to where they stand, is lined with terraced houses that aren't entirely uniform but have the same sloping roofs and chimneys. Many have kept their original red-bricked outer face. The street is dotted on either side with tall, thick, tree trunks that have had their branches sawn off, but verdant leaves and soft white flowers now decorate their stumps.

Despite herself, Isabel finds herself charmed.

It's a very different feel to the slick, new building they've been put up in next to the river. Lovely. Peaceful.

'It's up there,' Adam says, pointing up towards the top of the street.

'Lead the way,' Isabel says.

It's quiet. Isabel can hear the sound of children playing, a chorus of excited voices and childish screams, muted only by distance. There must be a school somewhere nearby.

Rampaul is waiting for them at the top where another road bisects the long slope. She has on a light, long black cardigan, white T-shirt, smart slacks, and sunglasses. She looks like a model for a lifestyle magazine.

When she spots them, she waves them over impatiently.

'Took you long enough,' she says.

At their side, Adam speeds up. 'Sorry boss, we got caught in some traffic,' he says.

Rampaul waves it away. She takes a deep breath and addresses Isabel and Voronov. 'Sorry for the short notice, hope you weren't expecting a lie-in,' she says, her dry tone removing any actual apologetic intent.

'We'll live,' Isabel says. She glances at the big building next to them. 'Is this it?'

It blends in perfectly well with the rest of the buildings in the street, but this one is bigger.

'Yup, let's go.'

They round the corner. It has a car park which stretches the length of the building, half hidden by tall, neatly trimmed hedges.

Stairs and a ramp lead up to the wide, glossy red front door.

Rampaul reaches the door and presses the button mounted on the wall next to it. A loud buzz echoes inside, loud enough that they hear it.

'They might be a bit pissed off at us, word of warning,' Rampaul says.

The door unlatches with a loud answering buzz. Rampaul pushes it open and immediately, Isabel feels the chill of the place pool out and pour over them.

'Why?' Isabel asks.

'Thanks to us they had to handle twelve bodies,' Rampaul says, heading for the Reception desk at the front where a young woman sits behind a tall counter. There's someone else at a desk behind her. He's got his back to them and Isabel can't see his face but he's wearing a deep-green cashmere polo neck that stands in contrast to his unusually pale skin. His closely shaved hair is a very, very white blond.

There's a radio playing somewhere, just loud enough to be pleasant. Isabel vaguely recognises the pop song that's wrapping up as the DJ starts speaking to her listeners.

'DI Rampaul and DC Duncan,' Rampaul tells the woman, gesturing between herself and Adam before nodding in Isabel and Voronov's direction, 'Inspectors Reis and Voronov are visiting us from Portugal to assist on this investigation.' She reaches for the pen atop the counter and clicks it twice, impatient. 'Where do you need us to sign?'

The young woman looks over her shoulder at the man who heaves a put-upon sigh without bothering to turn around.

'Let them sign in, Ginny.'

'Of course.' The woman, Ginny, stands from her desk and hands over a clipboard with the sign-in form.

Rampaul takes it from her but doesn't do anything, instead leaning on the counter and addressing the man. 'It wasn't me; you know,' she says, raising her voice, 'so stop throwing a tantrum and say hello. Jesus. You'd think you'd already know what an arse my boss is.'

The man snaps around so fast Isabel is surprised he doesn't break his neck in the process. He's got sharp, angular features and his nose may have been broken once or twice before. The cat's-eye thick-rimmed glasses take Isabel a little by surprise, but they suit him.

'It's always *you*,' he says.

Rampaul rolls her eyes. 'Not my fault, Dr Marlow,' she almost sing-songs. 'Like I said, blame this one on my boss.'

Isabel passes the sign-in form to Voronov and the two share an amused look at the bickering. But then the look lingers. Humour slips away from Voronov's face, leaving them just watching each other.

Yeah. It's easy to keep forgetting the distance she's been trying to enforce between them when it's only the two of them here to rely on for company and for complete trust. Being in each other's space in and out of work doesn't help her much either.

Isabel glances away and runs a hand over her hair.

'Wish you both luck in working with this one,' Marlow says, standing.

He's skinny but very tall. He towers over them. Even Voronov.

'She's a pain in the arse,' he concludes.

Rampaul shakes her head and turns away and starts walking off down the corridor. 'At least tell it like it is,' she says over her shoulder, 'you hate me because I don't put up with your crap and I'm pushy and that pisses you off.'

At their side, Adam smiles apologetically at Isabel and Voronov. 'This is normal.'

Dr Marlow rounds the counter, pace clipped. 'No. I dislike you because you do as you like without regard for the rules. Because of you I had to pull three extra people to work around the clock.'

Isabel tunes out their conversation.

This mortuary, with its varnished floor and tall, wide corridors, smells just like the ones she goes in and out of back home. The antiseptic smell, like that in a hospital, is so strong it feels like it will singe your nose.

Dr Marlow leads them through a set of double doors into a huge postmortem examination room. Isabel is used to mortuaries that are always tight for space. Doesn't seem to be a problem with this one.

It's cold and Isabel hunches her shoulders against the chill.

Dr Marlow is fast to suit up in protective equipment. 'Let me make this quick.'

The operating table is gleaming under the stark white lights in the room. On the far-right side of the room is a wall comprising twelve compartments, cold lockers, all of them locked. Dr Marlow heads straight over to them and partially slides out a body. He does a quick check of the tag attached to the body's toe and then indicates it with a nod of his head.

'My best guess is asphyxia.'

Best guess? 'Is the cause of death unclear?' Isabel thinks back to the video. She'd thought maybe a heart attack or a stroke, something of that nature. She hadn't expected asphyxiation.

Voronov walks over and leans in to read the name on the tag. 'Emanuel Francisco,' he says.

'Not just him,' Dr Marlow says.

Voronov stills. 'Who else?'

Dr Marlow rests his hands on the edge of the body tray and nudges his glasses up his nose. 'All bodies found at the scene at the embassy. To make matters more interesting, one thing I *am* sure about is they all died within the same time frame.' He checks the board in his hand.

Rampaul is impatient and makes a rewind motion with her hand. 'Roll it back. You're saying every single one of those people suffocated to death?'

Marlow sighs, frowning down at his notes. 'Like I said, I can't say for sure, but they all have similar signs. All the bodies have signs of petechiae – basically tiny haemorrhages – some are visible in the eyes, others apparent on the surface of the heart and other organs, certain patches of skin. Also, the presence of cyanotic tissue.' He sets the notes down. 'But what caused it? I can't say. Blood work should be back in another few hours, but unless that hints at something else, then I've got nothing for you.'

'But suffocation . . .' Isabel starts.

Suffocation doesn't immediately lead to death. It leads to unconsciousness. If they've died from it then it means sustained suffocation lasting anywhere from five to ten minutes.

In the video of Francisco's death there was no one else in there with him.

'I wouldn't have called you down here for this alone,' Marlow says. He turns back to Francisco's body and flips the sheet. 'See those?'

They all follow the point of his finger as he shows them.

'Here and here and here. See that?' Marlow says.

He's pointing to scratch marks. Vivid ones. All up Francisco's right wrist and hand, and then again on the left side of his face and his neck.

'Mr Francisco was also wearing make-up. Not to stereotype, but he doesn't seem the type. It wasn't very well applied but it did the trick. These were done before he died, they're no more than a few days old.'

Isabel recalls her and Rampaul's interviews yesterday with Cíntia and Moreno Security. The presence of concealed scratches doesn't bode well.

All of this new information, the asphyxiation, the scratches . . .

It's beginning to point to something much darker than she'd expected.

She meets Voronov's eyes and knows she's not the only one feeling this sense of foreboding.

# 17

Isabel turns her phone over in her hand as Adam pulls the car into one of the parking bays at the station.

The sun is baking down on them.

She's still mulling over Dr Marlow's findings.

'Isabel.'

Voronov is already outside the car and peering at her from the open door. He has one arm resting on the door frame and his head dipped. The sunlight is hitting him at full blast.

Rampaul is also out of the car and frowning at her. DC Duncan is in the front seat, peering at her through the rear-view mirror, apologetic.

'Oh, I'm sorry,' Isabel says. She grips her phone tightly and gets out.

She hadn't noticed the car stopping. She glances back down at her phone.

'Are you good, Reis?' Rampaul asks.

'Yes, I'm fine. Go ahead without me, I'll be right in.'

Rampaul nods. 'Let's go.' She gestures at DC Duncan to follow her.

Voronov lingers.

Isabel holds up her phone. 'I need to make a call; I'll be quick. Meet you inside.'

'Okay,' he says, pats the roof and heads in.

Isabel watches him follow Rampaul and DC Duncan into the building.

She turns her back on the building, unlocking her phone and scrolling through her contacts until she finds a name that she wasn't planning on seeking out so soon.

She doesn't hesitate though. Doesn't have the time or the patience to waste on being uncertain.

Putting the phone to her ear, she paces away from the car and towards the far end of the car park where a hotel situated some roads away stretches up into the sky and casts a shadow.

The phone rings, the ring tone sounding distant.

'Inspector Reis?' Dr Nazaré Alves's greeting is a mix between surprise and cautious pleasure.

'Dr Alves,' Isabel greets her in return.

There's a pause from the other side. 'I'm surprised you called me. I wasn't expecting you to reach out to me any time soon. Or at all, if I'm honest.'

Another police car drives into the car park, driving slowly past her, wheels crunching. Tucked into a corner in the shade is a small cluster of pigeons, pecking at French fries that someone must have dropped. Just outside the door leading into the police building is a group of four officers, some in uniform, some out of it, standing close together and frowning at the sun, rubbing at sweaty foreheads – it doesn't make them smoke their cigarettes any faster though.

'Truthfully, I didn't plan on it myself.'

'Oh?' Curiosity animates her voice, making it more familiar.

Isabel hadn't had any issues with Nazaré Alves; she'd enjoyed her company even, in the short time they'd known each other. She'd met her during a case a couple of years back where she'd needed an expert on Gifted and their abilities. Dr Alves had proved more than useful and interesting company. She knew her field and she was smart and perceptive with a good sense of humour. Exactly the type of person that Isabel liked to be able to call on for work matters.

The problem had occurred in the middle of Isabel's last major case.

Monitoring, Portugal's regulatory body for Gifted individuals, had caught a whiff that something about a case Isabel had worked hadn't been quite right. And, well. Isabel had been right. Dr Nazaré Alves was perceptive.

They'd shown up at her place of work to interrogate her. It hadn't gone too well for them. Except later on, Nazaré had sought Isabel out alone, and told her to be careful. That Monitoring was keeping tabs on her. At the time Isabel had been too pissed off and suspicious of her to appreciate the warning. It has been long enough since then though, and while Isabel can't say she trusts her personally, she does trust her in a professional capacity.

'I hear you've left the country,' Nazaré says, when Isabel doesn't elaborate. 'How are the English treating you?'

Isabel scoffs. Of course. 'Still keeping tabs on me.'

Nazaré sighs at her end. 'Would you prefer I lie to you?'

Laughter echoes in the car park and Isabel's attention is drawn back to the smokers. 'I'm calling because I need your opinion on something. Confidential.'

'Related to a case?'

'Yes. Can I trust you there, at least?'

Another sigh. 'Yes. Yes, you can, Isabel. I'm listening.'

'We've talked about control before.' The group of smokers are stubbing their cigarettes out, still loud, as they head in. A siren sounds, its wail piercing the air and making Isabel wince. She digs a thumb into her temple, the gestures subconscious. She's been exposed to so much loudness, consistent everywhere she goes here.

'You're talking about control of a Gifted individual over their affinity?'

'Yes.'

'Go on.'

'The case we're assisting with is unusual.'

'Is a Gifted involved?'

Isabel glances around her. Everyone has left. Just her and the pigeons now. They're still pecking at the fries.

As if in recognition, her stomach rumbles. What time did she eat last?

'No. Not that we know of.'

'Okay. What's making you consider the possibility?'

'Confidential, Dr Alves.'

'Isabel. With this, you can trust me.'

She grits her teeth. Feels the still tender side of her face and mouth throb at the motion. 'We have twelve people dead. They all died within the same time frame, I'd imagine give or take five or ten minutes. We have no way of knowing or narrowing it down further than that.'

'That's possible to do without using an affinity. How did they die?'

'Preliminary reports are saying asphyxia.'

Silence fills the line for a moment. 'Okay. I see. Not caused by anything else?'

'If it was, then the reason hasn't yet been identified. We're waiting for blood works. We might get some more information then.' Asphyxia could be caused by multiple different things. In a situation like this, with multiple people dying with the same symptom, the most likely offenders could be a drug overdose or inhalation of chemical substances. If administered together, both would come with their own complications. 'If someone has a telekinetic affinity, could it be done?'

Nazaré blows out a breath and Isabel can picture her adjusting the large glasses on her face as she considers the question. 'If, as you've said, they all died within the same span of time, and all in the same way . . . asphyxiation doesn't kill immediately either. Is it possible? I can't say that it is *im*possible. The Gifted individual would be a higher-level Gifted. I wouldn't place them below a level ten. But even that wouldn't be enough – they would have to have,' she laughs, incredulous, 'Isabel they'd have to have an insane amount of control. An insane amount. I'm not sure it can be done.'

Maybe not for people like Isabel or your average person.

For someone more regimented though, someone with a background in the military, even if their focus was not battle – did that make this type of control easier to attain? From Isabel's understanding anyone working for the military, no matter what the country, and no matter in what area of specialisation, even if they were working behind a desk, would have to undergo basic combat training. Sharpening control of the body and mind in whatever setting could easily lend itself to greater control of one's Gift as well. At least it's a strong possibility.

'Let's say they have both,' Isabel says, 'how would that even work? It's not like they'd be able to wrap an invisible noose around their necks.' Even with Isabel's hypothesis, she reckons that would be something out of a movie.

'No. My best guess would be in the form of pressure.'

'Pressure? I don't—' She's interrupted by someone speaking from Nazaré's side of the line.

'I have to go, I have someone waiting. But for something like what you're describing, with multiple deaths from the same cause? It would have to be extreme.'

'Right.' She starts making her way back to the station. 'Thank you. I'll let you get back to your day.'

'Isabel.'

The automatic doors slide open and Isabel steps inside, the loudness around her instantly surging back up to nerve-grinding levels. 'Yes?'

'If you need me, just reach out. If I can help, I will.'

'I'll keep that in mind.' They hang up after that and Isabel makes a beeline for the steps.

How she wishes that Nazaré's answer had been a straightforward 'no'.

'Are you sure it was a good idea calling her?' Voronov asks.

He's referring to her earlier call to Nazaré.

They've spent the last couple of hours checking through the CCTV and rotas provided by the embassy and since they were due a small break from the screen, Isabel and Voronov are on a lunch-hunting mission before Voronov and Adam head off to speak to Ramos's neighbours.

They would have to speak to the members of staff Isabel and

116

Rampaul had already seen yesterday. This time they would be going over the death of another colleague.

'No. But it wasn't a bad one either,' she says.

They find a tiny Italian deli a couple of roads from the station. It's small, with barely room for two people in its short aisles. The shelves are stacked floor to ceiling with all sorts of products. Isabel can see everything from biscuits to bottled sauces and drinks. Some are the same as things they have in Portugal, except the language printed on the labels is different.

The prices make Isabel wince. They queue up for the deli section. A short man in a grey T-shirt and a white apron chuckles as he talks with a customer, the two conversing in Italian as the man in the apron expertly puts the sandwich together. He doesn't watch what he's doing, all of it muscle memory.

The store has its aircon on full blast and while she hates the extreme cold blowing over her skin, it soothes the low-level aching of her head that has been almost constant since she stepped off the plane at Heathrow.

Even in this little store with so few people inside, the thoughts and emotions are continuous, a non-stop stream of consciousness like everyone else in this city. Isabel hadn't expected to be blocking thoughts at this level.

'Isabel?'

Voronov has edged forward in line. He's looking at her like he's said her name a couple of times.

Dr Alves. Right. Voronov had been the one to get Isabel out of the room when Nazaré turned up with a colleague and tried to catch her out at the station. He's one of three people, including Isabel, who knows how dangerous this situation is for her. It's no surprise he's not comfortable with the idea of her speaking to Dr Alves.

'I think we need to know what's possible,' Isabel says. 'We don't know anyone here.' She sighs, shoving her hand through her hair, frustrated. 'And we have no authority here either. In this, at least, I trust her information.' She sighs again. 'And she never lied to me about Monitoring or their intentions towards me.' If anything, at this point, Monitoring is the least of her problems.

'This case might not be Gifted-related at all.'

'I'd like to think it isn't,' Isabel says. 'But we both know there's precedent for something like this.'

'You're talking about the telekinetic at Colombo.' A few years back a teenager had caused a major incident at Lisbon's biggest shopping centre. Her Gift had spiralled out of control, and she'd taken half the building down with her.

'Yes.'

The conversation in Italian at the front continues, loud. The Italians seem to favour the same tone levels as the Portuguese. Which is to say, no moderation at all. It almost feels like home.

The bell sounds as the door opens and three chatty women walk in, purses in hand. Colleagues probably. They're dressed like city workers.

Isabel turns to Voronov to keep their conversation private. 'From what Dr Alves says, it would take a lot for a Gifted individual to manage to do that kind of damage, especially simultaneously. She said it would take a higher level. And a lot of control.'

The worker behind the counter gestures for them to come forward. Isabel smiles out of habit, greeting him before surveying the selection of food.

'The only person we think has witnessed anything is Gifted herself. We know she's Gifted from the articles you dug up and it was corroborated by Mackey and Bridges who were keeping tabs on her at the embassy. Then we have the reports from Grosz, from Cíntia Cheever and the security detail from Moreno. The scratches on Francisco's body. Sexual harassment in a place that's meant to be your safe haven from whatever you're running from. People crack.' She sighs and runs a hand through her hair. 'Without speaking to Pereira this is obviously all hypothetical, I know. I'm just saying it's possible.' She gestures to the options. 'What do you want?'

They put in their order, including extras for Rampaul and DC

Duncan, carrying on their conversation while their orders are put together.

'You're right though,' she says as they step back out, the can of Coke inside the plastic bag a cool spot against her leg, 'I don't want us to get ahead of ourselves. Dr Marlow said he will have the blood works soon, so I guess we're waiting for that . . .'

'And there's Judite Ramos,' Voronov says. 'Her death happens close to those of the people who died at the embassy. She's a member of staff there and the ambassador's secretary. Interviews with the security company and the office and facilities manager hint that Dr Pereira may have been the latest victim of the ambassador.'

There's something there, like a twisting, in the emotions normally kept so in check by him. 'What is it?' she asks.

Voronov stops as they reach the edge of the pavement. A delivery bike speeds past, almost clipping him, but he does nothing more than send a frosty glance the rider's way before turning to face Isabel fully. His forehead is scrunched, his eyes narrowed against the sunlight.

'Nothing. I want us to see this through.'

'Yeah. Me too.' The traffic on the road slows and Isabel takes advantage of it to cross. 'We'll check in with the chief. See if she's got anything new for us.'

The time to pull them off this case has passed and anyone who attempts to do it will find they won't get rid of them so easily.

# 18

Outside, night has settled. The building opposite the station is nothing but darkened windows reflecting the lights of the police building.

Isabel and Rampaul were in back-to-back interviews with the remaining embassy staff members. Voronov and Adam had spent the rest of the afternoon in West London, carrying out inquiries on Judite Ramos's murder. Marlow had reluctantly agreed that they would do their best to prioritise the autopsy for Judite after they finished the report on those lost at the embassy.

Neighbours heard nothing and saw nothing out of the ordinary. Most of them left early to go to work and came back late. The only one who had seen anything odd had been the translator next door, who had told them all that she knew already. They didn't even seem to know much about her other than that she had a boyfriend who would come over every now and then. Their description of the boyfriend matched Timothy Allen.

Adam and Voronov are about twenty minutes away from the station.

Isabel is powering down the laptop she's been loaned by the station and Rampaul is tidying the printouts of the rotas they had been combing through – not that they had rendered all that much information.

Rampaul is rubbing at the curve between her neck and shoulder, grimacing. 'Must have done something to it,' she mutters, 'feeling grimy. Want a shower and then my bed and nothing else.'

'Sounds like a plan,' Isabel says.

The young officer from the front desk appears at the door and raps her fingers on it quietly. 'DI Rampaul. There's someone downstairs wanting to speak to you, a Dr Eliana Cross.'

Isabel sets her laptop back down.

Dr Eliana Cross is Dr Pereira's boss. She is the woman mentioned in the articles Voronov had found on Dr Pereira and who DC Bridges had named as Dr Pereira's mentor.

Rampaul looks over at Isabel before setting her bag down again and turning back to the officer. 'Do me a favour and take her into one of the interview rooms for me, we'll be right there.'

Eliana Cross looks up when they enter the room.

Isabel closes the door behind them and she and Rampaul take the chairs on the other side of the table.

'Dr Cross, I'm DI Rampaul with the Met's MCIU and this is Inspector Reis with the Portuguese Judiciary Police,' Rampaul says, settling into her seat. 'Thank you for getting in contact with us.'

Isabel takes the seat beside her, giving Cross a nod in greeting.

She'll be taking a back seat in this interview. One, because Rampaul wants to be in control of the conversation, and two, because she's asked Isabel to concentrate on what she can pick up from Cross.

It's not a role Isabel is used to, or comfortable with taking, particularly with Rampaul's expectations of Isabel's use of her Gift.

But she's not on home turf and she's not in charge.

She doesn't know why she'd imagined someone rigid instead of this soft-purple-sweater woman. She's got olive-toned skin that is showing signs of age. She has dark circles under her eyes, but there is a feeling of vitality to her that is evident in the way she's sitting and the bright air of competence and intelligence stamped on to the proud slant of her chin and the way she's listening to Rampaul.

Her light-brown hair has plenty of grey among it and has been left to frame her rounded cheeks in soft waves. There's nothing about her face that would make her remarkable, but she is a woman who attracts the gaze and holds attention.

'Yes, of course.' Her accent is markedly different, American, though if you asked Isabel which part of the US she might be from, she wouldn't have the faintest clue. 'We've been searching for Dr Pereira. We're anxious to get her back home.'

Back home? Interesting choice of words. Not back to be tried for stealing US property. Not back to be dealt with. But anxious to get her back home.

Rampaul tilts her head to the side, considering.

'That's a very affectionate way of speaking about someone who deserted your organisation, Dr Cross,' Rampaul says, calmly challenging.

'Well, I wasn't just Anabel's boss. I was her mentor. I have been her mentor since we snatched her right out of high school. So yes, I want her home.'

'I see. No hard feelings, then, about whatever she took from you. Speaking of which, what *did* Dr Pereira steal from you?'

Cross gives her a thin smile. 'She never stole from me. I can't disclose the nature of her transgression.'

'You mean her crime? You might want to reconsider that, Dr Cross, considering the circumstances.'

Isabel takes some of the printouts they'd selected before coming in there out of the folder. She slides them across to Cross.

Rampaul gestures towards them as if she's inviting Cross to partake in a meal.

'In case you weren't aware of said circumstances,' Rampaul says.

Cross's smile fades. She shifts forward in her seat, and her gaze drops to the images laid out. 'May I?' she asks.

'Please, go ahead.'

Cross reaches out and drags the photos to her, one by one.

She takes her time, her eyes roaming over the images of those who had been found within the walls of the embassy. Her expression doesn't change.

When she's finished, she carefully gathers them all into a pile. She taps the edges of the photos on the desk to get them all in line. She pushes them back over to Rampaul and Isabel's side.

'I'm not sure why you're showing me these. Where is Anabel?' she says. 'I'm sorry for these people and their families. But I'm here for Anabel. She is my primary concern and if these are anything to go by,' she flicks the corner of the pile of pictures with her nail, 'and you didn't find her in there then she could be out there hurt somewhere.'

All Isabel is getting from Cross is an eerie calm. She's a fount of it. There's no uptick of nervousness or anxiety, no thoughts, no emotion.

It's possible that Cross is someone who just has impressive control of her emotions. She works with the US military; that alone would require a level of control most might not have. Add to that her lead role in ensuring Gifted effectiveness in combat situations and providing work to optimise that . . .

Isabel is sure Cross is an impressive woman in more ways than one.

Rampaul takes the photos back. 'I assure you, Dr Cross, we're as concerned about her wellbeing as you are. But it's our job to consider all possibilities. It's our understanding that Dr Pereira is a skilled telepathic Gifted herself. A level eight. And we also have reason to believe she may not have been having the best time in there. Gifts can be used in all sorts of ways.'

Cross tucks her hair behind her ear, revealing a dangling butterfly earring. It reflects the light with a wink. 'I've mentored Anabel from when she was very young. Have watched her become one of the best scientists to have ever worked in the US military and beyond. I know better than anyone in this room what she's capable of and what she isn't.'

'So you foresaw the stealing then?' Rampaul asks. 'Because by your logic, you would have seen that coming too, don't you think?'

'I understand where you're coming from,' Cross says, still no hint of any kind of any doubt coming across in her tone or her face, 'I really do. But it has nothing to do with her. As I said, if anything, she could be out there in danger.'

Isabel thinks about Moreno Security. They had been equally protective of Dr Pereira.

Rampaul makes a humming sound and sits back in her seat.

'The truth is you weren't there, Dr Cross. And after the incident took place, neither was Anabel. You're a smart woman. You know this doesn't look good.'

Cross leans over, hands spread on the table. 'I know that Anabel was taking refuge within the Portuguese Embassy here in London. And now, from what you've said, what you've shown me, I know a tragedy has taken place at that same embassy and that you believe someone caused the death of these people. The way I see it,' she says, 'there was an attack and you have no suspects and Anabel is a potential victim somewhere out in the city. Maybe dead herself. You said you're searching for her and yet you and your colleague are sitting across from me. So what are you doing to find her?'

She's not wrong.

They don't know what happened in there. Focusing on Anabel Pereira as a suspect could cost them big time if she turns up dead somewhere. There will be questions about why she was instantly viewed as a suspect rather than a potential victim.

'Our team are doing what they need to in order to resolve the situation. Unfortunately, we need to consider the very strong possibility that Anabel was the cause of what took place. Help us understand her.'

Cross sighs. She flicks a look at Isabel, assessing. Maybe because Isabel has stayed quiet throughout her exchange with Rampaul. 'Of course, I'm here to do anything I can. As I said, we want her home.'

Rampaul nods. 'Where is home exactly?'

Cross obliges. Answering questions with ease and without any apparent attempt to hold anything back. Home for Dr Pereira and Cross is Massachusetts. Dr Pereira lived with her fiancée off base before she disappeared. There were no concerns before that; she'd been going to work as usual, friends hadn't noticed anything different about her, her fiancée hadn't noticed anything different about her.

She gives them the details of the fiancée for them to follow up with her, a Miss Weir.

'What about as a Gifted individual. Did Dr Pereira have any issues with that? You said she's adept with her Gift.'

Cross shakes her head. 'Never. Those who worked with her trusted her. We work with many people who are Gifted, telepaths and telekinetics alike. Things have come a long way for us.'

Rampaul arcs an eyebrow, clearly communicating what she thinks of that statement. 'Regardless of the utopia you think you have, human nature is human nature. There's always one person or another that shows distrust. Or envy. Or fear. There is always something. It doesn't have to be related to her Gift. Tell me about what she was like at work.'

Cross goes on to describe Dr Pereira as meticulous, the type to always arrive early. Loved her job and wouldn't have given it up for the world.

A bit of a contrast to the actions Dr Pereira would have taken to end up in the situation they currently find themselves dealing with.

Isabel keeps a frown from showing on her face. Nothing is connecting here.

The more Cross describes the woman who had worked with her – honest, diligent, living for her job – none of it adds up. If she is all those things, then what pushed her? And why would she run all the way over here and not to her mentor?

Isabel eyes her as she continues answering Rampaul's questions, emotions still as a lake surface, not one ripple in them.

However, Isabel knows these things don't necessarily mean anything. It's one thing you see all the time.

Good people, even the best people, can make the craziest of decisions in the right circumstances.

# 19

They take Cross's details down. She's staying in a hotel in central London, not too far from the police station itself. She wants to stay close and be apprised of changes in the case.

Adam and Voronov arrive as Rampaul is guiding her out and Adam goes with her.

Voronov follows Isabel back to the case room.

'How was it?'

Isabel shakes her head, going back to where they had left their things earlier. 'Maybe she's been given some kind of special training due to her work with the military. I don't know. She's probably the only person since we arrived here who seems to actively keep her thoughts where they should stay.' And consciously aims to keep intruders out.

'What did she have to say?'

Isabel switches off the lights and closes the door behind her. They head for the stairs, shoulders close together. 'She's insistent that Dr Pereira has nothing to do with the deaths at the embassy and just wants to take her back home. Wants us to be doing much more to find her.' Also, it's not like they could explain that they're being asked to operate with a significantly smaller number of people than Isabel would expect for an investigation of this nature. 'It would probably make her feel better if we told her we'd like the same thing too. What about you guys, anything interesting come up?'

It happens then.

Isabel stops.

The faintest of tremors. As if she's standing on the ground right above a running train.

Voronov stops too, frowning.

It's over in a handful of seconds and if it weren't for Voronov she wonders if she'd be left thinking she'd imagined it.

The lights flicker, too fast for Isabel to do more than register that they'd gone out multiple times in quick succession.

'Aleks,' she says, even as she hears others in the office speak up.

The murmurs in the office die down quickly, devolving into grumbles about cheapskate bosses and how the building hasn't been upgraded in years. They settle back in as if nothing happened.

Isabel hurries to the stairs.

'What is it?' Voronov asks, staying close.

'You didn't feel that?'

'I did,' he says.

On the staircase, other members of staff are continuing on their way, some of them sending suspicious glances up at the ceiling, others frowning. There's no alarm though, just quiet exclamations of surprise.

She could be overreacting.

She's halfway to the ground floor when she smells it. It's faint. She stops on the landing and tries to breathe more of it in.

So, so faint. But it's there. Like burnt hair. 'You smell that?' she murmurs.

Voronov's staring down the brightly lit stairs, eyebrows slashing down, and lips forced into a grim flat line. He nods.

The burnt-hair scent manifests in places where strong telekinesis has been used.

They both head straight down, and Isabel almost runs head on into Adam, who is jogging up the steps with his head down. She manages to skid to a stop and would have fallen on her arse if Voronov wasn't behind her. He catches hold of her shoulders to steady her even as Adam jerks back, arms flailing to keep his balance.

'Inspector, sorry! I didn't see you!'

Isabel waves it off and ducks around him. 'Did the lights cut out downstairs?' she asks, straightening away from Voronov's steadying hands with a thanks.

'Uh,' Adam looks between her and Voronov, confused. He hurries to keep up with them. 'No – I mean, yes? They didn't really cut out, just flickered for a second. Why? Is the electricity out upstairs?'

'No. Where's Rampaul?'

'She was seeing Dr Cross to her car . . . what's going on?'

Isabel opens the door to the main Reception area, not checking her strength. It slams open, drawing the eyes of those waiting to speak to the receptionist on shift and the two women police officers walking in with a woman in cuffs.

She scans the space, but no one stands out. She heads for the exit.

Cold air washes over her face as she steps outside and continues on down to the pavement.

The street is less busy now. It's dark out, the streetlights are on, shining pools of brightness on sections of the road. People hustle past, everyone keeping to the same tight pace – tight enough that a couple speed-walking past her clip Isabel's shoulder.

Isabel spares a brief glance their way even as she scans the road, eyes catching on shadows in the corners of the street, the windows lit up from within, the flow of traffic further down leading to the main road. A couple of people go in and out of a corner shop.

Isabel looks in the opposite direction. There is a small recreational area further down the road. She can just make out the shadows of the slide and the swings from her spot in front of the police station.

She squints.

Outside the small playground, the streetlight highlights a familiar build.

Isabel feels her own skin ripple, the sensation travelling up her spine. It spreads to her shoulder blades and arms. It leaves every single hair on her body standing on end.

She takes a tentative step forward, something in her recognising what she's seeing but her mind not comprehending. Like a puzzle piece that you know belongs in the picture but you can't figure out where it fits in the frame.

When it hits her exactly what she's seeing, she stops. Her heart spikes, the veins in her neck throbbing.

'No . . .' she murmurs.

As if they hear her, the person starts to turn.

In the corner of her mind that shadowed presence she's been trying to keep buried stirs, like a tree shivering and shedding its leaves to expose its pointed branches.

'Isabel.'

She startles at the soft touch to her elbow, spinning to face Voronov. His hand hovers between them, his blue eyes focused on her, concern clear.

Isabel looks back at the playground.

It's empty.

There's no one there.

In the recesses of her mind, she hears her name, spoken like a promise.

Then that presence curls back in on itself and disappears.

'Isabel,' Voronov says, again. 'What is it?' He follows her gaze, trying to spot what has alarmed her. 'You saw something.'

She pushes her hair back from her face, body tight with tension. And beneath that, deep into her chest, what took root months ago begins to grow from her stomach and twist up into her chest.

Fear.

'Nothing,' she says. It comes out monotone, but at least her voice is steady. 'I thought I saw something, but there's nothing there.'

# 20

After they leave the station, Isabel and Voronov insist that Adam let them make their own way home. There's a metro station close to their place anyway.

Not one of their best ideas.

By the time they exit the station at the other end, Isabel's head is one big throbbing mess and she's holding back the need to throw up.

Voronov curses under his breath and guides her out and into the fresh air, moving her as far away from the bustling station as fast as her weakened legs will allow. He doesn't stop until they've reached a point in the road where the crowd is thinned.

Isabel rests against the wall of a closed shop, head leaning back to catch what little breeze is sweeping past, forehead scrunched, and eyes screwed shut in agony. Her throat bobs as she swallows convulsively, trying to stave off the threat of being sick.

At least if she needs to be sick now they are outside.

The train had been overwhelming. The carriage completely packed out, sandwiching her between Voronov and the crowd, people constantly jostling and their thoughts so loud, so insistent, so imbued with irritation, fatigue and resentment that she'd felt her defensive walls crumbling under the weight of it all.

'Stay here,' Voronov says. 'I'll be right back.'

She manages a nod and doesn't even bother opening her eyes.

Sweat drips down her forehead as she focuses on stabilising herself.

She hates that people in this city are so inescapably loud.

There are crowds of people, the buzz of conversation echoing in the streets where they're gathered together, most sporting one drink or another in their hands as they talk away the working day, others alternating between drinking and smoking outside the pubs on the other side of the road.

This part isn't so different from being back home.

Except the feel is different. The thoughts here float up, tangled in all colours of emotions to form a ceiling of *too much* above her head.

Isabel does her best to block.

London is made up of long populated roads and then alleyways that make Isabel think of different times, almost as if she's walking through a time machine.

Even here, so close to the new-build they're staying in, Isabel can see where the new veers into pathways and streetlamps that hark back to the Victorian era.

Slowly the acidic sensation in her throat begins to ease and she opens her eyes. Voronov is hurrying back over to her. There's a water bottle and a chocolate bar in his hand.

'Are you feeling steadier?' he asks as he reaches her. 'Here.' He hands her the water and the chocolate bar.

'Thanks,' she murmurs. When she sips the water it's blessedly cool and she closes her eyes again but this time in bliss. 'That's good.' She gulps down half the bottle before finally unwrapping the chocolate bar and taking a good bite. 'I'm better, thank you.' She lifts the chocolate bar. 'This helps.' She can hear how drained she sounds though, knows that there's no way she'll be of much use for the rest of the evening.

Voronov joins her, leaning on the wall too, arms crossed as they watch the evening crowds.

'You know, don't you?' she asks. 'You've been letting me get away with it for a while, but you've known something's wrong.'

He doesn't deny it. Instead he waits.

'It happened a few months ago.' She lets her gaze drift back to the pub-goers, twisting the cap back on to the bottle, 'after we wrapped up the Venâncio case.'

It was their last major case which they had closed a few months ago, investigating the murder of a youth worker which led to them uncovering a trafficking ring right there in the middle of Lisbon. That's when Gabriel Bernardo, a man who Isabel and Voronov had put away for murder on their first ever case together, had intruded in their lives again. If it wasn't for him, Isabel might not be standing here today. He went missing shortly after.

She wishes that had been the end of it.

Right now, inside her head, it's as still as their surroundings. Somewhere in her head, he's dormant too. She almost wouldn't be able to tell his presence was inside her mind at all if she didn't know what to look for.

But she does. And it's there. Tucked into a corner, shrunken in on itself as if by making itself smaller, blending in, Isabel will forget the voice in her head. That she'll forget that someone else's eyes sometimes try to see through hers.

'You told me Gabriel Bernardo had disappeared,' she says.

Voronov's eyes narrow. Whatever he'd been expecting it clearly wasn't a mention of Gabriel Bernardo. 'He did,' he says, 'they haven't been able to find him since he went missing from the facility he was being kept in.'

'He didn't disappear completely, Aleks.' She feels the tightness in her throat, along her jaw, has to wet her lips before she can continue. 'He's in my head.' She breathes out, clears her throat to get rid of the tremble in her voice. 'He's in my head,' she says again.

She sees the moment it clicks. At first his eyes are scanning her face, the space between his eyebrows wrinkling as he tries to make sense of what she's saying. But then his face smooths out, eyes widening as he understands what she's just told him.

Voronov had been with her when they comprehended the enormity of the horror of what Gabriel Bernardo had done to his girlfriend at the time. Embedded himself in her head. Embedded himself in her head strongly enough to be able to exert control over her and her actions as he wished.

He pushes away from the wall and turns to face her. 'How?' Voronov's voice is tight and there's the tell-tale flex of his jaw. As if he's working to contain himself. He is. Isabel feels that too.

He's normally so controlled, but when things impact him in a certain way, where something happens that has a more emotional edge to it, the natural control Voronov has in keeping his thoughts and emotions protected from someone like Isabel slips.

She sees the tendrils of fear, soft, their reach short, like he's pulling them back under control almost as soon as they escape.

'Isabel. How?'

She shrugs her shoulders and shakes her head, at a loss. 'I don't know. I don't know how.' But she remembers that night, with the salt of the water in her mouth, the dead weight of Gabriel's target in her arms, unmoving, the desperation of knowing that she couldn't win this. And then the reaching right for his mind and taking control. 'You know what I did up there on the rocks that night.'

They've never talked about it. Never. Even when they'd had to write up their statements of what took place when they arrested Gabriel Bernardo.

Voronov had brought her back from the edge that time.

Even now, he doesn't say it out loud.

'I think maybe it happened then. But it took me too long to notice something was wrong. Until a few months ago.' She wonders about that. About why it took so long for her to notice. Was it just that Gabriel was that good? Or was it that he hadn't been capable of doing anything about the connection he had made with her, earlier? Both are possible.

A Gifted of his level wouldn't have been left alone for long when incarcerated. Given what he had already proven he could do with his Gift, it's likely that they would have taken measures to suppress it or, at least, suppress his ability to use it effectively for some time.

But since hearing his voice, clear as crystal in her head, calling her name, she can recognise the moments when he'd been rousing inside her mind, settling in. Observing her. Observing *through* her.

The thought has goosebumps blooming across the skin of her arms and she curls in tighter on herself.

'Since then?' Voronov asks.

'Yes. Though I haven't felt his . . . presence until more recently. And back there at the station. When we got outside I thought I saw him.' She shakes her head. 'I didn't, of course.'

'You think he was the cause of the tremors?' Voronov asks, frowning.

'No. No.' She laughs, without humour. 'No, that was definitely something else.'

'Has he done anything? Would you know if he had?'

Isabel glances up at him with a frown. 'No. He hasn't done anything. He called out to me, once.'

Voronov moves closer. 'What do you mean? He spoke to you?'

The exhaustion that has been weighing her down since they'd exited the metro station is pushed back. She can feel the defensiveness building, feeding energy back into her veins, but not in the way she wants it to. When she answers, it's measured. 'Yes, he called out to me. He said my name. He hasn't said anything else since then.' She doesn't want to hold anything back, not now that she's finally telling him. 'But sometimes, I know he's there. Like he's checking in, or . . . tuning into what I'm doing.'

He stills. 'He can see what you're doing?'

She squeezes the bottle in her hand until the plastic gives with a crackle. 'I don't know. I can't say for sure. I've been doing my best to make sure that doesn't happen. Whenever he . . . is present, I've been able to notice and shut it down as soon as it happens.' She doesn't tell him that the way Gabriel taps into her mind and shows himself has been changing.

He sighs. He reaches up to rub at the back of his neck. 'Have you told anyone else?' he asks.

'Yes. My old Guide, Rosario, knows. I reached out to her when I realised what was happening.' Young individuals in Portugal were all assigned to Guides after testing as Gifted. A Guide usually helped them navigate their Gift, learn to acclimatise to it and live with it in their day-to-day life all the way until they legally became adults at eighteen. After many years, Isabel reconnected with Rosario last year.

'You haven't told the chief.'

'No, I haven't.'

He doesn't say anything else, and his agitation is chipping away at his barriers, his emotions spilling loose. Worry is in there. The fear there is for her too. But there's a good dose of anger, a simmer of it growing stronger as they stand there. She can't tell who that anger is aimed at.

Isabel nudges his shoulder until he turns and faces her. 'Aleks.'

He sighs and meets her eyes, face sober.

Isabel drops her hand back down to her side. 'Fala.'

'Is he watching right now?'

'No.'

'How do you know?' he asks.

She takes a deep breath, composing herself. 'I've got this under control. I can hold him back. He's not seeing anything because I don't let him.'

'Can you promise he won't do what he did with his girlfriend? He was controlling her mind and body, Isabel.'

'I'm not her,' she sighs, exhausted, 'we both know I'm different. You know that.' She looks at him. 'Please trust me.'

At that quiet plea, something eases on his face. 'I do trust you.'

Isabel had been worried about how he might react when she finally told him. She hadn't realised how much until now. Hearing him reaffirm his trust in her feels like an uncoiling of tension that has been fused to her for so long she had become accustomed to living with it. It drains from her now, and she slumps back against the wall again.

'Okay.'

Voronov takes the bottle from her and tugs her into his side. 'Come on.'

She nods and follows his lead, happy to lean on him as they make their way home.

136

'Do you think that that was Dr Pereira back at the station?' Voronov asks.

'The tremors?

'Mm.'

'I don't know,' Isabel says, 'but I don't think that it was coincidence. But why then?'

'If it was Dr Pereira, she could have been there for multiple reasons, maybe even to speak to us despite the risk of deportation. Or maybe for Cross.'

Isabel nods. 'If they're as close as Cross insists they are, maybe Dr Pereira found out her mentor and boss was going to be there. Maybe she wanted to see her.' Although that would pose other questions. How would she have known Cross would be there? And if she *had* been there for Cross, why would she have left without speaking with her? Why would she have revealed her presence there at all?

The tremors hadn't been noticed by everyone. They'd been faint and lasted only a few seconds and people hadn't been too bothered by one instance of flickering lights. They had occurred somewhere between Cross being signed out by Rampaul and Adam and her leaving the building.

As they follow the natural bend of the road and head to the river path Isabel has been making use of on her morning runs, she frowns.

'If it was her and we go with the theory that the people at the embassy were killed by someone using their telekinesis, then their presence there at the same time as Cross's could be a threat. Maybe Cross isn't connected to the embassy, but she's connected to Dr Pereira. We still don't know the circumstances that led to those people dying. It's possible that if it was targeted then, without knowing what rules we're playing by, Cross could be at risk for reasons we just don't know yet.'

There's more of a breeze by the riverside, though its warmth doesn't do much to help, but the lapping of the water is a balm to the senses after her experience on the metro.

Isabel murmurs a thanks and shifts out of Voronov's supportive hold to walk, feeling steadier. As soon as they get into the apartment though she's going straight for a shower and then collapsing for the rest of the evening.

'Or it could have been an unplanned emotional reaction,' Voronov says. 'That's what Nazaré Alves told you, isn't it? That something like that can trigger an explosion of someone's affinity, something strong enough to cause the collapse of a shopping centre or multiple people dying of asphyxiation at the same time.'

'Yeah. It could be.'

But then the question becomes: what would have triggered that burst of lethal emotion?

The only answer that makes sense is Cross.

# 21

The next morning Isabel sends Voronov on ahead.

She'd tossed and turned all night. She'd heard Gabriel calling her name in her dreams and when she'd woken up to a pitch-black room in the dead of night, her heart had frozen on the spot when she'd thought she'd seen his silhouette in the corner of her room.

She hadn't been able to sleep until the early hours of the morning, around 6.15 a.m. The sky was beginning to lighten into day.

Voronov had found her wrapped up in a thin blanket on the sofa, eyes gritty after having only just fallen asleep again and a headache that had her burying her head under the covers. She'd had worse before, but the aftereffects of their journey home the previous evening had drained her, and a night of anxiety and not a little dose of fear, had taken their toll.

Now, standing outside their building, a coffee in one hand and her phone in the other, waiting for her cab to take her to the police station, she writes a slow thumb-typed message to her brother checking in and apologising for not being in touch.

Right about now if she were home, she'd be hugging the hell out of her dogs to ease the knot in her chest that refused to leave her alone.

She has a few texts waiting for her attention. Two of them have been on her phone from the day she landed. One from her sister and another from her sister's fiancé. Both remain unread.

Isabel clicks out of the messaging app and checks to see how far away the cab is.

Getting public transport was clearly not an option.

'Inspector Reis?'

Isabel lifts her head.

She hadn't heard anyone approach her.

The woman is taller than Isabel by an inch or two but similar in build.

Her hair is pulled back in a ponytail. Her eyebrows are thick and lend her an air of severity, though the effect is ruined a little by the full mouth, an unexpected show of softness in an otherwise stern countenance.

She's dressed like someone who's come from an office, shiny, low-heeled black shoes, a black blouse and grey suit trousers. Even through her clothes, Isabel can tell she has compact muscle. The kind that packs power.

The woman reaches out a perfectly manicured hand. Her nails are glossy, oval and black. 'Joana Weir,' she says.

Isabel looks down at her hand and then at her face. The name rings a bell.

Everyone in this place has been loud enough to make Isabel want to tear her hair out. Then yesterday and today, she meets two people in a row whose thoughts and emotions aren't bleeding out of them like water flowing from a tap.

It leaves Isabel suspicious even as she feels relieved at not being bombarded with more uninvited thoughts.

Still, it's best to avoid touching her skin on skin. 'I'm sorry,' she says, nodding at her hand, 'I can't shake your hand, I hope you don't take it personally.' There are enough people around that she's not worried. But the odds on this woman, whoever she is, randomly coming upon her outside the place where she and Voronov are staying and randomly recognising her from somewhere unknown are pretty slim.

'Can I help you?' Isabel says, even as she searches her head for where she's heard the name before. Her tone isn't the most welcoming.

The woman, Joana, drops her hand. She doesn't seem offended. 'Sorry. To be honest I've been keeping tabs on you since your and your partner's arrival. I needed someone to speak to but wasn't sure about the police here.'

'Oh?'

Joana opens her coat and reaches inside. She hooks the ID around her neck and pulls it out so Isabel can see. 'I'm a journalist with the—'

It comes to Isabel then. Cross had told them about her.

'You're Dr Pereira's fiancée,' Isabel says.

That seems to startle Joana, as if she didn't think Isabel would know.

Joana quickly glances around them, as if she's worried someone overheard. She tucks her hands back into her pockets and walks closer to Isabel. 'Well . . . ex-fiancée. We broke up some months ago, but we've always been in touch. I've been speaking with her the entire time she's been at the embassy but then suddenly she cut off contact again. No reason. No replies to my messages.'

Isabel processes that. 'On Tuesday?'

Joana shakes her head. 'No. It was last week. I got worried so I got a flight out of Boston, came here to check on her. I tried to see her at the embassy but they turned me away. Then on Tuesday when I go to the embassy to try again, there's police all over the place trying to keep something under wraps and no one in there is picking up the phone either. I'm not stupid. Something's happening and I'm worried about her.'

Isabel narrows her eyes. 'You can go to the police here.'

Joana shakes her head. 'No. I've done my homework. I want to speak to *you*.'

When Isabel stares at her, unconvinced, she comes closer.

'An hour of your time. Let me buy you coffee. Give me one hour. Please? And then I promise I'll go on record and speak to the police and let them ask me any questions they want.'

# 22

The place they find is busy and full of families. It's decked out in heavy colours with booths and a carpeted floor. They have to wait about ten minutes for a table and there's a crying baby somewhere in the room.

The level of noise, both internal and external, is excruciating and Isabel's not sure how long she'll be able to handle it for. The cafe smells heavily of meat and something else she can't pin down, but which speaks to the fact that this is probably a cheap option for tourists in the city.

Isabel hands the menu back to the waitress with a thanks and a strained smile. She's ordered an omelette and chips, and can't help but think of the rushed toasts and coffee Voronov has scoffed down before rushing out of the apartment. Voronov is someone who is punctual to a fault, but Isabel's admissions and sick state of the previous evening had clearly left him worried. He'd only felt comfortable leaving after he'd seen her sitting up and drinking down some water.

She'd rather be having breakfast in his company and soaking in his calm. Even if whenever they're in the same room lately, it feels as if they're walking this ever-shrinking circle each time. She's not quite sure when it will happen but eventually, they'll have to stop and face each other. Face this thing that charges the air between them in every shared moment of stillness. This thing that is only about the two of them.

Joana Weir gives her order and the waitress says she'll be back with drinks and leaves.

Isabel makes herself comfortable. 'You said you're no longer together. But you're here.'

Someone else who is a long way from where she should be and who has openly admitted to visiting the embassy and attempting to speak with their missing person multiple times. She doesn't strike Isabel as a woman who doesn't understand the consequences of coming forward with this type of information.

'Well.' Joana reaches for the jug of water left behind by the waitress and pours herself a glass. She offers some to Isabel and Isabel nudges her glass out with a thanks. 'We were together a long time and despite the breakup, I still consider her one of my closest friends. I'd say if you were to ask her, she would say the same. Well. I would have. I don't know what's going on anymore.'

'You said you're a journalist,' Isabel prompts.

'Yes, I'm an investigative journalist, sometimes I work as a foreign correspondent, though I don't do much of that now.'

'You said you've been speaking to her while she's been here. Can you tell me why she hid in the embassy?' Isabel asks.

Joana takes a drink from her water and then sets it down with a shake of her head. 'No. She wouldn't tell me. I've already been interrogated in the US,' the smile she gives Isabel isn't a happy one, 'not the most pleasant experience. They thought I knew about what she planned to do.'

'Did you?'

'No, I had no clue. But thinking back on it now, I see some differences in her behaviour around that time. I think maybe it was something she'd been planning for a while.'

'Can you tell me what your conversations have been like since she's been here?'

'Well . . . I've worked on a lot of stories with a focus on Gifted individuals. Some human rights pieces, others uncovering some . . .' She sighs and then the corners of her mouth pinch inward. 'Let's just say some ugly environments and situations. Not to toot my own horn, but I've developed a bit of a reputation.' She meets Isabel's eyes. 'Something I think maybe you and I share.'

Isabel doesn't particularly want to touch on that subject at all – and the rest she can research on her own.

143

'I think that's why she felt she could speak to me about this, and I don't scare easily. I think the only thing that worried her was the personal element of our relationship. She's probably furious that I'm here. But I've dealt with more harrowing situations.'

Isabel raises her eyebrows, curious.

'The target of one of my investigations took up stalking,' Joana says, and she's speaking with a smile now, but her eyes don't match her mouth. 'Police didn't take me seriously. Followed me home. *Not* a fun experience.'

Isabel nods. Despite her cavalier tone, a situation like that is nothing short of a scene taken from a horror movie. 'I'm sorry that happened to you.'

'Me too.' She puffs out a big breath. 'Anyway. Anabel didn't tell me anything at first. We just talked everyday things. She was really down the first two weeks. Quiet. I got the feeling she was always on edge. I asked her how the people there were treating her, and she said she had no complaints.'

Isabel moves her glass out of the way and rests her arms on the table, leaning forward. 'Did she tell you why she took refuge at the embassy?'

'Bits and pieces. She was careful not to tell me too much. I'm not sure if she wanted to try and protect me and keep me out of it or . . . I don't know. But she asked me if she could count on me.'

'Count on you for what?'

'To go public,' Joana says. 'I was her backup plan in case the Portuguese government didn't play ball. From what she shared with me, she wanted them to grant her Portuguese citizenship, which shouldn't have been that much of an issue. Both of her parents are of Portuguese descent. But that wasn't all she needed from them. She made that clear to me. She wanted me to be her final card.'

'Okay, tell me.'

And Joana does.

Yes. Anabel had taken something from the US military – she said it was part of a research project they were conducting. She was part of that research team. It had been something they had been working on for years.

'Did she say what it was?' Isabel asks.

'No, she didn't go into detail about the research itself. Only that she'd been having trouble with the ethics of the project. She had voiced her concerns to her superiors.'

'Anyone in particular?'

'Her supervisor on the project, Dr Cross.'

Ah. Interesting. 'And?'

The waitress returns with a loaded plate in each hand. She sets a plate of fish and chips in front of Joana and the omelette in front of Isabel.

Isabel digs in and feels something settle inside her at the first mixed bite of the eggs and the fried potatoes. Not the best, but not the worst and she's too hungry to care at this point. She motions with her fork for Joana to continue.

The crispy coat of the fish crackles beneath Joana's knife. 'Her concerns were dismissed.'

'So, Anabel took matters into her own hands?'

Joana chews through a bite. 'Yes.'

'That doesn't seem extreme to you? If she's someone who is willing to ask you to break the news if needed, then wouldn't it have made more sense for her to have gone to someone in the US? Get them to expose whatever this is there, instead of coming to a foreign country, holing up at the embassy and *then* threatening to expose everything?'

This all seems like the behaviours of someone responding reactively, without thinking through consequences, which doesn't make sense. From what Isabel has heard and understood, Anabel Pereira is an extremely intelligent woman. She built strong relationships with those around her and had the trust of almost everyone who she had been close to. This is not the type of person to act without a plan.

Although maybe that's where everything went wrong. Her plan fell through. Joana has said that this was Dr Pereira's final plan and if that's the case then she'd never planned to go public with this in the first place.

What had she wanted?

'I thought the same thing,' Joana says. 'She didn't want any of this at all. She wanted a way out of the UK. The British work too closely with the US; the moment they realised she was here, they alerted the Americans.'

Isabel frowns. 'The extradition treaty – I'm not sure whether Portugal has one with the US too.'

'It does. The US has an extradition agreement with the European Union.'

'So, hiding at the embassy wouldn't have done her much good. They would have pursued the same course of action with Portugal.'

'Yes, eventually they would have.' Joana sets down her cutlery. 'Except for the part where the Portuguese Embassy never informed the US that they were harbouring her. No one knew.'

Then who informed the Americans? Another question is, if Anabel was already wary of the relationship between the UK and America being a danger to her escape, why had she come here instead of to another country?

'Why not go directly to Portugal?' Isabel asks.

Joana nods. 'She kept things about her last days in the US close to her chest, but there was a conference happening in London around that time, a pretty big-deal one for researchers working within the field of Gifted studies. Anabel is friends with one of the committee board members, Ian Russell. He invited her to attend as a key speaker.' She sets aside her cutlery and reaches for her phone, unlocking it and typing something in. When she finds what she's searching for, she sets it on the table face up and slides it over to Isabel to see.

Isabel drags the phone closer and peers down at it.

It's a website detailing an event that has already taken place: GIRC.

GIRC?

Without asking, Isabel taps the phone screen to view the details.

The Gifted International Research Conference took place at London Excel this year, earlier on, in July. She skims over the conference agenda, detailing speakers, companies and organisations that attended.

Anabel's name pops up along with a professional photo of her in action, presenting to an audience, either in the middle of a lecture or speech.

'She attended?' Isabel asks.

'Yes. There's a video of her keynote speech as well but it's mostly highlights. She talked about new areas of research and progress around the known effects of Gift utilisation on areas of the brain.'

Isabel pauses in scrolling through the content. 'That's what she was researching?'

'I think whatever she was working on went beyond that. But I know that was one of her key areas of focus. She told me so herself.'

Isabel looks back down at Anabel's picture.

She locks the screen and gives it back to Joana and goes back to her plate.

'This Ian Russell. Is he based here in London?'

'I think so. Don't know if he is based here in the city though, but I know he lives in the UK.'

Isabel nods.

They're both silent for a moment. Isabel makes quick work of her food, even as her brain continues to tick away. Though she's still cautious of this woman who has come out of nowhere to provide information their team happens to need, it's a welcome distraction. Isabel would rather be solving any problems but her own right now.

When she's done, Isabel moves her plate aside. She feels steadier.

Joana is watching her, curiosity in her eyes.

'What did she ask you to do?' Isabel asks.

Joana glances away then. She shifts in her seat. 'She sent me . . . some videos.'

'Of what?' Isabel asks.

The muscles in Joana's neck become more pronounced. As if her entire body were clenching. 'She was being sexually harassed.'

Isabel has a feeling she knows the answer, but she asks anyway. 'By whom?'

'I think maybe it's better if I show you.'

# 23

Isabel makes it to the MCIU's headquarters by 11.35 a.m.

She'd called Voronov as soon as she'd finished with Joana Weir and asked him to hold Rampaul and Adam there until she arrived because she had new information for the team.

Voronov is leaning against the wall outside their case room when she gets there, concern evident in his face and the once-over he gives her as she nears.

'Thanks,' she says, stopping in front of him and adjusting her bag strap on her shoulder, 'are Rampaul and Adam still here too?'

'Yes. What happened?'

Isabel sighs and nods at the door. 'I'll tell you inside.'

Isabel runs them through the unexpected meeting, slurping down hastily made, weak coffee from the kitchenette on their floor.

The activity at MCIU's quarters is in full flow but she blocks it all out, grateful when her walls hold even as she feels multiple minds weighing on it.

'She's been keeping her eyes on us which I still don't like,' she says as she types her password into her laptop. 'Apparently she's been tracking me and Voronov almost from the second we got to London.'

Rampaul is hitched up on the edge of one of the tables. 'Why you?'

Isabel's email opens up on the screen and she sees two emails from Joana Weir waiting. 'For the same reason you thought Voronov and I were sent here. We're notorious apparently.' She clicks on the email. 'I've got the details of where she's staying and her number and she's coming in tomorrow morning at nine for us to take her statement. We should make sure she stays put in the city.'

'Good. What has she sent us?'

'Videos, I think . . .' and they get up to huddle around her.

One email contains a link to a hosting website and the other contains the password to access it.

Clicking the link launches the browser and it takes them immediately to the website to which Joana Weir has uploaded the videos. Isabel types in the password and is given the option to download a zipped folder.

The folder holds two MP4 video files.

'I think it's these.'

The files are labelled AP Embassy 1 08.09.202X and AP Embassy 2 08.15.202X.

Isabel selects one of the files.

The video opens up into a still frame of a familiar room.

The annexe at the embassy.

A section of the frame is blocked off. The part that is visible is focused on a door.

Isabel clicks play.

A slight figure walks up to the door; she's in simple clothes, jeans, and an oversized jumper. The colours are muted because the room is in the dark and though there's a light illuminating her from somewhere, they can't see where. It's definitely not the main room light. Her hair is pinned up with a big clip.

She leans close to the door, hands pressed against its panels.

'*Yes?*'

A muffled response is heard but Isabel can't make out the words.

Dr Pereira doesn't move right away, just presses her forehead against the door and stays that way for a moment.

'*I'd rather we spoke in the morning.*'

Another response from the other party which they can't hear.

They watch as Dr Pereira visibly gathers herself, squaring her shoulders and standing straight, head held high. She shifts enough that she can open the door but also enough that the door can't open entirely without her giving way.

'We've spoken about this before, Mr Francisco. I don't feel comfortable meeting one on one like this, particularly in my private room.'

'Given the time-sensitive nature of your situation, I thought it would be best to come and update you as soon as possible. We all want this situation to be resolved and for this we have to be a bit flexible, don't we? I think it would be best to talk inside.'

Isabel keeps watch but already she has a sense of what they might be about to witness. She hopes she's wrong. She really, really hopes she's wrong.

'Correct me if I'm wrong, but isn't that the ambassador?' Rampaul says. Her grim tone says she also has some ideas about what they're about to see.

'Seems like it,' Isabel says.

The person on the other side of the door finally enters the room. Because of Dr Pereira's blatant reluctance, it's more like he squeezes himself in through the gap she had allowed in order to speak to him face to face.

He walks further into the room without hesitating, adjusting his suit jacket as he goes. Dr Pereira doesn't budge from her spot by the door, instead opening the door wider and standing in full view of it, crossing her arms over her chest, her back to the hallway as she keeps her eyes on Francisco. He walks around to the other side of her, using the door to shield him from any eyes that may come upon the scene. He stops there.

'Things aren't going very well in negotiations for you, Anabel.'

He lifts a hand. Dr Pereira flinches as he runs the back of his fingers down the side of her arm, her expression going stiff and her entire body straining as far away from him as possible without physically moving.

The recording lasts for five minutes and those are the last words spoken before the door is slammed shut.

Isabel watches it all play out, her chest growing hollow, forcing herself to keep her eyes on the screen and watch the assault take place.

It's something they should be hardened to.

Francisco has Dr Pereira trapped against the door. Her face is turned away and he's saying something again, too low for them to pick up.

Isabel feels her stomach turn.

When he finally stops, the harsh sound of his breaths filters through the speakers of Isabel's laptop. Dr Pereira shoves him away and yanks the door back open. 'Leave.' The word breaks in the middle, but Dr Pereira stands, resolute, hand tight around the doorknob, and she stares straight ahead.

Francisco adjusts himself, the motion crude. They can't see his face from this angle but they can tell he's watching Dr Pereira the entire time.

Then he tells her they'll talk in the morning and bids her goodnight.

He walks out and seconds tick away, with Dr Pereira still fixed to the same spot.

Then slowly, slowly, moving as if her body is waking up from a long coma, she closes the door. The click of it locking into place is gentle.

She lifts her head.

Isabel freezes.

Her eyes are focused right on them, boring into them through the screen.

She walks back across the room, her pale face getting closer and closer to the camera. There's an unnatural blankness to it. The sound goes haywire as the image on the screen moves fast, giving them a flash of ceiling. Then it goes black and the video ends.

Isabel swallows and pushes the laptop back, as if the distance will help soften the horror in the pit of her stomach. It's not enough though, so she gets up and paces away, taking in a deep breath as she does so.

She's grateful that Dr Pereira's thoughts at that moment are locked within that screen. If Isabel had had to hear them too . . . She drags her fingers through her hair, raking her nails over her scalp, trying to anchor herself in this room, and locks her hands behind her neck.

'I guess his death isn't exactly a loss,' Isabel says.

Rampaul rests her hand on her hips and blows out a breath. Her skin is a shade paler than usual.

Adam is staring at the floor, his fists clenched tight, and his eyebrows pinched together.

'I think we have a motive,' Rampaul says quietly.

Isabel thinks for a moment, and then says, 'I think we need to check the cameras for this building.'

Rampaul jerks her head up. 'Why would we need to do that?'

'Because we think she may have been close by yesterday. We think she may have been here. And I think she was watching Cross,' Isabel says.

Rampaul frowns. 'Why would you say that?'

'There was a disturbance in the building,' Voronov says, 'Isabel felt it and so did I. We weren't the only ones. It was brief and didn't stand out very much, so it was probably dismissed by most people in the building at the time.'

'And?' Rampaul asks.

'And I don't think it was a freak coincidence.' She blows out a breath. 'I think a telekinetic did it.'

Rampaul takes a deep breath. 'All right, well. At least now we have another place to start. But before that, we have an update too.' She gestures at Adam to speak.

Adam clears his throat. He looks uncomfortable. 'Dr Marlow sent us an update on the blood works for the deceased.' He wets his lips before continuing. 'All of them came back clean.'

Isabel takes a steadying breath. She shares a glance with Voronov.

'Given the nature of their deaths,' Adam continues, 'the lack of physical evidence and a high-level telekinetic Gifted's presence on the premises at the time of deaths, he believes the deaths were likely caused by an individual using their Gift.'

Rampaul crosses her arms, expression grave. 'We're officially classifying this as a Gifted crime.'

# 24

Ian Russell lives in an impressive period penthouse in a Victorian mansion block on Putney Embankment. The interior is painted white and flooded with light in all directions. Isabel can't help but think about what it costs to live in a place like this.

He sits at a large white dinner table that comfortably seats six people. His laptop is open in front of him and there are some earmarked books in a pile, along with a sheaf of papers with highlighted text. He doesn't bother to hide his annoyance at their intrusion and his wife, who he'd introduced as Tracy, stands at the kitchen counter, arms and ankles crossed, as the kettle boils despite Rampaul, Isabel and Voronov declining any refreshments.

Despite the obvious tension at their presence, he's more comfortable than most people would be if they were paid an unexpected visit by the police.

'Can we keep this short? We've got a lunch later and,' he waves at the stuff in front of him, 'as you can see, I've got quite a bit of work to get done.'

Ian Russell's light-brown hair is still wet from a recent shower. He nudges his round, gold-rimmed glasses up his nose as he stares up at them from his seat. He's wearing a long-sleeved casual dark-blue shirt, and a pair of slacks, slippers on his feet. He has pale-blue eyes that lend an odd detachment to his expression. His wife, a petite, dark-skinned black woman, is still in her robe, a soft pink satin one that covers her down to her ankles and matches the head wrap binding her hair. She's a beautiful woman but her face is devoid of any warmth.

The look Rampaul levels at him makes it obvious what she thinks of his lunch, but she makes no comment about it. 'We understand your time is precious, Mr Russell, we just wanted to check in with you about a couple of things and thought popping over might be more convenient than inviting you down to the station.'

The general feeling Isabel gets from him matches his tone, one of impatience and something else between arrogance and determination.

'Mr Russell, we're here in regard to your friend, Dr Anabel Pereira.'

Isabel picks up a spike. Not from him though. But from his wife.

At the mention of Anabel's name, she straightens away from the counter, busying herself with opening the cupboard as the kettle continues to boil. Isabel feels the sudden surge of emotion in her, like she's trying to tamp it down as much as possible but not quite succeeding.

From the corner of her eye, she notices Voronov clocking her shift in attention and he turns slightly to keep the wife in sight as well.

Russell pushes his hair further back from his face. 'Anabel?' He frowns. 'Why are you here asking about Anabel of all people?'

'We recently spoke to her ex-fiancée. Anabel has got herself into a tricky situation and Miss Weir is concerned. You organised a conference here, July was it? You invited her to attend as a key speaker.'

'Of course, she's one of the leading minds in Gifted research in the States.'

'So we hear,' Rampaul says, 'and here's our problem, Mr Russell. Your friend never returned home and now she's missing. We need to speak with her as a matter of urgency. Miss Weir made it very clear that you and Anabel are close friends, so we need to know if Anabel has been in touch with you. Maybe to ask for help or money.'

'Why would Anabel be missing? And there's no way she stayed behind after the conference. I would have known about it.'

'Miss Weir knew about it.'

He scoffs. 'Miss Weir needs to move on. Maybe Annie hasn't gone missing, maybe she's just trying to give her the slip.'

The affectionate nickname doesn't escape anyone's notice.

'Why would she need to give her the slip? According to Miss Weir, although their engagement ended, the two remained close.' Rampaul taps her fingers on the table as she considers him. 'I'm getting the sense you don't agree.'

'I have nothing against her,' he says.

Rampaul hums. 'Really?'

'It's nothing personal,' he says, 'I just didn't like how she was with Annie. You know how it is in relationships between Gifted and Regulars, there's always an imbalance of some kind. It's why most mixed relationships never work.'

Isabel blinks at him, incredulous. Is this man on something?

She darts a look at his wife. She has her eyes firmly fixed on the floor. Her hands are clenched tightly around her mug.

Voronov is watching him with narrowed eyes.

Isabel can understand why his wife is getting stiffer and stiffer in her corner. The dark tendrils of jealousy rising off Ian Russell are enough that Isabel thinks if she reached out to touch them, she'd feel them billow against the palm of her hand.

'There are always underlying issues,' he says, turning to check something on his laptop screen and running his eyes over one of the highlighted pages of text. He picks one up and shifts it to the side as if making note of it for later before continuing. 'There are always things neither wants to say. And most Regulars in those types of relationships seem to have an obsession, almost like they fetishise their partner. Leaves a bad taste in my mouth.'

'That's quite an opinion, Mr Russell,' Rampaul says.

When he smiles, it twists the corners of his mouth, until it becomes more of a sneer. 'I've done quite a few studies and written extensively about it.'

Isabel resists the urge to roll her eyes. It bothers her though, that there is a part of her that can't help but hear what he's saying and reflect back on her past relationships.

'And you're saying this is what took place in Miss Weir's relationship with your friend?'

'I think there was an element of that, yes.'

Obsession is a scary thing. Despite Isabel feeling very firmly that this man is an arsehole, they can't afford to dismiss this new information. Although Isabel would say, having spoken to Joana Weir, and standing here now with this man, she's not so sure she'd pin Joana as the obsessive one out of the two.

It makes her wonder why his wife, just a few feet away, hasn't left this man yet, when he's got such a vested interest in another woman. Some friendships really are that close though and maybe that's all this is. A particularly tight friendship where boundaries are a little blurry.

'Are you both Gifted?' Isabel asks, motioning between Ian and his wife.

He visibly reacts to that, pulling his attention away from the things he'd been fiddling with on the table and sitting straight, and gives them that smile again. 'Yes. Actually, we were both members of the Gifted Scientists Society at university, that's how we met. Both mid-level telekinetics, quite a rare thing among Gifted couples to be so well matched.' He clearly takes a lot of pride in that. 'We found out last week that we're expecting.'

Isabel wonders if he knows how he sounds. 'Congratulations to you both,' she says, even though Tracy is still avoiding any involvement in the conversation and goes on staring at that one spot on the floor as she sips from her coffee.

'It's quite something,' he says, leaning back in his chair, 'unfortunately pregnancy rates where both parents are Gifted are quite low, so this is an exciting time.'

Right.

When Isabel glances at Voronov to gauge what he's thinking she doesn't know what to make of the closed off expression he's wearing.

Rampaul sighs and looks at Isabel. Isabel gives her a slight shake of the head. She doesn't think there's anything else to get here, other than two people caught in what feels like an unhappy marriage.

For all that he's preached about the problems of mixed couples, the man seems blind to the problems in his own relationship.

Interesting, Isabel thinks, that he's spent so much time talking about himself, his thoughts, and his beliefs, even going so far as to tell them all what he thinks of his 'close' friend's relationship with her ex-fiancée, but despite their reason for being here, showing almost no concern for the safety of his said friend who they've told him is missing.

Tracy's reaction too. The heavy quietness, the disengagement, even when her pregnancy is spoken about – irritation or anger, maybe joy, maybe even resentment at having the information offered freely like she's not the one carrying a child or being asked for permission to disclose beforehand – there's nothing. Everything is being contained and Isabel gets the impression that she's close to bursting.

Rampaul pulls the conversation back on track. 'Well, we know you've got some work to be getting back to and that lunch later, of course, so we'll get out of your hair. But Mr Russell,' her tone makes it clear he'd better not be messing her around, 'this is a serious situation your friend is in. If Anabel Pereira reaches out to you in any way, shape, or form, I expect you to contact me ASAP. Am I clear?'

He nods slowly. 'Yes. Of course.'

Rampaul takes a card holder from the inside of her jacket and plucks one out which she lays on the table. 'My contact number. We'll be on our way.' She flicks a glance at Tracy. 'Have a good day, Mrs Russell. Thank you both for your time.'

Isabel nods at them both and follows Rampaul out, Voronov at her side, and they turn into the entrance area, split from the rest of the place by a wall of distorted glass.

Rampaul opens the door and steps outside, Voronov right behind her. Isabel follows, pulling the door behind her, about to close it.

Behind them, vicious antagonism explodes into the air, followed by hissed-out words Isabel can't quite make out but which she knows are coming from Tracy. That resentment that Isabel had sensed under the surface is bubbling over now.

' – how could you?'

'Calm down—'

Low, still said very low. But this is a place with high ceilings, all open plan and even whispers will carry, especially when spoken with such vim.

Rampaul and Voronov stop when they realise Isabel isn't following.

*What rules?* Rampaul had said.

Isabel meets Voronov's questioning look and turns back into the flat, walking quickly back into the open space of the kitchen and sitting room.

Tracy is stooped over her husband, finger in his face, her pretty face twisted in anger which quickly morphs into surprise when her gaze shifts up and meets Isabel's. She straightens away slowly, hand falling to her side, but can't get all the signs of her anger back under control, her chest still heaving with it.

She paces away from Russell, shoving her hands into the pockets of her dressing gown as she does so.

Seeing Isabel walking slowly towards him, his face turns pallid and the earlier arrogance that had been firmly in place when they had been speaking to him doesn't quite make it back in full force.

'Sorry,' Isabel says and knows she doesn't sound it at all. She stops shy of fully entering their living-area space again and tucks her hands into the pockets of her jackets.

Back home, this wouldn't have been an ace in the hole. Back home, Isabel would have had to disclose to these people right away what she was, taking out her ID, showing them her classification and level. Her Gift, although permissible in the field, couldn't be used without following the policies set out by the Polícia Judiciária.

Here, Rampaul has said, there are no rules.

Isabel addresses Tracy. 'You haven't said a word. Barely anything. You've been standing there in your corner, contained, feelings completely strapped in. But it felt more like someone who didn't want to blow up, than someone who is naturally reserved.'

'I'm sorry? I don't get your meaning.' It's the first time Tracy has spoken to them directly aside from when she'd greeted them after their arrival.

Isabel nods. 'Like you and your husband, I'm Gifted.'

Tracy stills.

Ian snorts but unlike earlier, his confidence is forced. 'Gifted officers in the Met? I thought that was a rare thing.' He darts a glance at Rampaul and Voronov who have followed Isabel back in.

'We're here to assist DI Rampaul and her team in this matter.' Isabel waves it away. 'And I can assure you I'm Gifted. My affinity is telepathy.'

Tracy pulls in a steadying breath, like she's trying to contain herself again, but it's not working as well as it had earlier. Through the thin material of her dressing gown, Isabel can see that her hands are fisted.

'So I want you both to think very carefully about what you say to us next. Up until now, I haven't made a concerted effort to listen in.' Isabel taps her temple to indicate their thoughts. 'I have found that people here in the UK are naturally very loud thinkers and the headaches haven't been fun, so I've been doing my best to block them out actually.' She looks from one to the other. 'You understand what I'm saying? Also, your whispering match was louder than you thought.' Isabel gestures at the spacious apartment. 'Echoes. Perhaps next time it might be best for you to wait until after the door is closed.'

Ian Russell's nose is scrunched up, forcing his glasses to dig into the folding skin over the bridge of his nose.

'Anabel has been in touch with you, hasn't she, Mr Russell? Your wife is upset with you because for some reason you've chosen not to share that with us.' Though in Isabel's opinion she thinks his wife is probably more upset about him sounding like he's in love with her and not in a platonic sense either.

'She hasn't,' he snaps.

'Really?' Isabel walks closer until she's standing over him just as his wife had been. 'Let me tell you what I think, Mr Russell. I think it's odd that we arrive at your door and tell you your friend is missing but you don't seem very concerned. You asked maybe one question in that entire conversation in relation to her being missing. But you know what else? I got nothing from you. Not the faintest hint of concern for someone who you've made clear is quite important to you. That's not a normal reaction, is it?'

'Just because I didn't verbally express—'

Did he not hear a word Isabel said? 'Neither verbally, nor in any other way, Mr Russell. There wasn't one ripple of concern in the emotions you were feeling as DI Rampaul was speaking with you. But if it makes you feel better, I can see for myself and confirm, right here, right now.'

He scoffs. The man actually scoffs. 'Please. You're wrong. And even if you weren't, that's not something you can just do, even if you are a telepathic Gifted. It's hard enough just for telepaths to correctly perceive and interpret emotions even at mid-levels, and you'd require touching for anything beyond that.'

Isabel rests a hand on the table and leans in close, staring straight into his face. She doesn't say a word.

Slowly, the smirk on his face dies out.

'Are you sure about that?' she asks quietly.

His nostrils flare as he forces himself to breathe slowly, easing ever so slightly away from her.

'Is there something you want to tell us, Mr Russell?' she asks.

'Upstairs.'

Ian Russell whips his head round to stare at his wife. 'Tracy!'

Tracy has moved closer, and she's got her arms wrapped around her middle. A stubborn jut to her chin. She doesn't acknowledge her husband. 'Second door on the left.'

Isabel backs away, glancing up at the ceiling reflexively, disconcerted.

She hadn't sensed anyone else in the house.

Voronov is already heading for the stairs, Rampaul close behind.

Ian Russell is glaring at his wife, but Tracy is pacing back to the kitchen. Her hands are shaking.

Like Isabel, she knows she's done something that she won't be forgiven for.

Turning on her heel, Isabel heads for the bottom of the stairs too and hears Rampaul call out.

'Dr Pereira? This is DI Rampaul with the Major Crime Investigative Support Unit. Please come out.'

Isabel can see Voronov's back. He's standing at the top of the stairs. It's only a short flight and the ceiling there isn't anywhere as high as that of the floor below. The roof of the building slopes downward in the opposite direction but it can still comfortably accommodate Voronov's height.

'Dr Pereira,' Isabel hears Rampaul call out again, 'I'm coming in.'

Voronov disappears as he heads towards Rampaul and Isabel starts up the stairs.

'Shit, *shit*! She's going down the fire escape!'

Shit.

# 25

'Damn it!' Isabel snaps round to look at the couple staring wide-eyed at her, their previous ire and resentment disappearing into incredulity as the situation actually seems to sink in. 'Where does the fire escape lead out to? *Where?*'

Unsurprisingly, it's Tracy who answers. 'It leads down to Glendarvon Street. She'll only be able to get on to Putney Embankment, the back end of Glendarvon is blocked off for road construction.'

The door slams into the wall behind Isabel as she darts out of the front door and heads straight for the stairs, the sound of Ian's yelling echoing out into the hallway as she goes.

The building doesn't have a lift and she rushes down the three flights of stairs to street level, nearly twisting her ankle on the last one when her right foot hits the ground and her foot turns on its side.

Isabel has her phone in her hand as she bursts out into the open, sun in her face, trying to get her bearings.

Voronov picks up on the first ring.

Isabel goes out into the street, looking left and right. 'Tracy said the fire escape leads down to a Glendarvon Street, it opens out into the main road along the river that we arrived by. The back of that street is closed off.'

'We're pursuing,' Voronov says, 'but we've lost sight of her. Oversized dark-blue hoodie and black bottoms. White trainers.'

Isabel starts walking, forcing her breathing into calm as she goes.

It's not very busy, the street tranquil with some people pausing at the side to watch the rowers as they row their crew boat along the river. Mostly people walking in twos or by themselves, with most of the traffic going in the direction of the bridge.

Isabel heads in that direction too. 'Heading in the direction of the bridge,' she says.

'Got it. One of us will follow along to the other end.'

'Okay. Call me if—'

She's tall, is the first thing Isabel notices.

As Voronov described, she has on a dark-blue hoodie; the hood is up over her head, and she has her hands tucked into its kangaroo pockets. Dark bottoms, white trainers. She blends in just fine. She could have been a local resident warming up for a routine run or cooling down after one.

'I see her,' Isabel says and crosses the street. She keeps her voice down. 'She's walking in the direction of the bridge.' Isabel falls in line, behind her. 'In pursuit.'

'We're coming.'

She follows her, steadily closing the gap.

Anabel isn't looking around. Just keeps heading in the same direction.

They pass a lively pub on their right, and Isabel can see where the path narrows, some of the path closed off by workers, forcing pedestrians into a bit of road that has been marked temporarily split off so that they can continue down the road.

Isabel speeds up further. She's careful to stay behind Anabel, not wanting Anabel to catch sight of her.

Up ahead where the works end, Isabel sees the split in the road. The left fork leads on to the bridge.

The sun is beating down on them. Isabel can feel the sweat gathering under her arms and in the dip of her lower back. She overtakes two people.

They're going to hit the bridge soon.

Isabel keeps her breathing steady; it feels like it's louder than she knows it is. Can hear it, as if it's whooshing right into her ear drums.

She's almost within arm's-reach range.

Anabel breaks into a run.

'Fuck.' Isabel darts forward. Her fingers skim the back of the hoodie. They hook briefly into the fabric, yanking the material off Anabel's head, but it slips off her fingers.

They're fully on the bridge now. Anabel is running faster than Isabel would have expected a woman of her build to.

Anabel shoulder-checks a huge man in a leather jacket she can't dodge in time and the man bursts into expletives, yelling across the length of the bridge at them as Isabel runs straight past him.

'Stop!' Isabel yells out. 'Anabel! Stop! We can *help* you!'

Isabel stops talking, can't afford to lose her breath.

People on the bridge are stopping to watch, murmurs going up all over. Out of the corner of her eye Isabel sees phone cameras coming up to record what's happening.

Anabel veers into the road.

Cars screech to a halt and a chorus of air-blasting horns sounds, one joining after the other as the domino effect ripples back down the bridge.

Isabel follows. Her heart jumps into her throat as a car stops way too close to her for comfort. She can't afford to spare the driver any attention. Her feet pound the ground and get her close again. She keeps her breathing under control and doesn't slow.

She's a runner and that's helping her, but she won't be able to keep up a sprinting pace for long.

But as long as she doesn't lose her, Isabel thinks maybe Anabel will tire before she does. She spares a thought for where Voronov and Rampaul are right now. They're probably too far back, still on the other side of the road. They've got no one to cut her off on this side.

Anabel's plaited hair whips from side to side as she pushes herself harder.

Isabel dodges around pedestrians freezing on the spot, clenching their limbs tight to themselves as she runs past.

Anabel slips into an opening on the right, quickly disappearing down.

Steps, fuck. Fuck.

Isabel follows, her momentum almost slamming her into the concrete wall encasing the small staircase leading down from the bridge. She can hear Anabel's steps but has lost visual.

When she comes out, she's behind a big, tall white building and clocks Anabel approaching the end of the road.

Isabel pumps harder.

Seconds later, Anabel veers left.

Isabel's going to lose her. She's going to lose her.

Isabel reaches the end of the building and turns left, her chest aching, muscles of her thighs burning, and slides to a stop.

Three different roads leading off that one turning point.

Her eyes jump from one to the other, to the other, chest heaving, top sticking to her front and back.

She can feel her phone buzzing in her back pocket now that she's stopped.

Isabel groans and drops down to her haunches, head hanging low, trying to catch her breath. She reaches back to pull out her phone and sees Voronov's name on the screen.

'Isabel. Where are you?'

Isabel huffs out a breath and rubs at her forehead. 'Other side of the bridge.'

She hears Voronov relaying the information to Rampaul. 'Do you have her?'

Isabel sighs, then she stands. Bystanders outside nearby shops and cafés are staring at her.

Isabel turns her back on them.

'I lost her.'

# 26

Voronov catches up with her when Isabel reaches Putney Embankment again.

'Are you all right?' he asks, falling into step with her.

'Yes. Just out of breath.' Anabel had given Isabel a run for her money. Literally.

By the time they make it back to the mansion block, Rampaul is herding both Ian Russell and his wife into the car.

A few of the residents lean over their balconies, one of them with a glass of white wine in hand as if this is the best entertainment she's seen all day. None of them seem to even consider pretending not to be watching this.

Isabel thought Portugal was bad.

She's surprised though, as Ian Russell gets into the car without much fuss.

Stopping by the car, she rests her hands on her hips. 'Sorry. I lost her behind the hotel. Managed to speak to a few people who saw the direction she went in. Too late for me to catch up but they said she headed for Putney Bridge station.'

Rampaul pats Isabel on the shoulder. 'We'll get Adam on the phone to TfL.'

Poor Adam, those people must be sick of him. He's been on the phone to them at least once a day, chasing progress on other routes that pass close to the embassy. The stations were easier than individual bus cameras. There were too many routes.

'All right. Are we taking them back to the station?' Isabel asks.

Rampaul nods, peering in at both wife and husband who are sitting inside completely silent now. Isabel is sure they're able to hear everything they're saying though.

'Yes. Mr Russell has some explaining to do and I want to hear what the wife has to say as well.' She gives Isabel an impressed look. 'Good job, Reis. Feel free to use your – let's call them listening skills? – more often.' She pats the car's roof, motioning for them to get in, and rounds the car to the driver's side.

'I'll sit with them,' Voronov says, already reaching for the door.

Isabel snorts and shoves him out of the way. 'Have you seen your size? You barely fit inside this tiny thing as it is. Go in the front.' She opens the door and finds herself face to face with Tracy Russell. She motions for her to scoot closer to her husband.

A touch to her wrist stops her before she can get in.

Voronov is looking between her and Tracy Russell. 'Are you sure it won't be too much?'

Of course, he'd notice. She pats his hand. 'I'll be fine,' she says, smiling, 'promise.'

It helps that when Isabel gets in, Tracy Russell shifts as far away from her as possible and plasters herself completely up against her husband.

When they arrive at the station Adam is waiting for them downstairs in the car park.

'I want them in separate rooms,' Rampaul says, shutting her door. Isabel and Voronov exit together and go around to the front. Adam is standing by one of the doors to the back, ready to let them out.

Isabel's gaze drifts over to Tracy. She's sitting calm as anything in the back of the car.

Neither of them is under arrest, so they could have made a fuss if they wanted to but that would have drawn more attention. Probably that was why both of them had got in the car without issue.

And, if Ian Russell's distasteful boasting was anything to go by, then they were going to have to be careful with Tracy if she's expecting.

Isabel doubts having a fugitive hiding out in her home is conducive to a stress-free pregnancy.

The more she thinks about it, the more she dislikes the man.

'Rampaul,' Isabel says, 'let us talk to her.'

Rampaul glances at Tracy as she steps out of the car after her husband. 'Is there a specific reason why?'

'I think she might talk to me.'

Rampaul thinks about it, watching the couple as they follow Adam into the building. 'All right. I want it recorded.'

Isabel nods. 'No problem.'

When Isabel and Voronov enter the room, Tracy is standing at the window, facing outwards. She doesn't turn around when they walk inside.

Voronov shuts the door quietly behind them and Isabel walks over to her. She gives her plenty of space, choosing to lean back against the wall instead.

'How are you feeling, Tracy? We've brought you some water, but we can get you something else, if you'd like. Tea or coffee?' Isabel is talking to the side of her face because she's doing exactly what she did back in her home, not making contact, body pulled in tight.

Isabel feels her out, mindful that she doesn't want to push her over the edge when she knows this is someone at the start of their pregnancy.

She's less contained now. Nerves pricking out of her shell, leaving little holes behind for Isabel to spot the deep soot of resentment and raw anger.

Voronov pulls a chair back from the table in the room, its legs briefly dragging along the floor before he sits. He sets down a legal pad and a pen handed to them by Adam before he'd gone with Rampaul to speak to Ian Russell.

Frankly, Isabel is happy not to have to listen to that man again.

Something about the way he'd spoken about Gifted and Regulars had left her feeling deeply uncomfortable. It doesn't help that, in general, he seems like a particular brand of arsehole.

There's a camera in the corner of the room recording everything so they don't have to.

'Tracy?'

Finally, she turns. 'What? Have I not already given you what you wanted?' That same anger that Isabel can see pooling around her feet like dust is evident in her voice now as well.

Isabel lets the harshness of her words fade before replying, calm. 'Not until you were pushed for it, no.' Isabel slides her hands into her pockets. 'If I hadn't caught the shift in you and your husband, then you would have let us walk out of there and allowed him to continue harbouring Dr Pereira. Something tells me you wouldn't have rushed to the phone afterwards to correct that mistake.'

Tracy tucks back a few of her twists. Her guard is all the way up.

Voronov leans forward and nudges the water in her direction. 'Why not take a seat?' he asks.

She seems to debate it for another moment. Then she makes her way to the other side of the table, pulls out the other chair and reaches for the water.

Isabel stays where she is. Maybe the distance will make her feel less ganged up on. Voronov is good at things like this, giving people the illusion of space. Even now, though he's seated near her, he's sitting back, hands relaxed on his lap, expression open.

Although most people don't want it to, his manner always disarms them to a certain extent.

Isabel should know. She knows he uses that same tact with her regularly, which is endlessly irritating.

'If you're hoping that I'll sit here and make excuses and tell you that he wasn't like this when I married him, you're wasting your time.'

Isabel tilts her head. Interesting take and not where she saw this going. 'Is that what people normally ask you?'

Tracy takes another sip of water before setting the glass down. She flattens her hands on the desk. 'My own family stopped speaking to me after I refused to break it off. He's always been like this, and I knew about it when I met him.'

'Like what?'

'Unimpressed by Regular people. Wanting better for our community. He's dedicated his entire life's work to it, and I support that.'

Right. 'So, you agree with everything he was saying earlier?' Isabel asks.

'I believe there are too many differences between Gifted and Regular people for relationships of that nature to ever truly succeed, yes.'

'Hmm. And you think that's why Anabel and Joana Weir didn't last?' Isabel asks. 'Do you also think that Miss Weir was unhealthily obsessed with Anabel?'

She doesn't reply so fast then. Her mouth snaps shut. 'I'm not as close to Anabel as my husband is.'

Isabel nods. 'Yes. I did get that impression. And yet you allowed him to harbour her in your home knowing she is a fugitive. I'm surprised you let that happen.'

No response.

'Or maybe you didn't. Maybe your husband went ahead and did it without even checking with you.'

Still nothing.

'But I suppose whether he checked with you or not isn't the question. The fact is she was there. How long has she been at your house?'

'Since Tuesday night,' she says.

'When did she get there? Morning? Afternoon? Evening?'

'She was already there when I got home.'

'When did you get home?'

She huffs out an impatient breath and rolls her eyes. 'I don't know. My meeting ran late that day, I left the office around six thirty in the evening, so maybe I got there at seven fifteen, seven thirty. I'm not sure.'

'And she was there when you arrived?'

'Yes.'

'What? Your husband didn't take you aside before you walked in? Explain that she was there? Or maybe contact you during your day, maybe let you know you'd need to talk about something? Because maybe this is just me,' Isabel says, 'but installing someone in your home who your wife knows you have questionable feelings about would warrant a conversation. Especially when that person is also running from the law.'

If looks could kill, Isabel thinks she'd be in a coffin right now being lowered into the ground.

'They're friends.'

'Of course. Your husband gave the impression of someone who's impressed by higher-level Gifted,' Isabel points out. 'Anabel is a higher-level telekinetic, isn't she? Higher than you.'

Tracy twists in her chair to face Isabel, resting her arm along the back of the chair. 'Yes. Okay? I'm not blind. I know that his interest in her goes beyond friendship. But that's all it is. *Interest.* He's never crossed a line and I trust him. As long as he remains faithful to me, then who his friends are and how he feels about them are none of my business. Yes, Anabel is a higher-level Gifted than I am. Yes, he's fascinated by that part of her. It is what it is. What do you want me to say?'

Well. At least she's not burying her head in the sand.

'What has she been doing while she's been staying in your home? Did she or your husband talk about how long she intended to stay?'

'Ian said it was temporary. That she was resolving a situation. He didn't think she'd be staying for longer than two weeks.'

'Why? What exactly was going to be resolved in two weeks?'

The crack of Tracy's hand on the table is loud. 'I. Don't. Know.' She's visibly worked up, her breathing elevated, her mouth sealed as she drags in air through her nose, chest lifting with it each time. She curls the hand she'd used to slap the table into a fist.

Isabel flicks a look at Voronov.

'Tracy. Are you aware of what drove Anabel to ask your husband for help?' he asks.

Tracy glances over her shoulder and, for the first time, uncertainty touches her expression. It's only there for a second before it's immediately smoothed over. She's quick in regaining control of her emotions. At least outwardly. Isabel still feels it. Just under the surface where it continues to bloom, spreading along her body.

'I said I don't know,' Tracy says.

'On Tuesday, the day Anabel shows up at your home, twelve people were discovered dead at the Portuguese Embassy in Golden Square, Soho. Anabel was the only surviving person who was on the premises that day and was identified as missing by the security team. We've been trying to locate her since then.'

Shock ripples through her, lending a vulnerability to her features that she's been taking pains to keep from seeing the light of day since they'd arrived on her doorstep. 'What? Are you saying she *did* this?'

'No,' Isabel cautions, 'but Anabel is the only person in a position to explain what happened that morning. We weren't lying to you and your husband when we said we were concerned for her. Joana Weir got in touch with me because she was worried. That Anabel happened to actually be in your home was unexpected.'

Tracy braces her hands on the sides of her chair, adjusts her seat, eyebrows heavy over her eyes as she works through this new piece of information.

Isabel rests her hands on the table and leans closer to her. 'We still have to find her. And you and your husband have already proven that you lied to DI Rampaul when being questioned. That alone is something you can get in trouble for. I believe you that *you* didn't know about what happened. Did you?'

Tracy shakes her head, no.

'Did you know she's currently a fugitive from the American authorities?'

She nods.

'Okay.' Isabel tries again. 'Tracy. Do you think your husband knows what Anabel is planning on doing next?'

Tracy studies her hands.

They're shaking.

'Yes.'

As the cab rolls to a stop in front of them, Tracy looks at Isabel.

Her defences are down.

'He's all I have, you know. My family . . . they don't – I made some decisions.'

The words surprise Isabel too. This woman has been wound so tight; Isabel hadn't expected her to give them anything more. Especially not anything of a personal nature like this, anything that would render her vulnerable. Tracy leaves a strong impression of someone who can't abide vulnerability, specifically her own.

Her words make Isabel think of her own family situation. 'You have tried reaching out to them?'

Tracy shakes her head. 'No point. I know how it will go.'

'Listen, I don't know your situation, but you won't know unless you actually get in touch and speak to them.' She glances at Tracy's hand pressed gently to her lower belly and adds, 'Especially at a time like this.'

Isabel walks over to the cab and opens the passenger door for her. 'I think whatever drew you to him – shared beliefs or ideals – think about what kind of parent that man will make, if he's risking the health of his pregnant wife for someone else and keeping secrets at this point in your life.'

Tracy doesn't respond to that.

She gets into the back seat of the car and relays her address to the waiting cab driver before reaching for the door.

'I hope you catch her,' she says.

She pulls the door shut and the cab drives away.

# 27

Adam tugs the door closed behind him and waves a hello to Isabel and Voronov.

'I think we're going to be here a while,' Adam says and glances round at the screen where they can see Rampaul sitting opposite Ian Russell. 'He's being stubborn. Says he was helping out a friend because he cares for her.'

Isabel shakes her head. 'Oh, he definitely cares for her,' she mutters. 'We've sent Mrs Russell home; we got a taxi to take her there.' Isabel would have preferred it if they'd had an officer do it, if for no other reason than to keep an eye on her and see what she did immediately after leaving the police station, but with their lack of resources for this case, which Isabel is trying her best not to dwell on, they didn't have that option. The taxi was the next best thing.

Isabel thinks back to the quiet woman they'd escorted out of the station.

'Mrs Russell is certainly not a fan of their relationship,' Isabel says, folding her arms, 'and they kept a lot from her. She didn't know about what took place at the embassy, but she seems certain her husband would have been aware. She also thinks that he knows what Anabel is planning.'

Adam lets out a low whistle. 'That's a big trust, isn't it?'

It is. It makes her wonder if at some point Anabel and Ian had some sort of intimate relationship after all.

Isabel glances at him. 'Have you already contacted TfL again?'

Adam winces. 'Yeah, I'll have to chase them on it first thing tomorrow. Still waiting on some of the surveillance footage for bus routes from around the embassy. I'll have the requests for

Wandsworth Borough Council surveillance near Putney Embankment put through today as well, hopefully before the end of the day.'

Isabel nods. 'While you guys finish off here, I can pitch in, you've been doing most of the heavy lifting with surveillance. Sorry about that.'

Adam goes a little red and waves it off. 'It's fine, boss.' He motions over his shoulder with a thumb. 'Better get back in there—'

There's a knock on the door that breaks up the conversation and the three of them turn to watch an officer come in, who Isabel recognises the officer who normally sits at the front desk on the MCIU's floor. She's usually there when they walk in first thing and is often still there late into the night.

'Sorry to intrude,' she says, and her voice is so small and high at the same time that Isabel is almost convinced it's put on. It sounds like a voice you'd hear in a children's cartoon. 'I have someone waiting on the line. It's in relation to the embassy case,' she says.

Adam steps around Isabel and Voronov. 'DI Rampaul is still interviewing Ian Russell, I can take it. Who is it? Is it a sighting?'

She shakes her head before nodding in Isabel's direction. 'They're asking for her, Adam. She said she wants to speak to Inspector Reis.'

Isabel blinks at her. What?

'She?' Isabel says. 'She who?' The only people who might phone her are the embassy staff members who she helped interview. Aside from that, for every other piece of the investigation including requests for information from the local businesses, everyone had been clearly directed to ask for Rampaul or Adam.

Isabel turns to Adam. 'It's your call. What do you want to do?'

'Uh.' He looks undecided. 'Let me check with the boss.'

Through the one-way screen, they see Rampaul pause in her interrogation at Adam's knock on the door. Irritation flashes across her face. Ian Russell barely registers it. She murmurs that she'll be a moment and he continues to stare ahead. Not even an acknowledgement. Rampaul comes out of the room. 'What are you doing?' she says, the words enunciated slowly and through gritted teeth. Definitely not happy about being interrupted.

Isabel is surprised when Adam stands his ground. She'd almost expected him to turn tail and run.

'There's a caller wanting to speak to Inspector Reis, it's about the incident at the embassy.'

The scowl drops off Rampaul's face and she eases back, the line of her shoulders relaxing as confusion settles in. 'With Reis? Is it one of the members of staff from the embassy?'

The officer who had brought in the message shakes her head, blond bob swishing around her thin chin. 'No ma'am. She won't disclose who she is. She's insisting on speaking with the inspector.'

Rampaul purses her mouth. Then she curses under her breath. 'Go,' she says to Isabel. 'Adam, you go with her. I'll finish up here.'

'Okay,' Isabel says and turns to follow the officer out, Adam and Voronov behind her.

The officer splits from them, telling them she'll transfer the call to Rampaul's desk phone.

It's already ringing from the internal transfer by the time they reach it.

Isabel goes around the partition and takes a deep breath, doing her best to seal out the whirl of voices around her. She's getting faster at phasing them out.

Taking the phone in hand, she sits down, gaze flicking up to Voronov and Adam, who are both hovering over her.

'This is Inspector Reis. Who am I speaking to?'

There's a pause and if it weren't for the background noise, Isabel would wonder if the call had dropped. But it's there. The low murmur of other voices filters through the line, along with distinct sounds, the rushing of a coffee machine, of orders being taken and multiple conversations layering one upon the other.

Voronov catches her eye. Adam stands beside him. Both of them waiting.

Before she can ask again, the person on the line finally speaks.

'Inspector Reis. My name is Anabel Pereira. We met yesterday.'

Isabel jerks her head up. Her eyes lock with Voronov's blue ones. Understanding that something is happening right now settles quickly over his face. She mouths 'Anabel Pereira.'

Adam's eyes go wide. He gestures quickly, winding his finger, motioning for her to carry on before he takes off back in the direction they had come from.

Isabel nods and focuses. 'I wouldn't call yesterday an introduction, Anabel. The police here have been searching for you for a little while now.'

'Yes, I know.'

'Why did you run?' Isabel asks.

'To protect myself. I don't have a deal in place with the Portuguese government yet and I'm outside of their sanctuary. As long as I'm outside embassy walls you'll arrest me. Put me on the next plane back to the US.'

Despite knowing enough about her background to expect it, the American accent catches Isabel off guard. There isn't a hint of any other accent. It's a pleasant voice, deep and poised. She doesn't sound as if she's in a panic or running scared, but some people are good at keeping their emotions contained. Maybe Dr Pereira is such a person.

True. 'Then why run away from the embassy?' Isabel asks. 'If you'd stayed in the building, even if they were granted access, the police here wouldn't have been able to remove you from the premises without violating diplomatic policy.'

She doesn't immediately answer.

'You think I don't know what it looked like, Inspector? What you guys would assume took place in there?' Her sigh travels through the line. 'They would have handed me over to the British police in a heartbeat.'

'We would have heard you out,' Isabel says. 'We still can. We only want to know what happened in there, Anabel. We've got families who are waiting for an explanation about why their loved ones are dead. It's the job of the police here to give them that.'

'And what about your job, Inspector? Why have you and your partner come such a long way from home?'

Isabel eases back in her seat. 'We're assisting for now.'

'Who asked you to do that?'

Voronov has rounded the desk and is standing next to Isabel now.

'Our boss. Who was asked by the Department of Foreign Affairs. So here we are.'

Anabel chuckles, the sound low and self-mocking. 'Right. Do they know what their officials get up to on foreign ground when they're supposed to be fulfilling their duties?'

Isabel takes a deep breath. 'We can talk about that too,' she says, 'if that's what you want.'

'It's not.'

'Okay. Then do you want to talk to me about why you called and asked for me?'

The sound of running steps has Isabel lifting her head to peek over the top of the partition. She sees Rampaul rushing down the length of the room, Adam at her heels. She stops short of knocking into the partition and grasps the top. She reaches across to tap Voronov on the shoulder and motions him closer. She asks him something in a hushed voice, eyes on Isabel.

'Joana told me about you.'

'You've spoken to Joana Weir? When?'

'She messaged me after her conversation with you. Said you were someone who might understand. Told me how to contact you. I did as she asked. I looked you up too.'

'And you decided she was right?'

'I don't know yet. I'm trying to figure that out.'

'So come in and talk to me.'

'I'll talk to you. If you do something for me first.'

Isabel narrows her eyes. 'I have no jurisdiction here beyond what the police here allow me.'

'It's nothing to do with the police. You won't need their permission for this.'

'I want to hear what it is that you want first.'

'I want you to find out whoever it was that Emanuel Francisco was speaking to about my proposal and citizenship and I want an update as soon as possible.'

'I think—'

'I'm not finished.'

Isabel waits.

'Eliana Cross. She's been in to see you.'

Isabel drags over a stack of Post-its and grabs a pencil, quickly scrawls on it: *She knows JW & EC spoke to us.*

She peels it off and then hands it up to Rampaul and Voronov. Adam leans in close to read it too.

'She has.'

'Was she alone?'

'Why?'

'I need you to tell me if she came alone or not.'

'That might be trickier. I don't know what your intentions are, you're refusing to speak to me, remember? Until we can understand what happened at the embassy, I can't tell you that.'

'Fine. But my first request?'

'I'll see what I can do,' Isabel says.

'Fine. I'll be in touch again soon. Speak to you soon, Inspector.' She hangs up.

Around her, its silent.

Isabel stares down at the mouthpiece in her hand. Then quietly, she replaces it on the receiver.

# 28

In the end, they don't get anything else out of Ian Russell. They send him off home with two officers on his tail to make sure he stays put and that if Anabel returns, they're there to step in. When Voronov asks Rampaul if her chief is okay with that, she waves it off, telling them to let her handle it.

As for Dr Pereira's call, there is no trace of the number called from. Isabel isn't surprised by that, and neither is anyone else in the room. So, they end up in front of the case board Adam put together.

Their lines of inquiry board, detailing what they're exploring, has a few more names on it now:

Anabel Pereira – US fugitive, Gifted, sole survivor of Tues 03/09, missing, witness/culprit?
Joana Weir – AP ex-fiancée, journalist
Ian Russell – AP friend, jealous of AP ex, Gifted, on GIRC conference board
Tracy Russell – wife of Ian Russell, Gifted, AP rival?
Eliana Cross – mentor/previous boss
Emanuel Francisco (deceased) – ambassador Portuguese embassy, SA perpetrator
Judite Ramos – murdered/related? unsure about contact w/AP

'Timothy Allen says Judite knew Francisco was sexually harassing Anabel Pereira,' Adam says, 'I'm working through her finance records to see if there was a payout, something to support the allegations. If Judite Ramos knew what was taking place and assisted in keeping it quiet and Anabel knows, that's a good motive for getting rid of her.'

Rampaul rocks back on her chair. 'At this point we know that the abuse was an open secret. So the people in the embassy that day are dead. Ramos, who was apparently helping him cover it up, is dead. And Anabel is out there on the loose.'

'Revenge?' Adam says.

'Still worth noting that the causes of death are different,' Voronov says.

'Doesn't mean it couldn't have been her,' Rampaul says.

'We can check with Cross if Anabel had weapons training,' Isabel says. 'Do we have the preliminary results from the crime-scene team or the autopsy for Ramos?'

Voronov crosses his arms. 'They had nothing to add to what they told us before. The house was clean. No sign of forced entry, any type of electronic device that can store information is absent from the house. No phone, no laptop, no tablet. We've also searched her office at the embassy and it was clean too.'

'We spoke to most of the neighbours on Ramos's road and the road where the houses back up to her garden,' Adam says, 'and no one heard any gunshots or unusual activity. We think it's possible the attack took place in the morning, maybe at a time when most people would be out of their houses at work.'

It's unlikely that there wouldn't have been at least one neighbour nearby in their home to overhear. That nothing had been heard at all means there were probably no screams for help or any significant disturbance. Maybe Ramos knew her attacker or maybe she'd never been given the chance to fight back or even realised she was in danger before being subdued.

If someone can murder multiple people with nothing but telekinesis, they can certainly subdue one person long enough to restrain them.

Voronov turns their attention back to the embassy deaths.

'Adam has finished putting in the requests for neighbouring embassy CCTV with Westminster Council,' Voronov says, 'and we received the footage from inside the embassy itself earlier today. We're waiting to hear back from Wandsworth Borough Council for Dr Pereira's presence in Putney.'

He's got two images projected up on the whiteboard.

Outside, the heat has given way to rain and it has started pouring down. The sound is loud enough to penetrate the walls of the building and fills the room with a constant rushing noise. All the rain does is amplify the humidity inside the room. The flimsy air conditioning of these rooms might as well not be there.

The heat here is different from the heat back home. It clings to the skin, leaving a sticky feeling that makes clothes feel unpleasant and suffocating. Adam had told them this is what they call an Indian summer over here. When she'd asked him why it was called that, he hadn't known either.

Isabel wipes the back of her wrist across her forehead as she grabs a chair.

Voronov settles into the seat beside Isabel and Rampaul stays near Adam, arms crossed over her chest as she takes in the images.

One of the images is a map of the area surrounding the embassy. Familiar names catch Isabel's attention: Hyde Park, Westminster, Buckingham Palace. But the embassy itself is in Soho so the map on display covers much further ground than that. The map is littered with red and yellow circles, with the number of yellow circles far outweighing the ones in red.

The second one is made up of three separate sections, a building plan that Isabel recognises as the embassy.

'I took on the tracking of the fugitive,' Adam says, 'so I looked mostly at our surveillance options around the embassy to see if we're able to catch her on any of the available cameras. I'm still in the middle of compiling a list of surrounding businesses we can query, to see if they have their own surveillance, but we'll also have to go around on foot and see if there are any others we can spot. Speaking to Westminster Council to see if they have a list of their own cameras.'

'What are the circles?' Isabel asks, leaning forward in her chair to read the names next to them.

'Red circles are Underground stations nearby; the yellow ones are bus stops,' Adam says. As he continues, he rubs the back of his neck. 'These are all potential routes that someone exiting the embassy may have taken.'

There are seven red circles, the closest two being Knightsbridge and Hyde Park Corner.

Clearly the more time-consuming ones will be the bus stops. There are ten that Isabel can see, and they'll have multiple routes at each one, and going in different directions.

That's a lot of legwork for a team of only four. Rampaul had made it clear that they'd been denied even the help of junior officers and Mackey and Bridges are already pushing the limits of how much they can help, having been reassigned.

Isabel wants to ask if they're being punished for something more than being foreigners encroaching on their turf.

'I have a list of all the bus routes corresponding with the circled bus stops,' Adam says. 'Now that we know she stayed in the area, our priority is shifting to figuring out at which point she left the embassy. Any sightings of her before or after the deaths of the staff will help us establish the timeline of events. In relation to her hiding out at Ian Russell's, at least the only nearby tube station is Putney Bridge, but if she continued on foot or took a bus then that will take us longer to figure out.'

'Whatever it takes. I'm worried she'll try to leave London at this stage,' Rampaul says. 'I'm a little surprised she didn't attempt it to begin with, though after speaking to her biggest fan, I suppose staying with him was the safest option for her. I don't think she's got many more places to turn to after him.'

'We've put watch requests out with TfL. I know it's always risky. It's like finding a needle in a haystack when we've got millions of commuters every day but at least it's out there.'

'Well done, Adam,' Rampaul says.

Adam glances at her in surprise, and after a moment gives her a tight nod, skin flushing pink under his freckles.

That it would be going much faster if they'd been given a few more officers to start combing through what they've already gathered, goes unsaid. Isabel reminds herself that although they have been directed to assist, they are practically guests here and it won't pay to make a fuss. Not right now anyway.

'Okay,' Rampaul claps her hands together, 'what else? CCTV from inside the embassy. We've got that too?'

Voronov nods and has his notebook in hand, the pencil tucked in through the spirals on top.

'Those are the floor plans of the embassy building. We have a total of five CCTV cameras in the building.'

He runs them through the position of each one. Three on the ground floor. One at the entrance, one facing the door into the garden and one more at the door used by suppliers. All of these are aimed to monitor people coming in and out of the building. The remaining cameras are set up at each landing.

Voronov's chair creaks as he gets up and walks over to the floor maps. He pulls the pen from his notebook to tap against the image. 'The one directly in front of the front door catches people walking in, same for the one at the garden door and the suppliers' door. None of them capture anything of what goes on on the floor itself. We have a little more luck with the other surveillance but not much. These are mounted on the walls and face the ascending set of stairs.'

'So, we see who is accessing each floor?' Isabel says.

'Yes.'

Voronov goes over to the laptop and the images on the whiteboard disappear and are replaced by six different viewpoints. They're easily recognisable as the security footage setup he's just explained.

The time stamps are for Tuesday morning. No one is in any of the shots.

'With the exception of the call we were able to witness due to it being an online meeting,' Voronov says, 'we haven't caught anything on camera.'

How can that be? 'What about the woman on the staircase?' Isabel asks. 'What happens to her should be visible.'

'It should.' He gestures at the time stamps. 'This is set to three minutes before the ambassador's death, based on the time shown on the video call.' The time stamp reads 07:37:11. He presses play.

The seconds tick by, all four of them silent and waiting.

When movement finally happens it's on the camera facing the stairs leading up to the second floor. The movement they get is minuscule. The hint of a head.

Then, as if being switched off one by one, beginning from the garden entrance camera, the cameras shut off, the screen filled with nothing but the bright grey of a white noise screen.

It happens in a matter of seconds.

Isabel blinks. 'What happened?' she asks. In the background, the footage continues to play. 'Was it tampered with?'

'I don't know,' he says. 'This lasts for twenty-seven minutes and then the screens return. By that time, you see the woman we found on the stairs leading up to the second floor, and then much later, you see us coming in. But that's it. Nothing else between that.'

Twenty-seven minutes. That's a big deal; a significant amount of time. More than enough time for someone to get in and out of the building and disappear. Within that time frame, twelve people die and a fugitive goes missing.

Isabel shakes her head.

'Gives us a time stamp to focus our outside surveillance canvassing on,' Rampaul says. 'Any guesses about the identity of the person we barely get a glimpse of nearing the stairs?'

Voronov considers the question. 'I think that's the woman we found on the staircase, but we don't see enough of her on the screen to confirm. That's the most likely scenario but I would be wary of making any assumptions.'

Isabel sighs, resting her head in her hand and rubbing a thumb over and over her temple, for once more out of habit than a need to relieve pain.

'Another detail for us to take note of is that the cameras went out in a particular order. This might not have any particular significance, but these are the times.' He sets his notebook on the table for them to see.

Camera 1 / main entrance: 07:40:23
Camera 2 / supply entrance: 07:40:20
Camera 3 / garden door: 07:40:10
Camera 4 / 1st floor landing: 07:40:35
Camera 5 / 2nd floor landing: 07:40:41

It started from the garden door.

Isabel looks at Voronov. 'Anabel was in the annexe. No cameras in the hallway outside the annexe?'

'No.'

Rampaul sighs and sets her hands on her hips. She shakes her head. 'Okay let's—'

She's interrupted by a knock on the door. The same officer who had alerted them to Anabel's call sticks her head in through the gap in the door. 'DI Rampaul?'

Rampaul straightens. 'What is it?'

'Chief is calling for you. There's an urgent call-out and he wants you and Keeley on it.'

Rampaul frowns. 'I'll be right there.' She shuts the door after the officer. 'I don't know how long this'll take.'

Isabel nods. 'We'll keep working away.'

'All right.' Rampaul nods. 'It's been a long one and none of us have been getting much rest. Call it a day for today. Get a break tonight. We'll pick it back up in the morning.' And with that she bids them a good evening and leaves.

Isabel stands. She walks over to the screen, eyes running over what they have.

Adam looks uncertainly at the door Rampaul has left through and at the computer.

Isabel glances at Voronov.

'It wouldn't hurt to take a break tonight,' he says.

'Okay then. Adam, let's start again tomorrow. Hopefully the remaining surveillance we're waiting on will have been sent.' She thinks about it. 'Might be a good idea to speak with the hotel Cross is staying in, find out the day she checked in and get a list of

188

guests who also checked in the same day. Then maybe we could use that to cross-reference with the flight manifest from when Cross flew in. See if we can figure out who exactly Dr Pereira is hoping came over with Cross.'

Adam nods. 'Okay, sounds like a plan. See you both tomorrow then.'

They gather their stuff and then say their goodbyes before parting ways for the night.

As Isabel and Voronov head out, Isabel sees that the space where Rampaul and her partner sit is empty.

She just hopes they're not about to lose their lead investigator too.

# 29

By the time they get back to Greenwich the rain has long since stopped but the scent of it lingers in the air.

The grounds are still stained dark from the rainfall, and little drops glitter on the leaves of the plants and shrubbery decorating the recreational space between the buildings.

Isabel sits on one of the benches, staring out at the view of the river that is straight ahead.

Night has settled. The sky is a stretch of black, no stars, no moon but the buildings across the river, clustered together, stand out like a beacon. The warmth that has persisted throughout the downpour earlier remains and Isabel is comfortable, grateful for the slight breeze that comes every now and then.

There aren't too many people out. A few here and there, walking past the space, maybe to get home from work or some on their way out in small groups, headed for a quick drink nearby.

Overall, it's quiet.

The lights from televisions, kitchens and living rooms light up the balconies that make up part of the building's exterior, lending them a warm glow.

Isabel hears familiar steps, the rhythm growing more distinct as they approach her.

She leans her head back in time to catch Voronov approaching the benches and coming around the side to take a seat beside her.

As he settles in, he hands over a coffee cup, setting his own aside before reaching into the white bag with its red-and-blue logo, taking out two packaged wraps and passing one over to her.

Isabel wrinkles her nose as she takes it. 'God, what is it?' she asks. It's late and neither of them had felt like cooking or hunting down a place to eat.

Voronov settles in, leaning against the back of the bench with a long exhalation. 'They didn't have much left,' Voronov says, 'which isn't surprising going by the time. I think we're lucky they were still open.'

'And that they had coffee,' Isabel muses, picking up the maroon cup and peeling back the lid with a cautious sniff.

Voronov gives a short hmm, getting to work on the plastic encasing the wrap. 'I wouldn't be too happy about the coffee just yet. Try it first.'

Isabel shakes her head and chuckles. 'Don't worry about it. Thanks.'

Neither of them speaks while they eat. Unsurprisingly, the chicken wrap leaves a lot to be desired, but it does the trick. She picks up the coffee and sighs.

She's managed to shake off the persistent exhaustion that has been with her since she arrived, no matter how much sleep she does or doesn't get. But now that they're outside the office and being given space to breathe, she feels every ounce of it weighing her down. She's content to stay exactly where she is and not move again unless it's to go to bed.

'This isn't bad,' Isabel murmurs, taking in the view.

Voronov makes a noise in agreement but doesn't elaborate.

He's finished eating too and is nursing his coffee with one hand, his other arm stretched along the back of the bench, fingertips almost close enough to touch Isabel's shoulder.

Unlike her, his gaze isn't focused on the view of the city in front of them but instead on some unseen point, deep in thought.

'What is it?' she asks.

Voronov gives a slight shake of his head. 'I'm thinking about what Ian Russell said.'

Isabel shifts, bringing a leg up on to the seat of the bench and letting her arm hang off the back of it to face him. 'That sorry excuse for a man said a lot of things,' she snorts and takes a sip of the coffee.

Voronov had been right; it isn't great either.

'When he talked about Anabel and Joana Weir.'

Ah. That. Isabel shakes her head. 'There are a lot of people like him out there. I guess we don't hear from that flipside of the coin too often.' Something she's grateful for. There's enough divisive bullshit out there already without people adding more to it.

'You didn't like what he said?' Voronov asks.

'I don't agree with it, no.' She thinks about Russell's wife. She doesn't feel sorry for Tracy. The woman clearly knows herself very well, knows what she's got into. Isabel imagines she knows exactly how to get herself out of it as well. She doesn't want anyone's pity. That would be insulting to a woman like her. 'The way he talks he makes their pregnancy sound more like his contribution to eugenics. There was nothing in what he said that sold his own relationship as healthy. Don't get me wrong, I'm talking about his relationship specifically.'

Voronov stays quiet, but that questioning look remains. Like he's patiently waiting for her to go on.

Isabel shrugs. 'I don't know. I guess to me it doesn't matter.' Though she can see where other people's views have probably influenced her own approach, given the relationships she's had so far. She's never been with someone else Gifted.

Not for the first time, she wonders how things might have gone differently if her dad, someone who had fully supported her and held no prejudice against Gifted people, had been around to raise her.

Instead, Isabel had grown up under her mother's disgust for what she was, and all people like her.

In a situation like that, where a parent is shunning, there's so much sacrifice on the child's part. Isabel hadn't been old enough to understand anything but the fact that her mother had pushed her away once she'd found out her daughter was Gifted. So being Gifted was the problem and, as a teenager, Isabel had tried to diminish that side of herself as much as possible even as she'd worked in her sessions with her Guide to learn how to properly use her Gift.

There had never been any joy in it for her.

Even now, Isabel can't tell whether that's due to her mother's views on Gifted people or whether it was the nature of her own Gift which was repellent to her.

There isn't a single point in time where Isabel can point to her Gift ever truly feeling like the gift her father had told her it would be.

Maybe as an extension of that, Isabel had never actively sought out people like her. She'd barely even interacted with people who weren't like her. She'd forged relationships and bonds with people only in her immediate sphere at work. She'd been lucky in that regard and found friends there. Being Gifted or not hadn't come into it. At least not on a conscious level.

Meeting Michael had been like that, just like it had been with other people she'd dated. People she'd got to know because they'd come into contact with her little sphere.

'Or maybe it did matter,' Isabel corrects, 'and I never realised it mattered.' She looks at Voronov. 'It shouldn't though. And it doesn't, to me, right now.' She glances away, eyes drawn back to the river. 'Does it matter to you?'

She guesses it might. For Gifted it's normal. For Regulars it means that the person you're with will always have an edge on you. It's enough to put people off before they've even properly started.

Maybe that's why Ian Russell thought it could never work, because some people might already be entering a partnership feeling off balance. It wouldn't be as much of a problem if people talked it out. The reality is that most will just paper over it and pretend there is no problem.

She blinks in surprise as Voronov holds his hand out to her.

Isabel flicks a gaze up from his hand to his face.

He raises his eyebrows expectantly.

Slowly, because she's not sure what he wants here, she slides her hand into his.

A small smile lifts the corner of his mouth, and he drops their hands down between them and turns his attention back to the river.

In an echo of his show of faith when they had started working together a few years ago, Isabel hears his answer in her head.

She lets out a small laugh, and follows his example, turning back to the view.

'Good.'

# 30

The entrance to her mother's house feels different.

Isabel isn't sure why. She hasn't been here in a long while.

Standing in front of it would normally make her feel queasy. She has so many feelings associated with this house, all of the good ones buried beneath the bad. The good ones are from too long ago and tied to a time when she'd still had her dad. When Isabel lets herself sink into them, they make her smile even as their thin-tipped ends softly press into her, puncturing through as if sinking into the soft flesh and leaving her bleeding.

Around her, Isabel hears the susurrus of tree leaves moving under the currents of the breeze. The plants in their terracotta pots placed all around the bottom of the house sway gently before settling back into place when the breeze abates.

She catches these details out of the corner of her eye. She wants to look at them directly but she can't.

Something is wrong.

This feels familiar. Not just the location, but this feeling she has. Like she's somewhere she doesn't belong.

What is she doing here?

It feels like a dream but not, at the same time.

Everything is vivid. She can feel the sun, dappling her face as its light filters through the leaves. The breeze is soft, rustling her hair, except that feels different too. The back of her neck is unprotected, it feels lighter.

The more she focuses on herself, the more things feel off kilter. Her centre of gravity is different.

And then she's moving forward.

One step after the other, gaze fixed straight ahead on the door to her mother's house.

Her mouth shapes words.

'Are you with me, Isabel?'

The voice is low, and deep. It vibrates in her throat, the vocal cords, not her own. It's not her voice but she knows whose voice it is.

The shock of it leaves her stunned for a moment, even as panic spreads through her, the fight or flight response trapping her, leaving her unable to take action. She feels her arm lift, not of her own volition, and a sickening feeling rises in her, but the body she's in shows no signs of reacting to any of her emotional or mental turmoil; it remains unaffected.

Here, so close to the door, she hears the familiar sound of the radio playing in the kitchen, a habit her mother has never broken even after her dad had died, music playing low as they go about their day. That radio was only ever turned off if neither of them was in the house or before bed. Otherwise, music flowed, always, sometimes the sound lowered, sometimes louder.

Her mother is home.

She watches as a man's hand reaches out to the door. She feels the solidity of the door beneath the knuckles as it – he – knocks twice.

Isabel stares fixedly at the door.

No. Don't come. Don't come. Don't come. *Don't come!*

The burst of violent will manifests itself, twists something in her, in this body that isn't hers but that she's been in once before, and she feels his surprise even as his body stutters, hand faltering to hover in the air aimlessly, like it doesn't understand who to obey.

*Stop!*

Is this real? Is any of this real?

Except the door in front of her clacks open and her mother's face peers out.

Isabel shoots forward, hand spread out to urge her back into the house—

'*– sabel!*'

Isabel blinks her eyes open, to a soft warm wind blowing her hair back from her face and sweeping over her bared legs. Her chest heaves violently, her mouth open and dragging in air just as hard. For a moment she stares out unseeing, struggling in the grip of the two arms banded tight across her chest.

'Isabel, *Isabel*! Stop!'

The words are uttered right above her ear.

Voronov.

He's plastered to her back. She can feel where his face is pressing into her hair; his tone, though urgent, is hushed. He's holding her.

Isabel reaches up, curling her fingers tightly around his wrists, anchoring herself as her eyes finally start to focus and she understands her surroundings.

She's standing on the balcony, inches from the edge. She's held back by Voronov's arms alone.

Oh God. Oh God.

The strength goes out of her legs as the situation hits her.

Behind her, Voronov curses and takes her weight. 'Hey, hey,' he says as he adjusts his grip on her, urging her gently to stay on her feet, 'you're fine.' He steps back, pulling her with him. 'Talk to me.'

They move back. Slowly. As slowly as she had moved forward towards her mother's house.

Voronov continues to walk back, Isabel stumbling back with him, never letting go of his hands. He's murmuring to her, talking to her as they go. What he probably doesn't realise is that where his words are soothing and trying to keep her with him, his thoughts are chaotic and uncharacteristically loud and indecipherable amidst the strong emotions pouring out of him. Fear, panic, confusion, creating a whirlpool that threatens to drag Isabel in.

She's trembling, badly. Her skin is cold. Shock is still in her, weighing down her limbs and her mind, making her slow.

Voronov shifts his grip on her, and she registers his apology. Realises he's apologising for pulling away from her and prying her hands from where they'd been squeezing his wrists. Her eyes fall on his skin, and she sees the imprint of her fingers there even in the dark. There are little half-moons cut into his skin too, red, where the rest of the marks she'd left on him are white. She'd held on so tight she'd stopped the blood flow.

He snatches up a blanket and lays it over her shoulders before striding back to the balcony doors and pulling them closed.

'Stay there,' he says.

She does as she's told, slowly adjusting the blanket over her shoulders and staring at the balcony doors.

Voronov flicks on the lights in the kitchen and the light spills out into the living room.

She hears the bubbling sound of the kettle being filled and Voronov going into the cupboards and dragging out mugs. Hears the clink of them as they're set on the counter.

She reaches up and catches the edge of the blanket slipping down her arm and pulls it up and tightens it around her body.

Her legs are bare. She's in her sleeping T-shirt.

The door to her room is wide open; she can see a corner of the bed. The blankets are at the end of it.

She hadn't taken the sleeping pills today. Had been tired enough from the day that she'd just taken a chance.

The worst part is, whatever that was, it hadn't felt like a dream.

She finally feels herself calming down, her thought process slowing to actually take in the pieces in front of her and slot them together.

She'd definitely been asleep. Whatever had taken place, she'd got up and walked out of her room, into the living space and to the balcony doors. She'd opened them and stepped outside.

Going by Voronov's actions, she thinks it's safe to assume that he'd interrupted whatever she'd been doing and held her back. His heightened emotion, bright and unsettled in the background even now, speaks to how close she had been to the edge of the balcony. Possibly close to going over.

The dream itself – it had felt too real. The smells and the sounds . . .

She stands up and goes straight to her room, still anchoring the blanket around her shoulders.

Her phone is on her nightstand. The screen lights up, telling her it's 3.23 in the morning.

In the dream, it had been daytime.

Still, she needs to be sure. She *has* to be sure.

She unlocks her phone, kissing her teeth when she goes into the wrong app twice, her impatience making her clumsy. She gets into her contacts list and scrolls down. Going over who would be best to call. Daniel is more likely to be on nights. Jacinta, who has been inundated from work from other districts, if she's not sleeping the sleep of the dead right now, then she's probably on a scene bagging and tagging.

She touches her thumb to Daniel's name.

The ring tone against her ear feels like it's piercing through her skull, echoing uncomfortably deep.

Outside she can hear Voronov moving around, hears the bubbling of the kettle. She watches the pool of light spilling in from the living room on to the floor of her bedroom as the ring tone continues.

Then: 'Isabel?'

Daniel's voice comes down the line, his voice thick and weighed down with sleep. He sounds exhausted and like he shouldn't be awake.

'Hey,' she says, 'didn't mean to wake you up. Thought you'd be on nights.'

There's a rustling on his side. It sounds like he's in bed. 'What's wrong?'

Isabel has known Daniel a long time. She, Daniel and Jacinta had met as students and risen through their careers together. Most of the time their relationship consists of ribbing each other, calling each other names, and always complaining. It's the way their friendship works. Despite always taking the piss, Isabel knows he's someone she can trust, and rely on. The fact that he doesn't bitch about her waking him up says a lot.

Distantly, Isabel wonders how she sounds right now.

'I'm sorry. I need you to do something for me.'

He's silent. Then, 'Now?'

'Yes. I know it's late, I'm sorry.'

'Stop apologising.' He sounds more awake now and there's the sound of more shifting in the background, an odd metallic echo that comes from moving around on a mattress. 'Tell me what you need.'

'I need you to go and check on my mum. Just make sure that everything is okay.'

'Yeah. Yeah. Of course. I'm on it. Do you want me to tell her you sent me?'

'No, no. Can you make something up? A neighbour calling in, something, anything is fine.'

'Of course. I'll call you once I've checked in on her.'

'Thank you.'

He makes a sound like he's about to say something else. He's well within his rights to ask her why she's calling him in the middle of the night to do this. He hasn't even asked if she's called her brother, why he's not the one she's speaking to right now asking for something of this nature.

In the end, though, he doesn't ask.

'Is Voronov with you?' he asks.

'Yeah,' she says. The blanket is sliding again. As if summoned, Voronov comes into view, a mug in his hand.

When their eyes meet, he lifts the mug and nods his head towards the sofa before disappearing from view once more.

'Okay. We'll talk later. Take it easy.'

'All right.'

They hang up. Isabel walks back over to the living room, her phone held tightly in her hand.

Her attention strays to her reflection on the balcony doors. It sends a shiver through her.

She turns inward, prodding the corners of her mind, seeking that dark, curled thing that she knows is there. It's made itself even smaller now. A parasite burrowing deep to keep from being detected, but Isabel knows it hasn't left. She feels the shape of it in her mind.

Voronov is sitting on the edge of the sofa, waiting for her.

There's a mug on the coffee table. 'Is that for me?'

'To warm you up.'

She nods and murmurs a thank-you. The scent of chamomile drifts up from the mug. She expects it to be blistering hot against her hand, but it isn't, just hot enough to do the job.

It's a comforting spot of heat warming the skin of her hands as Isabel sits down next to him.

It feels like a surreal moment. Isabel doesn't know if it's because she's still out of sorts from whatever just took place, the late hour, or the low lights, but she feels like right now she's sitting in a liminal space. That feeling of knowing something is coming, that where you are right now is temporary, like the lines of the world around you are blurred.

Isabel adjusts the blanket corners once more. 'What happened?' she asks.

He leans forward, elbows resting on his knees, eyes on her, searching her face.

They both know that he should be the one asking that.

But she needs to know what he saw, what he heard.

Not knowing what exactly she did while she was out of it is . . . it's a sobering feeling.

'I woke up when I heard you opening the balcony doors,' he says quietly.

She wonders if he can also sense it. The transitional feel of this moment.

It feels dangerously fragile.

'But it sounded off. It was taking you too long to open it and like you were struggling. I think that's what woke me up. I got up to see what was happening and said your name, but you didn't hear me.'

The knuckles of her fingers grind against each other where they interlace around the mug. The strength of her grip is enough that it feels as if even the webbing between each finger will bruise.

'And then?'

'You got the doors open and walked out on to the balcony. And then you kept walking and kept trying again and again, like the railing wasn't in front of you. You weren't responding to me and when I reached you, it seemed like you were sleepwalking.'

Sleepwalking.

'Why did you have to call Daniel?' Voronov asks.

Isabel takes a drink from the mug. 'I needed someone to go check on my mother. Aleks . . .' She forces herself to meet his gaze. 'I'm know I still haven't told you everything . . . and I'm sorry.' She shakes her head, at a loss here. She needs to figure this out.

There is a lot riding on what Daniel reports back.

'I don't want to lie to you though. I'm asking you to give me more time.' She tucks her hair behind her ear. She ignores the tremor in her fingers, hopes that he doesn't notice it. 'Can you do that?'

Voronov gives a slow nod.

Isabel feels the weight dissipate, leaving her, and sinks back into the sofa, letting her head lean against it. Her feet are cold. Her toes are aching. She probably rammed them against the balcony railing.

She rests the mug on her stomach, a small circle of heat that feels as if it is spreading out to the rest of her.

She stares at the ceiling. 'Feels like I'm always thanking you,' she murmurs.

'You don't have to.'

'I know.' She sighs.

# 31

'Isabel, I haven't heard your voice in a while. I was starting to get worried. How are you?'

Rosario, Isabel's old, assigned Guide from when Isabel had been a little girl learning what it meant to be Gifted and have a Gift, is warm on the phone, though her tone is tempered with a worried edge.

It hasn't been all that long since they'd reconnected. Isabel had been on edge, struggling with how her Gift had developed. Turning to any kind of professional would have spelled a very bad ending for her so Isabel hadn't known who to turn to. The only people she associated with safety in regard to her Gift had been her dad and Rosario. She'd lost one when he'd passed away. She'd lost the other when she came of age and the required legal Guiding support was removed.

Still. It had taken time to search and find where Rosario was then. It had taken even longer, once Isabel had found out, to drum up the courage to reach out and make contact. Eventually they had reconnected, and Isabel had risked it all, telling her the whole truth about the state of her Gift, about the suppressors she'd been taking.

She'd been the first one Isabel had called after she'd gone to bed one night and heard Gabriel Bernardo's voice in her head.

It's early morning and Isabel's eyes are aching, the very air making them sting, and she has to stop herself from rubbing them over and over.

'Sorry,' Isabel says, 'I meant to call but work happened, as it usually does. Me and my partner are in London right now assisting with a case.'

'Oh? They're sending you to London now?' Isabel can picture her in her wicker garden chair, having her morning coffee, a pair of show-stopping earrings in place. Sometimes Isabel wonders if she rolls out of bed with them already on. It doesn't matter what time of night or day Isabel sees her, she's always got a different pair on, big and bright and unmissable. She's always been that way.

'How is it over there?' Rosario asks.

Isabel steps out of the way of an officer going into the police station with an apology and crosses to the other side of the street. Opposite the station is a series of tall buildings, mostly offices going all the way up. Isabel thinks it's likely that they all house multiple businesses.

Though there's the children's park in one direction; on the opposite side is a quiet street, with a modest restaurant at the corner that's usually packed with police officers and further down a small shop keeping everything from everyday snacks to fruit, toiletries and probably every other emergency thing you could think of.

'Not great,' Isabel says, 'but we'll manage. The sooner we get home the better, but until then, we'll do our best.'

'Okay. I hope you're taking good care of yourself.'

Her words are edged with a warning.

Rosario is the only person who knows the extent of what Isabel is dealing with right now. She knows about her struggles with sleep, about needing to medicate, knows that Isabel is trying to think her way out of this trap she's found herself in with seemingly no way of escape.

Isabel lets out a steadying breath, scanning the road around her to make sure she's got at least some privacy. 'Something happened last night,' she says.

'Tell me.'

Isabel does.

Daniel had called back a few hours later to say he'd been to her mother's house. Isabel had been back in her room then, arm curled under her pillow, staring at the wall. Sleep was something far away that she didn't want to give in to, something she now mistrusts. As if she doesn't have few enough things to trust in right now.

It's getting harder and harder not to feel bitter over the turn things have taken.

Daniel had said her mother hadn't been the happiest at being interrupted from her sleep. Her sister had come to the door as well and all seemed fine with them. Daniel apologised for interrupting them, making an excuse that they'd had a report and since he was friends with Isabel, he'd elected to check it out himself.

No issues, no anything.

Isabel had thanked him and apologised for taking him from what was probably the first deep sleep he'd had in a long while. And she'd asked him to keep it to himself for now.

So, none of it had happened. It had all been something she'd dreamed up in her head.

Except that she can't shake the feeling that it hadn't been a dream.

There's also the fact of what both she and Voronov had left unsaid in the early hours.

The two of them have shared space enough times, over the course of several cases, crashing in each other's living rooms or even at the precinct, sinking into deep sleep too many times to count. He knows as well as she does that she does not sleepwalk.

Isabel hears Rosario take a deep breath after she finishes bringing her up to speed.

'Have you had any luck finding out where he is?' Rosario asks.

'No. Nothing. And then we were sent over here so it hasn't been easy. There are still a few contacts I haven't tried but I'd rather not involve them unless I don't have a choice.'

'Okay. Listen to me. I think this is your turning point. So far, it's been little things, hasn't it? You've felt him in there, moving around in your head, making himself known. You've been working to keep him out since you found out, to shut him down before he can try anything.'

Isabel nods even though Rosario can't see.

'You stopped him before.'

Isabel gives a short laugh before shoving her fingers through her hair. 'I didn't stop him.'

'Didn't you? You stopped him in his tracks that day on the rocks. You may not like how you did it. But if you did it then, you can do it again. Gabriel is an impressive Gifted individual and I'm not going to sit here and tell you that the breadth of what he can do isn't terrifying. But we both know you have your own advantages. You stopped him then and you can stop him now. But you have got to stop playing it safe.'

'I can't do that.'

'Why? Because it's against the rules? Because you can't look in someone's head without consent? Isabel, you're a smart woman. He is in *your* head. He is a danger to *you*. If he can do with you what he did to other people, those you are close to, who are in your day-to-day life, family, friends, colleagues – those people are also in his firing line.'

In her mind's eye she sees that hand that doesn't belong to her lifting, despite her best efforts, to knock on her mother's door.

'You don't think it was a dream either, do you?' Isabel asks.

'I don't know what it was, Isabel. But it certainly sounds like a lot more than a dream.'

# 32

Rampaul and DI Keeley are still working on the case Rampaul had been pulled into the previous day; she has left a message for them telling them to get in touch in case of any major developments, and Adam is running late, having messaged them to say he'd had a family emergency overnight, but is on his way.

It ends up panning out well because on their way in this morning, Voronov and Isabel had received a call from a very tired Daniel telling them they had finally got somewhere with Milena Amorim and Rogério Pessoa's personal secretaries. They were being granted a thirty-minute slot in the diaries of the two Portuguese foreign affairs officials who have been dodging them since day one. It went without saying that if they missed this window then they wouldn't be getting another one any time soon.

'What time is the call?' Isabel asks, setting down two cups of coffee on the table.

They're in the case room their ragtag team has been working in so far. Outside, on the main floor, it's quieter than usual. Isabel's not sure if this is because it's early on a Saturday morning. She and Voronov have spent most of their time tied to Adam and Rampaul so Isabel's impressions of how things work here aren't as detailed as they could be. She and Voronov still get mostly hostile looks every time they arrive – something that is shared by Adam, though they're more cautious when it comes to Rampaul – with the exception of two of the officers who are usually on Reception. They've started greeting her and Voronov by name.

Well, any progress is progress, she supposes.

Voronov checks his watch. 'We have about ten or so minutes to go.'

Isabel nods, going to her bag and getting her notebook out. She'd been working in the back of the cab on the way over on the questions she wants to get answers to, and she and Voronov had already gone over them and agreed them together.

They get settled in and join the call early.

The room is sufficiently soundproofed, and Isabel's not too concerned about anyone overhearing, particularly as they'll be speaking a different language. Isabel doesn't get the impression there are other people here who speak Portuguese. Portuguese people tend to make themselves known to each other almost immediately, when in another country. Isabel doesn't know why, but it's almost like an impulse, a need for the other person to know that you, too, are like them. She thinks it's less of a habit with the newer generation though, which she appreciates.

Voronov has set up the call on the laptop and connected it to the digital whiteboard so when they join early, all that comes up on the screen initially is an image reflecting them back to themselves. Isabel on one side of the table, Voronov on the other. The windows are open but Isabel can feel the heat building already. She feels it pricking at the back of her exposed neck. Her hair is pinned up to the back of her head with a large butterfly clip and she hopes the white short-sleeved T-shirt will do its job. According to the news the heatwave is going to last another four days. Voronov has dressed a little more formally today. He likes to look unfailingly professional when meeting with higher-ups.

He's clean-shaven in a fitted pale-blue shirt and navy chinos. It'd got him some very appreciative glances from some of the police officers when they'd arrived this morning. Isabel can't blame them. A well-turned-out man always draws the eye.

There's a little text on the side of the screen stating that the other participants have not joined yet.

They didn't talk anymore this morning about what had happened in the middle of the night. After they'd parted ways, Voronov had gone back to his room to get some rest until they had to be back in.

Isabel had returned to the living room, attention straying to the balcony again and again until she'd had enough of herself. She'd switched from the herbal tea to a coffee, fetched her laptop and spent what remained of the night working on the case and finding out what she could about Eliana Cross.

As someone working for the US military, as a researcher no less, Isabel hadn't had particularly high hopes. She doubted anything major would have been allowed to make it to the papers or online.

What she'd gleaned from her efforts had been a decent understanding of how brilliant and highly regarded Cross was in the US and in her field but there seemed to be some debate across different comment sections with people wondering if her research was in the interests of the security of the United States.

None of this necessarily meant anything. After all, Cross had not even been in the country when the incident at the embassy had taken place, but if she was in any way related to it then Isabel wants to know about it.

Anabel's words over their call make it clear that if nothing else, Cross is at least directly involved in Anabel's presence at the embassy.

That's enough to have Isabel looking into it for her.

They're not seeing the whole picture and she knows the rest of them on this case are feeling the exact same way. It feels like they have so much, but at the same time, nothing at all.

She's determined for them to squeeze as much as they can out of this meeting with Amorim and Pessoa.

Just then the image that had been on the whiteboard changes.

Whereas Isabel and Voronov had previously been taking up the entire space in the call window, now two familiar faces take up space along the top, each in its own window.

Milena Amorim's chin is dimpling from how hard she's pinching her lips together. Her black hair is pulled back severely enough that Isabel wonders how she's not in pain from it.

Rogério Pessoa's expression at least is a little more tempered.

He looks the same as he had in the video of the call he'd had with Emanuel Francisco. Shirt and suit, a wine-red tie snug to his throat, the top of it almost hidden from view by the skin of his neck and chin. His white hair is neatly combed back from his face.

Isabel shifts in her chair so she can lean forward, resting her arm along the table and her palm on the surface. Her notebook is face up in front of her and she has a pen in her other hand.

'Senhora Amorim, Senhor Pessoa, bom dia,' she says, 'I know you're both very busy people, so I appreciate you making time to speak to us today.' She was putting it generously and from the way Amorim's eyebrow twitches when Isabel mentions 'making time', Isabel makes a note to ask Daniel how he and Carla had persuaded them to attend today. She doubts it was pleasant. Maybe the chief threw some weight around to get it done.

Pessoa grunts, as if clearing his throat, and then nods. 'Well, of course. I understand the situation over there isn't very good right now. Naturally, anything we can do to help the investigation along, we'll be happy to help.'

Of course you are, Isabel thinks.

'Thank you. I'm sure you must already know this but just for the sake of clarity,' Isabel says, 'I'm Inspector Reis and this is Inspector Voronov. We were the ones asked to assist in the investigation of Emanuel Francisco's death. As I'm sure you're both now aware, the ambassador was not the only one to die at the embassy that day. This information is, at the moment, only known to the investigators on this case, the families of the deceased and yourselves.' Isabel drags her notebook closer. 'We're aware to some extent of why Dr Anabel Pereira had taken refuge at the embassy, and how long she'd been there. It's come to our attention that she was waiting on an agreement between her and the Portuguese government during this time.'

On screen, Pessoa's expression doesn't change. Almost like he'd expected it already. Although there's no way of him knowing that they had come into contact with Anabel herself and the information she would have divulged.

It's odd. Even when not actively using her gift, at this point in an interview, Isabel is accustomed to some level of feedback, at least on the emotional level. Isabel feels, surprisingly deeply, that one of her senses has been effectively locked off. It can't serve her here.

'We've also obtained proof that during Dr Pereira's time at the embassy she was subjected to sexual harassment, and one incident of sexual assault, by Emanuel Francisco. Were either of you made aware of this?'

Amorim is the one who reacts most noticeably, her mouth losing the bitter tightness that it has held since she joined the meeting and her eyebrows climbing up her forehead. Quite a feat considering how restrictive her hairdo is.

Then Amorim starts spluttering. 'If anything like that was happening, we would have been told. There are countless staff at the embassy and the office and facilities manager was personally responsible for ensuring Dr Pereira's wellbeing.'

'I see,' Isabel says. She gestures between herself and Voronov with her pen. 'Why *were* Voronov and I not informed about the presence of a fugitive during the time of the ambassador's death?'

That shuts Amorim up very fast, her lips snapping back into that irritated line.

'We had to be informed by the head of security here,' Isabel says, 'which didn't really make for a good look in front of the lead investigator of the MCIU. In fact, it actually set us off on the wrong foot, made it seem like we were deliberately withholding information from *their* investigation. Not the best way to ensure that we were able to participate in assisting them.'

'Ah, Inspector Reis,' Pessoa says; he gives a short cough, as if he's clearing his throat, 'I assure you that the intention of our department was not to withhold that information. However, that was *classified* information.'

Voronov, still leaning back in his chair and having been quiet so far, sits up. 'With all due respect Senhor, your department was aware of the reason we were being sent here. Surely you knew that we would be made aware that a fugitive was being held here and how that might impact this investigation.'

'Yes. But this was a matter of delicacy that was blown out of proportion when she was found to be missing.'

Blown out of proportion? Is this arsehole serious? She can't actually believe what she's hearing.

They cannot have been this stupid.

'It was withholding information from an active investigation,' Voronov says with a sigh that sounds like he's politely asking for patience, 'and we should have been informed before we even left Lisbon. We're lucky the British authorities didn't hold it against us. They could have made things very difficult for us.'

Isabel taps the table. 'Does the reason for not telling us relate to why you were keeping Anabel there?'

'She was there of her own free will,' Pessoa says, punctuating the end of the sentence with another grunt.

'Because you promised her something. What did you promise her?'

'There are some things that you don't need to know—'

'I'll tell that to the newspapers when this situation finally breaks out, shall I?' Isabel shakes her head. 'I don't think you comprehend the situation you have on your hands. How long do you think the families of the deceased will stay quiet if they don't start getting some answers?'

Amorim tilts her head back. Isabel didn't think it was possible for someone to look down their nose at others over a video call. Clearly, she's wrong.

'Getting those answers for them is *your* job, Inspector Reis.'

'I'll make sure to tell my chief you said that, Senhora,' Isabel says, 'and you can explain to her how you got her and her team involved in this just to throw them under the bus.'

That seems to shut her up.

'What were you promising Dr Pereira?'

Nothing.

Isabel glances at Voronov.

'Twelve people dead and allegations of sexual assault. She was under *your* care,' Isabel says. 'What were you promising, Senhor?'

Another of those grunts and clearing of his throat.

'Citizenship.'

'For Anabel? That seems like a simple request. A yes or no request. It's within your power to grant it but from the sound of it, you hadn't made up your minds yet. What was the hold-up?'

'And what were you asking for in return?' Voronov asks. 'I don't think governments would be willing to grant citizenship for no reason at all, especially when you consider Dr Pereira's circumstances. I would have thought that could potentially cause tensions between Portugal and the American government.' Not an ideal situation when there was such a huge gap in the weight of both countries. Portugal wouldn't want to antagonise the American government. But for some reason they'd risked it by not only giving Anabel Pereira a place to hide out, but by also negotiating on citizenship. What would make that kind of risk worth it for a small country like Portugal? How far up did this go?

'We can't disclose that, but I can confirm that Dr Pereira had information that was of interest to us, and likely other interested parties. In return for the information, we would have offered safe passage to mainland Portugal and citizenship. Emanuel Francisco was tasked with negotiating with Dr Pereira on the finer details of the terms being agreed to by both parties. Given the sensitive nature of the situation we were doing our best to handle it with care. As you rightly pointed out, there is our relationship with America to consider. We wanted to resolve the situation to appease all parties.'

'Is that what you and the ambassador were discussing on the call that morning?' Isabel asks. 'Because you see there's no sound on the video you provided for us, which is unfortunate. I understand you've been unable to provide us with a version of it that has the sound restored so we're in the process of procuring a specialist to work out what has been said.'

Again, Isabel feels that muted frustration. She knows her words have got a reaction. But it's all beneath the surface. And she's not there to be able to tell the difference.

'Yes, we were meeting to discuss his progress with Dr Pereira.' That's all he says before he falls silent again.

'And what did he report?' Isabel asks.

The flesh around his mouth wobbles with the echoes of another grunt. 'Well. We didn't get very far into his report before the incident took place.'

'The call with the ambassador started at 7.30 a.m.,' Voronov says. 'The ambassador died at seven 7.47 a.m. so you were on the call for roughly fifteen minutes. Were you speaking about the weather in those fifteen minutes?'

Isabel has to stop herself from smiling. Voronov is usually the more soothing presence in the interview room out of the two of them. Unfailingly polite, patient. She secretly loves it when he starts giving pain-in-the-arse people some sass.

Pessoa, though, remains stubborn. 'We didn't discuss it.'

Isabel sighs. 'Right, I see. Maybe you were discussing the sexual assault instead.'

Both Amorim and Pessoa start talking at the same time and she waves them off. She'll probably get in trouble for this later – they're definitely going to put in a complaint, that's the kind of people they are – but she's had enough. They're deliberately obstructing the investigation and she doesn't have time for this.

'I think we've spoken enough. Senhor, we *will* be getting a specialist to do what they can with that video. I'll leave it to you to decide whether you'd like to tell us what you spoke about yourself. Trust me, in the end, it'll be much better if you volunteer the information.'

'I don't appreciate your line of questioning or the accusations, Inspector Reis,' Amorim says. 'I will be taking this up with your superior.'

Shocking.

It makes Isabel wonder what she'd thought she was doing when she'd asked Chief Bautista to put them on the case. There was enough out there about Isabel and Voronov's previous cases for the woman to know that they were not the type to back down from authority.

'Of course. Do as you like. We'll continue to do our jobs on this end, Senhora Amorim, like you asked us to.' Isabel turns back to Pessoa. 'So. The negotiations were for Anabel Pereira's citizenship. And where do they stand now? Is that still on the table?'

This time Pessoa is definitely clearing his throat. Isabel refrains from telling him he needs to get that checked out.

'I think you'll agree that recent events change things. Dr Pereira is under investigation, and it would be irresponsible of us to grant citizenship to her before we understand what took place.'

Right. An investigation you are hindering for whatever reason.

'Dr Pereira also had parts of the agreement left to fulfil. In addition to the subject of her own citizenship, we can't grant citizenship to someone else in good faith without knowing anything about them.'

Isabel blinks, confused. 'What do you mean? You know her and her background, you even know more about why she's taking refuge here than the authorities.'

Pessoa coughs into his hand even as he waves her question away impatiently with the other. 'Of course we know about her circumstances and who she is.'

'Then what do you mean?'

'As parts of our negotiations, Dr Pereira requested citizenship not just for herself.'

Isabel sits up, finally hearing something of use.

'Who else?' Voronov asks.

'And that's where we have a problem, Inspector Voronov. We don't know.'

215

# 33

Adam returns just as Isabel and Voronov have finished wrapping up a call with their chief.

They both glance up when he opens the door to the case room slowly and quietly, as if he's trying to take up as little of people's notice as possible. He's carrying his hoodie in his hand, his blue T-shirt is rumpled, creases all along the back and the side.

'Sorry,' he says, closing the door behind him, and sets his hoodie on the desk.

Isabel pushes back from the desk. 'Is everything all right?'

He nods fast and looks at the screen that is still showing the pending screen from the call they'd finished with their chief.

'Yeah, yeah,' he rubs his hand over his eyes, 'my sister was on shift – she's a nurse – and my niece wasn't well, it was a rough night. It's all good now. What have I missed?' he says. 'They told me at the front DI Rampaul is still out on the other case with Keeley.'

'Are you sure?' Isabel asks. 'Voronov and I can survive a few more hours without you . . .?'

'Yes boss.'

Isabel accepts the subject change, nodding slowly.

'You are just in time, I think,' Voronov says, 'we were updating our chief on the investigation. We spoke to Milena Amorim, the person responsible for our presence here in the UK, and Rogério Pessoa. He was on the call with Emanuel Francisco when he died. They are both from the Foreign Affairs Department.'

Adam pulls out a chair and sits down. He pulls up the edge of his T-shirt to wipe his forehead where sweat is beading at his hairline, either from the heat or his rush to get here.

Despite the tiredness weighing down the skin beneath his eyes and slumping his shoulders, his eyes widen, alertness coming back. The feeling he'd carried into the room with him, a heaviness that had dragged itself in behind him, reshapes itself into something different, becoming needle-thin with concentration.

He sits up straight like a straight-A student about to shoot their hand into the air eager to be the first to answer a question.

'Did they give us anything?'

Isabel grimaces. 'They were mostly uncooperative. But they did give us something. Pessoa said that part of the negotiations with Anabel, which were being run by the ambassador, included a request for citizenship by Anabel. But this wasn't for just one, but two people.'

Adam narrows his eyes. 'For two people? Did they say who?'

Isabel shakes her head. 'No name. They haven't been able to find out who it was. Or,' she acknowledges, 'for some reason they don't want to tell us.'

Adam nods. 'Okay. Well, one of the reasons I was rushing over was because I found something. One second.' He jumps up and goes back out of the room and comes back with his own laptop. 'I had some time to kill at the hospital,' he opens his laptop, 'and finished combing through the neighbouring surveillance footage we received.'

Isabel shifts to peer over his shoulder at the screen, Voronov coming in to stand beside her.

There's already an image on the screen when it comes up.

'This is the boutique on the corner two roads over from the embassy.'

The angle of the camera gives them a view of the steps leading up to the shop and the iron spikes fencing it in. It gives them a window span of the front of the shop and then a wider view across the street from the camera.

In the freeze frame the time stamp is on the top right-hand corner of the screen. It reads: 08:15.

The quality of the image isn't bad. It's in colour, good enough that they can make out number plates on the cars and see the pigeons lining the overhang of a box-like coffee shop.

'Okay,' Adam says, 'now watch.'

He presses play and the picture starts moving.

Isabel leans further down, not wanting to miss a thing.

There isn't much activity for a few seconds. The timer ticks over into 08:16.

A woman enters into the camera's view from the left side of the frame on the same side of the street as the coffee shop. She's not walking too fast or too slow. She is in jeans, trainers and a black, zipped-up hoodie. The hood is up over her head and there's a black bag strapped to her back.

She is long-limbed and there's a quality to her movements that reminds Isabel of new-born animals out in the wild, with their long legs that they haven't quite learned how to walk on yet. Her hands hold on to the straps of the bag at her shoulders as she goes.

It takes her only a handful of seconds to cross the frame and disappear again, crossing the road. There's nothing off about her. Before she leaves the frame of the camera, she glances across the road. Then she's gone.

Adam pauses the recording. It's still at 08:16.

Without saying anything, he closes that window and opens up another one. 'I isolated by frame.'

He brings up another window that had been minimised on the desktop.

It's from the same camera. Except this one is zoomed in enough that they can make out the shadows of the people working inside the coffee shop behind the young woman whose face is looking right in the direction of the camera.

It's a familiar face. They've seen it in the pictures they've been able to find of her. Isabel had seen it herself when she'd chased her over Putney bridge.

'The incident at the embassy takes place roughly between 7.40 and 7.47 a.m. and we have Anabel Pereira moving away from the scene *after* the incident has taken place, so this means she was probably in there during that time, right?'

Isabel nods.

It's a snapshot but it holds weight.

'A couple of other things,' Adam says, straightening up and rubbing at his eyes. He gives his head a slight shake like he's trying to keep himself awake. 'I got the flight manifests. We have the date that Cross arrived. She landed on Wednesday evening, and she was here talking to us the next day. I'm checking the other names on there but so far nothing. The other thing is the autopsy report from Dr Marlow for Judite Ramos and the crime-scene report for it. Came through around eight in the morning.'

Isabel wonders how long he'd spent at the hospital that he'd had time to comb through the remaining CCTV and then still been there to receive the reports from the crime-scene team and the coroners.

'Did they find anything of note?' Voronov asks.

This time the sigh Adam lets out is a visibly tired one. He doesn't bother to hide it.

'Unfortunately, no. The crime-scene team confirmed that the house was wiped clean. No sign of forced entry anywhere. They identified the type of bullet as a .40 S&W. I checked. It's a firearm used frequently by the US military.'

Isabel frowns. 'It's odd, none of the neighbours have reported hearing anything but a shot fired should have been loud enough for someone to hear something.'

'There was nothing in the house that suggested an object was used to muffle the shot,' Adam says, 'but the perpetrator could have taken whatever they used with them. But it's likely that there would have been traces of that kind of object on the victim herself or at the crime scene, but there's nothing.'

'Hmm,' Isabel says. It could also be that the crime had taken place at a time when most people weren't home, maybe while most people would have been at work. It's a large gap.

'They could have used a silencer,' Voronov suggests.

'Does Rampaul know?' Isabel asks.

'Yes, boss, already forwarded the information to her as well.'

Isabel still doesn't know if he calls her that because he forgets himself or if it's a genuine show of respect. She's already told him plenty of times that he can call her Isabel. He could call her Inspector as well, just as he does with Voronov. She wonders if there's something she's missing.

'Did she give you any updates on when she'll be rejoining us?' Isabel asks.

Rampaul is the lead investigator in this case. Things are already complicated enough with Isabel and Voronov assisting in the case but without the power to make any official decisions. They need Rampaul for that. With her attention now split between two cases, their already depleted work force diminishes further.

'No, she asked that we keep her posted and said she's going to do her best to come back today and see where we're up to, but at the moment it's pretty touch and go.'

Isabel is curious despite herself. 'What's so important that they'd pull her from a case which now numbers thirteen people dead?'

Adam's expression turns sombre, and he reaches up to rub at the lobe of his ear, eyes sliding away from hers.

'It's a pretty dark one,' he says, 'family of four in Westminster, murdered. Neighbour found them.'

'I see.' Isabel blows out a long breath. 'It might be a while then before Rampaul can join us. We have Adam, and if there's anything major we can always reach her. Bridges and Mackey are still leading the ground searches for Anabel. Not sure we should delay anything.'

Voronov nods in agreement and turns to Adam. 'Then let's prioritise the flight manifests. If possible, we should push for someone to be dispatched to keep an eye on Eliana Cross and the ex-fiancée, Joana Weir. We already have eyes on Mr Russell and his wife so that should be enough.'

Adam gives a doubtful look. 'Not sure that will fly well with the chief, Inspector.'

Isabel looks at Adam. 'Give it your best shot? Worst-case scenario, I guess we'll have to sit out there ourselves where possible. What about Francisco's and Ramos's financials? Something isn't adding up here and,' she shrugs, 'maybe the money will tell us something.'

Adam gives them a tired but determined nod. 'Having trouble getting access to Francisco's finances but should be getting access to Ramos soon. I'll focus on it boss.'

'And let's give Daniel and Carla another call,' Isabel says, 'there's something else I want them to do.'

# 34

Unsurprisingly, and especially without Rampaul there in person to push the case, there is no clearance from the MCIU's superintendent to support the surveillance that their team needs. At least he agreed to allocating them a car.

'I could only get one,' Adam says. There's a hardness to his eyes that has been settling in more and more since the day he had collected Voronov and Isabel at the airport. The constant withdrawal of support and the way both he and Rampaul seem to have been singled out hasn't been discreet. Where at first the whispers and side-eyes were mostly directed at Isabel and Voronov, two unknowns, slowly they've been cropping up more and more whenever Rampaul and Adam themselves are present.

Isabel's taken a good look around. It's not so different in Portugal. The diversity isn't particularly stand-out in the police force and it seems to be the same here. Regardless of how this unit's chief is handling this, this is a high-profile case.

Isabel recognises when someone is being set up to fail.

She scrunches the empty packet of crisps in her hand, the crackling sound loud in the mostly empty café.

It's 7.30 a.m. on Sunday and she's tucked into a corner of a small French café across the road from the hotel Eliana Cross is staying in.

There's a queue of people lining up, waiting to get their turn at the counter, but barely anyone is occupying the plush seats. People are on their phones, scrolling on their screens, or talking in hushed voices – some in loud ones because they have their earphones on and don't realise their volume is way too high – waiting to order their breakfast on the go.

It's their third day of surveillance.

Adam obtained the list of check-ins for the day Cross had checked into the hotel in August and has been working away on cross-referencing the names with flight manifests for the date of Cross's arrival. He'd even gone a step beyond that, liaising with airport security to learn if Cross left Heathrow airport alone upon arrival.

So far, no hits. There could be nothing. Anabel could have sent them on a wild goose chase to buy herself some time. They would have been stupid not to consider it.

They'd had positive news from Carla and Daniel the night before though. They'd managed to find a couple of people in Foreign Affairs willing to talk to them about Francisco. They'd caught wind of rumours that had been squashed by the bosses. But rumours are difficult to contain. The more you try to suppress them, the more they come out in hushed conversations on a smoke break outside, or over a quick *bica* after lunch. People live for gossip. The more you're not meant to have a certain piece of information, the more someone will want it.

They'll talk about it among themselves. The obstacle arises when you're trying to get them to talk about it to outsiders. Like, for instance, the police.

They all clam up.

Except Carla and Daniel had found a few holes in the fence there. Isabel hopes they don't get cold feet at the last minute and that at some point today they'll have more information on what exactly Francisco may have been getting up to behind closed doors.

Isabel picks up the paper cup. The serrated texture of the cupholder doesn't do much to keep the scalding temperature of the drink inside from searing her palm, but she doesn't mind it. Instead, she plucks the plastic lid off the top and dips her head to get a whiff of the strong smell of coffee, inhaling it like she's taking a hit of something.

She should probably be easing off the coffee, but she hasn't slept properly since the night she'd woken up to Voronov grabbing her and pulling her away from their apartment's balcony railing. That had been two days ago.

Short naps were the most she'd been allowing herself and to make sure it didn't go beyond that, she stuck to the living room. The bed was too tempting. So she kept her laptop close and set her alarm for thirty minutes at a time, sipping on coffee or tea in between, the light from her laptop feeling like a thousand tiny little pinpricks stabbing into the dry surface of her eyes.

Voronov came out of his room in the morning and after finding her up each time, he hadn't said anything, but he had become more watchful.

She digs a thumb into her temple and takes a sip of the hot coffee, making a mental note to pass by a pharmacy and see if she can pick up some eye drops, anything to ease the soreness that she's been dealing with.

At least they'd finally be getting Rampaul back. They'd heard from her last night. The family homicide case she'd been working on with her partner the last week had wrapped up, with arrests made yesterday. It had been on the evening news, though it had been Rampaul's partner's face, and not Rampaul's, that had been on the screen.

She'd be back with them today so that was something at least.

Isabel keeps her eye on the entrance of the hotel. It's around the corner from a busy Oxford Street, right at the end of the street after a structure covered in scaffolding, but the building resembles a block of flats, and not the kind that Isabel is staying in right now, but like the ones she's seen in the clearly more deprived areas. She wonders if maybe in the past that's what it was before they converted it into a hotel. However, its entrance leaves no question that this is an upmarket hotel.

The entrance is wide and colourful, with plants bursting green on either side of its double doors and an overhang that is sea-green and a little translucent, the early-morning sun pooling over it to give it a soft glow. A quick check online had told Isabel that the six-floor building has a five-star rating and a popular rooftop bar with a spectacular 360-degree skyline view. The prices had her wincing.

There is only one entrance for guests, which is the one Isabel is staring at right now from her perch inside the café.

Cross had checked into this hotel the same day her flight had landed.

Despite Adam's efforts, he had found no links between guests who checked in the same day as Cross to the names on the flight manifest; he'd moved on to the surrounding hotels but still nothing. Cross's hotel also hadn't logged any calls to her room or from it. It was likely she was using her mobile phone for that. To their knowledge she hadn't received any visitors either.

As for Cross herself, Isabel had had a word with the staff. She didn't leave the hotel much, though they had seen her leaving a couple of times. They'd been helpful in checking key card times and Isabel had them send a copy of those records over to Adam. Aside from the day she had gone to the station for the interview, the breaks away from her room hadn't been that long, consistent with someone heading out to stretch their legs for a bit. There were some that were longer, particularly the ones in the evening, but those coincided with reservations made in the hotel's own restaurant. Some others didn't.

The day of the incident at the embassy, she had the only significantly large gap, from 8.37 a.m. to 3.03 p.m.

After Anabel's specific request for information regarding Cross, Isabel wants to know where she spent that six-hour block of time.

In the last three days Isabel has spent here, she's seen Cross leave the hotel twice. She hadn't needed the car she'd borrowed from the MCIU to find out where she'd gone.

One of those trips had been to a coffee shop a few doors down from the one Isabel is sitting in right now. She'd bagged a coffee and a pastry and then headed back to the hotel. The second had been a longer trip to an express grocery store, smaller than the bigger chains Isabel had seen dotted around, but Cross had spent some time inside browsing through the limited aisles and what they'd had to offer. She had bought a bag full of snacks and drinks. She'd been on her phone the entire time but mindful of being seen, Isabel kept her distance so she hadn't been able to hear any of it.

But she'd been close enough to use her Gift.

It was curious, then, that Isabel had gleaned absolutely nothing from her. Cross's barriers were high, and well formed. Maybe due to the nature of her work, that's to be expected.

Isabel ignores the voice in the back of her head that tells her that if she truly tried, she could get past them if she wanted.

Voronov hasn't done much better with his watch over Joana Weir, though at least he's seen more movement at his end. Unlike Cross, Joana Weir doesn't seem to enjoy being cooped up in the little flat she's staying in in Angel, Islington. She often leaves to go and sit in the park and work, and goes out frequently throughout the day to stretch her legs before returning. But other than that, he hasn't reported anything of note from his time keeping an eye on her either.

The problem is, they've only got so long. Other than the morning to evening watch, without the additional manpower, they have to leave to get some rest. Well. They're supposed to get some rest. Voronov does, anyway.

In Weir's case, there's no way to monitor if she has left her place at night. They've located the owner of the listing where she's staying but so far haven't had a response from them. Joana gets into the property using a code, but they don't know if those logs are viewable by the owner, or if they get any logs at all. There's no way to tell when she comes or goes unless someone is there to see it.

At least with Cross, Isabel can check with hotel staff.

She hasn't left though.

The vibration of Isabel's phone startles her out of her thoughts. Isabel sets her cup down. The noise of the phone gets her a few glances from those in the café queue that don't have their ears plugged by earphones or aren't on a phone call.

She sees her brother's name on it and picks it up with a soft smile. She misses him.

'Hey mano,' she says, 'how are you?' She lifts her gaze back to the entrance of the hotel.

'Good, good, just checking on my maninha who hasn't called once since she left for London,' Sebastião says by way of greeting.

Isabel winces even as she's comforted by the sound of his voice. 'Sorry, it's been intense over here. How are you? How are Tigre and Branca?' she asks. It hasn't been a week but she's missing her dogs more than anything. The warm enjoyment and love they invariably emanate are a balm to her always worn senses.

'They're good. They're good. They'll be all over you when you get back.'

'Hmm,' she says, 'and you?'

She hears his sigh across the line and he sounds as tired as she feels. 'I'm okay. I spoke to Rita. You didn't tell me you guys argued before you left.'

Oh great. This is the last thing she needs. 'Is that why you're really calling?' Isabel asks.

'No. I just want to make sure you're okay.'

'Because she told me she doesn't want me involved in their wedding anymore? Yeah. I'm fine. I didn't want anything to do with it in the first place.' Her sister Rita had kept her relationship with Isabel's ex-partner under wraps only to tell her the truth when the two of them got engaged. It had been the shortest family dinner of Isabel's life.

'Isa.'

'I don't have time to deal with whatever paranoia she's developed about her fiancé's association with me. She doesn't want me involved, that works pretty well for me. It's not as if she needs me there. She's got her precious mum there and she'll have you and tia.'

'Tia Maria is your mum too,' he says quietly.

Isabel shakes her head. A young mother and her little girl walk past the coffee shop window, the grey bunny in the little girl's arms bouncing around with her skipping steps. 'We both know she hasn't been my mother in a very long time.'

Sebastião doesn't say anything and that makes Isabel think back to a couple of nights ago, when she had been standing outside her mother's house, except it hadn't been Isabel herself standing there.

Daniel had checked in and had assured her everything was fine and nothing had happened. But now . . .

'Hey,' she says quietly, 'mano, is everything okay over there?' She tightens her hand on her coffee cup subconsciously and has to snatch it back when the drink threatens to overspill.

'Everything is fine, maninha. I just wanted to check you're okay over there. And because I'm missing you over here, hmm.'

Isabel relaxes back into her chair. 'Okay. Well . . . I don't know when we're going to wrap up here. But I'll let you know as soon as we've got a better idea.'

'All right. I love you, maninha.'

'I love you too.'

She hangs up and sets her phone down with a sigh, momentarily distracted by the conversation she'd just had and irritation at her sister. The messages Rita and her fiancé had sent her are still on her phone. Isabel had been debating deleting them both without reading them, but she hadn't been able to do it because some stupid part of her would feel guilty about it. Which makes no sense because she has no intention of reading them.

Her phone rings again. This time the display shows no caller ID.

'Reis here.'

'Good morning, Inspector Reis.'

Isabel stills and the hand that had the cup of coffee halfway to her mouth again freezes.

'Anabel,' she greets her calmly. 'This is a private number,' she says, her tone gently curious, but pointed. There aren't too many people she could have got it from. One was Joana Weir and the others were Ian Russell and his wife. Isabel doubts that Tracy

Russell would have given her anything, though given how much it took to get her to even talk to them last time, she wonders if Tracy would have let them know if her husband had been in touch with Anabel. She clearly doesn't like Anabel, but that is obviously not enough to have her throw Anabel under the bus again, no matter that she would personally like to see Anabel caught.

So, the likeliest source is Weir.

'How are you, Isabel? Do you mind if I call you Isabel?'

Isabel flicks the rim of the cup with her thumbnail, alert as the sliding doors to the hotel open and a couple walks out, and then another man, nose buried in his phone, behind them. The doors shut again, and the people walk down the side of the street.

'No,' Isabel says, 'I don't mind at all.'

'Good,' Anabel sighs in her ear; it sounds a little tired, and honest. 'It makes me feel more comfortable.'

Isabel nods even though she knows Anabel isn't there to see it. 'No problem. Then we'll both be comfortable. I take it you've been speaking with Miss Weir?'

Anabel makes a humming sound that is neither confirmation nor denial. 'How did it go? I wanted to give you time to do your due diligence.'

This time if she is in a public space, it's an enclosed one, and very quiet. Isabel doesn't pick up any additional sounds from around her. No faraway voices, not even ones that could be picked up from a TV being on nearby. Nothing that indicates movement or activity of any kind.

'We did,' Isabel says. 'We learned some interesting things but I'm not sure if it will be all that interesting from your perspective.'

'I'm sure it will be. What did the stiffs from Foreign Affairs say?' Anabel asks.

A woman with six dogs on a leash, looking as if she's being led by them instead of the other way around, walks past the entrance of the hotel.

Isabel tracks them as they get to the end, feeling a pang as, briefly, she's reminded of her own dogs, far away. She's been missing them and the comfort they offer every night she's been here.

'They said that they'll still fulfil the request for citizenship, provided that you're cleared as a suspect from this investigation and pending the information you promised to deliver to them, and the second citizenship will be granted only when you disclose the identity of who it is for, and then only if they deem it appropriate based on who that is.'

Anabel gives another one of those hums, followed by another sigh. She sounds, Isabel thinks, like someone who is deep in thought, and staring off into space as she talks. That's the image Isabel has of her in her head right now.

'Who is the second person, Anabel?' Isabel asks.

'Does it matter?' Anabel asks.

'If it doesn't matter then why withhold their identity? Things are complicated enough for you as it is,' Isabel says, 'not revealing the identity of the second person you want to bargain for complicates things further and I don't think you'd do that unless you had reason to. Someone to protect, maybe?' Isabel asks. Because the truth is, why else would she be keeping that quiet? She needs these citizenships granted as fast as possible and giving that name right away would have sped things along. She hasn't done that though.

So, it's one of two things. Someone she's either protecting, or someone who has a hold on her, pulling the strings to keep her from moving forward.

But a gut instinct tells Isabel it's more likely to be the former, not the latter. Not that that means anything. Nothing ever means anything without evidence to back it up.

'You want me to be honest, Isabel? I think I might actually tell you. But I can't just yet.'

'What *can* you tell me?' Isabel asks.

Anabel laughs softly. 'Not as much as I'd like to. Isn't it odd? Why do I feel like I can trust you?'

It's an entirely different conversation to the one they'd had the first time. Then, Anabel's self-assuredness had been clear, as had her determination to keep the police at arms length. She sounds different now. She sounds tired.

'You can,' Isabel says, 'but I won't lie to you. You know my presence here is in an investigative capacity. But I can promise you that if you're honest with me, then I will do my best to help you where I am able to.'

Anabel laughs again. 'There. See that? Why do I believe you? You would have thought I'd have learned my lesson by now.'

Isabel pulls her notebook out of her pocket, and the garish green mechanical pencil she'd swiped from Rampaul's desk a couple of days ago.

She flips to a blank page quickly and scrawls: *betrayed?* She draws a loop around it. Someone she's trusted in the past has definitely made a mark here. Doesn't mean it's related to their case. But details are everything.

'What about Dr Cross?' Anabel asks.

That's another interesting thing. That she still refers to her as Dr Cross. Not Eliana, not Cross. But Dr Cross. A sign of lingering respect? Force of habit? Or maybe they had never been as close as Eliana had implied they were.

'We're still working on it. Who are you hoping we'll find?' She quickly scribbles another note down. *Person expected – second citizenship?*

'I was just curious.'

Isabel lays the pencil down and picks her coffee up, eyes flicking back up to the hotel entrance. 'I thought you wanted to trust me.'

'To be honest, I didn't have much faith in your people doing as I asked.'

'It wasn't out of the goodness of our hearts,' Isabel says, 'you know that. Actually, that brings me to a different point. I'm hoping you'll be able to talk to me about it this time.'

'Okay. I guess that's fair. Ask your question, Isabel.'

'We have CCTV surveillance of you outside the embassy shortly after the incident took place. You were in a hoodie, with a backpack. The CCTV is from a small boutique shop across the street.'

Anabel falls silent.

Isabel eases back into her seat, swirls the coffee inside the cup, notes that there's less than half left and she'll probably have to wait a while before she can have another one. 'I do want to help you. But you have to let me.'

'It's not that simple.' Her words this time are short, more reminiscent of the first phone call where she had been all business. But they've built something here and Isabel doesn't want them sliding back.

'All right. Let's try this another way. Let me tell you what I know?' Isabel hopes she's reading this right, that she's reading Anabel right.

There's a pause. Then: 'Tell me.'

Isabel finishes the coffee, sitting up properly again. The bell over the café's door rings as a customer opens it to leave.

The hotel's doors haven't opened since the last people left.

'I know that you're an extremely intelligent woman. You sped through school, wrapped up university early and ended up in the military, leading on ground-breaking industry research within the Gifted field. I know that you speak at conferences and have written a good number of papers. You're a respected name in your field. Dr Cross has called you brilliant and Ian Russell considers you a highly talented individual and colleague.' And more than that, but Isabel leaves that out. Isabel lowers her voice and turns away from the other customers, wanting to keep this as quiet as possible because you never know. 'The question I'm asking myself is why would someone as intelligent as you, with all the respectability you've attained, take a risk as big as taking something from the US military, running across the world and then locking yourself up in an embassy. What kind of thing would lead someone as esteemed as you to bargain in this way?'

Anabel doesn't say anything else.

'Cross is someone who you've been working with since you finished university. You've been working closely with her for the entirety of your career. But from how you left, whatever it is you took with you, it's something you weren't able to confide in her. You don't trust her.'

The quiet persists and Isabel thinks maybe this is it and that she won't be able to keep her talking anymore.

She opens her mouth to try again but before she can, Anabel answers.

'Dr Cross is an incredible woman. You're right, she's been with me from the start. She was even there when I was in high school. Did you know that?'

'No, I didn't.'

'My family weren't the most well off financially, but I was lucky. Got my hands on scholarships, but I was moving quite fast. Dr Cross was able to help with that. I interned with her throughout my time in college. It was amazing. Exciting. I learned so much.'

She's been with her longer than Isabel had anticipated. It makes this entire situation odder. Despite the fact that it is no longer the case, there's a touch of wonder, of nostalgia, in Anabel's voice. Clearly this is someone she felt respect for, maybe even, great affection.

'But things changed.'

'What changed?' Isabel asks.

'We didn't have the same values.'

'Did you turn on her?'

'I'm sure that's probably how she feels. I don't see it that way. I respected her. I thought I could get her to listen to me . . .' Anabel scoffs. 'Now look at me. Look at this whole mess.' She laughs, self-deprecating, and then falls silent.

'Anabel,' Isabel says, 'are you responsible for the deaths of those at the embassy?'

Silence.

'Anabel?'

'Responsible . . . maybe. But I wouldn't be the only one. I don't think it would be fair to say I was the only one.'

'Who else? The ambassador? Cross?'

But Anabel doesn't give her any more. 'I hope . . . I do hope we get to speak again, Isabel. I mean that.'

There's no chance for Isabel to ask anything else. The dial tone beeps in fast succession in Isabel's ear before the line falls silent.

Isabel swears under her breath.

She sets her phone down, pushes her hair back from her face and glances over at the few words she'd jotted down in her notebook. She picks up her pencil and writes down Cross's name, underlines it twice and then sits back, staring at it.

She's involved here.

Whatever Anabel had found she'd gone to Cross with it first. Isabel's sure of it. But she hadn't received the support she expected. That or something else. It's the only thing that would have got someone like Anabel into such a vulnerable position and at the mercy of an unfamiliar government she'd inherited as part of previous generations of her family. It had probably been the next best option. Either that, or there was another reason she'd picked Portugal out. Given the nature of the projects she had worked on and her expertise in Gifted research, whatever she'd taken with her might be good leverage. Portugal has a reputation in the Gifted field, an unexpected one, given that it is a small country that otherwise keeps to itself. Still, if whatever Anabel has is good enough, there are plenty of other countries which will be willing to bargain with her for it.

What is it? What is it that she took?

'I need another coffee.'

Her head is pulsing with an ache that's been with her for a while now. It's due to the exhaustion and the constant pouring of her energy into guarding not just against the people outside her head, but the one hiding within it.

Before she can get up to go and grab another coffee – despite knowing she really should give it a bit of time – her phone starts ringing again.

This time the screen has DI Rampaul lit up.

Isabel picks up, checks the hotel entrance again as she takes the empty cup to go and toss it in the bin. 'So you've returned?' she says by way of greeting. 'I've got an update for you, actually.'

'It'll have to wait. How fast can you get here?' Rampaul says.

Isabel stops, frowns. 'I don't know,' she says, 'it's probably rush hour but hopefully not longer than half an hour. Why? What's wrong?'

'We're on the news.'

# 35

When Isabel reaches the car park at the police station, she sees Voronov up ahead, getting out of Adam's car.

'Hey,' she says, resting a hand on the roof of the car as she gets out. She's parked closer to the door leading into the station.

The sky is overcast today, and though it's already warm, the breeze has a chill to it that lingers in the shadow of the buildings towering over them. Right now, the building on the other side of the car park is blocking out the sun and Isabel feels the loss of warmth.

'Did Rampaul tell you?' she asks.

'Yes,' he says, stopping beside her and waiting for her to get her things out, 'it's on all the news channels here and it's spread quickly. It's all over the news back home as well.'

Isabel slams the door of the car shut and shrugs her bag on to her shoulder. 'To be honest, I'm surprised it didn't get out sooner.' She shakes her head. 'This has been handled all wrong from the start. We should have made a statement to the press days ago. This was always going to be bad if it was leaked.' She doesn't realise she's stopped for Voronov to open the door for her until he's already done it and then she scowls right after. 'Like he's got me trained,' she mutters as she goes on ahead. She doesn't miss the smirk on his face when he overhears it.

She hadn't realised how much she'd been holding on to the tension of what had happened the night he'd dragged her back from the balcony, until she feels it ease at the sight of his smile.

They still haven't discussed that night properly. By the time they've got back after being on stakeouts all day, neither of them does more than exchange a few words before falling into their individual wind-down rituals. Voronov's been making use of the gym downstairs and Isabel heads out for her run along the river, even if her body isn't too happy with how much she's been pushing it.

'Well, we have one more update.'

Voronov looks at her, falling behind her as they head up the stairs and a number of officers run past them on the other side, full speed ahead. 'Cross?'

Isabel watches them go for a second as she continues up, shaking her head. 'I was keeping watch and got a call from Anabel Pereira.'

Voronov stops, a step below her. Isabel stops too.

'Personal phone?'

Isabel nods. 'Yes. My best guess is she got it from Joana Weir. When I asked Anabel if she'd been speaking to her, she didn't confirm or deny. You were keeping watch. Did you see anything?'

Voronov's gaze drifts off past her shoulder as he thinks on it. 'Not that I saw,' he says. 'Each time I saw her outside, she didn't take or make any calls. If they spoke it would have been when she was inside the apartment. They could have spoken for hours, and we wouldn't know.'

'Yeah.' Isabel sighs and continues on up the stairs.

Voronov easily falls into step beside her. 'Anything?' he asks.

'I got the sense that things between her and Cross were more antagonistic than we might have expected,' she says. 'I asked her about the second citizenship request, but she kept her mouth shut on that. Got nothing out of her. But I'm wondering if it's related to the request she made of us, about someone coming with Cross.'

'If it's for someone who came in with Cross, why would she bargain on their behalf?'

Isabel bites her lip, shaking her head. 'I don't know.'

As they walk out into the main office, they spot Rampaul and Adam standing by the partition next to Rampaul's desk. It's the least put-together Isabel has seen her. She's wearing a rumpled grey T-shirt, black jeans and a pair of beat-up trainers. Her hair is up and although she is still striking, there's a visible layer of exhaustion over her.

She's got her arms resting on top of the partition and a foot tapping impatiently on the floor.

When she spots Isabel and Voronov heading their way, she straightens up and motions for Adam to follow her, walking up to meet them part-way.

'Sorry to make you guys rush, but we're pressed for time. The chief wants to speak to us.'

Isabel blinks. 'Us?'

Despite the situation, there's a grim satisfaction running through Rampaul that's palpable.

Given the severity of the situation, it throws Isabel off.

Rampaul is way too calm.

'Yeah,' Rampaul says, 'I think he wants to say hello properly this time. Let's go.'

Isabel watches her back as she starts towards the chief's office, still unsure about what she's picking up from Rampaul.

Voronov gives her a questioning look, but Isabel only shakes her head and follows after Rampaul.

The chief's office is one floor up from where Isabel and Voronov have been working with Rampaul and Adam. It's the only enclosed room in this open-plan space. Isabel has no idea what department this is. They've never gone this far up into the building.

Like the people downstairs, the staff up here watch them closely. Oh, they carry on their conversations, but their eyes keep flicking over to their procession like they're expecting fireworks. Isabel suspects they're about to get them.

Rampaul heads straight over to the one office. It has glass doors, but they can't see into it because the blinds inside are down. She raps her knuckles on the door and gets a curt 'come in' from inside.

238

Rampaul gives them all a brief look, as if telling them to brace themselves, and then opens it and goes inside.

The office that the door opens into is a spacious one. Definitely bigger than the one their chief has back at their precinct at home. Isabel hadn't expected it to be as cosy as it is, given what she's seen of the rest of the station.

Beige walls and a big window that lets in a good amount of natural light. The desk itself is huge and sits in the centre of the room. There's a small kitchenette in the corner, complete with a little fridge. Two very comfortable-looking chairs – are those *leather*? – are set out for guests in front of the desk which the chief of the MCIU is currently sitting behind. The name plate on his desk reads: Superintendent William McKinley.

Isabel is surprised when she sees him up close. He's wearing a neat white shirt and dark suit trousers, both fitting him perfectly well. His blond hair is thick and neatly combed back, his face is made up of strong bones and there's a severity to it that's marred only by big blue eyes that give him a touch of boyishness. Probably a very handsome man by most standards, but right now his thin lips pressed together in disapproval and the whirl of irritation and personal affront swirling around him, as if this situation had been done *to* him, makes him utterly unappealing.

He doesn't make a good first impression.

He doesn't get up and he doesn't greet them. Instead, he stabs a finger in their direction. 'Get in here and shut that bloody door.'

Isabel can't help thinking that Chief Bautista would eat him for breakfast.

It's unsurprising given the way that he's been directing this entire case. An unimpressive man with an ego. Even his presence is weak.

He's also forgetting the part where he is not Isabel's, or Voronov's, boss.

Still, she walks in after Rampaul, Voronov at her side, and Adam comes in last, pulling the door closed behind him.

'How did this get out?' he yells.

What was the point in Adam closing the door? Isabel thinks, at this rate, everyone and their grandmother can hear that.

Isabel folds her lips together and clasps her hands behind her. They haven't even seen what 'this' is, even if she does have a good idea.

Rampaul, standing closest to him, is resting her hands on the back of the chair on the left. Her response is calm and composed. 'I don't know.' Beneath it though, she is anything but. She's seething. And standing here, in the room with her, it quickly becomes apparent that she hates this man.

'You *don't know*? Remind me, Detective Inspector, who is leading this investigation?' He's spitting the words out through gritted teeth but at least he's keeping the volume down.

Rampaul stands straighter. 'Considering how *small* the team I've been given to work this case is, I think it's easy to see that the leaks did not come from us. *Maybe*,' Rampaul says, speaking fast when McKinley opens his mouth again to speak, 'it's one of the family members who still have not received any answers. Answers they might have already had, if this investigation had been afforded the resources that it clearly warrants.'

Well.

Isabel clenches her jaw and keeps her gaze somewhere else to keep the satisfied curl of her mouth down.

That was well delivered.

'Why do you need more resources?' McKinley stands and gestures at Isabel, Voronov and Adam standing in the back. 'The Portuguese government,' he says, and cuts a look at them as he practically sneers the words, 'were kind enough to lend us two of their best. One of whom, I'm told, is a telepathic Gifted. It's up to you how you handle the team you were given and if you've failed to put an asset to good use, then that's on you, isn't it?'

That wipes away any traces of satisfaction Isabel may have felt.

An asset.

At her side, she feels the quiet pulse of Voronov's anger stir, a nascent red.

She takes a deep breath. Her mouth stays shut. Probably for the best.

'I disagree,' Rampaul says. 'Inspector Reis and Inspector Voronov, as well as DC Duncan, have been doing exemplary work. But as I've said before, on more than one occasion, this is a high-profile case, with multiple deaths and the potential to disturb political relationships. The help we have been given is *not* enough.'

'Watch your tone, Detective Inspector.'

'Apologies for interrupting.'

Isabel glances at Voronov in surprise, as do McKinley and Rampaul. But whereas Rampaul doesn't seem to mind the interruption, Isabel can't say the same for McKinley. Red starts blooming at the point where the white collar of his shirt meets his neck, and it travels all the way up to stain his cheeks in blotches.

'It feels like we're getting carried away from the main point. I assumed we were asked to be here to discuss next steps and damage control,' Voronov says. He is as always, unfailingly polite, but there's frost in his tone and the stare he pins on McKinley is the kind that people usually reserve for pests crawling around in the gutter.

Rampaul nods. 'You're right, we don't have much time. What do you want us to do?' she asks. 'It won't take the press very long to figure out who is handling this investigation and they'll be knocking on our doors soon enough.'

'We're calling a press conference; the relevant media contacts have already been told and will be here at midday today. I want you and DC Duncan there. The statement is being drafted as we speak; go and liaise with the communications manager.' He rakes a look over Rampaul. 'Get changed into something decent. We have appearances to maintain.'

Rampaul grits her teeth. 'Of course.'

'I've already had a call about this from the higher-ups. Keep it short and concise. I don't want any panic, understand?'

'Yes.'

'Good. Get a report on my desk for tomorrow morning. I'll see what other resources we can allocate to this.'

'Thank you, sir.'

Assuming they've been dismissed, Rampaul turns, meeting Isabel's eyes and indicating that they should go.

'As for you, Inspector Reis,' the chief calls out.

Isabel pauses on her way out. 'Yes?'

'Shouldn't you be putting your skills to good use? That's why your boss sent you here, isn't it. You and your partner are the best of the best, I'm told. Solved quite a few high-profile cases. So, I'd suggest trying a little harder. If you can read minds, shouldn't this all have been made easier for you?'

Even Rampaul is frowning. 'Sir—'

Voronov has taken half a step back towards him and although she can't see Adam, she can feel his resentment, rising from his spot behind them, by the door.

Isabel holds out a hand to stay them as she turns to fully face McKinley. 'I think you're confused about something,' she says, deliberately omitting any kind of honorific.

It doesn't go unnoticed, and his eyes narrow on her face.

'I don't work for you, neither does my partner. Also, perhaps you should read up on the use of Gifts in the workforce. Using my Gift is not a requirement for my role and when I do use it, I do it at *my* discretion and no one else's. I'd suggest investing more time and money into this investigation if you want it to go anywhere.' She turns to go and then stops. 'I would be careful if I were you, sir. Now that the press is out there, if they were to ask me or my colleague about the case, and its progress, we wouldn't want me to be too honest about the reason why we're so far behind, now would we?'

He stands up so fast he almost knocks his chair back, hands laid flat on his desk.

'We'll see you at the press conference.' Isabel gestures for the rest of them to head out and then pulls the door closed behind her.

For a moment they all stand there, Isabel's hand still locked around the door handle.

Then she lets out a long breath.

'Okay,' she says, and lifts her hand to rub at her forehead, 'so, should we go and find out how bad this really is?'

# 36

It's bad.

They're back in their case room.

The buzz that had followed their arrival back on their floor had been noticeable. Seemed like enough had been overheard upstairs that it had somehow already reached the floor below before they'd even got there.

They'd ignored it all and headed straight for their room.

Rampaul had pulled up one of the news channels and they were watching the video now.

The reporter was outside the Portuguese Embassy.

'– told the incident took place in the early hours of last Tuesday morning and reportedly twelve members of staff were found dead. We have reached out to families, and they can confirm that there has not yet been a breakthrough in the investigation. However, our sources tell us that there is a potential suspect and that they are currently on the loose. The suspect is said to have been a US citizen who was being harboured by the Portuguese government, though details are still unclear as to why and how the two things may be connected. Francis, back to you.'

As the coverage stops and the channel switches back to the news anchor, the reel at the bottom of the screen continues to circulate the case as breaking news.

Rampaul mutes the monitor and walks over to the window, driving her hands through her hair before checking the watch on her wrist.

'I need to go home, get changed,' she says, voice low.

Now that they've stopped properly, the dark circles under her eyes are more apparent. She's still bursting with the same frustration and anger that had been spilling out of her since they'd walked out of McKinley's office.

'I wonder how they got this much information,' Voronov says. 'I understand the victims' families speaking to the press but they wouldn't have known about Anabel Pereira.'

Isabel leans back and crosses her arms over her chest. 'There are a few who could have done it. There's Grosz or Cheever. Maybe even Weir. Though Voronov has been on her tail so less likely to be her.' Again there was no way to know for sure.

Rampaul presses her hands to her eyes and takes a deep breath. 'Okay, get me up to speed. Where are we at?'

Adam does the honours. Takes her through what they got out of the conversation with the Portuguese Foreign Affairs officials, what they had Daniel and Carla following up back in Lisbon and the latest on the CCTV and Isabel and Voronov setting up shop outside where Cross and Weir are staying.

'Anything from there?' Rampaul asks.

'No,' Isabel says, 'Cross stays in her room, barely going out. The few times she has gone out it hasn't been for anything significant. But, as you pointed out up there,' Isabel flicks a glance up at the ceiling, 'resources are scarce so what exactly they're getting up to in the evening, we're less sure of.'

Rampaul nods. 'And Weir?' she asks Voronov.

'Similar results.'

'Which is to say, nothing?'

He nods. 'Nothing that stands out.'

'Of course.' She sighs and then mutters. 'Fuck, I'm tired.'

A brief thought intrudes, heavy and large, and bad enough that Isabel almost grunts under the weight of it.

It's not her own thought.

It's Rampaul's. A memory. Recent. It's sharp in its freshness.

The image that fills Isabel's mind in that split second is enough to make her stomach turn.

That of two small bodies at a kitchen table. Faces turned to the side, empty eyes open. Hands bound and limp on their laps. Blood pooling on the table from cuts on their necks, deep and gaping like a smile, the flesh drooping open. A woman at the head of the table, sitting up straight, head limp. Blood pouring from a similar wound cut into her throat. Her yellow T-shirt turned brown all down the front from where the blood had sunk into the material. And a man, hanging from a light fixture, his bare toes grazing the dinner table.

Isabel shuts her eyes against it, turns her face away to escape from it.

She doesn't have to. The memory is shoved down by Rampaul as quickly as it emerges.

This is the case that Rampaul had been pulled away to.

Isabel slides a look her way and finds her standing with her hands on her hips, eyes staring down at the floor.

'Rampaul,' Isabel says.

She lifts her head and meets Isabel's eyes.

Isabel sees the change in her expression when she realises Isabel knows. That Isabel has just seen what she saw. Her face shuts down and she turns away.

'I have something to add,' Isabel says. 'Anabel Pereira got in contact with me again today.'

Rampaul turns back to her and Adam, who apart from bringing Rampaul up to speed has been in the same spot, staring stonily into one corner of the room, since they returned from McKinley's, jerks his head up.

'What do you mean, she contacted you again?' Rampaul frowns. 'Is this the update you mentioned earlier?'

'Yes. She called me on my mobile phone. I don't know how she got my number but suspect it might have been from Weir.'

'And?'

'She still won't confirm or deny if she's the one who caused the deaths of the people at the embassy. But I told Voronov that I think maybe there could be a connection between the person she's requesting the second citizenship for and the person she had us checking for, to see if they'd arrived with Cross. Her relationship

246

with Cross is also not as nice as Cross wanted us to think. Something took place there, and whatever that is, I think it's directly responsible for Anabel's presence here in the UK and at the Portuguese Embassy.'

Rampaul glances at them all. 'Okay. So, we're taking a closer look at Cross?'

'I think it's worth it, yes.'

'All right. Let's go with it. It's the only thing we have that isn't a total loss. We need to find the connection here.' She looks at Isabel. 'You've spoken to Anabel twice now.'

'Yes,' she says.

'What do you think?' Rampaul asks. 'Do you think she did it?'

Isabel thinks about the conversations they had both times, how different they had been. There had been something in the second one that had felt . . . almost like resignation.

But like the interview they had conducted with Milena Amorim and Rogério Pessoa, it had been something done through a different medium. Not in person. With no way for Isabel to feel her way through their emotions in the conversation for an indication of what might be true and what might not.

'I think she's capable of it,' Isabel says slowly. 'At first I thought, wouldn't she be saying she was innocent if she was? Especially after I told her that the Foreign Affairs Department has said they still plan on honouring their agreement with her as long as she's cleared. But she didn't say that. She didn't say anything.' Isabel doesn't get it. 'If she did do it, she can lie and say she didn't. After all it's not like anyone survived to tell the tale. We have no witnesses or the necessary surveillance within the building. We know the deaths were caused by the use of telekinesis. But other than the olfactory trace it leaves behind in the space where it is used, there are no genetic markers, no fingerprints. There's no way to point to someone and say with absolute certainty that it was them. Even if they were the only person in the building with telekinesis at the time.'

'Isn't there?' Adam says. He says it quietly, almost like he hopes they won't hear it.

'*Is* there?' Rampaul asks.

Adam meets Isabel's eyes briefly and before glancing away, like he can't quite do it. 'Won't you be able to tell?' he asks.

Rampaul waits, expectant.

She knows Voronov is looking at her too.

'I think we have a press conference to prepare for,' Isabel says, 'and I've got a headache I need to get rid of.'

# 37

At 3.00 p.m., Isabel and Voronov stand at the back of one of the bigger rooms situated on the ground floor.

By the time the two of them enter, the room is packed to the brim with journalists.

As she looks around the room, Isabel wonders how many correspondents for American and Portuguese news are also in here, and many more besides that, on a case that has the potential to become a diplomatic disaster in more ways than one.

At the head of the room, cleaned up, are McKinley, Rampaul and Adam. There's a young woman in a two-piece white suit there too, clutching a clipboard to her chest and bending to speak to the three of them. Probably she is from the team in charge of comms. The conference itself hasn't started yet.

Isabel takes a deep breath and fortifies her walls.

The room is filled with noise. Noise crowding into every corner, every crevice, filled with greed and excitement and ambition, staining the walls of the room itself.

A few months ago, this many people in an enclosed space, with this level of excitement, would have had her on her knees.

It's still overwhelming now, especially without decent rest. It helps that she's finally started getting used to operating in such an environment. She hopes that this wraps up quickly.

The woman who had been speaking with Rampaul and Adam leans over the table that they're sitting at and speaks into the microphone.

'The press conference will now begin.'

'Thank you all for joining us today,' McKinley says. He's sitting on the far left of the table, all well put together and composed, showing a completely different front to what they had seen in his office a few hours ago.

'As you are by now aware, the MCIU is investigating the deaths of twelve members of staff from the Portuguese Embassy, located in Golden Square, Soho. The incident took place last Tuesday morning.' He glances to his side and gestures to Rampaul and Adam. 'Detective Inspector Rampaul is our Senior Investigative Officer on this case and has been working with the assistance of Detective Constable Duncan as well as Inspectors Reis and Voronov of Portugal's Judiciary Police. DI Rampaul will now provide you with a brief overview of the case facts.'

Rampaul leans closer to the mic.

'Thank you. In addition to what Superintendent McKinley has outlined for you already, I want to first assure the public that we are pursuing every possible lead with the assistance of the Portuguese Judiciary Police. Currently we have a strong lead where we are focusing our efforts.' She takes a deep breath and although it's probably not noticeable to everyone else, Isabel sees her visibly brace herself for what she's about to say next.

When she remains quiet and doesn't continue, McKinley turns to watch her, face calm.

She must see it because she takes a deep breath and speaks into the mic again.

'We have identified the cause of death and believe this was caused by a Gifted individual with high-level telekinesis.'

Isabel stares, her mouth dropping open as voices erupt in a frothing chorus, all clamouring for attention and wanting to squeeze their questions in.

This is – an announcement like this is—

Questions are being yelled out and the coalescing thoughts of so many people are reaching a fever pitch that is making Isabel's walls start to buckle under the strain.

She straightens away from the wall and leaves as she hears Rampaul attempt to restore order over the press crowd.

She walks fast, as fast as she can to put distance between her and that room. She doesn't even process the fact that she's left the building completely until she's already standing outside and striding towards the park at the other end of the road.

The road is lined with vans and cars that hadn't been there when they'd arrived earlier. Some of those are already getting tickets because of the way they've been parked. Isabel briefly watches the ticketing officer making his way down the road, stopping at one after the other.

The heat is thick in the air, heavier than it has been throughout the day, and she shrugs out of the light jacket she's wearing and wipes the back of her wrist over her forehead.

The headache has taken hold properly and sits squarely on her temples and the top of her skull. She would gladly dunk her head in an ice bucket but since that's not an option right now, she'll make do with some air.

She's in the park, sitting on one of the swings, feet pushing her to and fro, by the time Voronov finds her.

Isabel looks up when his large shadow falls over her, squinting up at him. Even through the clouds, the brightness is intense.

'Sorry,' she says, 'didn't mean to do a dramatic exit but the voices in there got pretty loud.'

'No one noticed.'

'You did.'

Voronov moves over to the other swing and Isabel watches with scepticism as the seat and the chains all creak under his weight.

'One day you're going to break something,' she says, 'I keep telling you. The swings are for children.'

He scoffs, the sound soft and kicking up the corner of his mouth. 'It will hold.'

Isabel sighs and leans her head against one of the chains holding the swing in place. There's a small voice in her head telling her that it has been grasped in many little hands that were most likely less than clean. But the metal is cool against her forehead and so she makes an allowance.

The road is quiet save for a few passing cars.

'That press conference,' she says.

Voronov leans forward, resting his arms on his knees, listening.

'What Rampaul just announced in there is going to have repercussions beyond this case.'

Voronov looks away. 'I know.'

'They didn't need to know that. There was no need for that to be out there. We could have disclosed that to the families privately and confidentially.'

'Rampaul isn't careless. I think that came from McKinley.'

'I think so too.'

The two of them stay there, quiet on the swings.

The silence is only broken when people start pouring out of the station some ten minutes later. It's the press, all of them exiting the building, chatter excited and loud as they head over to their vehicles. Some of them groan when they spy the ticket that's been left tucked beneath windscreen wipers.

Isabel's phone rings for the third time that day.

Rampaul.

'I guess it's time to go back.'

# 38

Isabel watches as Adam approaches the table, pints in hand and a big grin on his face. Rampaul follows behind him, holding two more.

The pub is pretty, like something out of a Shakespearean play, and it overlooks a small docking berth. It's packed to the nines, so Isabel has chosen a table outside, the furthest away from the building itself.

Voronov takes a beer from Rampaul with a thank-you as Adam sets one down in front of Isabel and then climbs on to the bench on the opposite side.

Rampaul lets out a heavy sigh and lifts the drink. 'Well. To the day being over.'

They all lift their drinks and say cheers to that.

Isabel takes an experimental sip, licking the foam off her top lip. The beer is heavier than she's used to, thicker on the tongue.

Rampaul swallows more than a few gulps at once.

To be fair, she probably needs it.

When they'd met back at the car park, whatever energy had been left in her was gone.

She sets her glass down with a thunk and wipes her mouth. 'I needed that,' she says. 'That press conference was a shit show,' Rampaul says, 'but it achieved what McKinley wanted it to achieve.'

Isabel narrows her eyes. 'And what's that?'

'It's taken the focus off his fuck-up and landed the problem squarely on the laps of the Gifted population.'

Ah.

Isabel gets it now.

It really is the same everywhere. The discourse that will emerge from today won't be about the police and whatever missteps they may have made, there won't be any further interrogation of the investigation itself, at least not for a while.

The discourse will go back to what it always goes back to.

How dangerous Gifted are. How there's one on the loose out there who has killed twelve people.

And like Isabel said, it will have repercussions that will go beyond this.

'Your boss is a piece of shit.'

'Yes, he is,' Rampaul says.

Isabel is on her second beer, has been nursing the last dregs of it for some time now.

She's not sure how far the others have gone. But the outside area of the pub has now filled with people coming for a drink after a long working day and to enjoy the warm evening. It's still early and the mood around them is buoyant.

Still. She doesn't want to risk drinking any more. She hasn't had a proper drinking night in a long time, and she has no idea what it will do for her defences.

At least the sound of the water is soothing as she leans on the railing, a little further away from everyone else. The slight distance helps and being here right now feels like a small slice of peace. It's nice to be around good feelings for once, when she's constantly surrounded by everything else on the opposite side of the spectrum.

In the water, two swans move leisurely through the water. Isabel watches them, charmed by the sight. She can't remember the last time she saw swans. Had she ever actually seen any in Portugal? She can't recall.

'Sorry I forced you all out.'

Isabel glances over her shoulder. Rampaul is walking up to her, another full glass in her hand.

'Do we look forced?' Isabel asks, lifting her own glass.

'Isn't that the same glass you've been holding on to for the better part of an hour? That must be disgustingly warm by now.'

Isabel sighs. 'That's more because I have some trouble with crowds, it gets noisy. It's easier on my Gift if I'm sober right now.'

Rampaul inclines her head. 'All right.' She steps up and follows suit, leaning her arms on the railing too.

'Listen,' Isabel says, tucking a strand of loose hair back, 'I'm sorry about earlier.'

'What are you talking about?' Rampaul asks.

Isabel keeps her eyes on Rampaul's face, wanting her to see the truth. 'I didn't mean to see it.'

Isabel watches realisation dawn on Rampaul as she understands what Isabel is referring to. That Isabel had caught a glimpse of her thoughts. 'So, you did see it,' Rampaul says, quiet, verging on curious. 'At the time when we locked eyes I wondered. The colour drained from your face, you know? You looked right at me, and I thought to myself, she saw it. But then I thought it was all in my head. Just because that's your Gift doesn't mean you'd see it.'

'And I shouldn't have. So, I'm sorry.'

'You don't have to apologise. I don't even understand how it works if I'm honest. Do you simply . . . pick things up?'

The sun creeps through the gaps of the clouds and streams down. Isabel turns her face up, enjoying the warmth as it spills over her head and shoulders. She's long since abandoned her light jacket at the table and her headache has faded.

'Something like that,' she murmurs, 'I have barriers in place to stop things from slipping in but sometimes things get in anyway. If emotions are too strong or I'm caught off guard and it happens too suddenly.' She shrugs.

'Isn't that something only higher-level Gifted have to worry about?' Rampaul asks.

'Hmm. I think what people don't realise,' she says, as she focuses inward and reaches out tentative fingertips into that corner of her mind, feeling for what she knows is there, to make sure it's still contained and hiding, 'is that like with everything else on this planet, there is probably a lot more we don't know about Gifted than we think.'

'You sound like you know something we don't.'

Isabel shakes her head. 'I know about as much as you do, I promise you that.' She sighs. 'Is it personal?' Isabel asks. 'Your boss? Because it seems personal.'

Rampaul laughs. 'You noticed, did you?'

'Is there someone out there who hasn't noticed?'

'No, you're right. But they love turning a blind eye.'

'Including your partner?' Isabel asks. 'He seems . . . interesting.'

'Oh, he hates my guts.' Rampaul smiles, but it's a cutting smile. 'He would love to see me fail. Still. I guess it could be worse. We work our cases and do what needs to be done. If he does his job and doesn't compromise my safety out in the field then I can work with it.'

But can you actually trust someone like that to always do the right thing and not compromise your safety? Isabel wonders. All it takes is one moment of indecision. One moment of spite. It's why she'd always been happy to work on her own until the chief had forced Voronov on her.

She can't really complain about how that has turned out.

Most people prefer to pretend when something that makes them uncomfortable is happening right in front of them. Makes it easier for them to go about their day. Law enforcement is the same except maybe more intense.

Rampaul straightens up and leans back against the railing. 'What about you?'

Isabel cocks her head, lost. 'What do you mean?'

Rampaul gestures ahead with a lift of her chin.

Isabel follows her line of sight.

Not too far from them, Voronov sits with Adam, the two of them talking over their drinks. He seems relaxed. At ease. It's nice to see.

'You mean Aleks?' Isabel asks.

'Hmhm.' Rampaul drinks. 'Things seem good there. Have you guys been partners long?'

'A while now.'

'That's all there is to it?'

Isabel blinks, for once, at a loss. 'What?' She glances back at Voronov and as if he's the one with the telepathy, he glances up as if he can sense that they're talking about him.

'The two of you seem close.' She shrugs. 'I know that doesn't always mean anything; some partners end up like family. And some end up as something else.'

Voronov has gone back to speaking with Adam.

'We are . . .' Isabel chuckles and shakes her head. She straightens up and downs the rest of her beer. 'Our lives are way too complicated for that.'

'Oh, you have someone? Or he does?'

Isabel laughs. 'No. We don't. That's not what I meant. Just . . . other things.'

'Hmm.' Rampaul reaches over and plucks the glass out of Isabel's hand. 'I don't want to hear it. I'm getting you another one of these. We deserve it.' She starts to head off.

'Rampaul.'

Rampaul stops and looks at her questioningly.

'Who really tipped off the press?' she asks.

Rampaul pauses, taken aback. But then she smiles a slow, hard smile. 'So, you do break the rules. I knew you had it in you.' She waves her off, leaving Isabel to watch her go, bemused. Isabel laughs and follows her, rejoining the others at the table.

Adam glances at her as she settles next to him. His cheeks are flushed and there are more empty glasses on top of the table now than when she'd wandered off.

'I haven't even been gone that long,' she muses. 'When did you find the time to do all this?'

'Wasn't just us, boss,' Adam says, 'DI Rampaul had some.'

'Yeah,' Isabel sighs, 'she's gone to get more too.' It's going to be a long evening.

Adam turns in his seat so he's facing her. 'Boss, can I ask you something?'

Isabel catches Voronov's amused look. 'Only if you tell me why you keep calling me boss.'

Adam blinks at her. 'Oh, well.' He finishes off his drink and then points a thumb in the direction that Rampaul went in. 'It's 'cause you give off the same vibes as DI Rampaul.'

'Oh,' Isabel leans her head on her hand and smiles, 'and what vibe is that?'

'Just no nonsense, don't really let people mess with you.' His eyes light up 'McKinley was being a real dickhead and you set him straight, didn't even bat an eyelash. Only other person in that place that isn't afraid to call him out on his shit is her, you know. It's why everyone gives her crap all the time. They know she's the best at what she does there, and they don't like it.'

No surprises there. A black woman standing out in that place? It's not the kind of thing that goes down well in an institution like theirs.

'What about you?' Isabel asks.

'Me?'

'Yeah. Why do they give *you* a hard time?'

'Oh.' He shrugs and pouts down at his drink, like he's a little kid. It's cute. 'I'm new. Well. More than anyone else in there anyway and I don't join in with their crap. Don't like that kind of stuff. And . . .' he rubs at the back of his neck self-consciously, 'well.'

Isabel senses the change in his demeanour, the seriousness. And the guilt. 'When I started out with the MCIU I was riding with DI Rampaul and DI Keeley. I messed up.' He swallows and doesn't meet Isabel's eyes as he explains. 'It was a pretty big case. Boss was up for a promotion if she cleared it and . . .' his mouth flattens, 'well. They wanted any excuse to kick her back down to earth. Keeley more than anyone. Couldn't stand that she was outdoing him.'

'I see,' Isabel says. 'Doesn't mean you have to feel guilty forever, hmm? You need to start making more noise.' She nods in the direction Rampaul had gone for more drinks. 'Like your boss. They'll keep pushing if they think you won't do anything. Trust me, we've been there ourselves once or twice.'

'Adam!'

They all turn as one to see Rampaul standing there, hand on her hip and glaring their way.

'Get over here and come help me with these drinks.'

They don't get back too late; it's a few minutes past nine in the evening when they arrive at their building in Greenwich.

There's a pleasant low buzz of conversation when they get inside, a good number of residents downstairs in the shared area, nestled into sofas and wine glasses in hand, the quiet melody of something that sounds like jazz playing loud enough to hear but quiet enough that people can comfortably talk without having to raise their voices.

Unlike the lively active energy of the crowd at the pub, this is more mellow, people winding down after their working day, fewer thoughts, quietened and slowed further by the addition of wine.

The feeling is almost contagious, especially with alcohol in her own system.

They walk to the lift in silence, close together, shoulders brushing here and there.

There had been a delicacy to their silence in the cab home that is new for them, and it makes something in her chest ache and feel like she has to breathe a little bit deeper to soothe it.

When they step into the lift, Voronov presses for their floor and leans back against the opposite side of the small space. Like Isabel he's carrying his jacket on his arm, the day too warm for them to have bothered putting the outer layers back on. His eyes are on her, and maybe it's from the alcohol, or maybe it's from something else but they're hooded as he watches her.

Isabel takes a deep breath and doesn't look away.

She knows this feeling. It's old, so old that it makes nerves tangle in her stomach, but it's not quite able to kill the excitement it leaves in its path as it travels through her.

The lift dings, the doors opening with a soft whoosh to two women standing outside talking, their conversation pausing as it arrives. They smile at Isabel as she steps out, nodding in thanks and goodnights, their eyes lingering on Voronov as he gets out too.

When the doors shut again, it feels like the floor is sealed in silence.

Voronov follows her to their door, a step behind her, and waits there as she digs out the key to let them in. Standing close. Close enough that she can feel his warmth emanating against her back, his thoughts like a calm wave lapping gently at the walls that have gradually grown a little smaller over the course of the evening to let her bask, even if for just a moment, in the happy emotions of others.

The door unlocks with a beep. Isabel tucks the key card away in her pocket again as she walks in.

She reaches for the light switch and her breath stutters out when she feels Voronov catch her other hand in his and tug on it gently.

The city lights pour in through the balcony doors, illuminating the dark interior of the room.

Isabel turns, her eyes falling to where his big hand is wrapped around hers and all she can do is stare at them. She swallows.

Voronov leans back against the door, one hand keeping her tethered, the other tucked into his pocket, his jacket threaded through the space there. His head is tilted back and in the dark, his eyes glitter as he looks down at her.

Isabel can feel the beats of her heart, like all of a sudden she's aware of its weight inside her and how it presses against her chest with each beat.

Voronov tugs on her hand again, and keeps pulling until Isabel steps close.

His jacket falls to the floor with a soft sound, and she feels the touch of his hand on the curve of her waist. It nudges her into closing the last gap between them. He leans down.

He presses his lips to hers like a question, a soft clinging of his lips to her. Like he's asking for permission. Like if she asks him to let go and stop, he'll do it right away, no questions asked.

He would. Because this is Aleks.

Isabel closes her eyes, lets her jacket drop to the floor too. She reaches up to curl her fingers around the nape of his neck.

She kisses him back.

# 39

'Yes, they've plastered it all over the place here too,' Bautista says. 'It's everywhere.'

Isabel winces.

It's ten in the morning and the phones here at the station have been ringing incessantly as a result of the press release the MCIU had done yesterday. What Isabel had missed at the end of it all was that in addition to telling the public about the cause of death of those who had died at the embassy, they'd also given the public information about who they were searching for.

It's a whole fucking mess.

At least McKinley had finally given them a bigger team to work with. They now had people watching Weir and Cross around the clock, as well as people on the tip lines. And because of what they had revealed yesterday, there had been a request for increased police presence on the streets because they didn't want the public to worry about a dangerous telekinetic Gifted wandering around ready to attack at any moment.

'Are our names out in the papers?' Isabel asks.

'No, not yet. Unlike the people you're working with over there, our teams know how to keep their mouths shut.'

Isabel sighs. 'To be honest Chief, if this hadn't come out then we'd still be stuck. The superintendent has been digging his heels in since we got here because he didn't like that he was being forced to work with us or rely on us in any way. If something big didn't happen, this would be going nowhere.'

'I'm not interested, and I'll be having words with the Foreign Affairs Department. They've caused a mess and I'm not letting them land that on my plate. Let's stop wasting time. Do you have any updates? Where is the fugitive?'

The door clicks back open and Voronov comes in, carrying a takeaway bag, and a cup holder with four drinks in it. The smell of bacon instantly fills the room and Isabel's mouth waters.

'Is that the chief?' he asks.

Isabel nods even as she holds out her hand for the food.

'Morning Chief,' he calls out and pulls the chair out next to Isabel, sliding the coffee her way.

'No new breaks here,' Isabel says, 'but the good news is that McKinley has finally lent us some manpower. Rampaul and Adam are briefing them now. They're going to send out a number of officers to start combing the city for Anabel Pereira. They disclosed her information in the news yesterday.' Isabel unwraps her breakfast, which they call 'muffin' over here, confusing, considering she thought muffins were small cakes. That's the English language for you.

She takes a bite of it though and it's pretty good, so she won't complain too much. She plucks the lid off her coffee.

'That manpower should have been there from the first day of the investigation. This is too little too late.'

'I don't disagree, Chief,' Isabel says, and leans forward so the chief can hear her properly over the crinkling of Voronov unwrapping his own breakfast. The two extra cups in the holder mean that Rampaul and Adam will probably be joining them shortly. 'But we *do* need it, especially if we want to wrap this up and come home, and this case is nothing but complicated.'

Chief Bautista makes a rude noise. Isabel can only imagine the kind of expression she's making right now.

Yeah. Chief Bautista would make absolute mincemeat out of someone like McKinley.

'Well, if you need some good news, Daniel and Carla should be calling you at some point today. Seems like they got something for you about Emanuel Francisco. I don't need to tell you both that sniffing around these people is trouble for us so be careful. Understand?'

263

'Yes, Chief.'

'Good. Now get back to work.'

She hangs up.

Isabel reaches for her phone, locks it, and tucks it away.

If they can find something to support evidence of repeated abuse carried out by Francisco, then even if Anabel Pereira is caught and charged, they'll have some evidence on her side.

Isabel would rather pretend she doesn't know why having that weapon in her arsenal for someone who potentially killed a whole building full of people is important, but she does know why.

For the same reason she hadn't been able to disengage completely from Gabriel Bernardo either.

It isn't simply that they are people like her. It's that they are people pushed into a corner by the societies they've been raised in.

She knows all too well what that is like, even if it doesn't change the fact that she is still here to do her job, which she will carry out regardless of how she feels.

Still. The last time she'd felt empathy hadn't exactly done her any favours. It only takes one look at her current situation for her to shake off any excess concern.

In the case of Dr Anabel Pereira, she knows even less than what she had known with Gabriel.

Maybe she wasn't pushed into a corner at all.

Maybe she's just someone who took something she shouldn't have and then hurt people in her attempt to escape being held to account for her crimes.

Even if Isabel's guts are telling her otherwise.

Someone raps on the door and Isabel and Voronov turn. Before they can ask the person to come in though, the door has already been thrown open and Rampaul walks in, bottle of water in hand and knocking back a little pill. Adam comes in right behind her. He's the most content Isabel has seen him despite the tiredness clinging to him. She thinks the shift in his relationship with Rampaul has contributed a lot to that.

'Is that coffee?' Rampaul asks, and her voice is croaky, like it wasted away overnight.

'Yes,' Voronov says, 'I thought we could all use it today.'

'You're a lucky woman, Reis, this man is a godsend. Adam, take note,' she says, plucking the coffee up and lifting the lid to blow a cooling breath over it. 'We can't linger though. Cross is back and downstairs. Seems she didn't take too kindly to us smearing her old mentee's face all over the British media yesterday. I think she's probably had a few calls herself that she didn't like. Reis, you're with me. Let's go.'

# 40

Cross is standing by the table when they arrive. Her demeanour is very different from the last time she had been here at the station.

Her hair is down today, the brown and grey waves stopping at her lower back, and her floor-length cardigan whirls around her ankles when she spins to face them after they walk in.

'You branded her as dangerous?' Those are the first words out of her mouth, sharp with accusation.

Rampaul pauses, coffee halfway to her mouth and then continues into the room like she hadn't heard anything at all and holds the door open for Isabel.

'Please have a seat so we can talk,' Rampaul says.

Cross stares at them stubbornly before yanking the chair back and sitting.

Rampaul pulls out one of the chairs, sits down and crosses her legs, cradling her coffee. Isabel takes a seat next to her.

'Inspector Reis here has had some interesting conversations with your ... *mentee*. She seems to have taken a liking to Inspector Reis,' Rampaul says. 'Isn't it odd that someone you claim to have been so close to would rather pick up the phone and speak to an investigator who thinks of her as a suspect, than reach out to an old mentor who has been with her for the entirety of her career?'

Cross's attention jumps to Isabel and though her face goes blank, Isabel feels the sharpening of her thoughts.

'Anabel spoke to you?'

Rampaul continues sipping from her coffee and doesn't respond. The look she gives Isabel says, *Over to you.*

Cross interlocks her fingers together but stays sitting ramrod straight. 'I didn't realise last time that you're one of the inspectors from Portugal assisting with the case,' she says to Isabel.

'That's right,' Isabel says. 'Dr Cross you clearly have a lot of respect and maybe even affection for Dr Pereira. But my conversations with her have led me to believe that that sentiment isn't entirely mutual. I also don't understand your presence here today. Do you have something to share now that you didn't the first time you spoke to us?' Isabel asks. 'It can't be that you're here just because of the press conference. Realistically, you should have expected that to happen at some point once you learned about the situation Dr Pereira was in, no? If you're only here just to defend Dr Pereira's honour, then you're wasting your time, and ours.'

She keeps her tone firm and to the point.

She wants to see what road Cross will take this time.

Cross's guard is up in a way it hadn't been last time. It's as if there's an invisible wall, erected between her and them. It doesn't feel like the natural barriers Voronov and people like him have in place, people who are private by nature. It also doesn't feel like the void of nothingness Isabel had experienced with someone else in the past, almost as if it was their Gift too. This feels deliberate, but not supported by a Gift, nor born of it either.

This is something learned.

If Isabel concentrates, she can almost see it, the same way she sees the colours that fill people's emotions and words. This has a muted shimmer.

Isabel reaches out with her Gift, brushing experimentally against it, feather-light, not to break, but to test. It stays put. She exerts a little more force, not much, the equivalent of pressing with one finger against an untested surface. And there's a give. It doesn't shatter under it, but it's almost like when you press into Plasticine and feel it mould around your touch.

267

It tells Isabel that if she really wants to, then she can tear it down.

'There was . . .' Dr Cross stops, she swallows, and sweeps her hair back from her face and on to one shoulder, tapping her fingers on the table, 'yes, our relationship broke down. But I haven't misled you about my relationship with Anabel. She was, and still is, someone I care very much about and someone who I want to keep safe.

'Why did your relationship break down?' Isabel asks.

'We had a difference of opinion on a project we worked on together.'

'Difference of opinion sounds very light for something that changed your entire relationship with someone you were so close to. Must have been more than that, no?'

'It was a *significant* difference of opinion.'

Isabel nods. 'Most colleagues will experience that at some point. Why was this a long-lasting issue, Dr Cross?'

'We work in a sensitive industry.'

'Yes, I read about some of your work. Your research revolves around the Gifted phenomenon. You and Dr Pereira both. And you have a world-renowned reputation. That's quite a feat. Congratulations.'

'Thank you.'

Isabel inclines her head. 'I haven't read anything about you yourself being Gifted.'

It seems that the topic is one that gives Cross confidence, because Isabel watches as her body language changes, relaxing, head lifting, assuredness returning to her posture. 'No, I haven't been blessed that way.'

Isabel gives a small smile. 'Blessed? I don't very often hear it referred to that way.'

'Most people are bigots, Inspector Reis.'

'Hmm. Dr Pereira is Gifted though. From the sound of it you must have greatly valued her input, seeing as her perspective and experience would have felt quite different to your own.'

'Actually, they weren't.'

'She's Gifted and you're not. That alone would mean that your perspectives are different.'

Cross shakes her head. 'I disagree.'

'Maybe that belief is what may have led to your difference of opinion.' Isabel scoots her chair forward, leans her arms on the table. 'The reason why you fell out with each other isn't something that Dr Pereira chose to tell me. But one thing she made very clear is that she doesn't trust you. Which is why I'm even more curious as to the reason for your presence here.'

If Anabel has something on this woman, and Isabel thinks it's highly possible that she does, Isabel wants to use it to make sure Cross understands that Anabel does *not* have her back.

Usually, when people understand that any loyalty towards them is gone, it becomes easier for them to bend.

Cross inhales, her chest rising with it as she lets her gaze drift off to the side. 'I still stand by what I said. But I think what you and your team did yesterday has made her desperate.'

'Why? According to you she wouldn't hurt a fly. She loses nothing by coming in. Interestingly, when I told her I would do my best to help her, she believed me.'

Something about Isabel rubbing in the fact that Anabel has been speaking to her, rather than speaking with Cross, is finding its mark. There's a possessiveness there that unfurls even with Cross's barrier in place, like soot.

She doesn't like the thought of Anabel needing anyone other than herself.

Isabel wonders how far that emotion extends.

Would it extend far enough that she would corner Anabel, if it meant Anabel would turn to her?

'And yet she isn't here, is she, Inspector? You had to make a public appeal to see if you can get her here.' Cross visibly reels her own emotions in and Isabel feels them recede. 'Are you familiar with what can occur with high-level Gifted individuals?'

It's a fair question. Cross doesn't know that Isabel is Gifted. Isabel never disclosed that information to her.

Interesting considering Anabel had clearly informed herself about all aspects of her circumstances so quickly.

'I'm well acquainted with that phenomenon, yes. You're referring to the appearance of sociopathic tendencies that occur as a result of brain damage, no?' Isabel says.

Rampaul smooths it over well, but Isabel sees that she caught her off guard.

The funny thing is, many people are scared of the unknown when it comes to Gifted. There's a natural fear that comes from knowing these people could have power over them. They know that the higher their level of ability, then the more dangerous they could be. But they don't know the ins and outs of why. They'll quote that they read somewhere that Gifted are this or that, or that there's proof that they can lose their minds. But none of them ever really look into the actual cause, the facts of what could lead to that. Or how truly rare it is, because the majority of Gifted people simply don't operate on that level of ability.

To be honest, Isabel isn't sure if them knowing would make the whole situation better or worse.

Except that often, where there is a documented, medical reason for it, then there is the potential for cure. Maybe knowing the facts would help reduce the fear that ignorance has spent decades rousing to a fever pitch.

'That's right,' Cross says, as she shifts in her seat to fully face Isabel, 'the higher the levels and the frequency with which the Gift is used, the more the usage begins to erode the part of the brain which allows us to have empathy. You don't lose a sense of self, but you start to desensitise, and it begins to impact your decision-making skills, or reason, should we say.'

'I assume you're bringing this up in relation to Dr Pereira.'

Cross adjusts the glasses on her nose. 'Yes. It's been a few years now and it's been a gradual change, but the symptoms often displayed by Gifted individuals going through this began to manifest themselves in Anabel's behaviour.'

'Such as?' Isabel asks.

'Disengagement,' Cross says, 'emotional disengagement from those around her. She broke off her engagement, she distanced herself from me, from her other co-workers. Less empathy for . . . individuals we work with in our research. We work with a lot of different substances, we go through trial and error, it's not always the most comfortable experience for those who have volunteered to work with us.'

You mean test subjects, Isabel thinks.

'Pretend I'm stupid, Dr Cross,' Isabel says and leans back in her chair, 'spell it out for me.'

'I stand by what I said the first time I spoke to your colleague here,' she nods at Rampaul, 'the Anabel I know is a trusted and good friend. But the person you are searching for isn't the same person. She's someone who is suffering from the effects of erosion.'

Rampaul sets her coffee down. 'So what you're telling us now is that Dr Pereira is in a state that means she could have easily been responsible for the deaths of those people.'

'Yes,' Cross says, 'especially if she feels under threat.'

The image of Gabriel standing on the rocks that day forms in Isabel's mind's eye.

Especially if she feels under threat.

Like someone being cornered in their safe space and having no means to get away from unwanted advances.

Or from an entire police force taking to the city streets to hunt you down and bring you in.

A very real, very immediate, threat.

Isabel can see Rampaul making that same connection.

'My hope in coming here before was that we'd be able to find her quietly, calmly, to allow me to take her back with me and get her the help she needs. Right now,' Cross says, 'she's vulnerable and without a safe space and yesterday you went on national TV and told everyone in this country, and others, to hunt her down. Do you understand why I'm here now, Inspector?' she asks.

Isabel sits back in her seat.

Yeah.

They have a ticking bomb in their hands.

# 41

Isabel rubs her hands over her face and groans.

'Reis, what do you think?' Rampaul asks.

Isabel drops her hands.

They reconvened in the case room after Cross has left, with a plea for them to call her as soon as they hear anything.

They kept the tail on her, just in case.

Isabel crosses her arms, wrapping her fingers around her biceps and squeezing. 'What she says . . . tracks,' she admits reluctantly. 'And we have seen this before, in one of our other cases.'

'What happened there?' Adam asks.

Isabel's eyes meet Voronov's. 'We caught him.'

Had Gabriel been desperate? All of his moves had been deliberate. He'd picked people off one by one. But you could say it had been an explosion of quiet rage. Of desperation. He'd known what would happen once people found out the truth about him and he hadn't been wrong.

But what had happened on that case, and what is happening here, feel different.

In Gabriel's case, catching him hadn't been the end of the story either.

Then, like a moth to a flame, she feels it. A stirring of that presence in her mind.

Isabel shuts it down.

'That thing she said,' Rampaul says, 'erosion. Is that what's happening here? How did she sound when you spoke to her, Isabel?'

'Sane. Like someone who understands what she's up against. But I spoke to her before everything was splashed across the news and before we told everyone about her existence. Whatever the reason is that led her to end up at the embassy, her safety there was compromised the second Francisco started harassing her. She couldn't leave because she was dependent on him persuading the Portuguese government to get her what she needed. All of these things would put most people under great mental and emotional strain. If erosion had started, then I'm thinking that would probably help speed it along.' But if Cross was this concerned about Anabel and really came all this way to resolve the situation and take her home 'quietly' as she had put it, why not tell them the truth the first time she spoke with them? Enlist their help and work together with them?

'I think,' Voronov says, 'that we should heed what Dr Cross has said and consider the implications of Dr Pereira suffering from erosion.'

For some reason, hearing Voronov say that feels wrong. It unsettles something in her.

'But it would be helpful if we had proof. She didn't provide us with any documentation. No scans or reports,' he says. 'That doesn't mean she's wrong, but we should be cautious.'

The pressure Isabel had felt moments ago eases.

'I think Inspector Voronov here has a point,' Rampaul says. 'Adam, follow up with Dr Cross. Speak to her and see if there's any proof she can provide to us of Dr Pereira's fitness. And as she's feeling so helpful, we also want to know the name and contact details of Dr Pereira's doctor. If we can speak to them directly, that would be great. Dr Cross may think she knows every-thing about Anabel Pereira, but there is such a thing as doctor–patient privilege.'

Isabel glances up. 'There is someone else we can talk to.'

'Who?'

# 42

They wait until the next morning to pay Joana Weir a visit.

It doesn't help that the press now know exactly who is working on this case. They've camped outside the station, taking up space and watching everyone who goes in and out of there like hawks. It had taken Isabel and Voronov an extra twenty minutes just to make sure they didn't have anyone following them on their way to her flat.

The flat that Joana Weir is staying in is accessed through a door in a small brick alleyway where the ground is cobbled, large stones paving the way, their surfaces gently rounded.

There isn't a number on the lacquered black door but next to it, screwed into the wall, is a set of buttons with a label beside them, reading Flat 1, Flat 2, Flat 3, in black pen. One of the letters is a little smudged.

According to the information she had given Isabel during their first meeting, Joana Weir is staying in the ground-floor flat, Flat 1.

'This is it,' Voronov confirms. 'The officer assigned to her confirmed she's inside right now.'

They had split up, with Rampaul and Adam going to pay Ian and Tracy Russell a visit to question them seeing as Anabel had stayed there for a couple of days. Hopefully they would have noticed something off with her.

The bell, when they press it, is something they can hear from further inside. A little tune that sounds familiar but would annoy the hell out of Isabel if she had to listen to it every time someone stopped by to visit.

Cars speed by on the high street a short walk up the road and Isabel can see people walking past, in both directions, some carrying shopping bags from the shopping centre up the road, others just going about their own business.

Inside, there's the sound of a door unlocking.

The door opens and Joana Weir peers out at them.

'Inspector Reis?'

She looks as if she's been caught in the middle of work. She must have been wearing contacts the last time they met because she's wearing big glasses right now. Her hair is pulled back into a low ponytail and she's in a pair of sweats and a T-shirt. She lifts her glasses on to the top of her head and squints for a second before the corners of her eyes relax.

'Miss Weir. Can we come in?'

'Yes, of course.' She steps back to let them in.

The hallway is carpeted but feels uneven beneath their feet and as she walks them to the open door at the end of the hallway, they pass a set of stairs leading up into the rest of the building. Their steps make an odd thudding echo as they go, as if the floor beneath their feet is hollow. It's the kind of sound the people in the second flat can probably hear.

They step inside the flat and Isabel realises that it is actually a studio.

The floors are made of wood, and the space has a kitchen unit with an oven, stove, sink and a microwave with storage above it. Directly in front of that is a small circular dining table, with enough room to comfortably seat two people, currently occupied by an open laptop and a notebook, the charger running from the laptop and up to the plug next to a shiny chrome kettle. Isabel can hear the sound of music, tinny and radio-like, coming from the earphones connected to the laptop.

There's a double bed facing a huge wide-screen TV and a door on the other side of the bed that Isabel assumes leads to the bathroom. A large, cushioned, pastel-pink chair sits on the other side of the bed. There's a suitcase, open on the floor beside it, and a backpack resting on its seat.

Most of the natural light comes from the window that runs the length of the back wall of the kitchen and a door there, with worked glass that opens out on to a tiny slice of garden.

'I wasn't expecting you. Sorry if you tried to reach me.' She gestures at the table before wrapping her arms around herself. 'I haven't been checking my phone. Buried myself in work as you can see.'

'We didn't call ahead. Sorry. But we needed to ask you some questions.'

'Is it to do with the press conference the police gave yesterday?' She walks back over to her laptop and presses a key. The music that had been playing stops.

'Yes, I suppose you could say that.'

Joana nods. She goes to the chair and tosses the bag that had been on it on to the floor. 'Please, sit.' She pulls the other chair from the table too and offers it as well. 'Can I get you anything to drink?'

'No, thank you.' Isabel says, and Voronov also declines.

'Okay.' She sits on the edge of the bed, fingers curling tight over the edge of it. She takes a steadying breath. 'Are you here to tell me you've found Anabel?'

'I'm sorry, but no,' Isabel says.

Joana drops her head, letting it hang. 'Right. Okay.' She lets out a nervous laugh before covering her face with her hands. 'Sorry,' she says, taking a deep breath, and Isabel wonders if she's about to cry. She doesn't though, just drops her hands again and gives them a forced smile. 'The past couple of weeks, and then yesterday, it's been a lot. It's taking a toll on me.'

'You could always leave,' Isabel says. 'You don't have to stay here, Miss Weir.'

'No.' She shakes her head. 'No. I can't do that. She's going to need me, and I need to be here for her.'

'Okay. Ms Weir, yesterday, after the press conference, Eliana Cross came to see us. She disclosed that she thinks Anabel is suffering from erosion. Do you know what that is?' Isabel asks.

Joana's eyes widen and her mouth slackens in shock, 'Yes, of course I know. She says Anabel has erosion? Why?'

'We're looking into that and speaking with Dr Cross about evidence she may have in support of her claim. You said that since your separation you've kept in touch with each other, with instances where Anabel was even trusting you with information about her situation that could maybe help her in the future.'

Joana lifts her hand to the back of her head, driving her fingers into the hair there. 'Yes.'

'Do you think if she'd found she was suffering from erosion, that she would have shared that information with you?'

There's not a hint of doubt on Joana's face. 'Yes. I do. She wouldn't have kept something like that from me.'

'You're sure?' Isabel asks.

'Yes. I am.' She holds out her arm. 'I'm happy for you to check yourself, Inspector. She would have told me.'

Isabel glances at her bare arm. There are long red lines all along the length of it, razor-thin and healed, like the skin has been scratched over and over. She doesn't comment on it, nor does she take what Joana is offering. Isabel doesn't need touch for something like this. She can feel the sincerity coming from her in waves.

But just because she believes it doesn't make it true. It's clear Anabel is well aware of how her ex-fiancée feels about her. Telling her something like that would have caused her to worry. It's possible that for that reason she would have kept it to herself.

Voronov scoots forward in the chair, the legs protesting the action. 'We still have to consider that this is something she might be experiencing. When you broke off your engagement, how was her behaviour around that time?'

Joana wraps her arms around herself and scoots further back on the bed. Her fingers press so deeply into the skin that Isabel can see where she's making dents in the flesh.

'It wasn't a good time for either of us,' she says, 'and we didn't talk as much before or after. We were both hurt . . . she was more subdued but then again so was I. It wasn't anything that stood out. Just two people grieving their relationship.'

'And before that? Leading up to the break-up?'

'I . . . no. She kept to herself more, but that was it. She was still Anabel. The same. There were things happening at work, with the project she was working on with Cross. I know that was having an impact on her. But she was the same. Tired. Disillusioned. But the same.'

'Be honest, has she been in touch with you since we last spoke?'

'No. She hasn't. I wish she would, you can even check my phone records, or whatever else you like. I'm not lying to you.'

'Okay. I believe you, but for the purposes of this investigation, it would be good for us to have that information on hand. It saves you a lot of hassle in the long run too.'

'Yes. It's fine.'

'Then I want to ask you about something else,' Isabel says.

'Okay.' She sits still, eyes on Isabel, unwavering and waiting.

'I've spoken to Anabel twice now.'

Joana sits up. 'What? When?'

'The first time was shortly after you and I spoke for the first time. The second was yesterday, before the release that went out. She called me on my mobile phone. My personal number. As you were one of the few people who had access to it, I thought you may have been the one to give it to her.'

'Yes, I left a message on our – my – house phone. It's the only way I can communicate with her now. She still has access to our answer machine. I never changed the code. What did she say? What did she say to you?'

'Not much. I promised I would find something out for her, which I did. Is there someone else who was close to Anabel and Cross? Someone on their team maybe?'

Joana dips her head, gaze fixing on a corner of the room. 'Um.' She scratches at her arm. The same arm she'd stretched out earlier. Isabel watches as new marks form under the drag of her nails. 'They were under NDAs, there wasn't much she did discuss. I only knew about Cross because they were so close. Before things went downhill, we'd go over to her house for dinner, catch up with them.'

'Them?'

'Cross has a ward; she's lived with her for the longest time. But she didn't really show up often, she was always at work. I can count on one hand the amount of times I saw her.'

'Was Anabel close to her? The ward? Do you remember her name?'

'Not really, the only time they crossed paths was at Cross's house and even then, she never mentioned her much. Think her name was Teresa. Something like that. The few times I was there, she'd just pick up her plate and go off somewhere else in the house. Anabel was always in the kitchen with Cross, talking away. It's why I didn't really accompany her there often. There was hardly any point when the two of them wouldn't be caught up in their own little world, so I stopped going. I think it was the same for her too.'

'Hmm.'

'What about anyone else close to Cross?'

'No. Sorry. No one.'

'Okay,' Isabel stands. 'If you think of anyone, anyone at all who might come to mind, get in touch with me right away. Okay? And if Anabel gets in touch with you, tell her I want to talk to her again. Nothing else. Just talk.'

Joana keeps her gaze on her, not agreeing, not refusing.

Then, slowly, she nods.

# 43

They are on their way back, Voronov at the wheel, when Isabel's phone lights up with a message from Daniel.

*Can you talk?*

'It's Daniel,' she says, and rings him.

He picks up on the second ring. 'That was quick. You really must miss me.'

Isabel sighs heavily. 'Please. Don't make me hang up on you. I don't have time to waste unlike some.'

'Imagine how much more time you'd lose if I hung up the phone now because you're being an arse, hmm?'

'Daniel, just tell us.'

'Voronov with you?'

'Yes, he's driving.'

'Okay, good. Carla and I spoke to a couple of people about Emanuel Francisco.' He sounds pained.

'How did it go?'

'They wouldn't talk to us unless we agreed to keep their names off the record. Apparently, there was someone who attempted to whistle-blow two years ago and it didn't end well for them.'

'There was a whistle-blower?' she asks, and Voronov sneaks a quick look over too, before he's back to navigating the traffic.

'Yes. We did try to find out their identity, but we couldn't. Everyone is keeping a tight lid on that.'

Damn.

'But we spoke to two people. One of them, she used to work at the embassy back when Emanuel Francisco was first given the post there in London. She was the secretary for one of the other higher-ups there. He didn't do anything to her, though she says he made some inappropriate comments once or twice. But she said every woman that worked in the embassy knew to avoid being alone with him.'

'But was it all hearsay from her?'

'No,' Daniel sighs, like this has taken more out of him than he expected, 'the month before she was transferred, she walked in on him cornering the nineteen-year-old intern in one of the upstairs bathrooms. Says the intern was terrified but when he laughed it off, she didn't say anything either. Just went with it and then got out of there. The intern never went back.'

Disgusting man.

'And what else?'

'The other one was the parent of . . .' he pauses there and then clears his throat, 'of another victim. This one went further back. Francisco still lived here and worked for the government then. She was a maid in his and his wife's house. Her dad tried to report him for rape.'

Rape. Isabel unclenches her jaw when she realises how hard she's grinding her teeth together. 'Tried. That means he didn't succeed. What happened?'

'Family didn't have much money. Couldn't lawyer up. He threatened to sue them for defamation. Said she wanted pay-out, the sex was consensual, but he was a married man and didn't want to hurt his wife.'

Isabel spits out a curse. Of course. These types of men are nothing if not predictable. 'So, they kept their mouths shut.'

'Yes. Sprinkled a little money on them too, to keep them sweet.'

Isabel shakes her head. She's feeling more and more glad the man is dead.

Seems like his inability to treat women like human beings ended up leading to the deaths of everyone else who had been in that building with him.

'Is there anything else?'

'No. No one else would come forward. But from the sound of it, Isabel . . . I think it's all one big open secret. I think the government knows about his reputation. They're just keeping it hush.'

'All right.'

'Does that help?'

When Isabel looks Voronov's way, his hands are clenched around the steering wheel tightly enough that the veins on the back of them stand out.

'Yeah. Yeah, it helps.' Isabel leans her head back on the seat. 'Thank you.'

Even Daniel sounds subdued. 'All right. Listen, wrap things up over there fast. Sooner it's done, sooner you're back here, hmm?'

'Yeah. We're trying.'

'Update me later.'

'Will do.'

She switches the phone off and drops it in her lap. She digs the palms of her hands into her eyes. 'This is a mess, Aleks.'

'The financial records for Ramos show signs of irregular amounts being deposited into her account from an offshore account,' he says, 'Adam is getting the bank to trace where they came from. Going by what Ramos's boyfriend said, it's safe to assume those will come back linked to Francisco.'

Her phone vibrates again.

It's Adam this time.

'Adam. We're on our way back. Is everything okay?'

'Boss, the surveillance team on Cross called,' he's speaking so fast Isabel almost doesn't understand what he's saying, 'they are reporting that they just saw Anabel Pereira go inside the hotel.'

'What?' She sits up so fast the seat belt jams in its hold over her shoulder, cutting into her skin, and she has to pull on it to loosen it. 'Are they sure?'

'He says she matched the description. She walked in about five minutes ago. DI Rampaul and I are heading straight over and there's already a unit on their way.'

'Okay. We'll meet you there.'

She hangs up and turns to Voronov. 'How fast can you get us there?'

Voronov checks the satnav. 'Another ten minutes.'

# 44

It's the parking that takes them more time, but when they get there, the unit is already in the lobby of the hotel, Rampaul and Adam at the centre. Guests milling around are staying well out of their way but don't actually leave the building, openly staying to satisfy their curiosity.

Some of them must recognise Rampaul and Adam from the press conference that had aired because whispers start filling the room, thoughts spilling fast and messy. Others start palming their phones.

Isabel eyes them up and grabs the nearest officer. 'There are people getting ready to record whatever is about to take place. I'd advise you all to clear the guests out of here before we do anything further.'

She sees his chest puff up, knows what's about to come out of his mouth and spears him with a look.

'If you don't do as I say right this second and this ends up plastered all over the news or the internet, I'll make sure to tell your boss exactly who fucked up here. Understand?'

His mouth snaps shut on whatever he was about to say, and he gives her a tight nod. She watches as he grabs another colleague, and they head towards the guests.

Rampaul is speaking to what appears to be the manager of the hotel. That's Isabel's best guess. His attire is smart casual, and he has his name badge pinned to the outer pocket of his shirt. Not the kind of uniform Isabel is used to seeing on a hotel floor, but it fits with the relaxed vibe of the reception area.

Isabel and Voronov walk up to her and Adam.

Rampaul sees her coming and wraps up her conversation with a nod before turning to them.

'Good, you made it in time. We have half the unit around the back where the emergency stairs come down on to the street. The rest are coming up with us. Cross is in 302.'

'She hasn't come out yet?' Isabel asks. She checks her watch. Between the time Adam had called her and now, it had been about twenty-five minutes.

'No, not yet.'

Isabel surveys the group of officers gathered in the foyer. Unlike the ones she's seen up until now, these ones are decked out in bulletproof armour, and they have guns with them.

The lobby is empty now, save for the manager. 'We're sure she's gone up to Cross's room?'

Rampaul nods at the manager. 'The staff confirmed she went to Cross's floor.' She turns to the uniforms waiting. 'Let's go. Keep this quiet and keep it contained. Adam,' she says, 'stay here in case something happens. I want someone keeping an eye on the situation here.'

They split up, the unit taking the stairs while they cram into the lift to take them up to the third floor. The manager is with them too, squeezed into a corner of the lift, his skin shiny, a film of sweat gathered along his temples.

'This is quite a bit of manpower,' Isabel says. 'Not overkill?'

'Unfortunately, no,' Rampaul mutters, 'McKinley insisted.'

That bastard again.

'Given what she's suspected of, there was no way I was going to win that argument.'

When she puts it like that, Isabel can't say she would have done any better.

There's a precedent for this to go incredibly wrong.

But something feels off about this.

'What's wrong?' Voronov asks, voice low. He's standing right behind her, and he's bent down to say it as quietly as possible, but in the enclosed space, everyone hears. Rampaul shifts closer too, waiting for Isabel to respond.

'It doesn't make sense to me,' Isabel says. 'Why would she come here? She's too smart for this. And she did not want to go to her for any help. If there was one thing that came through loud and clear in our conversations, it was that. Now she waltzes in here on her own? Out of nowhere?'

Especially after expressing her distrust in Cross. Not to mention she'd know they would have eyes on this place.

No. This – something about this is wrong. There's also the fact that for someone who had claimed to want to help so much, they had yet to get a call from Cross to tell them that Anabel had waltzed into her hotel. Unless she was doing her best to keep that information from them. Not an unlikely possibility. Isabel had got the impression that she'd resented them having the upper hand from the start so this would fit in with her character perfectly.

No. It's more that she's finding this difficult to believe from Anabel's angle.

But at the end of the day, Isabel doesn't know her. Maybe Anabel had just been very good at getting Isabel to feel some kind of connection with her.

She's not made of stone. She can admit when she's been wrong.

She's not ready to admit that yet though.

'I get that, Reis,' Rampaul shifts to face her, 'but they saw what they saw, and they reported it. We can't let it go unchecked.'

Isabel nods. 'I know. I know.'

The lift dings as it arrives at Cross's floor.

The armed members of the unit file out first, heading straight in the direction that the manager sends them in.

They move quietly, their steps barely audible.

It's a good thing Anabel isn't a telepathic Gifted, because she would have clocked them from the second they'd all stepped into the Reception area downstairs. The thoughts of these people are loud. Too loud.

They're muttering in their heads, repetitive phrases that no doubt keep them focused and on point, present and on the task at hand.

The hallway is like the rest of the hotel, in keeping with a modern and free-spirited style. The floors are wooden, and the walls painted a neutral white. Plants stand dotted along the way.

It's clean, the smell one of freshness that makes Isabel think of a forest.

Having said that it's a relatively short corridor and Cross's room is at the very end.

They line up alongside the wall.

The unit leader checks with Rampaul.

She nods and he steps forward to knock on the door but doesn't announce himself.

There's a sound from inside the room, of something falling and crashing to the floor. 'Yes? Who is it?'

That is definitely Cross's voice. But there's no other sound. No footsteps coming towards the door, no more commotion either.

Isabel casts out her senses, like a net, spreading it beyond the walls in front of them, stretching the web as wide as she can to try and catch anything.

She locks in on Cross fast. This time, her barrier is only half-formed. A sign that she's been caught off guard and the knock at the door had raised her suspicions. She's pulling it up now, even as Isabel moves fast to try to capture whatever emotion or thought leaks out of her in those moments.

There's just one. Like a knife, jutting up and out. Panic.

But there's nothing else. No other stray thought for her to lock on to.

She looks over her shoulder at Voronov and lowers her voice. 'I can't sense anyone else in there. Only Cross.'

'Do you think she's there alone?'

Isabel shakes her head. 'I don't know. Anabel's extremely adept at blocking. I didn't sense her last time, in Ian Russell's house.'

The door clicks open and Cross walks out only to stop short when she sees the suited-up team right outside the door; she backs away as soon as she spots the guns, shrinking from them.

'What—'

Rampaul makes her way to the front as the team push past Cross into the room. Isabel follows Voronov in, her gaze taking in the space.

It's bigger than the studio flat that Joana Weir is staying in but one look is all they need to see the entire whole thing. Just a large pretty room. Cross has retreated further. The TV mounted on the wall is on, set on an all-day news channel. Her laptop is on the bed, on its side, and there's a mug, broken, tea spilt across the floor and on the side of the bed.

One of the team members comes back out of the small space where the bathroom is.

'Nothing.'

'What? What is this? What are you doing? Are you *insane*?'

Rampaul walks up to Cross. 'One of our men saw someone matching Dr Anabel Pereira's description walk into your hotel and the hotel staff confirm that this person got off on your floor. This was approximately,' she glances at the face of her watch, 'half an hour ago.'

Cross stares at them, wide-eyed behind her glasses, and slowly shakes her head. 'No.'

Isabel comes out of the room.

There's a neon sign indicating the emergency exit at the opposite end of the corridor.

'We should have your people downstairs check out the street-level emergency exit,' she calls over her shoulder, striding to the exit.

She pushes down on the bar mechanism and the heavy door opens with a groan into an enclosed concrete staircase. It's lit only by emergency lights dotting the ceiling in an intentional crumb-by-crumb path leading the way out to safety.

Isabel can hear the sound of her own breathing, as quiet as it is, echoing in the stairwell.

'Anything?' Voronov asks from behind her.

'If she was ever here, then I'm pretty sure we've missed her.'

'We'll make sure it's clear.' It's the man who had taken the lead in approaching Cross's room. He heads into the stairwell first, members of his team close behind.

Voronov touches a hand to her shoulder. 'I'll follow them.'

'Okay.'

She grabs his hand before he goes, wrapping her fingers around the bare skin of his wrist. *Be careful.*

He looks at her surprised.

His mouth softens ever so slightly, and he nods.

Embarrassed, Isabel lets go and goes back to the room.

When she gets there, Cross is pacing back and forth, her robe, a flowery silk that is probably more expensive than Isabel's whole wardrobe put together, trails after her, almost settling before she spins back around.

Rampaul is leaning against the wall, arms crossed, eyes pinned on Cross.

When Isabel walks in, they both look her way.

Agitation is palpable, creating waves in the air like heat on tarmac.

'Voronov went with the rest of the tactical unit; they're checking that there isn't anyone hiding in the stairwell.'

Rampaul gives a slow nod and then tilts her head in Cross's direction.

'Cross has something to tell us.'

'Oh?'

'Yes. She was here,' Cross spits out, like they're forcing the words out of her mouth.

'Really?' Isabel says. 'Now why would she do that.'

'I told you; you made her desperate.' She turns to them. 'And despite what *you* may think, Inspector Reis, I'm still one of the people she trusts most. She came to me because she needed help. She knows she's cornered.'

'What did she say?' Isabel asks.

'She doesn't think the Portuguese government will honour the promise they've made.' She's wringing her hands, rubbing them together over and over, her tone fervent, the same feeling peeling off her body in curls that Isabel could almost reach out and touch.

Isabel slides her hands into the pockets of her jeans. 'And she came to you for . . . what exactly?'

Cross stops pacing and glares at her. 'Like you, I'm not on my home turf, Inspector. But I belong to the organisation that is holding her responsible for what she took. My opinion and my advice hold weight.'

'So, you're saying she's come asking you for help going back?'

'Not in so many words. She knows I can't promise anything. But I don't think she's planning on waiting for me.'

'What do you mean?' Isabel asks.

Cross shakes her head. 'I don't know. I guess we'll all have to wait and see, together.'

The tactical team sweep the whole building and don't find any traces of her. Rampaul gets more people to come down and comb from Oxford Street outwards; they spend a good four hours out there. They even check the room of each guest as a safety measure and every other room in the hotel.

They don't find her.

At 11.35 that night, Isabel receives a message from Joana Weir:

*She wants to meet you. Tomorrow, Covent Garden station. She said to be early, she'll find you.*

# 45

Isabel doesn't like this. It's too packed.

She's standing on the corner of the street where Long Acre meets Neal Street, tucked between the trio of trees that reach as high as the surrounding buildings. Her back is pressed to the brick of the building behind her and she's under the shadow cast by the branches and their leaves.

Her position gives her a good view of both of Covent Garden Underground station's exits. It also gives her a decent view of the way back from the square and either side of Long Acre. It'll have to do.

The weather has turned, temperature dipping from the extreme and abnormal heat they've been seeing the last couple of weeks. There is still a lingering warmth, enough that all Isabel is wearing is a hoodie over her T-shirt and jeans. She's got her running trainers on and the cap Sebastião had put on her head the day he'd gone to the airport to see her off. Anything can happen and she wants to be sure she can move in the right way if needed.

Directly across from the station's exit, leaning back against a sunglasses shop, is DC Duncan. He's out of uniform for once, similarly dressed to Isabel except he's left off a hoodie. A blue-and-green checked shirt is tied around his waist, and he has his arms crossed over his chest and his phone in his hand.

For someone who usually exudes nervous energy, Isabel is surprised at how at ease he seems in this situation. She'd half expected him to be nervous, but he's fine, and if she didn't know him, she wouldn't suspect him of being there for any reason other than waiting for someone he was supposed to be meeting with.

She knows Rampaul and Voronov aren't that far away either, both of them together at the end of Long Acre, and more officers, including Mackey and Bridges, are spread throughout. The threat of more negative press leaking out into the public domain had made persuading the superintendent to lend them more people on this a little easier.

But it's a Friday afternoon, quickly descending into evening. There are two pubs at the opening into the square and they are already packed, people spilling out of them to talk outside, clustered around both buildings, drinks in their hands.

The space between the buildings on either side is filled with two-way traffic, tourists and people heading home or wandering the city all falling together.

On top of it all is the noise. The sheer level of noise that's clogging the air around them. Isabel is almost grateful for the constant stream of it that she's been subjected to since her arrival because even though it's jarring, she's now had enough practice in toning it down.

Isabel checks the time, shifting in place. She tracks the faces of the people passing by her, waiting.

Her phone vibrates in her hand.

She flips it up. The number unknown.

Isabel catches Adam's eye and answers it. 'Inspector Reis.'

'Right in front of the station, Inspector.'

Isabel spots the tall, lanky woman turning her back to her, pulling her phone away from her ear. She's wearing a thin black duster jacket and has her hair in a long plait. Anabel.

She sets off down the street, past Adam, heading straight for the square.

Isabel pushes off the wall and hurries after her, keeping her in sight, weaving in and around people. She doesn't risk another look at Adam, leaving it to him to alert the others.

Anabel cuts a quick path through them all and keeps her head down.

Isabel grits her teeth as people ram into her as they go the opposite way. Every time she comes into contact with someone, she feels the spike of emotion, too quick and fleeting for her to guard against, like quick jabs of a needle to the skin. Too weak to do much damage by itself, but like this, the oversensitivity has her flinching with each touch.

Someone slams into her side, laughing loudly and apologising, and something splashes over the sleeve of her hoodie, the distinct smell of beer instantly sinking into the fabric.

Isabel curses and shoves them away and follows Anabel right into the piazza. The road surface changes to thick, wide cobbles beneath her feet.

She follows Anabel, hoping the rest are behind her. She can't lose her. She doubts they'll be able to get her to this point again. They'd considered the chances that Anabel would either try to split Isabel from them or make a run for it. The former, Isabel can live with.

As Anabel cuts across the square, the stream of people increases, coming from other streets leading to the centre of it.

People mingle under the arches and others sit out on a restaurant terrace above their heads, watching the world go by, completely unaware of what is happening below them.

Anabel is high-risk. They couldn't agree to meeting her in a public space without fail-safes in place, considering what they suspect her of doing.

They slip out of the square, down another, narrower street lined with restaurants. The roads here are not as crowded, but there's still barely space for Isabel on the slim pavements.

Another person knocks into her shoulder, but she barely pays it any mind now, she's too close, Anabel ahead of her with no one to block their way.

Anabel's plait slides from her shoulder on to her back as she quickly glances behind her. Her gaze locks on Isabel briefly before she's back to facing forward, picking up her pace.

They continue this way for another five or so minutes, Isabel rushing across roads to avoid cars and hurrying to keep Anabel in sight after sharp turns into other roads.

That's when they come out into the open, the cluster of buildings they'd been winding themselves through opening up into the view of a bridge and the London skyline. The giant Ferris wheel that is the London Eye is directly in front of them. This part of the river lacks the quieter feel that Isabel has found on her morning runs.

Anabel slows. She slides her hands into her pockets as she makes her way over to the bridge, her pace changing to that of someone out for a stroll. She tips her face up to the sky and Isabel hears the deep breaths she takes as she finally pulls up beside her.

'Sorry,' Anabel says, glancing at her, 'but your people aren't very discreet, you know?'

They turn on to the concrete bridge. 'They're not my people.'

Up on the bridge, the breeze has a mean, cold edge to it. It peels tendrils of Anabel's hair, and they blow into her face. She nudges them away with a slight smile. 'Ah, that's right. You're like me. You don't belong here either.' Her eyes sweep over their surroundings. 'I was hoping maybe we could all go home.'

To passers-by, they must look like two friends enjoying the city. They're walking so slowly now. Slow enough that anyone they hadn't lost in Anabel's little maze walk could catch up to them in no time, and their path hadn't been complicated enough to lose anyone tailing them. No, Isabel doesn't think it had been Anabel's intention to lose anyone. So why do it?

'We can do that,' Isabel says. 'Isn't that why you wanted to speak to me?'

Up close, Anabel has a small beauty mark above the right side of her lip. It's to enough miss, but as Anabel smiles at her, it moves too, catching her eye. It's the only remarkable thing on an unremarkable face, a face that must have come in handy for someone hiding out in the city. She doesn't respond though.

Cars drive across the bridge, cyclists intermingling with them. There are a couple of street artists along the way, one sitting on the pavement, on a cushion, back against the guardrail. A boxy black radio sits next to him, the music blaring from it irritatingly loud. He sings along as he focuses on his sketches. His work is on display, the sketches covered in glossy plastic and pinned in two rows to the ground by pebbles.

Anabel walks past him, eyes wandering over his work, and she offers him a smile. The smile he gives her back is more of a grimace than anything else.

She keeps going almost until they reach the next street artist. This one is sitting on a stool, moving his pencil over the pages of his sketchbook to render an image of the young woman sitting on the stool in front of him. At her side her friend is giggling.

Anabel drifts off to the side and leans forward on the guardrail, bracing her elbows on it and clasping her hands together. Beneath them, the Thames cuts a path through the city.

Isabel stops too, lays a hand on the guardrail and faces her.

The sound of music thunders up from the river and she glances down to see what she assumes is a party cruise, moving slowly towards the bridge's underpass.

'Why are we meeting here?' Isabel asks.

'Maybe I wanted to see something pretty before it all comes to an end. You saw Joana.' She's smiling again, something small and softly sad. 'How did she look?'

'Tired,' Isabel says, 'like you do. She's worried about you. She wants to find you and wants you safe.'

The face Anabel turns to her is completely sober. Without the softness of teasing or a smile, the planes of her face turn harsh. There's no emotion in her eyes. In that moment Isabel looks at her and thinks of the faces of the bodies left behind at the embassy and thinks, yes. This woman could have done it without batting an eyelash.

'I didn't do it,' Anabel says. 'And we're here because I wasn't the only one who has been keeping a close eye on what you've been doing.'

Isabel steps closer. Anabel is taller than her, so she has to tilt her head back to meet her eyes. It doesn't take a big leap to know who she's talking about. 'Cross? Why did you go to her hotel yesterday?'

The corner of Anabel's mouth twitches at the name.

'Tell me what happened at the embassy,' Isabel says. 'Tell me so we can figure out how to help you. Right now, there's nothing we can do. One thing that I've learned about you is that you're an extremely intelligent woman. You know how this will go if you don't give us something.'

Around them, people continue to go about their daily lives. Behind the grey clouds the sun is making a valiant effort to come out, lining them in gold.

'Last time we spoke, you were talking to me, until Eliana Cross came up. And now you're bringing her up again.'

Anabel clenches her fist before facing Isabel completely. She steps closer.

Here Isabel sees it. The sallowness beneath her eyes. She's got the eyes of someone who hasn't slept well in a long while. Her collarbones are prominent where they peek out from the neckline of her T-shirt and her skin lacks life.

'She's here because I've got something she thinks belongs to her,' Anabel says, 'but she's wrong. She's the one who has something that doesn't belong to her. It took me a lot of time to get to this point.'

'What happened at the embassy?' she asks again.

'I didn't do it.'

'Okay. But you were in there. Tell me who did. Tell me what happened.' Isabel drops her voice even lower. 'We have families waiting to know why their loved ones died the way they did. They went to work in the morning, and they never went home. That's all those people know. The team need to give them something more than that.'

Anabel stays quiet.

'You were there when it happened. If you didn't do it then you can tell us what you saw, what you heard.'

One thing that Isabel is coming to realise is that higher-level Gifted are able to protect their thoughts and emotions to a degree that renders them practically impenetrable. Isabel has encountered a few, though she has never known their exact levels. It's one thing they have all had in common.

Anabel is no different. Not one thing leaks past her defences. Isabel wishes something would leak though. Anything to give her something to go by. The only one who can tell them what happened in there is Anabel.

All of a sudden, Anabel's head snaps up and she turns. She swallows tightly.

She swings back to Isabel and grabs her wrist, her grip hard and her nails digging into the sensitive skin of Isabel's inner wrist. She yanks Isabel close.

At the same time, a sudden flash of emotion reaches Isabel – a familiar one. Voronov. He's close by.

Isabel stills when she feels Anabel's breath wash over the curve of her ear.

'You can't let Eliana take her back,' Anabel hisses.

Isabel draws back but doesn't try to remove Anabel's hold. Anabel's eyes bore into hers. 'Take who back? Who else is involved with this? And I can't give you anything, Anabel. Not unless you tell me what I need to hear.'

'I don't have time—'

'Then you shouldn't have taken me on a chase through London when you should have been telling me how to help you. I can't do anything for you unless I know what's going on.' These bits and pieces of information that mean nothing on their own are adding to the frustration building in her chest. She needs Anabel to give her a connector. And she needs to do it fast because she can feel Voronov getting closer. At this point Isabel's certain she could pick him out anywhere. But if he's nearby, that means so are the others. Right now, what they're seeing is a potentially highly dangerous suspect, trapping one of their own on a bridge full of people.

The exact type of high-risk situation Isabel hadn't wanted them to end up in. There are too many chances for something to go wrong.

'Was it because of what Francisco was doing to you? We have the evidence for that. Joana has handed it over. We can build a case to—'

Anabel gives an emphatic shake of her head. 'No.'

She tightens her grip on Isabel's wrist and this time, Isabel does wince; she can't tamp down on the instinctive need to defend herself and locks her other hand over Anabel's hand in turn.

'Anabel—'

Isabel's attention shifts then, her gaze drifting from Annabel's face and settling over her shoulder.

There's a movement behind Anabel, nothing out of the ordinary. Just people walking. Isabel isn't sure what's distracted her, but she draws back from Anabel enough to focus.

'Inspector,' Anabel says.

There's a loud crack, like the sound of a firework going off, but close, too close, and sharper.

It hits Isabel's face like warm rain, in an arc, from Isabel's throat up to her cheek.

Isabel blinks. There's a ringing sound in her ear.

People are running.

Isabel looks up at Anabel.

Anabel's eyes are wide. Her mouth is opening and closing. A gurgle sounds. She sways back, like she's going to fall, and Isabel moves before she thinks about it, catching her shoulders and letting out a grunt as Anabel's knees collapse under her, her hands going to her throat.

Before her hands press down on it, Isabel sees it. A huge hole, black at the centre, a cluster of ripped flesh and tissue blown outward, gleaming with blood even as it seeps from the wound too fast.

Isabel eases her on to the ground as gently as she can, helping her sit and kneeling beside her, heartbeat going overtime. She can feel it in her throat, in her ears, a hot pulse that she needs to ignore to focus.

The shot came from behind Anabel.

Where are they?

Anabel's shoulders shake under her hands with each wet choking sound she makes; she's wheezing, chest heaving.

'Anabel,' Isabel forces her voice into calm, 'Anabel, help is coming.' Isabel wraps her hands around Anabel's where they're pressing over the wound. They are streaked with thick red. 'We need to press harder. This will hurt.' She pushes away the feeling of it. The slipperiness of her hand over Anabel's. Of how warm and heavy the blood is as it coats both their hands. Isabel can see the entry wound on the back of the neck. It looks almost innocuous compared to the wound on Anabel's throat. She presses a hand there too, hard and Anabel makes a wounded sound. 'They're coming.'

And they are. She can hear DC Duncan's voice loud as it requests an ambulance. She can feel Voronov's tightly leashed emotions, overwhelming, coming straight for her.

And she feels—

Isabel's head snaps up and locks on brown eyes. Freezes when she takes in the familiar closely cropped white-blond hair.

Elvira.

She's staring not at Isabel but at Anabel on the ground.

Her body is bent inwards, a hand clutching her head, and her chest is heaving, and heaving, and heaving. She's dressed like everyone else, except she's not panicking and running away like they are. There's a gun in her hand.

'Nnn . . . no . . . d-d-do—' More blood bubbles out in Anabel's attempt to speak.

Isabel tries to think. She's unarmed, nothing on her that will help her protect herself or anyone else on this bridge, so she keeps her hands where they are, tight around Anabel's throat.

She's not going to make it. Isabel knows that.

Anabel is slumping, sliding lower on to the pavement. The blood, despite Isabel's best attempt, is pouring out beneath their combined hands and fingers. It's soaking into the front of Anabel's T-shirt.

Someone is yelling Isabel's name now. She hears them.

Beneath them the ground shakes.

Elvira is gone.

'Fuck,' she spits. Useless, she's being so fucking useless right now. Anabel is dying.

Anabel slides her hand out from beneath Isabel's and grabs on to her wrist once more.

'No, don't, we have to keep pressing—'

'S'okay – loo-loo – k . . . hea—' She tightens her grip on Isabel, deliberately digs her nails into her skin. '*Look.*'

There are tears gathering in the corners of Anabel's eyes. One overflows and slides down her temple. But her eyes are fierce. No shock there anymore, but an intensity to them as she stares in unhinged determination.

Isabel closes her eyes.

She looks.

She is still in Anabel's mind when someone slides one arm under her arm and another around her waist. Someone murmurs her name against her temple as she's drawn up and away.

*Sister. She's my sister. Save her. Sav—*

The connection snaps, a string cut off that brings Isabel fully back into herself. The abruptness leaves her disorientated and it takes her a moment for her surroundings to come into focus.

'Are you back?'

Isabel blinks at Voronov steadying her.

'Reis.'

Isabel hears Rampaul calling her name.

She's rushing past her, giving Isabel a quick once-over as she runs over to where Adam is on the ground.

'Reis, are you okay?' Rampaul calls back at her even as she's kneeling beside Adam.

'She's gone, boss,' Adam murmurs.

He has Anabel's head resting on his knees. Her bloodied hands are still over her throat, limp. Her clothes are sodden. Her eyes stare unseeing up into the sky.

The clouds have cleared, and the deeper sunlight casts an eerie light on the river.

The sound of sirens bleeds into the air and there are officers at either end of the bridge now, locking off pedestrians, others in the middle of the road redirecting traffic.

'You're bleeding,' Voronov says.

Isabel blinks at him. 'What? No, I'm . . .'

She hadn't felt it at all.

There's a tear in the material over her shoulder and she can see the skin beneath it, split open and red, bleeding too. It hadn't gone through her but grazed her instead.

'Oh.' She lifts her hand to tend to it, but Voronov catches it gently before she can touch.

'Let's wait for a medic to see to it,' he says.

Isabel sees her hands. Anabel's blood is everywhere, under her nails, in the creases of her knuckles, swathes of it on the mounds of her palms. There's not an inch of skin left clean.

'Is it hurting?'

Slowly she shakes her head, still staring. She swallows hard, can't keep her eyes from drifting back to Anabel, lifeless on the ground. 'I don't feel it.'

Adam and Rampaul come over to her, their faces grim. Adam is staring down at the ground, his hands fisted at his side.

'You moved fast, Adam,' Isabel says softly, 'well done.'

He glances up at her at that, then drops his gaze to her hands. 'Should have been faster.'

'For now, we've secured the scene,' Rampaul says, 'ambulance is on its way but it could be a while. Can't believe this. They're going to want our heads on a platter.' She laughs but there's no humour in it. 'Lost the only lead we had. Got officers searching nearby.'

In her head, Isabel gathers the images she'd glimpsed, ones that Anabel's barely there presence had forced her way, opening door after door after door of memories to shove at her, too many for the time they had left.

'We have something,' Isabel says.

That gets the attention of all three of them.

'She asked me to look at her memories. Before.'

Rampaul stands straighter. 'Her memories of what happened at the embassy?'

'More than that. And . . .' She still remembers the look on the shooter's face.

Elvira's face.

It was the look of someone who had just had their heart ripped out.

'I saw who shot her.'

It hadn't been anyone in the embassy who killed those inside the building.

'What? Who?' Rampaul asks.

The sirens are louder now. At the end of the bridge, Isabel spies people with their phones out. She moves away from Voronov and goes to crouch next to Anabel, blocking their view.

'Elvira. From Moreno Security. Anabel's sister.'

# 46

Adam is the one who goes to Ian Russell's home with news of Anabel's death. He takes two officers with him. Rampaul stays on the scene to oversee the moving of the body and coordinate the witness statements of those who had been on the bridge at the time the shot had been fired.

Isabel and Voronov head to the nearest emergency room to get her wound seen to and end up at the A&E of Guy's and St Thomas' Hospital.

'You didn't have to stay,' Isabel says to Voronov. She's sitting on the bed while the doctor carefully finishes with the stitches. He's been standing by the door as if expecting that someone new is going to come barging in and he's making sure he's the first thing they'll see.

'Rampaul and DC Duncan have everything in hand for now,' Voronov says, watching the doctor closely as he works. 'Now that there is no longer a search for Anabel, Mackey and Bridges are probably there too.'

The doctor sends an amused look at Isabel from above his mask, eyes crinkling. 'Slashed my hand making dinner a couple of months ago, bleeding everywhere. Wife was annoyed at the cleaning up she was going to have to do. Would've been nice if she'd stood by the door making sure I got treated well instead. Mostly I just got yelled at. So, count yourself lucky, Inspector.'

Isabel allows a reluctant smile to show, though she's too tired to give it more than that. 'Oh, don't worry, Doctor. He's yelled at me before too, don't be fooled.'

The doctor chuckles as he continues. From the door, Voronov lets his head fall back, some of the tension easing from his shoulders.

The bullet had done more damage than she'd expected, and she'd been seen right away. They'd given her a shot for the pain when they'd cleaned it.

She hadn't realised she had blood on her face and neck until Voronov sat next to her with some damp paper towels and proceeded to wipe it off as if they weren't in the middle of a packed emergency room waiting to be seen.

Her skin is pebbled all over, cold having settled in as she'd sat mostly bared down to her waist while the doctor has worked on her. Her T-shirt and hoodie are a lost cause, but she's got nothing else to put on, not until she returns to the apartment.

A few moments later the doctor steps away and surveys his handiwork. 'Well, it's not too bad. It's in a tricky spot so be careful with it, not too much movement with this arm, and if you have to, then keep it small. The stitches will take care of themselves. Keep it clean and dry, and if you have any concerns go to your nearest doctor, but you shouldn't have any problems.'

Isabel thanks him and slides off the bed as he writes the prescription for painkillers and leaves them so she can get dressed.

She tugs one of her sports bra straps back up but leaves the other one off. She considers her T-shirt and hoodie, not sure about how to tackle them.

Voronov crosses the room and picks up the T-shirt. 'Just leave one sleeve off. It'll feel awkward but that will do, right?'

'Right,' she says on a sigh and lifts her arm obligingly when he indicates it. 'Where are Rampaul and Adam now?'

'Rampaul is heading back to the station. They managed to gather statements from those on the bridge. Adam left the Russell's and is on his way to Moreno Security to speak to them about Elvira.'

Isabel pops her head through the neck hole and pulls it down. She tries to be careful even though she can't feel any pain right now. What she doesn't feel now she'll feel later. 'Did Ian Russell say if he heard from Anabel again?'

'No. He says she didn't contact him again after she ran when we went to his place.'

'Right.'

Voronov reaches for the hoodie next and holds it out for her to shrug into.

'Let's head back too.' The hoodie's sleeve hangs empty over her shoulder and the T-shirt is stretched awkwardly across her chest and arm, but she'll live.

Voronov glances at her and for a second she thinks he's about to tell her she should rest. She knows that's what he'd like to be saying. He's not hiding his thoughts from her. He never has.

'Okay,' he says, 'let's see if we can grab a taxi.'

# 47

They arrive back in North Greenwich in the early morning. The sky is shifting into nascent pink.

Isabel doesn't move from the passenger seat. Her eyes are on the lightening sky over the river. Despite the warmth that has persisted since she'd landed in London, she's cold. The radio DJ is talking over the start of another song, her voice calming. She lets it wash over her. She's still wearing the blazer Voronov had put over her and she pulls it closed over her chest. The movement brings with it a hint of Voronov's scent and Isabel closes her eyes, dipping her head and breathing it in. It's that same clean scent that's always on him. It's soothing.

Right now, Isabel is happy to stay right here. She leans her head back against the head rest.

Then the radio cuts off.

She's aware of Voronov opening the door on his side, the car shaking briefly before he slams it shut.

The door on her side opens from the outside. Isabel opens her eyes again, head rolling to the side. A cool breeze, touched with the scent of the river, drifts inside.

Voronov stands waiting for her, holding the door open. In the encroaching dawn, the blue of his eyes is different, darker. 'You're tired,' he says, 'let's go.'

Slowly, feeling like it takes half of her energy to do that much, Isabel nods and undoes her seat belt. She gets out, leaning into Voronov's touch when he adjusts the jacket on her shoulder. He shuts and locks the door and wraps an arm around her upper back, fingers curling over her other arm and guiding her forward.

Normally this is where she tells him she can walk by herself. In fact, she would've been rolling her eyes over him opening her door, even though he does it all the time.

But right now – right now she badly needs to lean on someone. Echoes of Anabel's thoughts remain inside her head as the sensation of her blood spraying across Isabel's throat and face lingers. The heat of it. The weight of it. It had been cleaned away at the hospital, but Isabel knows if she reaches up she can trace its exact path with her fingers.

She has to keep her barriers up. Especially now, when her energy is so low, when the quietness of this city as its residents finally sleep, are *finally* quiet at all, could lull her into a false sense of security.

Voronov leads her into the building.

The ride up to their floor is silent. Isabel avoids looking at her mirrored reflection. Voronov doesn't move away, remains a warm presence at her side. Steady. The lift stops with a ding and the grinding of metal as the doors open and they wind their way through the building silently, the sounds of their steps absorbed into the carpeted floor.

Behind the doors they pass, Isabel gets nothing but soft drifts, wisp-like thoughts that are more akin to faded whispers, coloured like clouds. They belong to dreams and after so much loudness, only having to deal with this much feels like bliss.

They reach their door and Voronov lets go of her to unlock it. The lift doors ding again as they slide closed further down the hall.

He holds the door open, motioning with a nod for her to go inside.

Inside, the barest touch of light comes through the balcony doors.

Isabel makes a beeline for the sofa, toeing off her shoes as she goes and leaving them where they land. She collapses into the softness of the sofa, pulling the blazer around her even tighter and closing her eyes.

She doesn't open them even when she senses Voronov come close. Or when he touches her shoulder.

'Not here, come on. Get some proper rest.'

She huffs out an annoyed breath and allows her eyes to slit open. He's hunched down between the sofa and the coffee table, balanced on the balls of his feet. His skin is pale in the gloom.

He looks tired too.

'You know,' she says, her throat scratchy, and her voice coming out hoarse as she laughs a little and ignores the smarting of her eyes, 'I'm really tired.'

He doesn't say anything, and she knows he gets it. That she's not talking about feeling physically worn down, although right now, she feels that too. He knows she's talking about more than that.

The touch of his hand on her shoulder changes, his long fingers covering the cusp of her shoulder, and he kneads at the muscle there with his thumb. 'Do you want to talk about what happened the other night?' he asks, voice just as low.

Isabel snorts and shakes her head, pressing her cheek into the soft seat of the sofa. 'Haven't you looked outside? Or checked the time? It's morning already, Aleks.'

'I know.'

The stroking stops and his hand stills.

When she opens her eyes again, he's easing himself down in front of her, sitting down. He scoots until his back rests against the coffee table at the centre, getting comfortable, his touch sliding away until he's just sitting and waiting quietly.

Isabel pushes herself up to a sitting position too, groaning quietly at the effort it takes.

Maybe she should have had a shower, got changed and eaten something before having this conversation. But if she'd done that, if any of those things had sobered her in any way, she doesn't think she'd be sitting here right now, finally saying what she'd probably needed to tell him from the moment things had changed.

Voronov rests his hands on his knees, clasps them together.

Isabel shifts her gaze over his head to the balcony doors. From this angle she can't see the river. But she can see the sky.

'I think Gabriel got the better of me,' she admits. She gets up and skirts around the sofa, heads for the bathroom instead. She needs to wash this day off if she stands a chance of getting sleep of any kind. She shakes her head. Tired but determined. 'He won't manage it again.'

When she finally does look at him, he's watching her.

'Thanks for . . . you know.' She gestures at her face; the blood is gone now but there are still dried red spots on the neck of her T-shirt. 'Being there today. I'll see you in the morning.'

Stepping inside, she closes the bathroom door behind her.

# 48

She's woken up by her phone ringing.

She doesn't even know when she'd fallen asleep, but she's not surprised she gave in. When you put minimal sleep together with the last couple of days, and then getting shot on top of it, it'd be more surprising if she hadn't sunk under at some point.

The vibration of the phone makes it drift across the surface of the living-room table.

Groaning, and pressing a hand to the wound on her side, Isabel pushes herself into sitting.

The whole place is doused in muted light. The curtains have been drawn over the balcony doors but they're not thick enough to keep the daylight out entirely. The TV that she'd left on must have turned itself off some time ago.

A blanket which had been draped over her slithers down on to her lap.

She takes hold of the fabric and glances at the door to Voronov's room.

It hadn't been there when she'd curled up on the sofa earlier on.

The phone continues to move across the table, and she makes a grab for it.

She doesn't recognise the number on it. The time on the phone tells her it's gone quarter past three in the afternoon.

Pulling herself back takes more energy than she expects.

She rubs her tongue over her teeth, trying to dissipate that cotton feeling. She answers the phone. 'Yes?' Her voice comes out hoarse and her throat feels dry. She gets up to go into the kitchen for water.

She doesn't sense Voronov is anywhere in the building.

'Inspector Reis.'

Joana Weir's voice carries through the phone. Not the calm and composed way she normally speaks. It's weighted by grief but also something else. She sounds panicked.

'Miss Weir,' Isabel says. 'Are you all right?'

'No. I – I need to see you right away. It's important.'

Isabel stops. She sets aside the glass she's filled with water. 'Okay. Yes. Of course. I can come to you—'

'No, I'm outside your building.'

Isabel pulls the phone away from her and stares blankly at the screen. 'Okay. I'm coming down. Wait there.'

She doubles back towards her room and calls Rampaul as she does.

Joana Weir is sitting at the kitchen table opposite Isabel, her hands around a cup of tea Isabel had made for her nearly half an hour ago, when the front door finally opens to let in Voronov, followed by Rampaul and Adam. Isabel isn't sure she's taken so much as a sip from it.

She lifts her head to watch as they all walk in, nudges the hood still over her head all the way back. Her hair is dishevelled beneath it, strands sticking straight up like they've been rubbed against a balloon and made to stand by the static. Flakes of the pastel-brown nail varnish on her fingernails are gone along the edges, like they've been scraped away by teeth. There's a simple gold band on the ring finger of her left hand that hadn't been there before.

She's kept her big dark backpack wedged between her chest and the table ever since she sat down after Isabel had told her to make herself comfortable.

The heavy grief she had brought with her into the kitchen has expanded to coat everything in the apartment. Its weight is oppressive, like a weighted pitch-black blanket that swallows you whole.

Isabel leans back in her chair, her own mug long empty. She winces as the action causes her wound to smart.

They got here quickly.

'Miss Weir,' Rampaul says, I'm sorry for your loss. She brushes her hair behind her ear, eyes sharp as she takes in Joana's hunched-over figure and the full cup of tea she's clinging on to.

Joana stares at them blankly.

Isabel had warned her she'd have to call in Rampaul and that she'd have to wait to tell them everything. Joana hadn't been happy about it but had acquiesced to Isabel's request that she wait. Even so, the tension that has her sitting with muscles locked tight hasn't eased one bit during the time it has taken them to get here.

Slowly, as if it hurts to unfurl from her hunched position, Joana puts some space between her and the bag, straightening away from it to get at the zip and reach into it to drag out the laptop inside.

'This belongs to Anabel,' she says. Her voice is thick. 'She came to me, before . . .' She pauses, collects herself. 'Before.' She sets the laptop down. 'She gave me the username, the pass-words. Showed me the folder with the evidence and told me I could do what I wanted with the rest.' She opens the laptop and as it boots up, its light washes over her face, a pale-blue glow making the skin beneath her eyes and around her mouth look sallow.

'When?' Rampaul walks to the kitchen counter, braces her hands on it, keeps her posture open and her voice low. 'When did she come to see you, Joana?'

'Yesterday. It couldn't have been later than seven in the morning.' She seals her lips tight.

Isabel glances at Rampaul but decides to ask later why that hadn't been picked up by the watch they'd had on her. If they hadn't heard about it, then that means Anabel had got in and out of where Joana was staying without being seen by the officer on shift.

'Why did she come to see you?' Rampaul asks.

Joana looks up at them. Anger rises in her, thick, eating up the grief slowly and enveloping it. 'She knew what was going to happen when she agreed to meet you,' she says to Isabel. 'She knew she wasn't going to get out of there alive. You see,' her eyes start glazing with tears, and she blinks even as her lips stretch in a wide, humourless smile, 'she's been one step ahead of us this whole time. All of us.'

Isabel stares at her. 'How could she have known? Why walk to her death? She wanted to get out.'

The tears hover along the rims of Joana's eyes. When they spill, they leave wet tracks down her cheeks that she wipes away.

'The ward. Eliana's ward.'

Isabel's eyes narrow. 'The one you mentioned, at the dinners. Teresa. What about her?'

Joana lays her hands on the laptop, the touch almost reverent. 'Anabel asked me to go and give this to her. She even told me where to find her.'

'The ward?' Rampaul frowns. 'She's here? In London?'

Joana pulls a bright orange Post-it from her pocket. 'She wrote it down here.' She pushes it across the table to them.

The address written on it doesn't mean much to Isabel. She hands it over to Rampaul and Adam who are hovering behind her. Adam frowns, leaning closer to it.

'Anabel wanted me to tell her that everything she needs to get a new start is right here. She asked me to tell her to take it and get out.'

The second citizenship.

Don't let Eliana take her back. That's what Anabel had said.

'This is Elvira Smith's address,' Adam says.

The sister.

Cross's ward is Teresa.

Teresa is Elvira.

Anabel's sister.

Isabel drops her head into her hand and digs her thumb into

314

her temple. 'Wait.' She looks at Joana. 'When you say she was ahead of everyone, what do you mean?'

But even as she asks, she understands.

From the start, this had seemed like too risky a situation for someone as smart as Anabel. She'd backed herself into a corner by coming here. There should have been countless ways for her to work out and get what she needed from the Portuguese government without needing to leave American soil. Instead she'd risked opening up an entire manhunt on herself.

Her choice had been deliberate. The conference, the embassy, the negotiations. If what Joana says is right, and she'd prepared for the possibility of her death in that way, then she'd known how each and every major player was going to act here.

Except the deaths at the embassy. How do they play into all of this? And there's still Ramos's murder.

Isabel reaches for the laptop.

'Show me,' she tells Joana, 'Show me exactly what she wanted Teresa to see.'

The folder Joana shows them contains enough information that they don't even know where to start. It's a mix of things that she has obviously been collecting for a very long time.

There are folders containing saved emails that date back years. Others are reports and transcribed notes.

And then some are recordings.

The email exchanges are mostly between Anabel and Eliana Cross. There's talk of data and subjects, scientific jargon and graphs, images of what they're sure are brain scans labelled by subject, befores and afters, comparisons. They're able to deduce that each title refers to the subject, an affinity, and a level. The number that follows that, Joana informs them, is the level of erosion.

'Is this the information Anabel was planning on handing over?' Isabel murmurs.

She doesn't read all of it, but she reads enough to understand what they'd been working on. What they had managed to achieve.

They'd figured out how to stall erosion.

Not a quick fix, to lower someone's level of skill, to help contain the Gift itself, like the pills Isabel herself had taken for years of her life.

No. What they're looking at right now is a clear progression from fast erosion of higher-level Gifted to a complete slowing down of it altogether, if what she's seeing is correct.

Isabel swallows, her throat constricting.

This is huge. If this is what Anabel took, there's no way they wouldn't want her head on a chopping block.

Then they reach the first recording.

It begins with a long-drawn-out breath.

Then:

*'She's using Teresa.'* It's Anabel's voice. Hollow, monotone. *'She's using her and there's nothing I can do about it.'*

Joana is staring at the laptop like if she stares long enough, then Anabel will follow her voice right out of it and be in front of her again.

'Did she tell you?' Isabel asks.

She nods. More tears spill, flowing quietly down her cheeks. 'It's why . . . it's why she left me. She'd been dealing with,' her breath hitches in her throat, once, twice and she presses the inside of her wrist over her mouth as she breathes through her nose, her whole body hitching with sobs she's trying to contain. 'She'd been dealing with this all along and I had no clue. I didn't even know she had a sister. She never told me. She never told me.'

'Did she explain? When she came to you with this?'

She sniffs, the sound wet, and she swipes her wrist over her mouth and nose. 'Teresa was young, but her Gift developed fast. Spiralled when she was very young. Apparently, Anabel's parents couldn't cope. She says they split when they were young enough that Anabel didn't even remember her.'

'And then?'

'Teresa knew about her. Shows up when Anabel is in college. Teresa is already with Dr Cross by then. That's how Dr Cross

316

finds Anabel, gets to know her, brings her in. She keeps her around because Anabel is brilliant. Because of course she is. She said things were fine for a while, though Anabel grew apart from her family. Couldn't forgive them for giving Teresa away, for not telling her.'

Fuck.

'Teresa's erosion started early. But they didn't have enough data then, the early studies were insufficient. So, they tried something else.'

'What did they try?'

'Anabel says according to Cross they found a way to keep her from using her telekinesis.'

'Like the S3 pills?'

'No. Conditioning. Through . . . various means. Anabel says Teresa showed her the scars once.'

Oh God.

'Apparently it worked. Teresa was able to function without worry, she even served in the military. She was pulled eventually. There was an incident with a member of her team. She put him in hospital. Anabel says he never left. No one understood what had set her off, but something did. She blew up, used her Gift at levels that were . . . difficult to defend against for the average person. Cross apparently stepped in for damage control.' She taps the screen with her finger. 'But it's all in there. What led to her blowing up that way. She'd become Cross's lab rat. Cross used Anabel against her. Told her she would leave her too, if she realised just what dangerous levels her Gift had reached. Of course, Anabel knew nothing about it.'

'How did she find out?'

'She said it was an accident. She found the logs they'd been keeping on Teresa. But there was no way to get her away from Cross. Because Cross has guardianship. She raised her concerns, tried to raise it with higher-ups. They didn't listen and warned her if she pushed then she would end up off the research project and without access to Teresa. She said what Cross achieved with

317

Teresa was too groundbreaking for them. They weren't going to risk losing that.'

'And what was that? From what you're saying the erosion didn't stop.'

'No. But she had a high-level Gifted individual at her beck and call. Able to use her Gift at her command and with deadly precision. You can see how that would be of use to the US military.'

*Meu deus.*

'So, she needed to get her out of there. And there's nowhere that Teresa can go, without Cross. And she needed somewhere where she wouldn't be under US government control.'

Isabel takes a deep breath.

She can see the wild look in Teresa's eyes as she'd taken in her sister's body.

'Did Teresa know? What Anabel was planning?'

'Anabel said she did.'

Something she'd clearly planned so meticulously . . . but Teresa had been a factor she couldn't fully control herself.

Maybe telling Teresa had been her mistake in all of this.

'The deaths at the embassy,' Isabel says, remembering Anabel's assertion, finally, that it hadn't been her. But she had refused to say who had caused them. 'That was Teresa.'

'She found out about what Emanuel Francisco was doing to Anabel. She lost control.'

Silence falls over the room.

'Teresa showing up there yesterday . . .' Isabel says, 'that was a hit.'

'I came to you because I don't think Anabel is going to get what she wanted.'

'What do you mean?'

Joana gestures at the laptop. 'Teresa doesn't give a shit about this. Imagine you killed your sister because someone else had a hold on you. The one person who was trying to tell you they loved you and that they were getting you out. What would *you* do, Inspector?'

318

Isabel remembers the tremors of the bridge beneath her as she'd struggled to keep pressure on Anabel's wound, the shouts of the officers yelling at everyone to get back.

She turns to Rampaul.

'Where's Cross?'

# 49

The station is surrounded by press.

Coverage had intensified following the public shooting of Dr Anabel Pereira with blurry footage of the event. They clamour around the building's entrance, stretching up on tiptoes, microphones in hands being shoved aggressively into the faces of anyone heading into the building, even with police officers out there telling them to stand back.

Isabel watches from the back seat of the car, next to Voronov, silent, eyes tracking the journalists standing around the gate into the car park shouting questions at their car as Adam drives them through.

'Jesus Christ,' he mutters as he navigates the car through the narrow space, police officers there too, holding back the crowd. 'Idiots are gonna get run over at this rate.'

Rampaul sits next to him in the front passenger seat, gaze steely and focused ahead of them.

The sky is heavy with thunderclouds, with rumbles following them all along the way but not one drop of rain touching down in that time.

It's nearing 6 p.m. now, and it should be light outside. Sunset isn't until 9 p.m., but the storming clouds have left the roads dark, and the air permeated with the earthy scent of oncoming rain.

They'd stayed with Joana Weir until another officer had arrived, Rampaul pacing in the background and on the phone to the chief. Isabel had left it up to Voronov to call up their own boss and update her on the developments. She'd stayed close to Joana instead as Adam had patiently taken down her statement, taking her back over the details.

Joana had obliged, eyes puffed up from a combination of tears and constantly wiping them away, all while she'd stared straight ahead.

Rampaul issued the order for Cross to be collected at her hotel and brought to the station as quietly and discreetly as possible. It wasn't until they'd had confirmation that the officers assigned to watch her were on their way back to the station with her that they too left for the station, leaving Joana at their place with two officers in attendance.

They're all feeling the strain of the situation.

Somewhere out in the city right now is a high-level telekinetic Gifted who has killed thirteen people – possibly fourteen. They don't know for sure whether she is also responsible for the death of Judite Ramos. They're still waiting for the lab to report back on the bullet collected from yesterday's crime scene and the one that had been found in Judite Ramos's house.

But more importantly, this is someone who has a clear track record of harming others when they lose control of their Gift.

Isabel thinks about the spiel Cross had given them when they'd stormed the hotel, thinking it was Anabel who had arrived there.

She'd adjusted the truth nicely. It must have been convenient for them to have shown up at her room, thinking it was Anabel in there. When she'd talked about erosion, probably everything she had said had been the truth. Only the erosion itself had been happening to Teresa. Not Anabel.

Isabel guesses Cross had at least been telling the truth when she'd said they'd had a disagreement.

If I had pushed, Isabel thinks, if I had just broken that barrier down, I would have seen it all. Anabel would be alive right now.

She grinds her thumbs into the upper sides of her nose, kneading there, head dipping with it.

'Isabel,' Voronov says.

She doesn't lift her head. 'What?'

They haven't talked since the night before. He was gone this morning before she'd woken up and then Joana had called.

There'd been no opportunity to have a conversation about the mess that had been yesterday.

She nudges that away. They don't have time to think about that right now.

'Is it your wound?'

'No. It's fine.'

They get through the gates and park as close as possible to the back door.

Isabel gets out before Adam has even turned off the engine, needing air.

The others follow.

Rampaul walks to her. 'Reis?' She darts a look at Voronov. 'Are you good?'

Isabel heaves a sigh. 'Sleep-deprived. That's all.'

The expression on Rampaul's face says that she doesn't buy that, but she doesn't push it.

They don't linger outside, not with all of the press there, holding their cameras up to try and get something over the car-park gates.

Rampaul opens the door for them and goes in, and they follow her.

The door in from the car park leads to the downstairs area closest to the big rooms where they hold press conferences.

Rampaul's partner, DI Keeley, is there, shoulder leaning against the wall. He stands to his full height when they're inside.

'Took your time,' he says.

'Funny, your interest in this case seems to have manifested out of nowhere. Just like the press. Wonder if the two things are related,' Rampaul says, striding past him without sparing him more than a glance. 'Cross is here?'

'Upstairs. Third floor in twenty-two. Got two officers with her.'

They're walking so fast along the corridor that people dart out of their way to keep from being walked over.

That same tension is worse inside the building, packed into the air. It has the same weight as forty-degree sun on tarmac. Oppressive and unshakeable.

'McKinley isn't happy,' Keeley says.

'Well why don't you go and comfort him for me, then, Tom. Right now we've got a bigger problem on our hands.' She stops, the action too sudden and forcing Keeley's big body to wobble dangerously to a stop, almost knocking into another officer going in the other direction. 'What's McKinley doing about the press? What's he doing about finding the dangerous individual out there who we might have caught on to sooner if we'd had help, hmm?'

Then while he's standing there, grinding his teeth to dust, she walks around him like he was never there.

Isabel doesn't blame her one bit.

Adam gives him one mean look as he follows after her. It's the first thing to make Isabel feel a touch of humour in the past few days. He should show his no-bullshit side more often. It would definitely get a few people off his back.

There's one officer posted outside who tips his head to them in greeting.

They stop outside the room.

'Reis,' Rampaul says, 'do you feel up to being in the room?'

Isabel glances at her, surprised. She's been in the room with Rampaul a couple of times.

'I know I don't have the right to ask you this,' Rampaul says, 'I'm not your boss, and I know you have rules that you have to abide by. But if you go in that room with me and there's some way for you to push her so we can get as much as possible out of this, then I'm asking you to do that.'

Isabel considers what she's actually asking. 'You know how that will look if you get any information out of her that way?' Isabel asks. 'That press briefing has already caused damage. It won't take much to make things worse.'

'Listen,' Rampaul steps closer to her, 'I'm not going to stand here and pretend I know what you face day to day in this scenario. But if what Joana handed over to us today all checks out,' she glances at the closed door of room 22, 'then that person in there is a real piece of work and I don't want her setting one foot out of this country until she's been judged here. Anything you can get me to help ensure that doesn't happen, I will take.'

Isabel is conscious of Voronov at her side.

Part of her is teetering on the edge. It takes her back to the first time they'd been introduced to each other, and she'd been told Voronov was going to be her partner.

That feeling of waiting for the moment when someone will turn on you.

At her side, Voronov is silent, doesn't try to steer her either way.

'All right,' Isabel says.

Rampaul eases back, satisfaction adding a cat-like gleam to her gaze. 'All right,' she says. 'Good. Let's get in there then.'

Isabel glances over her shoulder at Voronov.

She's been blocking everyone out so hard since she'd woken up that there's no way for her to sense what he's thinking at all. If she really wanted to, she could. They both know that, and she sees that knowledge on his face.

'Adam,' Rampaul says, addressing him but narrowing her eyes on Keeley where he's stopped a few steps behind them, watching them with a face like stone, 'I need you to keep an eye on the progress of the search. Keeley,' she says, 'bring Adam up to date on numbers dispatched and what's coming in through calls. I want him ready to brief me by the time we're done here.'

Voronov moves back. 'I'll stay here and assist.'

'Good. Reis, come on. Let all the boys play together. We've got work to do.'

Isabel isn't sure what she expects to find when they walk into the room Cross is being kept in.

The room is more chilled than the rest of the building and has no windows. It's the size of a cubicle, just enough space for about four people, and even then, not much beyond that. There's a table with two chairs on either side and a camera mounted in the corner of the room.

Cross sits with her back to the wall, a plastic cup filled with water set on the table in front of her.

Rampaul steps in first, Isabel following and pulling the door closed. Cautious, she opens herself up, feels the way it changes her own posture, shoulders expanding and sharpness settling in.

Too sharp. She can trace Voronov, Adam and Keeley's progress away from them, their emotions leaving breadcrumb-like trails.

But from Cross, there isn't much. Just an air of cool competence. She places a lot of reliance on that flimsy barrier of hers.

Isabel isn't feeling as morally conflicted about tearing it down this time.

'It seems you lost one of your greatest assets yesterday, Dr Cross,' Rampaul says. She takes one of the empty chairs on the other side of the table.

Isabel stays by the door. The getting up and sitting down tugs on her stitches and to be honest, she wants the height difference, wants to be able to look down on Cross. She wants Cross to feel it: the discomfort of being under a microscope and taken apart in front of people who hold more power than she does.

And if Isabel doesn't feel up to examining that urge right now, she can make peace with herself later.

'How many times do I have to tell you people that Dr Pereira was more than a colleague to me? She certainly wasn't an *asset*.'

'She's not talking about Anabel,' Isabel says.

She waits until Cross meets her eyes. Brown eyes, calm, grief nowhere to be seen. There's no hint of redness, no hint of skin gone soft and shiny from no sleep. This woman is ready for anything they throw at her.

Isabel reaches for that shimmer of a barrier, except this time, instead of pressing against it, testing its give, she sharpens herself, sharpens her gift and like a claw rends it from top to bottom, its edges falling open like torn gossamer. Cross flinches, one eye closing like she's been pricked, but there's no awareness of what has just happened. Isabel wonders, with a detached sense of curiosity, how it had felt.

'She means Teresa.'

It's as if the air around Cross crystallises. Just as quickly, it melts, reshapes itself. Cross doesn't miss a beat. She frowns. 'Teresa? My ward? Why are you bringing her up?'

'This is where I tell you that playing stupid isn't going to help your case any longer. You see, you were right,' Rampaul says, and her voice is like honey, the voice of someone who knows she's caught her prey, 'Dr Pereira *was* a very smart individual.' Rampaul points at her. 'She outsmarted you. Did you know that?' Rampaul smiles.

'If you're going to keep me here, then I hope you'll start making some sense. Otherwise, I want to go back to my hotel so I can start packing my bags and go home. There's nothing left here for me. Which wouldn't have been the case if you'd all done your jobs better from the beginning.'

'Oho,' Rampaul laughs, smile widening, 'Dr Cross, you are one impressive liar. Does it hurt to keep your face that straight?' Before Cross can reply, Rampaul uncrosses her legs and leans forward. 'Let me tell you one more thing. Dr Pereira wasn't the only person who was backed into a corner and made desperate. Because of you, right now, there's a level-ten, military-trained, telekinetic Gifted who is very unstable and responsible for the death of her own sister.'

Cross narrows her eyes. 'Like I said. You need to start making sense.'

'How desperate do you think Teresa feels right now, Dr Cross?'

'Look—'

Isabel interrupts her. 'Dr Cross, I apologise. I think there's something I should have made you aware of when we first met,' she says. 'I can tell when you lie.'

Cross stills.

Isabel can feel her trying to fortify herself.

It's not a hard thing to fortify the walls that shield your thoughts from others, especially not for people who are used to it. Who are taught how to envision it, how to calm themselves, compartmentalise.

Maybe, if Cross's affinity was telepathy, it would be a different issue.

'Not that I need to,' Isabel says. 'You see, Anabel left us a very well ordered and very complete body of evidence. Put our entire investigation to shame by mapping it all out for us. I think, for your sake, it might be a good idea for you to tell us everything, from start to finish.'

'There's nothing for me to explain. I came here to help Anabel, reason with her, and take her home. I don't know where all this nonsense is coming from.'

'So, you're saying you don't know Teresa is in London. And yes, I *do* mean your ward.'

Cross adjusts her glasses. 'If Teresa is here, then no. I don't know anything about it. She has no reason to be here.'

'You gave her reason to be,' Rampaul says.

'Rampaul,' Isabel says, and makes her way to the empty chair next her, 'I don't think she understands.' Isabel sits and folds her arms on the table. 'I think you've overestimated your control over your ward. She didn't come back to you, yesterday, did she?' Isabel asks. 'Teresa. She didn't come back to you like she was supposed to.'

Unbidden, and against her will, Cross's mind drifts, flashing for a second to the memory of a door that won't open and a clock that keeps ticking. Waiting. The recall erupts unbidden, unwanted, and spilling through her broken walls.

'I feel like you're ignoring what I said about lying,' Isabel says.

Isabel cuts into her mind in the split of a second.

She doesn't have to search hard. Despite Cross's excellent blocks, behind them one memory, recent and shining with a myriad of emotions – guilt, resentment, sadness, relief – shines through.

She recognises the hotel room they'd visited even as she takes a moment to orientate herself from Cross's vantage point in the memory. It's the hotel room Cross has been staying in since her arrival in London.

Isabel sinks into the memory and as she settles, she feels the give of a mattress beneath her and understands that Cross is sitting on the bed.

Standing by the door, with her arms crossed over her chest and a blank expression, is Dr Anabel Pereira.

The memory is fraught. Anabel's face is clear one moment and then blurry the next. The feel of it as a whole is unsteady.

Cross is tense. Isabel can't feel the physicality of it but it's in the echo of the memory, in the way Cross remembers feeling in that moment, like the tightness of her muscles is attached to her memory of it. It feels full of foreboding.

Anabel's fingers dig into her arms. She stands ramrod straight. Her gaze, locked on Cross, feels like an ice pick right through the forehead.

'Do you know what you've done?' Anabel asks.

Isabel's head tilts back under Cross's command. The first time she had done this, she'd felt trapped, anchored into place. Now she's used to the claustrophobic sensation of sitting within someone else's memory. Of seeing through their eyes and their eyes only without being able to look beyond what that person has interpreted from their surroundings and line of sight.

'That's on you. You should have stayed put and seen your, and my, commitment through. That is what would have been of *actual* help to your sister. Your contribution.'

Anabel shakes her head slowly, her mouth pressed into a grim line. 'Not one bit of what you were doing was helping my sister. What you were doing was removing her agency.'

'Teresa is suffering from erosion – by limiting her access to her Gift we're buying more time for us to—'

'Bullshit. Bull. Shit. Eliana. If that's true then why did you send her to the embassy? What was she supposed to do there?'

'Why are you asking me? She was here for you. For your plans. So you could bag your negotiations with the Portuguese. Take her and the research with you. Betray me. Betray your country.'

'You betrayed *us* first. When you started to condition my sister into a military puppet.' Anabel visibly reins herself in. 'Now I didn't ask her to be there that day. *You* sent her. I want to know why you'd order a hit on all those people.'

'I didn't send her to kill those people,' Cross says.

'Oh,' Anabel says, as understanding dawns on her face, shifting her expression into something incredulous, 'just me then?'

Cross doesn't deny it. 'You took our *research* and offered it to another country. You stole from us. And you're currently conspiring to steal one of our greatest assets and the most important test subject we have. We've invested years into this. Millions of dollars. You thought that you'd just be allowed to do what you wanted? Grow up, Anabel. You're smarter than this.'

'Teresa isn't an asset. She trusted you. And if you sent her to get rid of me, you failed.'

Cross shakes her head. 'Anabel. Do you think the Portuguese are still going to help you? Their investigation is pointing to you. You ran from the scene. You have a motive. They didn't protect you while they had you. I *am* sorry about that. But this was all your choice.'

Anabel takes a step forward but Cross doesn't give her the chance to say anything more.

The room shifts for Isabel as Cross stands.

'There are two ways that this ends for you. You turn yourself in to the authorities here and assume responsibility for the deaths of the embassy staff. Do that and I'll do what I can for Teresa, I'll look after her until the very end. I love her as much as I love you. You have both been like daughters to me. But you stay on this path, then you're not giving me a choice. This time, I can guarantee you that she won't stray from the task I've set her. I'll make sure of it. It will go exactly as planned.'

Isabel pulls out of Cross's memory.

It dawns on her that what Anabel has successfully stolen, that precious asset that turned her into a fugitive, isn't the research she was using to bargain for citizenship.

What Anabel succeeded in stealing, was her sister.

Taking the research had been bait. She'd known Cross would come after her and she'd known Cross would use her sister to do it, removing Teresa from the watchful eye of the US military.

When Isabel refocuses, the interview room settling back around her, Cross is staring at her and Rampaul is sitting calmly, her gaze on Isabel as if she's done this with her a million times. Only the feel of concern emanating from her lets Isabel know that she hadn't been one hundred per cent sure Isabel was okay.

Cross keeps her eyes on Isabel's face, unmoved. But her thoughts are quicksilver-fast. She doesn't entirely believe what they have told her about Anabel having evidence that lays culpability at her feet. But she knows it's a possibility and is cautious enough to be trying to think her way out of it; at the same time, she's focused entirely on Isabel, waiting for what she has to say, understanding that something has changed.

The way she thinks is quite remarkable.

Isabel had once read a book about memory, how it works, how to lock certain things away and how to pull them back up. Cross's is like that, everything in neat compartments, perfectly ordered, unhindered by emotion. She's systematically going through her mind map, thinking of what else Anabel had had access to. What she may have been able to squirrel away before she ran off. She already knows what Anabel took in relation to their research. What she doesn't know is what she'd got her hands on in relation to Teresa and that Isabel has just seen exactly what she was responsible for, handed out by none other than Cross herself.

'Imagine you're given away as a child because you're different. Can you picture that for me?' Isabel says.

Cross freezes.

'Now imagine that you know about this, but you find out you have a sister and that you find her and that she accepts you and loves you.' Isabel gentles her voice. 'How nice would that be? And now imagine, someone who was meant to protect you starts doing awful things to you – in the name of helping you, of course – and you ask the one person you trust to help you and they find a way.'

Cross's nostrils flare and she sits back in her seat.

'And now that person, who was fighting so hard for you, is dead, by your own hand, all because they were trying to save you.'

Isabel leans forward a little more, lowers her voice enough.

'And it's all because someone manipulated you into doing it. *Forced* you into doing it. What do you think you would want to do to such a person?'

'That is an interesting hypothetical story.'

'It's a story about your arrogance. You're able to sit here calmly and *lie* to my face, because you're under the impression that when she comes to you, you'll be able to get Teresa to do as you want. The problem is that you've greatly overestimated your power over her. And I don't think you're ready for what is coming your way next. We could have picked you up at the airport. You trying to escape was not a worry for us. Despite what you may believe, I don't need you to corroborate anything. DI Rampaul explained to you. We have enough evidence without your cooperation.'

'Then why *am* I here?'

Ah. There it is. That arrogance, unhidden now, coating her words.

The arch look she's giving Isabel actually fits her face much better.

They've been looking at a fake this whole time.

Rampaul shakes her head, as if she can't process the level bold-faced lying happening right now. 'You're here for your own protection, Dr Cross. You're responsible for a loose cannon and we have a good idea about who she wants to talk to about her sister's death. The one *you* ordered her to carry out after you failed to blackmail Anabel into taking responsibility for the deaths at the embassy.'

Cross responds but Isabel doesn't hear it.

She glances at the door. She frowns.

Something feels off.

Cross speaks again but she doesn't register it.

'Reis?' Rampaul asks. She's close, her tone is calm.

It's like a blanket has been dropped on the entire building. Everything is silent.

Rampaul reaches for her, hand on her shoulder. 'Reis.'

Isabel frowns and stands. She heads for the door. 'There's something—'

Suddenly there's immense pressure. Like when a plane takes off and the air presses into your eardrums, and gravity tries to suck you back down.

Above them, a loud pop sounds and glass flies everywhere.

Cross yelps. Isabel hears Rampaul curse and hisses through her teeth when she feels a line cut across her cheek, hot and fast.

The room falls into blackness.

# 50

Yelling voices rend through the quiet that had felt eternally long a moment ago. Isabel hears the sound of the door swinging open but there's no light out in the corridor either. She instinctively jerks back, crashes into Rampaul who reaches out a steadying hand.

'What the hell is going on?' Rampaul asks.

Isabel yanks her phone out of her pocket as the officers who had been posted outside ask if they're okay. She can hear the sound of running, heavy running, and the blaring of radio communications though it's hard to make out the words when there are so many overlapping at once.

'Sorry, Detective Inspector, we're not sure,' one of the officers responds. 'The lights have all gone out. There's yelling up and down the building about it, they're trying to communicate over radio, but the frequency is off, sounds like they're asking for reinforcements downstairs.' He's speaking calmly but there's a shakiness to his voice that he can't mask. Several officers run past him, nearly knocking both men who'd been keeping watch outside their room into them.

The light from Isabel's phone illuminates the dark and she shines it around the room. It casts an eerie pale glow over all their faces. It touches only their cheeks, their throats, the bridges of their noses. It leaves eyes set deep within faces, shrouded in black, gleaming in the dark.

Isabel hadn't heard Cross's chair crash to the floor, but it lies on its side, and she stands pressed into the furthest corner of the room, palms pressed to the walls either side of her, shoulders halfway up to her ears.

'Rampaul,' Isabel says, 'I think we might have a situation on our hands.'

Rampaul taps at her ear with the palm of her hand 'What?'

Isabel's phone starts ringing. Voronov. Isabel puts the phone to her ear and shoves past the officers in the doorway. She motions for them to stay where they are and stops outside the room, looking down the length of the corridor.

She sees nothing but the small neon-green of an arrow at the far wall, indicating how people should get out in the event of a fire.

'Aleks, where are you guys?'

'Stay where you are,' Voronov says, voice blunt and short, 'we're coming to you.'

'Why?' Isabel asks. 'What's happening? I felt something change and then—'

She cuts off as she feels a tremor beneath her feet, small, but there.

'She's here. She's attacking the building,' Voronov says.

Fuck. 'Okay, okay.' Isabel whirls around to go back to the room—

A sudden violent shaking of the building throws her off balance, tripping her up. She flings out a hand to steady herself but misses, falling forward instead. The phone drops from her hand and her head connects with something hard.

Pain. It ripples out from her temple, so acute that for a moment her breath traps in her throat. She hits the floor.

'Reis? Reis?'

That's Rampaul's voice but she can hear Voronov too, except his voice is much fainter.

Isabel presses a hand to the ground to steady herself. 'Ugh.' There's a ringing in her ears. She opens her eyes and presses a cautious hand to the side of her head.

Rampaul is on her knees in front of her. There's broken skin on the bridge of her nose, a trickle of blood slipping down from it. One side of her face is illuminated, and Isabel sees the door to the interview room they'd just been in is shut.

'What was that?' Rampaul asks. She sounds winded.

Isabel follows the source of the light to her phone. She snatches it up, gritting her teeth against the dizziness that swirls all the way down to her stomach.

'Aleks?' she says and feels wet heat drip down on to her mouth, tastes the saltiness and metallic coat of blood on her tongue. She wipes it away from under her nose with her T-shirt.

'She's trying to find her. We're on the first floor. She's on the ground floor. Electricity is down, everyone down here is arming themselves.'

'She's coming for Cross.'

Rampaul's gaze shoots up to her face, the downturn of her mouth grim.

'I think so. Adam and I are on our way up to you. Stay in the room, keep Dr Cross inside.'

The floor trembles beneath her feet again. Isabel grits her teeth. A thought flits through her mind, of a scene from a few years ago on the news in Portugal. Half of a shopping centre collapsed. The building had looked like someone had scooped out its insides and smashed the contents into the ground beneath.

A young, untrained, high-level telekinetic had done that.

'Got it,' Isabel says, her heart banging against her chest, 'be careful on the way here. We've got two officers with us, they're inside the room with Cross right now.'

'Okay. Keep your phone close, we're coming.' He cuts off the call.

Rampaul is watching her, and Isabel knows her expression isn't reassuring.

'A human being is doing this?' Rampaul asks. There's a determined set to her mouth that doesn't entirely mask the way her eyes keep flickering, unable to look away from the ring of darkness outside of the phone's torch light.

Dust falls from the ceiling. The shaking doesn't stop.

From inside the room, they hear a panicked wail.

'She needs to shut up,' Isabel says, 'unless she wants to be found faster.' Isabel steps closer to Rampaul. 'Voronov and Adam are making their way up.' Isabel looks back down at the exit sign. 'We wait until they get here and then we figure it out.'

'This building is full of police, someone will get to her before she makes it past the first floor,' Rampaul says but even as she speaks the building around them continues to stir, the shaking not as severe as what had thrown them around before but still bad enough.

This is the person responsible for killing twelve people within a twenty-minute window.

Instead of agreeing with her, Isabel focuses on the task at hand. 'Brief them in there, they'll have to be ready to move. I'll stay here and flag Adam and Aleks. There's barely any light, we need to make sure they see us.'

'Yes, all right.' Rampaul opens the door back into the room, dipping back inside.

Isabel curses her own stupidity and switches on the torch app on her phone and immediately, the hallway illuminates from one end to the other.

She glances back into the room, hearing Rampaul speak in measured tones, and her eyes meet Cross's wide-open gaze.

It's sinking in.

Disgust filters through Isabel and she turns away and heads down the corridor, past the lift to the main staircase of the building.

She can hear them downstairs. Someone shouting orders. All the sound is coming from the floors below and nothing from the floors above.

She tilts her screen to light the way ahead, checking behind her too. Rampaul is standing by the door now, watching her go.

Isabel stops in front of the central staircase. She shines her phone light on it.

The light bounces off the walls. The skylight over the stairs is cracked and water is sluicing down from it. She hears rain, though she has no idea when it started coming down.

Isabel peers down into the centre.

That same pressure is still there, but not as heavy.

*Where the hell are you, Aleks?*

'Where are they?' Rampaul's question reaches her.

Isabel shakes her head, still staring down into the stairwell. 'I don't see them,' she says.

She catches movement below.

A face is tilted up towards her.

Isabel is staring straight down into the wide eyes of Teresa.

# 51

Isabel backs away and speeds back down the hallway.

'She's coming,' is all she says. 'Get Cross out of there. Head for the emergency staircase.'

Rampaul's *fuck* echoes in the hallway before she turns and hisses orders into the room. By the time Isabel is almost to them, Rampaul has got Cross by the arm and is dragging her to the emergency exit. 'You two,' she says to the officers with them, 'cover us.'

The tremors increase. Isabel can hear the officers right behind them as they head for the exit.

Dust begins to fall in waves.

They hit the staircase. Isabel doesn't look back. 'Pick up the speed now.' The planes of her back feel exposed and goosebumps spread down her arms and up her neck.

'I need to call Voronov and let him know, so we're about to lose light.'

'Okay. Everyone step carefully, move fast but quiet,' Rampaul says.

The moment Isabel switches off the torch, the concrete space falls into shadows; the light from her screen weak now, Isabel quickly dials Voronov again and the second she puts the phone to her ear, they're plunged into complete darkness.

She presses her hand to the wall, willing her eyes to adjust and forces the rising panic down.

The dialling tone sounds too loud in the silence of the enclosed space, accompanied only by the echoes of their harsh breaths as they move as quickly as they dare.

They follow the turn of the staircase.

'Isa—'

It feels like they're being stalked by a monster in the dark. Isabel whispers as loud as she dares to. 'We're moving. Heading to the lower floors. She was almost up to our floor. We've cleared Cross out and are heading down to the ground floor through the emergency stairs.'

There's a noise above them. Isabel feels like ice is being poured down her spine.

She freezes where she is.

From somewhere beneath her, she hears the sounds of hitched breaths that she knows are coming from Cross.

It sounds like concrete splitting.

'Rampaul,' Isabel murmurs.

'Yes?' Her voice sounds a little further away. Isabel thinks they're still moving.

'Keep going,' Isabel breathes.

She stops and turns on the phone torch again. She shines it up the centre of the stairwell.

The officers that had followed behind them aren't there.

Isabel didn't hear a thing.

And then she sees it, the shape of her separating herself from the shadows above them.

She's only human but right then, she doesn't resemble one.

The eyes fixed on Isabel's face are animalistic, devoid of any kind of lucidity.

It's like staring into nothing.

'Rampaul,' she calls down, 'run. *Run.*' Isabel braces a hand on the handrail and jumps down to the quarter landing ahead, nearly knocking into Rampaul and Cross.

Fuck, fuck, fuck, fuck.

There's an awful sound. Loud and deafening, Isabel mistakes it for thunder at first but it's inside the building.

The speed with which they're going down the stairs is hard and every step reverberates up Isabel's shins painfully.

They hit the ground floor.

It's not thunder.

It's the sound of something on the floor above them collapsing.

A thick cloud of dust plumes into the air, spilling over on to the ground floor with them.

They don't get much further than that.

Isabel slams into Rampaul's back and she grunts as it sends them both crashing to the floor.

Isabel's hand hits an object when she lands, her fingers tangling in something soft that slips between them.

Her heart almost seizes up and she recoils. Hair. It's hair.

'*Jesus!*'

That's as far as she gets before she feels herself lift up.

It's the oddest, most surreal feeling. Like her reality is changing, and then the air is whistling past her face, cold and fast. Her reflexes are the only reason she's able to wrap her arms around her head and curl into herself seconds before she connects with the floor again.

Nausea rises up fast, and Isabel shoves herself back up just quickly enough to cast up the contents of her stomach.

'Teresa . . .'

That's Cross's voice. Isabel looks up with a groan. She notices that there's emergency lighting on this floor along the ceiling, pale-green lights that provide enough visibility for someone to follow but not enough to make everything out in detail.

Isabel can just about make out the dark shapes littered across the floor.

'Teresa, I need you to talk to me, okay?' Rampaul.

Rampaul is hunched over, cradling an arm to her chest, the other out in front of her, palm out, like she's coaxing a wild animal.

Looking at Teresa standing there, she might as well be one.

Her hair is plastered to her head, her mouth slack, her breathing completely off, making it seem like she's hyperventilating.

Cross is on her knees, hands clutching at nothing around her neck. 'Please don't . . . please *don't*—' Her pleas turn into a cough, another cough, and then a gag.

340

Isabel staggers up. Everything hurts.

But she forces herself to focus, stretching across the space between them, like her mouth is yawning open. She wades through the waves of ink-black emotion pouring out of Teresa. Isabel doesn't know how to describe it. It's not anger, it's not rage.

It feels like a madness.

Isabel pushes past it. There are no walls around Teresa. She's not trying to hold anything back.

She's unleashing everything she has.

'Isabel!'

Voronov. That's Voronov's voice. She hears the steps running up behind them, more than just two people, but she doesn't dare tear her eyes away from Teresa. She feels like the moment she does, that will be it. That will be the moment that they're done for.

Reinforcements, good. Great.

It might not work very well against a woman who can simultaneously choke everyone on this floor to death.

Which begs the question of why she hasn't.

Isabel and Rampaul are still very much alive.

'Teresa,' Isabel says, and at the same time envisions a warm, soft lapping wave of blue, lets it lap at the fringes of the sheer emotion pouring out of her, 'I was there, with Anabel when she . . .' she picks her word carefully, 'passed.'

Cross is wheezing. Her feet are kicking on the floor, her shoes squeaking against it and leaving dark marks. Teresa holds her in place.

Rampaul stares at Cross in horror. She can't see what's causing her to choke because there's nothing.

Isabel licks her lips and starts walking forward. She ignores the shaking of her hands and the hiss of her name behind her.

'You were the last thing on her mind as she passed. You know that, right?' Isabel continues talking, keeps pushing as much calm Teresa's way as she's able to. 'Your sister fought hard for you, so that you would be free. Teresa – *Teresa*. If you kill Cross here, you

will never be free, and your sister will have died for nothing.'
Isabel stops a few steps away from her.

She reaches out her hand, palm up.

'If you let go of her right now, and take my hand, I can help
you. I can show you,' she drags in a steadying breath when her
voice breaks, 'I can show you the last thoughts your sister shared
with me. Because they were meant for *you*, Teresa. Hmm?'

Awareness flickers there, brief. But there.

Cross drags in a huge breath, the sound loud and desperate.
She collapses to the floor like a puppet whose strings have been
cut, her head hitting the floor with a thud.

Isabel keeps her eyes dead ahead. Teresa's attention is on her
and her outstretched hand.

Her chest is still rising and falling, her breaths audible, and it's
almost like there's no intelligence behind her eyes.

Isabel keeps holding her hand out.

'I'll show it to you,' Isabel says softly, 'I promise. Your sister
said she wanted to trust me. I need *you* to trust me now. Let me
show you. Let me help you.'

Teresa's hand twitches at her side.

Isabel holds her breath.

It feels like no one else is breathing around her either.

Teresa raises her hand and reaches for hers. It takes everything in
Isabel not to flinch away from the touch, to force her fingers to close
around Teresa's. Up close, even in this light, Isabel can see the resem-
blance to Anabel, now that she knows to look for the right markers.

Same mouth and nose. Same lanky frame that looks ill equipped
to move the way she had moved after them, with all the grace and
coordination of a trained killer.

Which Isabel guesses, in a way, she is.

Isabel feels her own lips tremble as she forces them into a smile.
'There, see?'

Teresa doesn't react, doesn't so much as blink. When her lips
part, all she says is: 'Show me.'

Isabel takes a steadying breath and nods.

It's different, showing someone else her own memory. Not something she's ever done before.

It's easier, so much easier when all of Teresa is opening up, reaching for her, eager for what she's about to be shown.

Her yearning is so desperate, so painful, and inescapable, that Isabel's chest feels constricted with it. Behind her closed eyelids, she feels the prickle of tears.

She unfurls the memory gently, as if revealing a firefly in her cupped hands. She slips inside Teresa's mind and shares it with her. She doesn't hide anything, pours as much detail into the memory as she can recall.

She feels the devastation of Teresa's Gift as she hears Anabel's final thoughts, pleading with Isabel to save her sister.

Isabel doesn't detach herself when she draws back from sharing the memory with her. She stays in Teresa's mind, not threatening.

Their eyes remain locked and the police station and the chaos around them fade away. She sees the lucidity in Teresa's gaze.

Hears the first tentative thoughts she sends Isabel's way, for Isabel to hear only.

*'She promised she'd find a way to get me out. Once she understood what the purpose of the research really was, the aim of the project . . . she gave it all up for me. To protect me. Even though she knew I was losing myself a little more every day. She came first. And I would follow. She knew Cross would send me after her. She planned everything right until the end. But she put her trust in the wrong hands.'*

'How?' Isabel asks.

*'I came to see her at the embassy that day. Under the pretext of giving her another book but really it was because Cross had told me to. She said Anabel was experiencing erosion too. That she wasn't thinking about us. That this whole thing was a side effect of her reasoning being impacted. I was supposed to convince her to come back so we could get help together. Convince her by force if I had to. Anabel wasn't expecting me. I overheard that pig talking to his colleague in Portugal. Up until*

then I didn't have any clue. She didn't tell me what he'd been doing to her. But that fucker was talking about it to his little friend like it was a joke. He knew she wouldn't leave because we needed that citizenship.'

As she talks Isabel through it, Isabel sees it all, freely offered, a faint reel, like the flickering of a 35 mm film. It moves all around them, surrounding them so that Isabel sees nothing else but that.

'I – blanked out for a moment. When I came back to, they were all dead. Anabel came out of her room and she just – she . . . she'd never looked at me like that before. Like she believed I was beyond saving. She told me to go.'

'And did you?'

Teresa gives Isabel a slow nod. 'She disappeared too. I couldn't find her. Cross told me she'd turned her back on me. I remembered that look on Anabel's face and I believed her.'

Isabel takes a deep breath. 'Did you kill Ramos?'

The flickering images fade away and Isabel finds herself standing over Judite Ramos's unmoving body, her chest heaving, the gun warm in her hand. In Teresa's hand.

'Why did you go after her? She wasn't in the building when the others died.'

That brings back a hint of that same killing intent Isabel had sensed as she'd been hunted in the darkness of the stairwell.

'Even if Anabel had turned her back on me, I still couldn't forgive what was done to her. Judite knew. She knew all about it and all she did was help that bastard cover it up. Cross approved it. She told me to take care of her and swipe her things. We knew what Anabel had gone through would come out and you would think she murdered those people at the embassy. That you would think she went after Judite in revenge. She was meant to run back to us. To ask us for help. We would have gone back. Cross would have made sure they didn't punish her. Everything would have just gone back to the way it was before – before she tried to save us both.'

She's crying. Teresa's crying but she doesn't seem to realise it. Her face barely twitches, no sobs catch in her chest, no hitching

344

breaths. Only the wet gleam of tears on her cheeks as her eyes fill and the tears spill until they drip from her chin.

*'But she never betrayed me. She never turned her back on me. She loved me. And I killed her because I believed everything Cross told me. Because she managed to turn me into her fucking pupp—'*

A shot rings out.

Isabel jerks back.

Pain rips through her midriff and she doubles over with a cry, ripped out of the shared space she'd been inhabiting with Teresa.

Her hands instinctively go to her stomach even as Voronov shouts her name.

Her ears are ringing and her hands tremble as she pulls them away from her stomach.

Her hands are clean as she registers that the pain isn't hers. It's an echo of the mind she's still connected to.

Isabel's knees give.

Teresa glances down at her stomach. There's a hole that hadn't been there before. She reaches down to touch it with the hand that had just been in Isabel's grasp.

On the floor, on her knees, is Cross. There's a gun in her hand and it's still pointed at Teresa.

That's as much as Isabel has time to process.

Teresa collapses on to the floor, clutching her stomach. When she raises her head again, any semblance of humanity is gone.

Around them, the building shakes.

It's not the same small tremors as before. This time, it's shaking down to its foundations.

Teresa curls in on herself, pressing both hands to her stomach. Her eyes never leave Cross.

'This is on you.'

Isabel sees it. Sees what she's planning, how she's shaping it in her head for her Gift to follow.

'She's going to bring the building down.'

Rampaul reaches down to haul Cross to her feet, begins

dragging her away. 'Everyone *out*!' Her voice booms. 'She's trying to bring the building down. Out, *now*!'

Isabel turns, finds Voronov already striding towards her, Adam on his heels, sweating and dragging his leg behind him, barely keeping himself standing, and half a dozen others behind them, all of them armed.

'No one is leaving.'

As soon as she hears those words, Isabel feels that same pressure that she had felt in the interview room. Except this time it's worse. Bad enough that she staggers under the weight of it.

She's not the only one.

Is this what it had felt like? For the people at the embassy?

The pressure is coming from all sides, compressing her chest.

Isabel can't comprehend this level of power.

She buckles under it, too focused on breathing herself to notice the same happening to others.

*I have to try again. I have to connect, somehow.*

Except there's nothing there. Not even the faintest traces of self, when she throws herself into Teresa's head, pummelling herself with brute strength powered by desperation.

But there's nothing.

Nothing but a determination to crush every single thing in the room with her.

Erosion.

A second shot rings out.

Isabel is looking right at Teresa when it hits.

A small black circle is suddenly right there, to the left side of her forehead. Red splatters the floor behind her.

The pressure dissipates like it had never existed and Isabel fills her lungs with air even as Teresa falls back.

She collapses on the floor, she doesn't move again.

It takes Isabel a moment to convince herself to move. When she does, it's to find Voronov, feet braced, and arms still positioned in a firing stance.

# 52

The police station is closed, indefinitely.

Due to the damage it sustained, the building is deemed too unstable to resume regular operations. The MCIU along with the other units that had been housed in the building are split up, setting up temporary camp at other police stations and some in less appropriate government buildings.

It's in one of these buildings, an office block belonging to the Royal Borough of Kensington and Chelsea, that Isabel and Voronov witness as Rampaul and Adam sit across from Dr Eliana Cross, her two lawyers on either side of her, and take her through the events that led to the destruction of the police station and the deaths of fifteen people in total, two of those Anabel and Teresa. It makes for an odd scene, with Rampaul's arm in a sling and Adam's leg in a cast.

There's no trace of the defiance, the cocky arrogance, that Cross had displayed so unapologetically in their interviews before.

She'd thought she was going to die, stared death in the face, a threat she had created herself.

It's several days of interrogation, going over every single detail. Combined with Joana Weir's statement and the information gathered and left behind by Anabel, the MCIU were confident they would get a good result once this went to trial.

The bigger problem was the frosty tone that the narrative between the UK, Portugal and the US had taken.

The allegations of sexual abuse were out there now too, and the Portuguese Foreign Affairs Department, particularly Amorim and Pessoa, had been thrown under the bus for how everything had gone down. The investigation there will continue for some time.

The day of the last interview is the first night Isabel and Voronov actually head back to North Greenwich to pack for the flight that will take them back to Lisbon the next morning.

It's a silent ride home.

# 53

'Well.' Rampaul holds out her good hand, for a shake. 'I won't say it's been a pleasure, because . . . well.' Her jacket hangs off one of her shoulders where her arm is cradled in a sling, pressed to her chest.

Rampaul had showed up in the morning to pick them up and drive them to Heathrow.

They're stopped outside the entrance to departures at Terminal 2. They've got two hours to go until their flight.

Isabel takes her hand and grips it tight. 'I think you mean to say, thank you for the help.' She's smiling though she can feel how tired it probably looks. She can't wait to be in her own home and getting into her own bed, her dogs beside her, and sleep for a week.

'Hmhm.' Rampaul turns to Voronov, holding her hand out to him too.

'If you and Adam ever want to visit,' Isabel says, 'for *non-working* reasons, give us a buzz. You both probably need a holiday after all that.' Then she laughs at herself. 'Listen to me. Correction. We *all* need some time off after all this.'

Adam was headed back to the hospital this morning for the procedure on his leg that would keep him out of commission for some time. The injury had been a bad enough break that ultimately the doctors had advised surgery to set the bones in place using a metal plate.

'I'll tell him,' Rampaul says. 'Have a safe flight back. Let me know when you land.' Then she slides her sunglasses into place and, with a final wave, heads back to her car.

They watch her get in and drive off.

Isabel glances at Voronov.

'Are you okay?' he asks.

Isabel sighs. 'I'm glad to be going home.'

By the time they land in Lisbon, it's close to midday.

The sun is blasting as they head outside, the heat wildly different from the sort that had been present throughout their stay in London.

Here, Isabel feels like she can breathe.

They walk towards the exit in a silence that's weighted by exhaustion.

Walking down the ramp, Isabel spots Sebastião standing by one of the kiosks, a newspaper rolled up and tucked under his arm. His eyes are scanning the crowds exiting the ramp and she sees the moment when he spots her. His entire face softens with it and just then she wants nothing more than to hug her brother into next week and not budge.

She turns to Voronov and finds him deep in thought.

'Hey.' She reaches for his shoulder and waits for his blue eyes to meet hers. 'Sebastião is waiting for me. But I don't want you alone. Can I . . . can I come by later?'

She thinks about how he's kept to himself since the night at the station, pulled into himself.

Some warmth seems to come back into his face at that, but he starts to shake his head. 'I'll be fine. You should rest. Spend time with your brother. I know you've missed the dogs.'

She sighs. 'Stop. I'm too tired for this. I'll just show up anyway.'

A ghost of a smile appears on his face. 'All right.'

Isabel scoffs, steps back and shakes her head. 'Okay. I'll see you later.'

The next couple of weeks are going to be messy. But right now, she doesn't have the capacity to think beyond making it home.

Her brother smiles when he sees her, but she can already spot the concern pulling at his expression.

Still, when he wraps his arms around her, she drops her bag and hugs him tight.

'Ah maninha, I missed you.'

Isabel buries her head in his shoulder. 'Yeah. Me too.'

She doesn't know how long they stand there but when she pulls back, she's about to demand to know where her dogs are when she finally catches it.

She'd felt so relieved to be home, to *see* him, that she'd read his concern for her and not looked beyond it.

But now, she feels it, a tension and a worry that feel rooted elsewhere.

Isabel draws back, hands going to his shoulders as her relief at being home evaporates.

'Sebastião,' she says. 'What's wrong?'

She watches as the joy at seeing her fades from his face.

He shakes his head. 'I don't know how to explain it. And I'm worried about how . . . how . . .' He sighs and rubs his eyes. 'Come on. They're waiting.'

'What?'

During the drive home, she stares at him in confused silence, his behaviour leaving her too afraid to do what she shouldn't and just take the information he isn't giving her.

The sun is high up in the sky when he finally pulls up. Except they're not at her house. Not even at her street.

Isabel stares at the door of the house she grew up in.

'Sebastião. Why are we here?'

She doesn't come here. This is not her place.

He stares back at her. 'I'm sorry. I asked Daniel not to tell you. I'm sorry, Isa.'

Then before she can ask again, she hears the door open.

She stiffens as her mother comes into view and is about to curse Sebastião out for even bringing her here when Rita, her sister, comes out behind her mother too.

Her arms are wrapped tightly around her middle and her face is set in stone.

And then her mother does something that leaves Isabel stunned.

She rushes to close the distance between them, her familiar face creased into something like panic and worry as she heads straight for the car and yanks the door open.

'Isabel – oh my God, Isabel—'

She wraps her arms around her and pulls her in close.

Isabel sits frozen in the same spot, arms stiff at her sides, staring ahead.

'. . . Mãe?'

Over her mother's head, Isabel's eyes meet her brother's. There's a grimness there that chills her.

And what she's known all along is confirmed.

It had never been just a dream.

'It's okay,' her mother says, 'you're home now.'

# 54

Chief Bautista answers Isabel's knock at her door with an impatient invitation to enter. Her voice sounds more gravelly than usual and when Isabel opens the door, two coffee cups in hand, Bautista is knocking back two pills and washing them down with water.

Bautista glances up at her as she shuts the door behind her, sealing off the noise of the precinct. Her eyes drop down to the coffee cups.

'If you're bringing me bribes this means I'm not going to like this conversation.'

Isabel shrugs but doesn't correct her. She holds the coffee over the desk and waits for Bautista to take it before she sits, resting her own on her lap. 'Do you have time right now?'

Bautista leans back in her chair, nudging her keyboard aside and putting her cup on the desk. 'Should have asked that before you sat down.'

When Isabel doesn't respond, Bautista narrows her eyes.

'What's this about, Reis? Are you here to request some time off?'

Isabel picks at the plastic lid of her cup. 'Not quite.'

A pause. Then Bautista lets out a long sigh. Uncovering the cup, she takes a drink of the coffee. Isabel can't help a small wince. That's not a regular coffee. There's a reason why Bautista's voice always sounds ruined; between the inhumanly strong coffee she likes to drink and the packets of cigarettes she goes through in a week, it's a miracle that a ruined voice is all she has to deal with.

'I expected something like this after Monitoring sent those two here to "discuss inconsistencies" and yet only asked to speak to you. It took a little longer than I expected.'

Isabel shifts forward in her seat. 'Chief . . .' Nerves clog her throat and her chest feels too tight. When she can't go on, she has a drink of her coffee instead. Maybe she should have added a splash of alcohol to it. Might have been more helpful.

Bautista pulls open the top desk drawer, taking out a pack of Marlboro Lights and a lighter. She takes one out and puts it between her lips, lighting it and taking a deep drag.

It's not until she lets out a stream of smoke that she speaks. 'Is it because of your level?' She hooks her little finger into the glass ashtray sitting at the corner of the desk and pulls it over to her.

Isabel inclines her head. 'In part.'

Bautista tsks. 'Well don't beat around the bush. Let's hear it.'

So Isabel takes a deep breath and takes Chief Bautista all the way back to the Gabriel Bernardo case. She lays it all out for her, from the way her Gift exploded during the case to what method she used to keep Gabriel from killing again, all the way through to the incident in London.

By the time she stops, Bautista's cigarette has finished, and she sits in silence for a moment, eyes on the cigarette packet. Isabel wishes she'd open the window in the room wider.

With deliberate care, Bautista takes another cigarette out.

'You're telling me you're compromised.'

'I am.' She forges on. 'Chief, my level—'

Bautista waves at her to be quiet. 'Stop there.' She gives Isabel a hard look through tendrils of smoke. 'Reis, do I look stupid to you?'

Isabel frowns. 'What do you mean?'

'In regard to your level, outside of any mandatory retesting, you keep that to yourself. You keep your head down and you do exactly as you've been doing to get those level five results for now.'

'But . . .' Isabel scoots to the edge of her seat. Her coffee has long since been abandoned on the chief's desk. 'If they find out the truth about my level and they think you knew—'

Bautista raises her eyebrows. 'And why would they think that?'

Isabel is speechless.

'My primary concern is Gabriel Bernardo being inside your head. That's something I can't ignore.'

'I understand.'

Bautista scoffs. 'I doubt it. What were you planning on doing here today? Resigning?'

Hearing it said out loud is hard.

Isabel loves her job. She loves her team.

But the reality is that she's compromised.

She's not going to be the reason her colleagues are placed in any kind of danger. No matter how much every inch of her rejects the idea of leaving.

'You're not resigning. Don't be stupid, rapariga.'

Isabel blinks. 'What?'

'I'm putting you on extended leave. Deal with this, Isabel.' She jabs her finger on the desk. 'I expect you to figure out how to get that bastard out of there and lock him out for good. I'm not losing one of my best to this mess. Get your old Guide to help you or find a specialist – I don't care. You get it done. Understand?'

Isabel gapes at her. 'Chief—'

'*Understand?*'

Isabel shuts her mouth. She nods. 'Yes, Chief.'

'Good. Now get out. You've already ruined my week and I don't want to see your face. Have an extended leave request filled out and on my desk by end of play today.'

Isabel gets up. 'I will.'

All of a sudden, she feels tired. But mixed in with it is relief too. Relief that she doesn't have to let go of this place just yet. Relief that Chief Bautista will always be Chief Bautista. An immoveable wall that is as protective as it is frustrating.

As she opens the door to leave, Isabel looks back over her shoulder and finds Bautista watching her with a sober gaze.

'Thanks, Chief.'

After a moment, Bautista nods.

Isabel leaves the room.

She pulls the door closed behind her.

She spots Voronov's tall frame at their desks talking with Jacinta. Daniel is leaning on Isabel's desk and Carla stands beside him, arms crossed, listening.

Jacinta sees Isabel first and taps at the watch on her wrist with an exaggerated look of impatience.

'Isabel, hurry up! At this rate I'll never recover from the hole of hunger in my stomach.'

Voronov looks up at her and their eyes meet.

Isabel takes a deep breath and makes her way to her team.

# Acknowledgements

It's unbelievable to me that we have reached book three of the Inspector Reis series and I cannot stress how much I couldn't have done this alone. This book in particular has been a long journey and so many people helped me reach the end of it.

I want to give a huge thank you to my agent Oli Munson at A.M. Heath and Jo and Sorcha from the Hodder team who showed me such patience and support throughout this process. An additional thank you to the Hodder team for delivering me into the wonderfully capable hands of Kate who has been so supremely cool and a dream to work with. Here's to a few more books together!

Thanks to the Trash Fictioners who I started out on this crazy novel-writing ride with, the OG City MA Creative Writing (Crime Novel) lecturer team who got me here and our Theakstons Squad. You all represent the best of the crime writing community!

Thank you to my absolute rocks, Lori, Audrey, Lyn, Imaan, Myra and Emily who have been at my side for so long and kept me going even when I found it impossible to keep moving forward. I love you all very much and will always be grateful for your friendship and support. I look forward to more of our crazy, midnight writing sessions and fangirling.

A special thank you to Sade, Nadine, Richard and Melissa. Forever grateful for the lunches, dinners, reviving cousin's trips, and the rambling, daily voice note exchanges that kept me sane.

To Fernanda and Helena. I love you both very much. You are my world. Thank you for always being there.

And finally, to everyone who has picked up an Inspector Reis book and spent time in her world, I'm eternally grateful and I hope you stay with me for the remainder of her journey.

All the love,
Patricia x

'Patricia Marques debut takes the classic crime novel and the evocative setting of Lisbon, and utterly transforms both with a fascinating speculative twist. Pacy, immersive and brain-shiveringly clever. A brilliantly original crime story' **Philippa East**

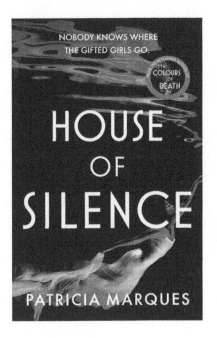 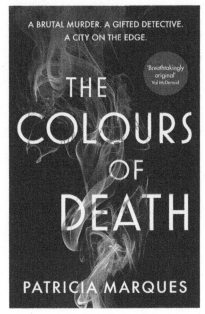

Follow Isabel as she heads back to Portugal for the final instalment of the Inspector Reis series, coming Spring 2025 . . .